THE GIRL FROM GUERNICA

THE GIRL FROM GUERNICA

KAREN ROBARDS

THORNDIKE PRESS
A part of Gale, a Cengage Company

LIBRARY OF CONGRESS CIP DATA ON FILE.
CATALOGUING IN PUBLICATION FOR THIS BOOK
IS AVAILABLE FROM THE LIBRARY OF CONGRESS.

ISBN-13: 978-1-4328-9620-1 (hardcover alk. paper)

Published in 2022 by arrangement with Harlequin Enterprises ULC.

Printed in Mexico
Print Number : 1   Print Year : 2023

This book is dedicated with love
to my three sons —
Peter, Christopher and Jack —
and to my beautiful new
daughter-in-law, Delanor,
who married Peter and joined our
family on March 7, 2020.

■ ■ ■ ■

PART ONE: GUERNICA

■ ■ ■ ■

1

April 25, 1937

To laugh and dance and *live* in the teeth of whatever tragedies an uncaring fate threw in your path was the Basque way.

The stories Sibi's mother told, stories handed down through generations of indomitable women, painted those defiant sufferers as heroes.

Sibi feared she was not the stuff of which such heroes were made.

She was hungry. Her feet hurt. And she was afraid. Of those things, afraid was the worst by far. She was so *tired* of being afraid.

A knot in her stomach. A tightness in her throat. A prickle of unease sliding over her skin. Familiar sensations all, which did not make their sudden onset feel any less dreadful. Sixteen-year-old Sibi — Sibil Francesca Helinger — pushed back a wayward strand of coffee-brown hair that had escaped from the heavy bun coiled at her nape and

9

frowned out into the misty darkness enshrouding the Calle Fernando el Católico. Her pulse thrummed as she clung to the desperate hope that she was not seeing what she thought she was. Since the fighting had moved close enough so that the residents of this ancient village high in the western Pyrenees could actually hear gunfire in the surrounding hills, fear had become her all-too-frequent visitor. But this — this was different. This was because of something that was happening *now,* right before her eyes, in the wide, tree-lined street just beyond where she stood watching the regular weekly celebration on the night before market day.

Have we left it too late? The thought made her mouth go dry.

"I want a sweet." Five-year-old Margrit's restless movement beside her reclaimed her attention. Gripping the child's hand tighter, Sibi cast an impatient glance down.

"There's no money for a sweet." Or anything else, Sibi could have added, but didn't.

"But I *want* one." Round blue eyes in a cherubic face surrounded by gold ringlets stared longingly at the squares of honey and almond *turrón* being hawked to the crowd by a woman bearing a tray of them. The yeasty aroma of the pastry made Sibi's stomach growl. For the last few weeks, she and her mother had been rationing their diminishing resources by skipping the evening meal so that the younger ones could eat.

"Ask Mama to buy you one later."

Margrit's warm little fingers — which Sibi kept a secure hold on because, as angelic as the youngest of the four Helinger sisters looked, she wasn't — twitched in hers. "She won't. You know she won't. She'll say she doesn't have any money, either."

That was undoubtedly true. In fact, Sibi had only said it in hopes of placating her little sister until their mother returned. Thinking fast — Margrit had mostly outgrown tantrums, but not entirely — Sibi was just about to come out with an alternate suggestion when thirteen-year-old Luiza jumped in.

"You know we're poor now, so stop being such a baby." Cross because she hadn't been permitted to go to the cinema with a group of her friends, Luiza spoke sharply. The thick, straight, butterscotch blond hair she'd chopped to chin length herself the night before — "Nobody has long hair anymore!" she'd wailed in the face of their mother's horror — had already lost its grip on the rag curls she'd forced into it. She looked like she was wearing a thatch of broom straw on her head, but Sibi was far too good a sister, and far too preoccupied at the moment, to point that out.

"I don't *like* being poor." Margrit's lower lip quivered.

"None of us do."

"I *specially* don't like —"

Luiza cut her off. "You're whining. You know what Mama said about whining."

"I am not . . ."

A match flared in the street. Tuning her sisters out, Sibi focused on what the brief incandescence revealed as it rose to light a cigarette — *red tip glowing brightly* — before arcing like a tiny shooting star to the ground. Sibi looked beyond the cigarette to the dark shape behind it. The dark *shapes* behind it. She *wasn't* mistaken. Soldiers — *their* soldiers, the loyalist Republicans, their uniforms unmistakable — poured into the street from seemingly everywhere. And the numbers were increasing . . .

Her heartbeat quickened. *Does no one else see?*

Biting down on her lower lip, she glanced around. The crowd clapped and swayed to the rollicking music of the highly prized town band and ate and danced and played games and — She concluded that no one else did. The village leaders who were present appeared unaware: Father Esteban talked to the woman behind the refreshment table as she ladled out a bowl of spicy fish soup for him; His Honor the mayor played *mus,* the popular card game, with three friends; the Count of Arana, the town's most prominent citizen, stood with his arms crossed and a stern gaze fixed on his fifteen-year-old daughter, Teresa, as she walked away from him with her hand tucked into the arm of . . . Emilio Aguire.

Sibi's stomach gave an odd little flutter.

Watching them reminded her of just how much of an outsider she was here in this quaint small town with its red-roofed white houses and narrow cobbled streets. Emilio was her age, he was the handsomest boy in school and he had been kind to her. She had hoped . . . But no. To hope for anything where he was concerned was foolishness. She and her mother and sisters were only temporary residents. She worked as a part-time waitress and her mother had worked in a dress shop before being fired three weeks ago, when the shop owner's husband had displayed too much interest in her. And that, of course, had immediately become a topic for much discussion among the town gossips whose gleeful suspicions that the former Marina Diaitz, now Helinger, who had come home with her children but without her husband, was a floozy were thus seemingly confirmed. All those factors combined to put them near the bottom of the social ladder in this place where the wealthy local aristocracy had been comfortably in place for generations, and they, with their German father, would have been outsiders, anyway. And Teresa was beautiful and rich and — Well, there it was, foolishness.

She had no time for foolishness.

Glancing at those in her own party — Luiza and Margrit, and their other sister Johanna, all bunched close around her, and their mother, Marina, dancing merrily with the baker Antonio Batzar beneath the colored lights strung above the makeshift dance floor in hopes of securing a scarce loaf of tomorrow morning's fresh bread — Sibi felt her heartbeat quicken.

Intent on their own concerns, they appeared oblivious to anything else. As usual it was up to her, notorious as the family worrier, to think about what might happen, to catch and make sense of what the rest of them missed.

Tonight, it was that their soldiers, their last line of defense against the surging rebel Nationalists, appeared to be coming together en masse to slink like starving cats past the Sunday night festivities.

These were the same war-weary, battle-scarred troops that had been camped out in the forested peaks surrounding the town since they had fallen back after the savage attack on the neighboring village of Durango that had brought the nine-month-old civil war as close as its ancient churches and rambling streets. In the days since, thousands of panicking refugees had flooded the town. The warships of Generalissimo Francisco Franco, commander in chief of the rebel forces, had blockaded the Basque ports. Food had become scarce: along with bread, milk and meat were almost impossible to obtain. People were hungry, frightened. The war that had been safely on the other side of the country had changed direction so fast that the residents of these sleepy villages high above the Bay of Biscay had been caught unprepared. But unprepared or not, in a new and terrifying offensive the newspapers were calling the War of the North, the fighting was now rushing like a wave toward their front door.

The soldiers were all that stood between them and the enemy forces determined to destroy them. And the soldiers were leaving.

Sibi's breathing quickened as she registered the numbers, so many, stretching out in a growing column that pushed through the less determined movements of the people coming and going from the festival like a boat through water. Looking toward the station plaza with its dim yellow lights, she saw a newly arrived train puffing smoke as it practically vibrated with eagerness to be gone again. Soldiers, dark shapes rendered unmistakable even at that distance because of their uniforms and the guns they carried on their backs, were already loading shipping crates and boxes aboard.

The train would hold only a fraction of the soldiers that were coming — but still they were coming. No, *going*.

The ones that weren't heading toward the train station were turning toward the Renteria Bridge. Or, in other words, taking the road out of town.

We should have gone weeks ago.

She'd known it, felt it with every prudent instinct she possessed. Eleven months earlier, they'd traveled with their mother to this, the town of Marina's birth, because Marina's mother, their *amona* Elisabeta, was on her deathbed. At that time, the civil war had not yet begun, the journey had been safe, the area had been safe and the

16

plan had been that they would be gone no longer than a month or two. Then to everyone's surprise, *Amona* had lingered on until January.

After that there was the funeral, and then *Amona*'s belongings to dispose of and other matters to settle, which Sibi had known was only a small part of the story. In the meantime, the civil war had raged, with much fighting centered on Madrid and Guadalajara and Málaga in the south. Finally, alarmed as the war turned in their direction, Sibi had broached the theretofore largely avoided topic of leaving, of going home to Berlin and their father. Her mother had regarded her out of pained eyes that reproached her for bringing the sensitive subject up. But at least Mama had listened — then discussed it with the whole close-knit network of relatives and friends and neighbors who lived around them at the bottom of Calle San Juan in the Old Quarter, otherwise known as the poor end of the street in the poor end of town.

All had insisted that there was no hurry, that in this remote village that was revered as the cradle of the ancient Basque people, the seat of their cherished democracy, the home of the Sacred Oak that had served as a symbol of their freedom since the fourteenth century, they were safe.

Mola won't dare attack here. Everyone was sure.

In the face of her mother's silently pleading eyes, Sibi had abandoned the argument, praying that everyone was right. But she had worried.

As you always do, Mama had said. Which was true. But in this case, she felt she had good reason.

The forces under the command of the Nationalist General Emilio Mola, leader of the Northern Offensive, were known to be merciless.

As far back as July, at the very beginning of the uprising, he had announced that this war would be one of extermination against all who stood against him.

The Basques stood against him. And now he was heading in their direction.

"Look, that lady has *mouchous.*" Tugging on Sibi's hand again, Margrit pointed toward a woman bearing the soft, almond-flavored cookies on a plate. "Can I have —"

"No." Sibi's tone was shorter than usual because her attention was focused on what was happening in the street beyond the fair.

With the soldiers gone, the town would be unprotected.

They would be unprotected.

18

Sibi could taste the fear now, sour in her mouth. Everybody knew the stories, even the ones that weren't considered fit for the ears of young girls: the enemy burning whole villages, shooting soldiers even after they surrendered, carrying out mass executions, slaughtering entire families, violating women at will, raping and killing children and even nuns. In their push to wrest control of the country from the duly elected Republican government, it was said that the Nationalists stopped at nothing.

And now the White Terror, as it was called, might be coming for them.

The column of soldiers stretched out into the darkness farther even than she could see. It was growing, widening, filling the street.

She couldn't stand it. She had to know what was happening.

"Here, hold on to Margrit." Thrusting the little girl's hand into Luiza's, Sibi turned away.

"Mama said we should stay together." Shy Jo, aged nine, clutched at Sibi's coat. Feeling the tug on the worn-thin wool, Sibi checked and glanced at her. Jo's black-framed glasses, too big because they were hand-me-downs from Luiza, slid precariously down her slender nose. Thick-lashed chocolate brown eyes in a square-jawed, high-cheekboned face that still retained some of its childish roundness, long coffee-colored braids tied up with scraps of red ribbon — except for the glasses and hair-style, delicately-made Jo resembled Sibi to a remarkable degree. The difference was in their personalities: as the eldest, upon whose thin shoulders the cares of the family consistently fell, Sibi had never had the luxury of being shy or frail.

"Is something wrong?" Speaking at almost the same time as Jo, Luiza gave Sibi a wide-eyed look.

"I'll be right back." Without really answering either of them, Sibi freed her coat from Jo's fingers and added a stern, "Be good," to Margrit as the little girl, registering the change in minders, whined, "You're hurting," at Luiza and tugged experimentally at her hand.

"Stop it. *Chiqueada.*" With a shake of her head, Luiza muttered that last half under her breath.

"I am *not* spoiled." Indignant at the charge, Margrit stamped her foot and tried harder to pull away.

"All of you, stay here." It was an order, given as Sibi slipped away. Ducking beneath the linked arms of the lustily singing merrymakers behind her, she stepped into the street. The slide of her too-big shoes, handed down from her mother, against the blistered places at the backs of her heels made her grimace: it would be nice, one day, to once again have shoes that actually fit. The clap of her rope soles on the cobblestones, like the shuffling march of the soldiers in front of her, was lost beneath the exuberant wail of the accordions as the song reached its crescendo. Here, away from the warmth provided by the fires burning in barrels, the air was cold enough to make her shiver. It smelled of pine and cigarettes and the livestock that had been brought in to be sold at tomorrow's market. Pulling her scarf up around her head, she hesitated, scanning the lines of men in hopes of spotting a friendly looking face.

So many. Along with the refugees, they had poured into the area by the thousands in recent days until it seemed as if every inch of space was clogged with them.

She'd hated their presence. But now . . .

A group of three came toward her, on the outside of the line and moving more slowly than the others, one man drooping as he was helped along by two of his fellows. Sick or wounded, she thought, and the thought was accompanied by a rush of hope that perhaps this was no more than an evacuation of the infirm. After all, the hospital was full to overflowing. Perhaps these men were being taken elsewhere for treatment.

"Excuse me . . ." Darting forward, she tugged on the arm of the outermost soldier, an officer, she thought from the five-pointed red star on his cap. Laden down by a pair of rucksacks and a collection of weapons slung over his shoulder, he had an arm around the injured man's waist. "Can you tell me — where are you going?"

His eyes glinted black at her from beneath his beret. "We're pulling back."

Her pulse pounded in her ears. "But how can you leave us?" Fueled by fear, the question burst from her throat.

Another soldier, overhearing, answered. "We're going no farther than the Cinturón de Hierro. What's that, thirty-five kilometers away? No distance at all."

The Cinturón de Hierro, or girdle of iron, was the massive wall of artillery and antiaircraft guns that had been set up around the nearby industrial capital of Bilbao. And yes, Bilbao was as close as he said. Still, as an attempt to reassure, his words had done anything but.

Their town stood squarely between Bilbao and the Nationalist Army.

"But what of us? What will we do?" She felt cold all over as she tried to calculate what the soldiers' departure might mean for her family. Theirs was a household of women, of girls — they would be more at risk than most. If the enemy was coming, should they leave now, following the troops? Or should they go up into the hills and hide? Or —

"You'll be in no danger once we are gone." The soldier touched his cap to her and, quickening his step, walked on.

"How can you say that?" she called, but he was gone. She clasped her hands together in agitation as she glanced back down the street at the oncoming sea of men.

There had to be someone who could tell her more, provide advice, direction. She felt woefully inadequate to evaluate the situation on her own. Her effervescent mother could rarely be brought to face anything unpleasant at the best of times, and certainly going home to Berlin and their father, whose letters had made it increasingly clear how displeased he was growing with their absence, would be unpleasant for her, Sibi knew. Her parents' marriage was not the happiest, and Marina *was* happy here in the town of her birth. But the thought of what might happen if they stayed made

Sibi's heart beat faster. And there were Luiza and Jo and Margrit to think of as well as herself.

We can't stay here. We can't.

"You heard him. We're in no danger." The speaker was Señora Rosen, the stout, middle-aged wife of the fire chief. Her tone was comfortably complacent.

Other voices joined the conversation as more people gathered around: neighbors, fellow townspeople.

"The soldiers are the target, you understand. Mola will pursue them, and leave us in peace." The wealthy and important Señor Unceto, owner of the arms factory at the southern end of town, patted her arm. Around him, people nodded solemn agreement.

"How can you *know*?" Sibi turned toward him, but he was already talking to someone else and didn't answer.

The street overflowed now with soldiers, while increasing numbers of onlookers formed a shifting line along the curb. A few were grim-faced, while more waved and smiled at the departing soldiers as if they were watching a parade. In the background, the music, the dancing and the festivities continued unabated. Excitement rather than dread hung in the air as the carnival atmosphere of the night before market day spilled out beyond the boundaries of the square.

Except for the exodus of the soldiers, all was continuing on as it always did. Surely if there was danger, there would be some —

"Sibi." Margrit's breathless cry brought Sibi's head sharply around. It was followed a split second later by the full weight of Margrit's small body crashing into her legs. "Sibi, come quick!"

Taking a staggering step back, she grabbed her sister's shoulders to steady herself and looked down at the little girl. "What is it?"

Margrit's eyes were round as coins. "It's Jo! She's in trouble."

2

"Slow down. I can't understand a word you're saying." They were on the far side of the square, rushing through the hive of activity surrounding the setting up of the stalls. As she spoke, Sibi planted her feet on the square's last few meters of trampled grass, refusing to take another step despite Margrit's frantic efforts at towing her along. The garbled explanation her sister was busy throwing at her over her shoulder made no sense, and Sibi was wary of letting Margrit pull her out into the rabbit warren of back streets and alleys behind the square, especially with so many strangers in town for market day. "Stop. Where is Jo?"

"The man got her! I told you!" Clearly frustrated at having been brought to a standstill, Margrit rounded on her. Her plump cheeks were flushed crimson and her blue eyes blazed with alarm. It was that rather than the determined tug Margrit gave to her hand that persuaded Sibi that, whatever this was, it was deadly serious.

"What man?"

Recognizing capitulation when she heard it, Margrit darted out into the street, dragging Sibi along behind her. "The mean man!"

They dodged through the chaos created by heavily loaded carts and livestock being driven toward holding pens and the general commotion in the crowded streets.

"Where is Luiza?" Whom she had counted on to keep the younger ones safe.

Margrit cast a guilty look back. "I, uh, kicked her, and then I ran toward Mama to see if she would buy me a sweet, but the dancing stopped and I couldn't find her, and then Jo found me and — *There.*" Margrit slowed her headlong pace as she pointed to a run-down building. Two stories tall, white with a red tile roof like most of the town's structures, this one had a cracked and dingy facade. A covered oxcart waited out front. It appeared to be unattended. "She's in there!"

"Margrit, you have to —" *Tell me exactly what happened,* Sibi was about to say when she was interrupted by a wordless cry. They were almost at the building's door, which was slightly ajar. Otherwise, with all that was going on around them, she never would have heard it.

Every cell in Sibi's body froze: the cry came from Jo, and it was shrill with fear.

"Stay here," she ordered Margrit fiercely, releasing her hand, but when she shoved through the door, Margrit — of course — was right behind her.

"Jo!" Sibi's voice echoed through the building. A gray wedge of light from the open door kept it from being completely dark. A few chairs pushed to one side were the only furniture: otherwise the room was empty. The smell of damp combined with a pungent, ammonia-like odor made her nose wrinkle. A wavery yellow light at the top of a flight of stairs drew her eyes.

"Jo!"

"Up here!"

At the high-pitched fear in her sister's voice, Sibi abandoned all thought of caution and raced up the stairs. Margrit scrambled after her.

Bursting out into what she saw from the light of a lantern placed on a crudely made wooden table near the top of the stairs was a large open space piled high with crates, Sibi stopped short at the sight of Jo in the grip of a hulking *paysun.* Her glance took in wide, stooped shoulders, a wild mass of grizzled hair and, as his head snapped around toward the new arrivals, a swooping mustache outlining a threatening snarl.

Jo's eyes were huge with fright, her cheeks shone wet with tears and her mouth trembled. The man was roughly the size of the bullock out front, and he was holding Jo in front of him by both thin arms.

"Get your hands off her!" Fists clenched at her sides, Sibi stayed where she was by an exercise of pure will. Every instinct she possessed urged her to rush at the man, to try to pull Jo away. But how stupid would it be to put herself, too, within his reach?

"She let my animals go." His eyes were small and vicious as they slid over Sibi. She knew what he was seeing: skinny and of no more than average height, she was all eyes and masses of hair. A whisper of a girl, no threat at all: she read the conclusion in his face. "She opened the cages. I caught her in the act."

"He was going to k-kill them. Dogs. For meat!" Jo's voice shook as she squirmed in an unavailing effort to free herself. Her glasses were in imminent danger of sliding off the end of her nose. In the too-big black coat that had once been Luiza's, with one red ribbon missing and the braid it had tied unraveling, she looked as young as Margrit, and far more defenseless. "I heard him talking to some man who was going to sell the — the pieces at market! He said no one would know they weren't rabbit — ow!"

"That's a lie! You shut your mouth!" The man jerked Jo up on her tiptoes. Her glasses dropped to the straw. Sibi's gaze automatically tracked them — glasses were difficult to obtain and expensive — before darting back to Jo's terrified face.

"Stop it! Let her go." Sibi strode toward the man like she was the one who was bullock-size before sanity prevailed, fortunately while she was still beyond his reach, and she stopped. At least his focus was on her now, and he was no longer shaking Jo.

"Sibi." Jo's eyes, shining with tears, met Sibi's despairingly.

In response Sibi's fists clenched so tightly that the sharp crescents of her nails dug painfully into her palms. Her little sisters' faith in her was infinite, she knew. Their mother was warm and fun and beautiful and bright, like a fire they all gathered around for warmth. She told them stories and sang to them and loved them from the bottom of her heart, but it was to Sibi that the girls turned when things went wrong. Always she'd been there for them, a confidante and playmate as well as a protector, taking care of them as needed, letting them into her bed at night when their parents quarreled, shielding them from as much of the world's harshness as she could.

With the blind faith of a younger sibling, Jo was counting on her now.

Sibi had never felt so helpless.

"You can't sell dogs as meat. It's against the law." Sibi wasn't sure that was true, but from his reaction — a threatening growl — she thought it might be. "If you don't let her go, I'll send my other sister here for the police."

She dared not look around to check on Margrit even as she gestured in her direction, but a sound from behind her told her that she was still there. Sending the little girl running for help was the very last choice she wanted to have to make. There was so much that could go wrong with that that the mere idea was hair-raising. As for herself, she was not leaving Jo.

"Oh, you will, will you? That's good. That's *good.* They can lock this little *emagaldu* —" he gave Jo another shake "— up until she pays me the money I'm out for my animals."

"Don't you dare call her a whore. She's nine years old!" Bouncing up and down on her toes with impotent distress as Jo burst into rattling sobs, Sibi thought of their empty pockets. "And we don't *have* any money. Please, just let her go!"

His face contorted with anger. Roaring, "I want my money!" he jerked Jo up higher — she gave a frightened cry as her feet left the floor — and shoved his face close to hers. "If I don't get it, maybe I'll cut *you* up for meat."

"You let my sister go!" Quick as a flash, Margrit hurtled past Sibi to throw herself against the man's legs, sinking her teeth into his thigh with all the ferocity of which her five-year-old self was capable. Bellowing, he grabbed a handful of golden curls and yanked her head back. Riven with fear, abandoning all thought of caution in the face of disaster, Sibi threw herself into the fray before he could do anything else, only to be met with a sweeping blow that flung her, and Margrit with her, to the ground.

Landing hard, she didn't move for a stunned instant. Then a possibility burst through the tide of panic surging through her. She stood and clapped a hand to her chest as she remembered what was there — the one thing of value she possessed. "Wait! I've got something — I can pay you!"

He stopped shaking a sobbing, trembling Jo to look at Sibi. "You have money?"

"I have . . . something." Delving inside the collar of her coat and blouse, Sibi pulled out the necklace their grandmother had given her, as the oldest granddaughter, days before her death. "I have this."

"What is it?" He watched suspiciously as she unclasped the necklace with unsteady hands. It was a pendant, a single stone on a delicate gold chain.

"Sibi, you can't — *Amona* —" Jo squeaked in protest. Sibi stepped as close to him as she dared, the pendant dangling from her fingers. His eyes fastened on it greedily.

"It's a ruby." She held it up so he could see it better. The dark red stone was no larger than her little fingernail, but it gleamed enticingly in the lantern light. "It's worth something." He leaned close, peering at it — a mountain of a man, dwarfing her, reeking of the alcoholic drink Patxaran and stale sweat — and she thrust it at him, gritting her teeth against the urge to take a step back. "It's all we have."

Taking one hand off Jo, he snatched the necklace, looked at it hard, then shoved Jo to the ground. "*Go.* Before I change my mind."

Galvanized, Jo scrambled toward the stairs. Catching sight of Jo's glasses in the straw, Sibi snatched them up in passing as the three of them fled.

"What possessed you to do something like that?" Sibi said to Jo a short time later. Now that they'd dropped to a walk and caught their breath and the safety of the square was in sight, she was equal parts shaken and angry.

"It was all my fault," Margrit said. Shivering, she pressed close against Sibi's side.

Sibi's grip on her sister's hand was firm. "What did you do?" There was resignation in her tone.

Margrit hung her head. "While I was looking for Mama, I saw this little dog grab this big fish out of a tub by one of the stalls and run away with it. It was really funny, because the fish was bigger than the dog, and I followed it. Then Jo found me and she said I should come back but I said no, because I wanted to see where it was taking the fish. So Jo came with me, and we followed it until it ran into that building. There wasn't anybody there, we didn't think, and the door was open. We could hear lots of dogs barking, so we went in." Margrit threw a quick, defensive look up at Sibi. "That part wasn't just me, Jo wanted to go in, too."

"I wanted to see what was wrong with the dogs," Jo said.

Of course she did. "Go on," Sibi said.

Margrit said, "The dog went up the stairs so we did, too. That's when we saw the cages, and all the dogs. The little dog had left the fish on the floor and was using her teeth to try to open one of the cages. There were puppies in it, so I thought she might be a mother dog and they were her puppies. Then we heard somebody coming up the stairs and we hid. The mean man and another man came in and they talked about how they would cut them up and say they were rabbit meat and sell them at the market tomorrow. They went away again, and that's when Jo started opening all the cages and letting the dogs out. I tried to help, but it was hard and I couldn't get any open. Then we heard the man coming back and I hid again but Jo wouldn't stop until all the dogs were out and he came upstairs and caught her. That's when I ran for help."

"I'm sorry about your necklace, Sibi," Jo said.

"I'm sorry about it, too," Margrit said.

"There you are, you brat!" The voice was Luiza's, and they all looked toward it. She stood at the edge of the square near the amusement stalls, her fists planted on her hips as she glared at Margrit. "I've been looking for you everywhere!" Her gaze shifted to Sibi. "She kicked me and ran away, and —"

"I already told her," Margrit said, and stuck out her tongue.

"You —" Visibly seething, Luiza broke off whatever statement of loathing she was meaning to address to Margrit as her sisters reached her. To Sibi she said, "I'm never watching her again. Never, do you understand?"

Turning, she stomped away, but didn't get far before breaking into a run. Sibi saw why: their mother, her quick step and lustrous black hair unmistakable even in the uncertain light, hurried their way.

"Mama!" Margrit exclaimed with delight. Pulling her hand from Sibi's, she raced toward their mother, streaking past Luiza to reach her first.

"Here." Sibi pulled Jo's glasses from her pocket and passed them to her. Jo put them on. By that time they were close enough to their mother and sisters that Margrit's voice carried clearly.

". . . all the dogs. Every single one." Margrit's pride in what she was recounting to their mother was unmistakable.

"Holy Mary Mother of God." Lifting her gaze from her youngest daughter, Marina fixed an appalled gaze on Jo as she and Sibi reached them. "Johanna Marie Helinger, you can't have done such a thing!"

"I had to do it. They were so scared, and some of them were so little. See!"

Thrusting a hand into one of her coat's two large pockets, Jo pulled out something not much bigger than her palm. It was black and . . . furry. It took Sibi a second to realize that what she was looking at was a very small puppy, its dark eyes blinking sleepily, its paws dangling free. Along with the rest of them, she watched in surprise as its head lifted and a tail about the size of her little finger began to wag.

"Is that one of those dogs?" Marina looked from the puppy to Jo in disbelief.

Jo gave a guilty nod. "She was in the last cage. She got her foot caught when she tried to jump out. She was just hanging there whimpering and I couldn't leave her and the man was coming. By the time I got her free the man was there so I stuck her in my pocket so he wouldn't see her. Then he started yelling and grabbed me."

Casting her eyes heavenward, Marina shook her head. Then she frowned direly at her two youngest. "Never do such a thing again, either of you. Do you have any concept of how much danger you put yourselves in? Jo, set the puppy down. You know we can't keep her. Our living situation is too unstable. And you four have school, and I —"

The bells of the Church of Santa María began to toll the hour, interrupting. The familiar deep resonance pealed out over the town, cutting through all the getting-ready-for market-day noise, echoing out into the hills: it was eight p.m.

"— have a job," Marina continued when the tolling stopped, and broke into a wide smile. Sibi was struck by how beautiful their mother, with her delicately-boned face, flashing dark eyes and slender figure, really was. "Come, we have to go. I have to pick up my smock. Antonio's offered me a job at his bakery, and I start tomorrow."

"Antonio?" Sibi lifted her eyebrows, a little unsettled by the familiarity with which her mother had used the name, while Jo exclaimed, "That's wonderful!" and Margrit said, "Will we get bread?"

"I've known him from childhood." Marina bestowed a quelling look on Sibi. Then she smiled impishly at the others. "And yes, it's a wonderful thing. And we will get bread."

"And maybe some honey?" Margrit asked.

"You are such a little glutton," Luiza said. "Mama, that's what started the whole thing. She wanted a sweet."

Marina sighed, shook her head and took

Margrit by the hand. "Come on, girls. Jo, put the puppy down."

"Mama, please, can't we take her home with us? Just for tonight?" Jo begged as they all started walking.

Marina's lips pursed. "All right, bring her. But it's for tonight only. Tomorrow you have to find her a home."

As they passed through the tall iron gates that opened into the crowded street, Marina looked at Sibi. Voice low, she said, "Stop frowning. You worry too much. My getting a job is *good* news."

Except for the part where they shouldn't be planning to stay here, and the new job and the excitement Marina was obviously feeling about it was going to make it even harder than Sibi had expected to persuade her mother that they needed to go. Marina had married and given birth to Sibi, her first child, at eighteen, and many times over the years Sibi had felt far older than her mother. This was one of those times. She thought of the soldiers leaving, of the war rushing toward them, of the gunfire in the hills of late and the makeshift air-raid shelters rigged up with sandbags and wooden support beams in the cellars of various buildings around town and what had happened in Durango, and her stomach tightened.

Antonio waited for them at the bakery, and ushered them inside, although it was closed to patrons until morning. Sibi had never paid much attention to him before. Now she did, and was moderately reassured: he was quite old, and plump, and unhandsome. But he was jolly, and seemed kind, and his attitude toward Marina was respectful.

A short time later they were back on the crowded street.

"See? I told you this job was a good thing." With the black smock the baker had given her hung over her arm, Marina sent a sidelong smile toward Sibi as Sibi finished the last delectable bite of the *etxeko bikotxa,* a buttery pastry filled with black cherry jam, that the baker had given each of them.

They were nearly home, for which Sibi was thankful. She was cold, and tired, and, once again, afraid. They'd passed the firehouse; the big front door was open, which it never was at night, so she'd seen the firefighters readying the horse-drawn truck for possible emergency use. Grim-faced men carried supplies into the bomb shelters that had been erected in the wake of the attack on Durango. Packed full of soldiers, the train left the station at last with a salutary blast of its horn that made her shiver. The open fires and braziers of the refugees camping in any available space flickered orange through the darkness, not just in the village but in the surrounding hills, as well. The sight would have been beautiful if it hadn't been for the implications.

Luiza and Jo walked in front of them, petting the puppy and talking about something that the street noise kept Sibi from overhearing. Margrit, her hand in her mother's firm grip, was busy licking the jam out of her second square of cake, which she had acquired from Marina, who had given her own piece to her youngest.

With her sisters either too preoccupied or too far away to overhear, Sibi met her mother's gaze full-on.

"The job *is* good. Or it would be good, except —" She took a deep breath. When she continued, her tone was urgent. "Mama, we have to leave. We can't stay here any longer. It's too dangerous. See all the soldiers in the streets? They're evacuating to Bilbao. When they're gone, the town will be unprotected."

Marina's smile died. "Where would we go? There's fighting all around us."

"We could go home." Before her mother could say anything, could argue as Sibi saw from her expression she meant to do, she rushed on, desperate to get the words out. "We'd be safe. We wouldn't have to worry about money all the time. We —"

"We can't go home." Marina's lips had tightened.

"I know you and Papa have your differences, but —"

"Sibi, stop." Marina made a quelling gesture. "It's nothing to do with that. We'd be putting ourselves in far more danger if we tried to get through. Everyone — the relatives, the town elders, Father Esteban — say it is safest to stay here and let the war sweep past us. Which it will do." Her stern expression faded. "Anyway, we can't go anywhere right now. We don't have the money."

Sibi's stomach knotted. "How much could it cost to take the train to Bilbao, where at least there are soldiers to protect us? We could sell something."

"What? Your *amona*'s necklace was the only thing of real value we possessed. And we don't have it anymore."

Sibi was left momentarily speechless. If she'd thought of something else, done something else, to save Jo —

"Your locket." She nodded at the silver locket Marina always wore. Engraved with the initials of her four daughters, it had a

42

small photograph of her with her girls inside and rested just below the hollow of her throat. "We could sell that."

Marina's smile was wry as she touched the delicate oval. "You know how much it's worth to me. But to anyone I might try to sell it to, it has no value. It's not even real silver."

"There has to be something —"

"I know we need to leave here," Marina surprised her by saying. "But there's time. We don't have to solve all our problems tonight. And now that I have a job again, everything will be better. Just you wait and see."

3

Home was the top floor of a half-timbered house in the Old Quarter, where the wood-frame buildings stood wall to wall and the smoke-scented streets were narrow canyons that multiplied every sound, including occasional bursts of hopefully celebratory gunfire that made Sibi flinch. Hundreds of permanent residents were packed tightly into the area, with many rooming houses and dwellings providing shelter for multiple families. Tonight, the Old Quarter was bursting at the seams with people, and Sibi was glad to get indoors.

"Señora, could I speak with you?" Their landlady, who lived in the lower half, stepped out into the hall.

"Take the girls on upstairs," Marina said quietly to Sibi, and stopped with a polite nod.

Once upstairs, Sibi tried not to worry about what the landlady wanted as she helped Margrit get ready for bed, then followed her into the room all four girls shared. Margrit promptly scrambled into one of the two low-slung beds where she curled up and pulled the covers up around her neck. Jo sat cross-legged on the floor in a pool of lamplight, the puppy on her lap, frowning with concentration as she tried to wrap a scrap of red cloth around its back paw as it squirmed and licked whatever part of her it could reach.

"What are you doing?" Sibi asked.

Jo looked up at her. "Ruby's foot is cut from where it got caught on the cage. I'm bandaging it."

"Ruby?" Sibi asked.

"Because you traded your necklace for her."

Sibi made a face. The trade had been for her sister, not the dog, but she saw no point in talking about it further. What was done was done, and there was no changing it.

"Hold her still." She crouched beside Jo. "I'll tie it for you."

The puppy licked her face as she finished.

"Sib, can you help me with my hair?" Luiza asked from the doorway. She was in her nightgown, with about half her hair rolled up in rags. The colorful cloth ends stuck up around her head, making it look as though butterflies perched in her hair. She peered more closely at the puppy, then demanded of Jo, "Is that one of my curlers tied around its foot?"

Jo responded with a guilty grimace. "It was all I could find. And it was just the right size."

"Stay out of my things." Luiza shot Jo a warning look. "Sibi, are you coming or not?"

Sibi stood up to go help Luiza.

"Get ready for bed, Jo." Marina appeared in the doorway. As their mother entered the room, Sibi saw that Marina was carrying a large box. To confine the puppy for the night, she guessed. In response to the question in Sibi's eyes, Marina said, low-voiced, as they passed, "She's raising the rent. She said she kept it low for your grandmother, but now . . ." Her voice trailed off.

Sibi's stomach twisted as she followed Luiza into the hall. *One more reason to leave.*

"Make sure it's tight," Luiza said as Sibi rolled the first section of hair up and tied off the rag. Seated on a stool in the small washroom, Luiza stared unhappily at her reflection in the mirror as Sibi did as instructed. "I don't want the curl to come out."

"Why are you so concerned about your hair all of a sudden, anyway?" Sibi asked, running a damp comb through the next section before winding it up and tying it off, too. "Oh, wait, I know. That boy you and Alma were talking about."

Luiza stiffened. "We were not —" Her eyes met Sibi's through the mirror. Sibi gave her a teasing look. Luiza broke off, then smiled sheepishly. "So maybe we were."

"The boy in question wouldn't be Mikel Gorka, would he?" Sibi rolled up more sections of hair.

"How did you . . . ?"

"I have friends, too. I hear he thinks you're beautiful."

Luiza's face pinkened. Her expression was suddenly vulnerable. "Really?"

"Yes, really." Sibi tied the last rag off with an extra flourish. "All finished. Now leave. I have to get ready for bed."

Luiza smiled at her. Then she left.

The lamp had been turned down so that the room was deep in shadow when Sibi walked back into it. Still in the trim black dress she had worn to the festivities, their mother perched on the side of the bed Jo and Margrit shared, telling the little girls a story about Tartaro, the mythical one-eyed giant who could always be outwitted by a quick-thinking human. Listening to Marina's soft voice as she slipped into her own bed beside Luiza, Sibi felt some of the worry twisting her insides start to ease.

As much danger as existed outside the house, as real as she knew the problems facing them were, the bed was soft and the covers were warm and Luiza, already asleep beside her, was a familiar, comforting presence. After their mother finished her story and extinguished the lamp, Sibi listened to her sisters' breathing, watched Marina walk to the doorway and turn back to look at her daughters, then heard her say, as she had done every night for as long as Sibi could remember, "Love you always."

Too tired to respond in kind, Sibi smiled a sleepy answer. And suddenly everything bad seemed very far away.

So far away that she was able to push the fear out of her head and fall asleep to thoughts of Emilio Aguire.

It was, therefore, something akin to a dream come true when, to her mingled surprise and confusion, he came loping up to her in the school plaza the next afternoon. Officially, school had been canceled as the town prepared its defenses in the light of what had happened in Durango, but the younger children and the older girls had met for classes, anyway, and the older boys had been put to work in the school plaza

48

filling sandbags for the air-raid shelters that were hastily being built.

The previous night's cold and mist had burned away with the rising of the sun. By that time, a little after four p.m., it was a perfect spring day. The sky was a clear cerulean blue dotted with gossamer white clouds and the temperature was balmy. Many people were on holiday for market day — as the saying went, "Not a stroke of work gets done on Mondays" — and the school plaza was crowded, as was the entire town. The mood was convivial as all the serious trading had been completed and the town prepared for another celebratory evening.

Sibi was on her way to her job at the Taberna Vasca restaurant, which was always particularly busy on market day and even more so now given all the refugees. But first she needed to walk Margrit to their mother, who was finishing her first shift at the bakery, which, like the restaurants, was one of the establishments that stayed open and busy. Luiza, whose curls had held up surprisingly well, was with them, having also just finished classes, while Jo had rushed back to the flat to get the puppy, because another home had been found for it. She was to meet them at the bakery.

Sibi had a good grip on Margrit's hand as she hurried across the grass in an effort not to be late for work. The three of them wore the pleated black skirts, thick black stockings and long-sleeved white blouses that were the uniform of their school, as did most of the other girls among the throng in the plaza.

"Sibi! Sibi, hold on a minute!" The boy's voice calling to her made her look around. The flutter in her stomach when she saw the speaker was Emilio made her grip on Margrit's hand tighten.

"Ow," Margrit protested, trying to yank her hand free.

Sibi paid no attention, beyond loosening her grip just the smallest bit. She stopped as the black-haired, dark-eyed boy skidded to a stop beside her.

"Sibi, hello." He brushed a lock of his too-long hair out of his eyes. "I saw you in the square last night."

"She saw you, too." Margrit looked up at him with candid appraisal before Sibi could collect herself enough to reply.

"I'll take her, Sib." After one quick glance at her older sibling's face, Luiza stepped into the breach, grabbing Margrit's free hand. "You can catch up to us." Then, with a growled, "Come on," she towed their irrepressible youngest sister away.

Pinning on a smile in an attempt to mask her discomfiture, Sibi looked at Emilio. "I was there with my family."

Sounding casual was one of the hardest things she'd ever done. Boys were new to her, and this boy — he was enough to make her go weak in the knees.

"I was wondering — are you going to the dance tonight?" He smiled engagingly. Her heart thumped. The hollow feeling in the pit of her stomach — who would have guessed that a pair of thickly lashed dark brown eyes looking into hers could cause *that*? "Because a group of us are going and I thought you might like to join us."

"I — I —" She was stuttering, she realized, and took firm hold of herself. She had *some* pride, after all. She wanted to accept so badly that it was a physical ache inside her, but there was nothing she could do. "I'd like to, but I have to work."

"Oh."

Did he sound disappointed? She thought he did.

"I'm really sorry," she added.

He glanced down, then looked back up at her again. Those brown eyes searched hers, and she felt their impact clear down to her toes. "Do you work every night? Because maybe —"

The bells of Santa María began to peal, interrupting. Since the attack on Durango, lookouts with binoculars had been stationed on the rooftops of the tallest buildings in town — the Carmelite Convent, the churches, the parliamentary building — and the violent ringing of the church bells at this unusual hour constituted a warning, as everyone knew.

Like Emilio, like probably everyone in town, Sibi instantly looked skyward. It took a minute, but then she spotted it: a single airplane, no larger than a bird at that distance, banking lazily above the pine-covered mountains to the northwest.

"It's a White," Emilio said.

A "White" meant an enemy airplane. A cold finger of dread slid down her spine as she watched it pass over the jagged mountain peaks, circle above the ancient church that crowned the summit of Monte San Miguel, then swoop around the perimeter of the valley toward the river.

"It's leaving," a man behind her said, relief palpable in his voice. Sibi didn't even glance back to try to identify the speaker. Her hand shielded her eyes as she tracked the progress of the airplane. With the small part of her mind that remained available to register anything else, she was aware that everyone in her vicinity was doing the same.

The sighting of a White airplane in the skies near the town was not uncommon. For the last few weeks, especially, they'd been spotted regularly on the horizon. Several times, one or a pair had streaked directly overhead, only to disappear into the distance. But the attack on Durango had made the town jumpy. A watch was kept. When an airplane appeared, the church bells rang. Everything stopped as the town held its collective breath.

The airplane followed the river, growing smaller, receding from view — until it changed course, curling back around toward the town.

Sibi's chest grew tight.

"What's it doing?"

"Where's it going?"

"It's coming back!"

The alarmed voices were drowned out as more bells began to ring. The Church of San Juan. The Carmelite Convent. The Monastery of Saint Augustine. All pealed wildly in deafening warning.

Sibi barely heard the noise over the roar of the blood rushing through her ears.

Is this it? What she'd feared: an attack.

Sunlight glinted on silver wings as the

airplane nosed downward.

She stood frozen, watching as it came in low above the Renteria Bridge and bore down on the town.

"Avión! Avión!"

"It's going to hit us!"

"Take shelter!"

A hand grabbed hers. "Run!"

Emilio took off running, pulled her with him. Heart pounding, she ran as fast as she could, but with the airplane closing in it didn't seem nearly fast enough. Her legs felt heavy, her feet weighted with fear. Margrit, Luiza — they were somewhere out there, on the open street, headed toward the bakery. Her mother, Jo — where were they?

She didn't know. She couldn't think. There was nothing she could do — except run. The drone of the airplane's engines filled the air, filled her ears, approaching fast, growing loud as an oncoming train in a distinctive, hair-raising growl. Screams, shouts, the crowd scattering, everyone fleeing in different directions: a kaleidoscope of panic.

"Look!"

"What's it doing?"

"It's slowing down!"

A glance back in response to what

sounded like a thousand terrified cries found the airplane gliding low above the train station — and releasing three cylindrical objects from its belly, one after the other, that fell lazily through the air.

Sibi's heart leaped into her throat as she realized exactly what she was seeing: bombs being dropped on Station Plaza. The plaza that, on this day in particular, would be jam-packed with refugees and revelers and visitors waiting for a train to take them home from market day. The Hotel Julian was nearby, with its guests and busy restaurant. The dress shop where her mother had worked was there. Thoughts of Señora Varga, the proprietress, and Isabel and Jacinta and Carmen — her mother's coworkers and friends — flashed through Sibi's head. There was a sweet shop that, at this time of day, would be filled with children and —

One after the other, the bombs flipped over and nose-dived toward the plaza, then disappeared behind the tall church spires and tiled rooftops that blocked Station Plaza from her view.

"Take cover!" someone screamed.

"In here!" Pushing her head down, Emilio hauled her inside — what? a shelter? a cave? Something gray and dark and cylindrical that smelled of damp — just as the bombs hit.

The resultant explosions shook the ground, boomed through the air, knocked her off her feet. She cannoned into Emilio, who caught her, then pulled her down with him onto her knees as a geyser of fire and smoke blasted skyward from Station Plaza.

"Cover your head," he cried and, dry-mouthed and shaking, she did. Huddled between him and the cold concrete wall, she listened in horror as a shower of debris rattled down on their shelter like hail.

A moment later screams, muffled by distance but no less terrible, exploded from the direction of Station Plaza, along with shouts of warning and thuds as larger chunks of falling debris landed. She registered so many things — an acrid burning smell; the warm press of bodies crammed with her into what she recognized now as the large drainage pipe that was under construction just beyond the school plaza; the distinctive clang of the fire alarm — in what seemed like the blink of an eye, while her heart thumped and her pulse raced and her stomach went all hollow with fear.

"It's leaving!"

"Look, the airplane's going away!"

"Praise the Sacred Mother!"

56

The voices belonged to others who'd taken refuge inside the pipe. Even as they multiplied until the questions and exclamations became impossible to separate into anything coherent, even as they became indistinguishable from the ringing in her ears, from the noise outside their shelter, from the dizzying shock that had taken possession of her senses, those around her began to stir, to clamber to their feet, to peer outside.

Sibi looked up to find that she could see out through the open end of the pipe, see the absolute chaos enveloping the slice of town in front of them. People poured out from houses and cellars and storefronts, some shouting and shaking fists at the sky, some gathering up friends and loved ones, many running toward Station Plaza where thick black smoke rolled skyward.

"Is it over?" The question was on everyone's lips.

A brave soul ventured to step out of the pipe. He scanned the sky, called back, "It's over. The airplane's gone."

More people emerged from the pipe. The sense of relief was palpable.

The most terrible thing imaginable had happened, but they had survived.

Sibi rose cautiously — she had to duck

her head, because the pipe was not tall enough to allow her to stand upright. Her knees weren't quite steady, she discovered.

She took a shaken breath.

We have to go. Today. A second later the reality of it hit her. The train station was almost certainly gone. What could they do — walk to Bilbao?

If we have to. Before it's too late.

4

"All right?" On his feet beside her, Emilio was forced to duck his head, too. His eyes on her face were dark with concern. His hand curled around her elbow. The handsomest boy in school — an hour ago, she would have been simultaneously beset with nerves and over the moon at such attention from him. Now she was barely aware of who it was who stood beside her.

She pulled her arm free. "I have to go. I have to find my sisters."

Margrit would be terrified. Luiza, too. But they were somewhere out there on the street in front of her, and that street was untouched, which meant they were unharmed. And Jo — the route between the Old Quarter and the bakery did not go through Station Plaza, where a column of black smoke streaked with orange tongues of fire climbed toward the sky. Jo should be unharmed. And Mama, in the bakery, would have escaped the bombing, too.

For the briefest of moments, Sibi closed her eyes and sent her most fervent thanks to God. Then she sent up another quick prayer for those who had not been so fortunate.

"We've been bombed," someone said on a slightly stupefied note as if such a thing was impossible to believe. Others repeated it, with variations but no lesser degree of disbelief. Sibi stepped out into the same bright sunlight, with the same blue sky and green grass, as before. But instead of the delicate scent of the gazania flowers lining the paths the air smelled of burning, and instead of happy chatter and birdsongs and ordinary street sounds the overwhelming uproar of a grievously wounded town filled her ears.

"I'll go with you." Emilio was beside her, talking to her, but Sibi barely glanced at him. He stayed with her as she strode along so she must have responded with something affirmative, or maybe she hadn't and he was just coming with her, anyway. It didn't matter: she had no time or energy to spare for him. She was busy visually skimming all the tumult in the long street that stretched downhill in front of her for the sight of a pair of curly blond heads presumably racing toward the bakery.

With single-minded determination, she dodged her way through the tide of would-be rescuers rushing toward Station Plaza.

". . . . call for help?" One man screamed the question at another.

"Phone lines are down! Can't get a message out!"

"The army —"

"They're not coming. No one's coming!"

"Wait." Emilio grabbed her arm. He was a few paces behind her; she'd been walking fast, bobbing up on her toes to look for Luiza and Margrit, and had pretty much forgotten all about him. When she glanced around, impatient at having been stopped, she saw that he was looking skyward again. His expression was enough to jump-start her heart. "There's something — *there.*"

He broke off, pointing, his hand tightening on her arm. She barely noticed his fingers digging into her flesh as she looked toward where he pointed, to the north, shielding her eyes against the sun, to see what, at that distance, appeared to be a trio of pale birds soaring through a gap in the mountains.

Heading toward the town.

Dread shivered through her.

Others saw the same thing. Stark horror made the voices sharp as broken glass.

"Look there!"

"They're coming back!"

"Bombers!"

Three airplanes, in a tight vee formation. Sibi's stomach dropped clear to her toes.

"More Whites." Emilio let go of her arm to clamp a hand around her wrist as, frozen in place, Sibi watched the approach of the distinctive twin-engine airplanes. *"Come on."*

His jerk on her arm galvanized her. Along with everyone else, they started to run. The drone of the airplane engines growing louder and louder was the most terrifying sound she'd ever heard. Church bells clanged in hysterical warning. Screams of terror, sirens wailing, people scattering in every direction, taking cover: scenes from her worst nightmares made real.

On the heels of a woman dragging a young child by the hand, she and Emilio clattered down steps into a cellar storeroom. The open door bore a sign: *Refugio* was scrawled in paint on cardboard.

The airplanes flew so close above them as they rushed inside that the growl of their engines rattled her teeth. She glimpsed the variegated colors of brown and tan and green on the wings, heard a whistling sound —

The cellar door slammed shut behind them.

Darkness. Ominous silence. A feeling of doom —

A blast shook the floor, the walls, the ceiling. Another followed, then another and another in quick succession. Sibi's heart hammered. Fear rose in her throat like bile. Emilio wrapped his arms around her. She buried her head against his chest.

The bombs fell in a relentless barrage. She kept her eyes closed tight and bit her lip to keep from crying out. The building swayed. The timbers above their heads seemed to groan.

The room grew hot and stuffy. All the oxygen seemed to have been sucked away.

Children cried. Around her, continuous prayers from dozens of throats were sent winging skyward.

"Padre nuestro —"

"Dios te salve, Maria —"

"— y del Espiritu Santo —"

She tried praying herself but the words wouldn't come. Dizzy and sick, cold with fear, she gritted her teeth and set herself to endure. Dust sifted down from above. The floor heaved. After a particularly violent hit that made her fear the whole building was coming down on them, part of the ceiling buckled.

Through it all, she and Emilio clung together as the only support the other had in an insane world. When the silence finally came, when the sounds of bursting bombs and airplanes roaring overhead stopped at last, it took Sibi — all of them — several long minutes to realize it.

Like Emilio, like everyone else in the shelter, she seemed to be suspended in time and space, not breathing, not moving.

Waiting.

To live, or die.

Because waiting was all they could do.

"It's stopped." Finally someone said it, a woman, she didn't know who. The words held a tentative note, almost posing a question, because of course it was impossible to be sure.

Sibi lifted her head, looked around, registered details she hadn't noticed before. Tomas Garza, Xabier Fernandez, Amaya Camus: schoolmates she just now realized were in the shelter, too. Señora Echauri, who taught math; Señor Kermen, the barber; Father Marco from the monastery — they were all there, along with maybe two dozen others she didn't recognize. Pale-faced, sweating, emanating fear as palpable as a smell.

Everyone in the shelter seemed reluctant to move.

Outside sounds — shouting, running feet, the clatter of wooden wheels on cobblestones — told of activity in the street.

Maybe the bombing really had stopped.

Sibi took a deep breath. Emilio looked down at her.

"You hurt?"

She shook her head. *No.*

"Are they gone?" someone asked, and people started to stir.

Daylight along with a plume of dust spilled in as someone cautiously opened the door.

She and Emilio, as the last ones inside before it was slammed shut, were right beside it. The cellar was not completely underground, and a sideways glance was all it took to focus her attention on the bedlam in the street. Feet raced past, as well as animals and the tires of what she thought, from the screeching siren that was briefly loud enough to fill the cellar, was an ambulance. The din was unbelievable. The smell of smoke was strong.

Then Sibi heard something that made

every cell in her body snap to instant attention.

"Margrit, stop! Margrit, come back here!"

Luiza, her voice shrill with fear.

Her little sisters were out there.

Shoving away from Emilio, Sibi bolted for the stairs.

5

The scene Sibi ran out into was horrific.

"Luiza! Margrit!" she screamed.

People, animals, carts and debris clogged the street. Clouds of dust obscured everything. Thick black smoke billowed skyward from so many points she couldn't begin to count them. Buildings — buildings she knew — collapsed into piles of rubble, some of them burning. Every single window shattered in the structures that remained standing. Shards of glass lay everywhere, glinting in the golden glow of the late-afternoon sun. Clothes, books, papers, dishes, every conceivable human possession, strewn about as if a giant had grabbed the town, turned it upside down and shaken the contents out. At the Bank of Vizcaya, the only thing left was the enormous iron vault. A dray horse, one of the two that ordinarily pulled the fire truck, lay on its side, partially buried beneath the pile of bricks that had been the firehouse, obviously dead. A woman in a blue dress hung limply over a destroyed wall, also dead.

People worked with desperate haste to pull others from the ruins.

A terrible scorched smell made it difficult to breathe.

And everywhere, *everywhere,* was the frantic clanging of the bells.

The bells.

Icy fear shot through her as she was struck by the realization that the bells had not been ringing during those final minutes she'd spent in the shelter.

They'd started up again. Just now. What did that mean? She could hardly bear to think —

Please, God, not more airplanes. Not more bombs.

"Luiza! Margrit!" She was frantic, shielding her eyes against the blinding angle of the sun, staring searchingly down the street. There was only chaos and destruction and —

Even over the bells, she heard them: the angry drone of airplane engines.

Her heart lodged in her throat as she whirled around.

There! There they were: small airplanes, smaller than the bombers. Single-engine

68

biplanes, flying in pairs, coming in low over the school: Heinkel 51s. She knew because her father had helped design their engines.

"*Avión! Avión!*" The cry rose from what sounded like a thousand throats at once.

Terror froze her in place. Her heart thumped. Her mouth went dry. She couldn't drag her eyes away as the airplanes separated, curving out over the town.

As lethally elegant as a stiletto, its silver skin painted fire orange by the sun, one airplane bore down on the very street where she stood.

She pivoted, screaming, "Luiza! Margrit!" as the airplane passed right over her head. So low she could see inside the open cockpit, see the pilot in his leather helmet, see the sun glinting off the goggles he wore to protect his eyes. So low she could see the landing gear tucked up against its belly like a bird's claws. So low she could see the white tailplane with its distinctive black saltire cross.

The high-pitched *thrum* of its propellers turned her stomach into a pit. The *whoosh* of its passing robbed her of her breath. The gust of hot acrid wind that followed in its wake ruffled her hair, blew up her skirt.

The staccato chatter of machine-gun fire electrified her. It seemingly came out of nowhere, a rapid burst of sound.

It was only as bullets started raking the street in front of her, tearing chunks out of the cobblestones and zinging off automobiles and thudding into wooden carts and doorways and ripping leaves from trees and blasting through living bodies with the kind of savagery that cut them in half where they stood that she realized what was happening: the airplanes were strafing the town. They were turning their double guns on the unarmed citizenry.

Chasers — that was what the He 51s were called, because they could fly fast enough and low enough to chase their targets down. Just as they were doing now.

People fled in every direction, only to be cut down without mercy. She could barely hear their screams over the pounding of her heart. Bullets sang through the air, raining down in a silver curtain of deadly hail. Bodies — body parts — went flying. Bright red gushers of blood sprayed everywhere.

As she followed the path of the airplane with disbelieving eyes, a fresh terror hit her like a lightning bolt. The sun shone on a curly golden head flying just ahead of the carnage. There was Margrit, bolting straight down the center of the street. Not far behind her ran Luiza, screaming Margrit's name.

The chaser bore down on them.

The hair stood up on the back of Sibi's neck. She started to run. She had to get to them —

Ahead of her, machine-gun fire raked the street, blasting through everyone in its path.

"Margrit!" Luiza's terrified cry pierced the uproar as the volley tore up the cobblestones behind her: *ratatatatatatatat.* She flew after Margrit, legs pumping like pistons, skirt flying, the blond curls that were still holding their shape this time bouncing with her every step.

Helplessly watching even as she ran full tilt, knowing she would never reach them in time and also knowing, with some small, icily coherent part of her mind, that there was absolutely nothing she could do that would make a difference even if she did, Sibi felt as if time stopped in that moment.

Bullets hit Luiza in the back with such force that she was lifted off her feet. Crying out, jerking hideously, she hung suspended in the air for the space of maybe a heartbeat before being flung forward to smash facedown on the cobblestones. Even across the distance that separated them, Sibi could see the spurting blood that instantly stained

Luiza's white shirt scarlet.

"No! Luiza!" Her sister's name ripped from Sibi's throat with explosive force. A burst of anguish so intense that she thought she might die of it knocked everything out of focus. The chatter of the machine-gun fire, the collapsing bodies of the victims, the raw-meat smell of freshly spilled blood — it all seemed unreal suddenly, as if she had been flung into an alternate universe where she could only observe from a distance.

Until she saw Margrit craning her neck to look back at Luiza on the ground, at her, she didn't know. But the five-year-old's terrified face shocked Sibi back into the present, had her screaming Margrit's name even as she ran right past Luiza. Luiza, who lay spread-eagled and ominously still in a growing pool of blood.

Margrit tripped and fell.

Bullets smacked into the street where she lay before the strafing moved on, merciless and deadly, as the chaser continued its terrible attack.

Sibi reached Margrit, threw herself to her knees beside the little girl. The child was breathing: she could see that much. Her white shirt was still white. There was no sign of blood.

Sibi touched her. "Margrit."

To Sibi's vast relief, Margrit rolled over and launched herself into her arms. Sibi hugged her tightly. The child was trembling, crying, but she was alive and seemed unhurt and for that Sibi thanked God. While Luiza —

Her heart shivered as she glanced back at Luiza.

"Sibi!" The timber of Margrit's voice went shrill with terror. She pointed over Sibi's shoulder. "More airplanes!"

Breath catching, Sibi looked up.

The bigger airplanes were back. The bombers. Another trio in vee formation. Coming in low from the north.

Her heart almost stopped. Fear twisted her stomach, dried her mouth. For a moment, a terrible moment, she couldn't move, couldn't speak, could only watch them come.

The bells went wild. Screams rent the air.

"I don't want to die." Margrit buried her face in Sibi's shoulder.

There was no time. The airplanes would be upon them in an instant. And they were out in the open, in the middle of a devastated street in a burning and nearly flattened town.

Her shaking, sobbing little sister gave Sibi the strength she needed.

73

Ordinarily she couldn't carry Margrit. The child was too heavy for her.

But in this time of *extremis* she did it. Clamping her arms around Margrit, she picked her up and ran.

The nearest shelter was in the cellar of an already partially collapsed building.

With Margrit's arms locked tight around her neck, she managed to leap over a pile of fallen bricks at the base of the stairs and stumble through the cellar's open door.

They'd no sooner made it inside than someone slammed the door shut behind them — and a heartbeat after that the bombs hit, one after the other, thunderclap after thunderclap.

Sibi felt the shock of each blast with every cell in her body. The sound was deafening. The shelter was black as pitch, suffocatingly hot and airless.

Closing her eyes, praying with every breath, she held on to Margrit while her heart hammered and the world shook and, finally, an ominous rumbling filled her ears.

The rumbling turned into a roar as the building collapsed.

The next sensation Sibi was aware of was heat: an uncomfortable, baking heat. She lay flat on her back on a surface that felt like stone, her arms flung out on either side of her. Her legs were straight, her feet buried up to the ankles in . . . something. The idea that she was entombed took possession of her, and she struggled uselessly against whatever was holding her down even as she tried to make sense of where she was. Something was heaped around her and close above her, forming a rough ceiling a few centimeters above her face. She knew it was there because when she breathed her breath came back at her, and when she turned her head her hair brushed against it.

Where she was, what had happened — terrible images chased each other through her mind. Her heart began to slam in thick, panicked strokes. A long shiver made her clench her teeth against it.

She took a breath, opened her eyes.

And saw nothing. A darkness so impenetrable that she might as well have been blind.

The air was thick and hot. Dust filled her mouth, clogged her airway. She coughed, turned her head, coughed some more.

An ominous crackling sound put her every sense on alert.

The heat, the sound — was there a fire?

She struggled once more in a compulsive attempt to free herself, until a shower of dirt and dust spilling down convinced her to stay still. That same awful clarity that had claimed it before took possession of her mind.

She was buried alive. Unable to escape. Barely able to move. Trapped in the rubble of a possibly burning building.

Margrit. Where was Margrit?

"Margrit." Her voice was hoarse, choked by dust and fear, and far too soft to penetrate what felt like the mountain of debris around her.

No answer.

She thought of Luiza, lying out there in the street, bloodied and — Her mind shied away from *dead,* but however much she didn't want to face it she knew it was almost certainly the truth.

The horror of it was nearly impossible to take in. Her whole body throbbed with anguish.

Please, God, not Margrit, too.

She'd been holding her sister when the building fell. She had to be nearby.

They'd been near the door. Whatever had kept the rubble from crushing her might have saved her sister, too.

She spat out dust, called out desperately. *"Margrit. Margrit."*

"Did you hear something?" A voice from

76

outside penetrated her prison. A man's voice, muffled, but the fact that she could hear it at all told her that he must be nearby.

Dragging the thick, hot air deep into her lungs, she began to scream.

6

"Hold on. We're going to get you out of
there."

Closer now, his voice was the only thing
keeping Sibi from complete, utter and
ultimately destructive panic. It was the same
steady, compelling voice that had first
reached her as he'd asked whoever was with
him if they'd heard something, then told
them to be quiet while he listened. Then
he'd spoken English, a language she'd
learned in school along with French and
Latin and was reasonably fluent in, just as
she was fluent in her mother's native Basque
and Spanish. When she'd cried out to him
in answer, though, she'd instinctively done
so in her own native German. She realized
that only when he replied in the same
language, flawlessly.

Who is he? None of the townspeople — at
least none she knew — spoke German. Or,
for that matter, English.

Basque, Spanish and in a few cases French were the languages of the region.

The question flickered out of her mind almost as quickly as it had appeared. What did it matter? He was, quite simply, her best hope of survival.

Fear seized her as she realized she could no longer hear him, or anyone at all. They — him, along with two or possibly three others out there with him — had been talking among themselves, quietly enough so that she couldn't quite understand the words, before going silent. How long ago? She couldn't be sure.

Her head hurt. Her ears rang. She felt dizzy, disoriented.

"Are you still there?" she called fearfully into the darkness.

"Yes." His voice again, deep and reassuring.

"Don't leave me."

"I'm not going to leave you. Give you my word."

Relief washed over her, and there was a pause during which she simply lay still and breathed. As she listened to him shout an affirmative answer — in Spanish — to someone asking if there was anyone left alive under there, she took as much of an inventory of her body as she could. She wasn't in acute pain — more like discomfort — which to her mind meant no vital systems were severely injured. If she was bleeding she couldn't tell it. Being unable to move was what was terrifying. Her heart raced every time she thought about being trapped, about how helpless she was, so she tried not to, although as the minutes passed that grew increasingly difficult.

The cavity where she lay made her think of the wall ovens used by Antonio the baker for baking bread: a shallow arched cave designed to radiate heat. The stone floor beneath her back was uneven, and parts of it dug into her spine. The air was grainy with dust. It smelled of old mortar. She was trying to ignore what else it smelled like — something burning — when his voice came again, once more in German. "Hello? Can you hear me?"

"Yes." She had to spit the grit out of her mouth before she could continue. The chalky taste lingered on her tongue. She tried to swallow. Her mouth was so dry it was difficult. "My sister — she's somewhere under here, too."

"We'll get her out. We'll get both of you out."

A chilling thought hit her. A flutter of panic quickened her breathing.

"What about the airplanes? Where are they?"

"Gone. You don't have to worry. They won't come at night."

It was night? "What time is it?"

"About ten thirty, give or take."

Shock shivered through her. Had she really been lying there unconscious for so many hours?

"Margrit." Desperation sharpened her voice as she called out.

Margrit didn't answer.

"Is Margrit your sister?" Steady and calm, his voice reached out to her again.

"Yes. She's five —" She broke off, coughing, as more dust sifted down.

"We'll find her." His voice soothed. She concentrated on it with fierce determination, clinging to his promises as if they were carved in stone. "Are you hurt?"

"I don't think so. At least, not badly. As far as I can tell."

"That's good. We're going to dig you out. It shouldn't be too long."

"Is there a fire?" Her voice shook. "It's so hot, and . . . I smell something burning."

"Everything's under control. Just stay calm."

It wasn't a direct answer. So what did that mean? Something she was better off not

81

knowing?

Stay calm, he'd said.

Sibi closed her eyes and called on every inner resource she possessed to try to comply. It was so dark — darker than the darkest night. Not being able to move anything much besides her head, knowing that she was trapped, that a collapsed building that could collapse still more at any second was piled on top of her, that if a fire was creeping toward her she couldn't get away, made her heart pound and her breathing come fast and shallow.

Knowing that Margrit was under there, too . . . She couldn't bear to think about it.

Despite everything, though, she was alive. That seemed to fall somewhere within the realm of the miraculous. Unless she wanted to lose her mind completely, she had to believe Margrit was alive, too.

Bullets slamming into Luiza; Luiza falling and lying motionless in a pool of blood . . . Sibi thrust the horrific images out of her mind.

She couldn't bear it. Couldn't bear it that Luiza might be dead. Couldn't bear it if something equally terrible had happened to her littlest sister, too.

By now she'd deduced that what was holding her immobile was a slab of heavy masonry attached to a giant wood beam, possibly one of the roof joists. At a guess the beam itself weighed close to a thousand kilograms, and it was being held just far enough off the floor to keep her pinned in place without crushing her completely. By what? She didn't know. She did know that if whatever it was moved, or if by some horrible mischance the beam itself shifted, she would almost certainly die.

"Keep talking, sweetheart, so we can find you," he called. More thuds, along with a series of clinks and scraping sounds, accompanied his voice. While she knew that those were almost certainly the sounds of rescue working its way toward her and not the mountain of debris on top of her shifting before it collapsed and crushed her, she had to fight off a stab of panic. "What's your name?"

Sibi wet her lips. "Sibil Helinger. Sibi."

"Pleased to meet you, Sibi. My name's Griff."

"Griff," she said. A harsh-sounding name, and not one with which she was familiar. American? She thought perhaps. Which would match up with the brusque quality of the English he'd spoken earlier.

"That's right." A pause filled with the sounds of more debris being shifted followed. Sibi cringed as a long, ominous creak sounded directly above her head. "How are you situated? Are you curled up under something?"

"I'm flat on my back in kind of a hollow space. There's a beam and part of the ceiling or a wall on top of me."

"Is your sister near you? Can you see her? Touch her?"

"No." Anxiety gripped her. "But I was holding her when the building fell. She has to be close." She broke off, coughing. "I have another sister. She's out there on the street. She was shot. The airplanes shot her."

"Shot her dead?" There was a kind of rough sympathy in his voice.

"I . . . don't know. There was a lot of blood." It was growing increasingly hard to talk, let alone breathe. The air seemed to thicken by the second as more dust and sediment sifted into the small pocket around her face. With her arms pinned there was no way to even brush the dust away.

"We'll check on her. Once we get you out."

"And my other sister. Margrit. Once she's out, too."

"Right. After we get you both out." A pause. "How many others were in there with you?"

"I'm not sure. Someone shut the door.

There were people — there had to have been — but I didn't really see anyone else. And I — I don't hear anyone now."

Though the shelter had been dark with shadow after the brightness of the street outside, and there'd been no time to look when she'd rushed through the door with Margrit, and she'd been in too much of a frenzy to notice anything beyond herself and her sister, anyway, someone had shut the door behind them. And there had been others in there, as well, and even in the building itself when it fell, as she was only just now realizing. The fact that no one else was crying out for help, no one else was making a sound, horrified her with its significance.

Was she the only one in this hellish pile left alive?

"Sibi?" His voice again.

"Yes?"

"You doing all right?"

She realized she'd been silent for a while.

"Yes." She coughed as more grit choked her. Her head hurt. She felt dizzy, nauseous. And really, right now all she wanted to do was rest.

"Keep talking." There was a pause during which he seemed to be waiting for her to say something. When she didn't — she couldn't think of anything, and besides, talking required a lot of effort, which she couldn't quite force herself to make — he asked, "How old are you?"

From somewhere she dredged up the strength. "Sixteen."

"Sixteen." He drew the word out. "So tell me, what's a nice German girl like you doing in a place like this?"

She swallowed. "I'm only half-German."

"Oh? How is that?"

She told him. Haltingly, with numerous pauses that he had to prod her out of, she told him about her parents, and their not so perfect union. Told him about her sisters, about Margrit and Jo, and Luiza with her freshly curled hair lying possibly dead out there in the street. About her *amona.* He kept her talking even when she was so exhausted she could barely think. Her growing dread of him giving up and leaving her alone in the dark, her fierce need to not lose the lifeline that was his voice, was what kept her going, what kept her from closing her eyes and drifting away.

"Do you go to school?"

"Yes."

"What's your favorite subject?"

"Physics." Even to her own ears her voice sounded weak. Reaching deep down inside herself, she found the will not to succumb to the lassitude that wanted to drag her off into unconsciousness.

"Physics?"

She heard the surprise in his voice. Which, to her, was no surprise. People always reacted that way. What they didn't appreciate was the effect that having an autocratic scientist father directing the education of his firstborn child, combined with her own apparently natural bent for the discipline, had on her choices.

"Yes. And math."

"Interesting."

He kept talking to her, and she kept responding even though staying awake was now a pitched battle between her survival instinct and the demands of her body.

"Sibi. We're getting ready to remove what's left of a wall. It could get loud."

Eyes shut tight, braced for the worst, she lay there and listened in terrified silence to what sounded like the building falling around her.

Until a particularly violent crash shook the ground, caused whatever was over her head to groan threateningly and made her cry out even as her eyes flew open. It was an instinctive reaction she couldn't control even though she knew she would see nothing —

Except the tiny sliver of a crack in the wall of debris to her right.

As she blinked at it, an electric thrill shot through her.

"Griff." She had to shout to alert him over the sounds of the digging. "I see light. There's a crack, and a bright white light's shining through it."

"You see light?" He sounded freshly energized. He then shouted to somebody who wasn't her, "Stop!" and the sounds stopped.

The light vanished, to be replaced by a faint orange incandescence.

It had to be from a fire.

The terror was back, slamming into her, reminding her that she was alone and trapped and —

"Do you see the light now?"

"No." Her voice shook. "But I can see the fire."

"I told you, you don't need to worry about that. We'll have you out of there long before it becomes a problem. Tell me when you can see the light again."

A moment later the bright light was back, shining through the crack.

"Now."

"All right. We've got you." There was no mistaking the triumph in his voice as the light apparently pinpointed her location for them. "Don't go anywhere."

Under less dire circumstances that would almost have sounded like a pathetic attempt at a joke, and it almost would have made her smile.

Then she heard an exclamation, and a curse. The light shifted so that she could still see its brilliance, although it was no longer shining directly through the crack.

The men were talking, but she couldn't quite make out the words. From the tone of them, she got the feeling that something unexpected had happened.

"Griff," she called in trepidation.

"Sibi." There was a quality to his voice that sent a chill down her spine. A sudden gentleness she found foreboding. "We've found your sister."

7

"Margrit?" Terror clutched at her. His voice — she could tell from his tone that, as good as the news was that Margrit was found, there was more that was not so good. *Oh, please, God. "Margrit."*

"She can't hear you. She's unconscious. But she's alive. She's breathing."

Sibi exhaled. "How bad is she?"

"I don't know. I can't tell. Can you hold on a little longer while we get her out?"

"Yes. Yes, of course." She could feel the blood pumping through her veins, thundering in her ears. "Griff." Her voice broke. "Please save her."

It was an impossible thing to ask of him, she knew.

"Do my best."

Except for the shifting light filtering in through the crack, the space where Sibi lay was once again as dark and suffocating as a tomb. She barely noticed. Every sense she possessed focused on the muffled sounds of shovels grating against stone, on the low-voiced conversation of what she was fairly certain now were three men plus Griff, on the absolute silence from Margrit.

That silence chilled her to the bone.

"We've got her out." Griff's shout filled her with relief.

"Margrit." She called frantically to her sister.

"She's unconscious, remember?" Griff replied. Then, to someone else, he said, "Go. Make sure somebody looks at her right away, would you?"

"Griff." In her agitation, Sibi made a sudden, abortive movement that bought down a shower of dust and grit and only reinforced how immobilized she was. Her body twitched as darts of pain shot through her arms and legs. Inhaling what felt like a lungful of dust, she started to cough.

"Keep still. She's on her way to the hospital. We're coming for you now."

Sibi closed her eyes.

She didn't know how long they worked to reach her. It could have been minutes or hours. What she did know was that, as she lay there in that coffin-like space, it felt like an eternity.

"Sibi." A hand, strong and warm, closed

around hers. *My hand must be free of the rubble.* The unexpected contact startled her, made her pulse leap. "Got you."

Her fingers clutched his like she would never let go.

"Get me out of here. Please."

"That's the plan. Hold on just a little longer."

With a quick squeeze he let go. Her fingers, bereft, curled into a ball.

"Close your eyes," he directed, and she did.

He talked to her, and she listened, and counted the metallic scrapes of the shovel — *one, two, three, a hundred* — until she felt a whisper of air feather across her face. *Moving* air. It felt warm — far too warm for a spring night — but still markedly unlike the suffocating closeness she'd been trapped in.

She sucked it in.

Her eyes popped open.

The ceiling that had enclosed her was gone.

A livid red incandescence colored everything. Shaking her head, blinking, she did her best to dislodge the dust that clogged her eyelashes and coated her skin. Even with her lids no longer so heavily weighted down, her flat-on-her-back position limited her field of vision. All she could actually see was the building's wreckage piled high around her and, directly overhead, a swath of night sky.

A strange, cloudy, pink-tinted sky that pulsed with flickering bands of red and orange. A terrifying sky that, nevertheless, in that moment looked absolutely beautiful simply because she could see it.

A beam of white light hit her in the face, blinding her. A torch, she realized, squinting against its brightness. The person holding the torch dropped with a thud from atop the nearest mound of rubble into the crater that formed a semicircle around her head: a tall, dark-haired man in a leather flight jacket. His boots crunched on the sediment surrounding her, and then he crouched beside her.

"Hello, sweetheart." He shifted the focus of the torch from her face, running it over the beam and attached blanket of masonry and other debris that still lay on top of her. She recognized his voice instantly.

"Griff."

"Yup. You ready to get out of here?" He turned the torch on her again.

"Yes. Oh, yes. Please."

His fingers, warm and gentle, brushed her face, and she realized he was whisking the worst of the dust away. She frowned up at him, blinking, trying to bring him into focus. With the red glow lighting up the world behind him and his torch, it was difficult to get more than a general impression of his appearance. Still, she was able to discern the outlines of a square jaw, wide cheekbones and a high, broad forehead. His shoulders were broad, too, silhouetted against the light. His dark hair was short and wavy and he seemed relatively young — midtwenties, perhaps. More than that she couldn't really tell.

"Careful. Jack both ends up at the same time. On my *go*." He spoke English again, directing his words to whoever was with him.

"Gonna be tricky. We'll get it up there, but I don't know how long it'll stay," a man answered.

"Just get it up there." Griff looked at her, switched back to German. "We're going to lift this beam, then I'm going to pull you out from under it. It'll happen fast. Understand?"

Even as her stomach cramped with fear — if something went wrong with what they were planning, she could be crushed to death in an instant — she nodded. "I understand."

His hands worked their way beneath her shoulders. His fingers hooked into her armpits. There wasn't much room for him to maneuver: the cavity around her head barely held them both. He crouched directly behind her now. His face was deep in shadow, but she could see the gleam of his eyes — and he must have been able to see the fright in hers.

"Steady," he said. "I'll get you out in one piece. Count on it."

Sibi's heart thumped, but believing in him was the only choice she could make and stay sane. "I am."

He smiled at her. She could just see the curve of his mouth. He raised his voice to address the men with him. "On the count of three. One. Two —"

"Now." The shout from one of the men she couldn't see had her bracing herself, had Griff's grip on her tightening. *"Three."*

The weight of the beam on top of her lifted — and then she was yanked violently out from beneath it, dragged across stone and rubble and, as Griff shot upright and pulled her upright with him, wrested free. As the truth of that hit her she went light-headed with reaction.

"Got her," Griff yelled to the others.

The beam crashed down, shaking the

ground, sending up a cloud of dust, making her shudder.

"All right?" he asked. They stood, her back to his front, with her leaning against him and his hands still hooked in her armpits.

"Yes. Oh!" Electric jolts of pain shot through her as her legs automatically tried to bear her weight before buckling. She sagged, and would have dropped to the ground like an empty suit of clothes if he hadn't been holding on to her.

"Whoa, there." He slid an arm beneath her knees and scooped her up. "I've got you."

Sibi found herself shivering like she would never stop. "I thought I was going to die under there." Even her voice shook.

"Not on my watch."

His eyes were deep-set and hooded, their color impossible to determine in the uncertain light as they swept over her. But there was a calm competence in the way he carried himself that was reassuring. For just the next little bit of time what made the most sense was to trust him, to give up the struggle to stay strong in favor of letting this stranger who had just become so enormously important in her life make the decisions. Surrendering to pain and fatigue and the aftermath of deep and abiding terror, she allowed herself to relax in his arms. Her head dropped onto his shoulder because she simply didn't have the strength to hold it up any longer. Her eyes closed.

"You're safe now," Griff said. His voice had gentled. "I'm not going to let anything happen to you."

She believed him, she did, but her body continued to be slow to get the message. Her head reeled, the world spun and she hurt all over. The sensation as the circulation started to return to her limbs was excruciating. It felt as if a thousand wasps were crawling over her skin, stinging her with every step.

She wet her lips, or tried to. Her throat and mouth were so dry. "Is there any water?"

"Soon, I promise." Griff was moving with her, turning. "First let's get you out of here."

"Jesus, that thing was heavy," a man said, presumably to Griff, from somewhere above them. "Broke the hell out of one of the jacks."

"Take her, would you?" Griff asked. Sibi felt herself being lifted, felt a second man taking her weight. As she was transferred from one pair of strong arms to another she opened her eyes.

From her new vantage point in yet another

stranger's arms high above the pit where she'd been trapped, the view was shattering.

The world was on fire.

8

The devastation was so immense Sibi could hardly take it in.

The night seethed with a horrible red glare. Giant tongues of flame leaped heavenward everywhere she looked. Great black swirls of smoke twisted into low-hanging clouds that billowed above what was left of the town. Skeletal remains of burned-out buildings were limned with orange. Other buildings, not yet destroyed, blazed angrily. Fire consumed the jagged splinter of what had been the Church of San Juan's spire even as she realized, from its position, that that was what she was looking at. So many landmarks were missing that there was no other way to tell. In the hills around the town, pillars of fire lit up the darkness like a thousand candles. The sight was almost beautiful, until she realized that each flaming column must be one of the *caserios,* the farmhouses that nestled on the steep slopes, the homes of people who had raised their families and made their livings there for hundreds of years. From the numbers, it didn't look as though many had escaped.

Her throat tightened. How was it possible that everything was just *gone*?

A hot wind blew in off the back of the fire, dragging across her face, ruffling her hair. It carried glowing red sparks in such numbers that the night seemed alive with infernal fireflies. The smell of burning stung her nostrils. The sound of the fire — an approaching monster's ominous roar — sent gooseflesh racing over her skin. Above it she could hear men shouting, the crash of collapsing structures, the clang of metal on stone and on metal and a high-pitched keening that wrung her heart as she identified it as multiple voices wailing in pain — or grief.

Hell itself couldn't have been more horrific.

"My God," Sibi breathed.

"God had nothing to do with it." The man holding her sounded grim. Except for registering that he was stocky and fair-haired and speaking American English in reply to her muttered, *"Mein Gott,"* she had barely a thought to spare for him. She couldn't tear her eyes away from the ghastly scene in front of her.

The street she knew so well was unrecognizable, destroyed to the point of oblivion. From the top of the street, where she had hurried along the sidewalk with Emilio what seemed like a thousand lifetimes ago, a wall of fire advanced steadily toward them, consuming everything in its path. Ahead of it, flames jumped from place to place like living creatures, soaring upward with a shower of sparks, then dying back only to blaze up again somewhere else. On their side of the street, an advance guard of flames raced to within three buildings — three towering piles of debris — of where they stood. It fed upon the remains like an angry, howling beast, twisting into a sky-scraping monolith as it found fuel apparently to its taste.

So close. So terrifyingly close.

Its intense heat took her breath; the rushing, popping sound it made sent her heart galloping. The angry orange glow it threw colored everything, fell over them where they stood.

How many people were under there, still buried, as the fire reached them? How many lay helpless in its path?

Luiza.

"Give her to me. Get the jack that's left."

Griff was beside them, speaking to the other man in the same American-accented English even as he reached for her. The other man handed her over and Griff started to move away with her, lurching slightly over the uneven terrain. To her he spoke in German. "Can you put your arms around my neck?"

Her arms had been immobilized for so long that lifting them was difficult. Every movement brought pain, but she gritted her teeth and did it, anyway.

"Hold on tight."

"You're American, aren't you? Who are you? What are you doing here?" She focused on his face because she couldn't bear to look at anything else. His eyes glinted at her beneath thick dark brows. His nose was straight, his mouth well-cut but thin.

"Captain James Griffin, US Army Air Corps, lately assigned to our embassy in Spain. I'm the assistant military attaché under Colonel Stephen Fuqua. We got word of what had happened here and I was sent to take a look. You just met Sergeant Ray Iverson. Also with me is Private Tim Lynch. Private Hank Phillips took your sister to the hospital." A quick glance at her. "You don't have to be afraid of us. We won't hurt you."

"I'm not afraid. At least, not of you." She took a breath. "My other sister. She's out there on the street. She — she — I don't know if she's alive. An airplane shot her. *Machine-gunned* her."

She broke off, unable to continue as the horror of what had happened to Luiza caused her throat to close up. And the rest of her family — given the scope of the destruction, she could no longer assume they were safe. Panic wrapped itself around her heart. How could she live until she knew they did, too?

She must have made a sound or otherwise signaled her distress, because his arms tightened around her.

"Let's get you taken care of first, and then I'll look for your sister and we can take the rest from there."

"She was in the middle of the street. Right up there." Sibi nodded in the direction she meant. The place where Luiza had fallen had been opposite the barbershop. The image of the sign being struck by the same fusillade of bullets that had hit Luiza was imprinted on her brain.

"I'll check on her just as soon as I can."

Around them there were more voices, more desperate plights.

"Take the other end. *Hurry.*" The urgency in the command was no less spine-tingling because it was muted by distance.

Originating from the shattered shell of what had been the building two doors away, it drew Sibi's attention to the frantic efforts of a pair of men attempting to rescue what she assumed must be more survivors from the bombed-out ruins. Even as she spotted them, a finger of fire made the leap from the newest towering blaze, racing toward where the men tore at the rubble. The flames were almost upon them when one grabbed the other and hauled him, cursing and struggling, away.

"Maria! Maria!" the struggling man screamed as the other man shoved him into the street and forcibly held him there.

"Can't we try to put it out?" Sibi's voice shook as she remembered the destroyed firehouse. "With a bucket brigade or —"

"There's no water," Griff said. "The bombs destroyed the lines."

Sibi said no more. There was nothing to do but watch in anguish as in a matter of moments the entire pile was engulfed in flames. The man who'd screamed for Maria dropped to his knees in front of the conflagration, raising his arms to the sky, weeping as he loudly berated God. The other man hovered helplessly over him.

"Poor bastard," Griff said, moving faster.

"Why? Why would anyone do this?" Sibi

whispered, sick at heart.

Griff shook his head. "I can't answer that."

"We don't get out of here, that'll be us," the fair-haired man — Sergeant Ray Iverson — said from behind them. "Fire's coming on fast."

Sibi registered the warning with the small part of her mind that wasn't wholly riven with horror.

The difference between life and death was so small.

"If you hadn't come when you did, the fire would have caught us. We — Margrit and I — would have burned to death," she said to Griff. The prospect made her dizzy.

"But we did come," Griff said. "No point in thinking about what might have happened. The important thing is what did."

He was right. She knew he was right. Dwelling was useless.

"Margrit and I weren't the only ones inside this building. I know we weren't. What if there are others still trapped?"

"We've been here digging, and calling, for a while now. We uncovered a couple of bodies, two men, near your sister. We've seen no one else, and no one else has made a sound. Maybe the rest escaped before we got here."

And maybe they didn't. Maybe they were

105

still buried under the rubble. Maybe —

A white blouse turned red with blood. A headful of blond curls against the cobblestones. As the terrible image rose without warning in her mind's eye, Sibi's stomach turned into a pit.

"Maybe they're dead." Her voice was a mere breath of sound. "Maybe —"

Luiza's dead, is what she was going to say. But she simply couldn't assume such a thing. Even if all that remained was the merest sliver of a possibility that her sister had survived, she would cling to it.

"Maybe they're lying under there unconscious," she said instead. "Like we were."

"If they're dead, there's nothing you or I or anyone else can do for them. As for the other —" His voice broke off as whatever was beneath his feet gave way with a sharp *pop.* Sibi caught her breath and clutched his neck tighter, but he recovered his balance and went on. There wasn't time to waste. The fire churned toward them. Smoke blew everywhere.

"There's no time left to look for anyone. I know," she said. As terrible as it was she knew it was true. The fire was so close now that the heat engulfing them was enough to make her feel like her skin was crisping. Griff hunched his shoulders and bent his head over her in an effort to protect her from the worst of it, but there was no warding off the sparks that swirled around them, flaming out on the smooth leather of his jacket, stinging her bare arms, burning tiny holes through her skirt and blouse and stockings. Looking down her legs, she realized that her shoes, those too-big shoes, were missing.

The slithering sound of something collapsing distracted her. Everywhere she looked, for as far as she could see, people dug desperately among the ruins, were loaded into carts filled with what from their cries she thought must be the injured, pushed wheelbarrows piled high with belongings, staggered away on foot as they attempted to escape the inferno. Others simply sat stunned atop piles of rubble and on crumbling stoops and on the ground and watched the fire come.

Mama, Jo — where were they? For the first time, the question she'd refused to allow herself to consider crept into her consciousness: Were they even still alive?

"You get the jack, Iverson?" Throwing the question over his shoulder, Griff half leaped, half slid down the sloping outer debris field. Glancing at the street below, Sibi watched a dog run past. A pack of dogs. As she looked more closely, the dark shapes moving over the cobblestones resolved themselves into animals — dogs, cats, chickens, sheep, a pig — fleeing the fire.

"Lynch has it. I've got the shovels."

Griff turned his head to yell, "You back there, Lynch?"

"Right behind you, Captain."

Sibi barely registered the exchange. She was now almost entirely focused on trying to identify the spot where Luiza lay, or had lain. The fire threw dancing shadows everywhere, making it difficult to get her bearings, or to discern what — or who — was or was not there.

Please, God, please, let Luiza only have been wounded. Please let her not be dead.

Griff had just stepped down into the street when, on the cobblestones a little way to her left, she saw maybe six or seven people lying in a row. The shifting shadows coupled with the flickering red glow made details difficult to discern, but it struck her that they looked odd, their motionless bodies in unnatural positions, their clothes ripped away —

Her breath caught as she realized what she was looking at: a lineup of the dead.

"Señora Casellas." The name came out as the merest breath as the identity of the closest of them hit her like a brick. A plump, cheerful woman, Juana Casellas was mother to a brood of children, including one of Margrit's closest friends. The small body lying next to her was — Sibi's throat tightened — Katalin, her youngest, aged no more than two. "I know them."

"Don't look." Griff's clipped recommendation came as he hitched her higher in his arms to keep her secure and kept walking, clearly intent on carrying her past the gruesome sight. Along with the animals, living people stumbled past, singly and in groups, some weeping and wailing, some stunned into silence. Most of them skirted the bodies with their eyes averted: Why see what you couldn't help?

"Make way! Make way!"

Griff checked at the cry, which came as a donkey cart careened past with a clatter of hooves and wheels. It passed maybe a meter in front of them to stop beside the bodies. The donkey between the shafts was on a leading rein in the grip of a wild-eyed local. With shock Sibi recognized that local as Jose Rodriguez, twentysomething son of the general manager of the munitions factory. Usually handsome and laughing and a favorite of the ladies, he was streaked with soot and his face was twisted with emotion.

Both donkey and man were breathing hard and dripping sweat, as was a second man who was with them. Despite the blindfold that had been tied around the donkey's eyes to keep it from being panicked by the fire, the animal shook and heaved as the men dropped the leading rein to rush toward the bodies.

"What are you doing?" The shout, directed at Rodriguez, came from someone on the street as Griff regained his stride to move on past. Wide-eyed with horror, Sibi watched over Griff's shoulder as the two men grabbed Señora Casellas by the arms and legs and threw her into the open-ended cart.

"Collecting the dead." Rodriguez picked up baby Katalin and gently deposited her limp body atop her mother's as he spoke. "The fire — they will be unrecognizable. We can't just leave them to it. They are our people."

At the sight of the little one sprawled out on her dead mother's chest, Sibi had to clamp her lips together to keep from crying out. Her eyes dropped because she couldn't bear to look any longer, but the sight that met them was no less gruesome: a jumble of mangled limbs; heads lolling at unnatural angles. Bloodied and torn, the bodies were positioned haphazardly, one on top of the other, some stiff and ungainly in death, others charred —

Sibi's eyes locked on blond curls, a familiar face.

Her heart clutched.

Luiza.

9

Luiza lay on her back near the bottom of the pile. Her head dangled limply off the end of the cart. Her mouth was open and slack. Her eyes were closed. Even in the pulsating orange light her skin looked gray.

Dead. There was no doubt.

"My sister —"

"Easy." Griff held her so that her view of Luiza, of the cart, was blocked as he strode away. Deliberately, Sibi thought, and for that she was almost grateful, though not entirely because losing visual contact with Luiza was wrenching. She closed her eyes, took deep breaths, fought to stay strong. Griff continued. "I'm sorry, sweetheart. Really sorry."

The cart started to move, the clatter of the wheels like an electric shock. Her eyes opened and she jerked upright in Griff's arms in time to see the cart bumping away down the street.

"No! Luiza!" Sibi struggled to get free, straining after the cart even as Griff's arms clamped tight around her, holding her in place. An instant later she accepted that there was nothing she could do. Luiza was dead, there was no fixing it, and her body — her *body* — couldn't just be left to burn in the street.

"Where are you taking her?" Sibi's cry, directed at Rodriguez as the cart rattled away, was all but lost beneath the tumult. It didn't occur to her that she was still speaking German, and Rodriguez wouldn't understand even if he heard, until one of a group stumbling past turned his head to frown in her direction. She heard him say, "A German," with loathing in his voice, and watched him spit on the ground.

With an electrifying sense of shock she realized that her German language, her German heritage, in his eyes made her one of the enemy. The *hated* enemy.

The enemy *she* hated.

The chaser that killed Luiza had been a Heinkel — a German airplane.

How incredibly monstrous was it that Luiza had been killed by an airplane powered by an engine their father had helped design?

"Iverson, find out where they're going," Griff ordered over his shoulder, and Iverson ran after the cart. To Sibi, Griff said, "They'll have set up a makeshift morgue, a place to collect the —" he hesitated, as if he searched for the right word "— victims."

At the thought of Luiza as one of the *victims* to be laid out in a morgue, Sibi felt sick. *Eternal rest grant unto her, oh Lord . . .*

"Are you all right?" Griff looked at her with concern.

"No more speaking German." She'd switched to Spanish, which she'd heard him use, uttering the warning in a strangled tone.

"No? Why not?" Griff replied in Spanish, too, as he deposited her in the front passenger seat of an open, military-style automobile with a small American flag attached to the front. He took off his jacket and wrapped it around her as she huddled there shivering. Beneath it he wore a white shirt. His shoulders looked very broad.

"The airplane that shot Luiza — it was a Heinkel. An He 51." In case he didn't comprehend the significance of that, she added, "A German airplane."

He paused whatever he was doing to give her a sharp look. "How do you know that?"

"I know airplanes, I know what they look like. And I saw the insignia. I'm not mistaken, believe me. It wasn't the Whites who did this. They were *German* airplanes."

Griff frowned at her.

"Taking them to the Casa de Juntas. It wasn't hit. Priest there saying rites for the dead." Iverson was back, speaking English, throwing several objects that were heavy and metallic sounding — shovels? He'd said he was carrying them — into a compartment in the rear.

"Did you understand what he said, Sibi? Your sister is being taken to a priest. They'll take care of her." When she didn't reply, he added, "Here. Drink," and offered her a canteen. She stared at it blankly. He held it to her lips. She understood then, and swallowed as he tilted it for her. The water was warm and stale, but welcome. It bathed her tongue and throat, splashed down into her stomach.

"Need to go." Iverson addressed that to Griff. There was no mistaking the urgency in his tone, or the significant glance he cast at the fire roaring toward them. With an answering nod for him, Griff cautioned Sibi, "Not too much at once. It'll make you sick."

When she kept drinking he took the canteen away.

She licked the last drops from her lips. Then she pulled his jacket on, putting her arms in the sleeves, zipping it up. It was far too big — she rolled up the cuffs as best she could — but she was *so cold.*

"Where's Lynch?" Already in motion, jogging around the front of the vehicle, Griff threw the question at Iverson. When Iverson jerked a thumb over his shoulder, Griff yelled, "Lynch!" in that direction with enough volume to make Sibi wince.

"Here, Captain. We got more passengers." Lynch ran up, panting. He was younger than Griff or Iverson, maybe twentyish, tall and gangly, with a bullet-shaped head and big ears beneath a peaked cap. More than that she couldn't tell in the garish orange light. He carried an old, frail, clearly unconscious woman in his arms. Another elderly woman and man, their arms around each other, stumbled along behind. All were covered with dust, and the woman Lynch carried looked to be in dire shape. "We need to get the *señora* here to the hospital."

"Jump in." With Griff now behind the wheel, the others piled in. Iverson crowded in next to Sibi, which put her in the middle between him and Griff, and the rest wedged into the back seat. They took off with a jolt and a grinding of gears.

Thick black curls of smoke tumbled after them. The street was pocked with huge craters left by the bombs, which they had to dodge, and clogged with debris. Desperate townspeople dug through the wreckage everywhere Sibi looked, calling out to each other and their missing loved ones and God as the clock for survival ticked down. A few *gudaris* — Basque soldiers — were on the scene, doing their best to direct a rescue operation that was so vast in scope that they seemed to know it was hopeless even as they went through the motions.

All the buildings, every single one for as far as Sibi could see, had been hit. Most were completely destroyed. She registered that with stunned disbelief as they bumped their way through a once-familiar landscape that was now unrecognizable.

A haze of smoke lay over everything, making sinuses sting and throats burn. The smell —

It made her grimace.

"The smoke smells different. Almost . . . sweet," the old man in the back said in a reed-thin voice. It was the first time he'd spoken, and Sibi recognized him as Señor Elizondo, who worked in the bank next door to the fire station. A dapper little man in his forties, he had routinely cashed her paycheck for her, and she had served him and his wife numerous times at the restaurant. With his hair white with ash, his newly stooped posture and lined, crumpled face, he appeared to have aged twenty years in the course of the day. The woman with him — the conscious one — was his wife.

"That's what human beings smell like when they cook." Lynch's reply, given in the same Spanish Señor Elizondo had used, was horrifyingly matter-of-fact.

Sibi's stomach turned inside out.

The smoke was everywhere. She couldn't *not* smell it. She barely managed not to gag.

People were burning. Maybe even . . . people she knew.

The thought was so hideous, so unspeakable, that she instantly rejected it.

"Shut it, Lynch." Griff's response was sharp. As always, when the three Americans talked to each other, it was in English. He glanced at Sibi. At whatever he saw in her face, his voice gentled. "It could be anything. Wood. Pine smells sweet when it burns. So does oak. Cooking supplies. Sugar."

Sibi nodded, pretending to accept the comfort he was trying to provide, although in some deep atavistic place in her soul she knew that it was Lynch who had it right.

"Here." Griff reached into his pocket, pulled out something, handed it to her. "It's clean."

118

"It" was a folded square of white linen — a handkerchief. Even as she accepted it, she realized that, despite her best intentions, despite the fist she pressed against her mouth to hold back any untoward sounds, she was weeping. Hot tears slid down her cheeks in what felt like an unstoppable stream. She mopped her eyes, her face. The linen was instantly damp and grimy. The tears kept falling. She hated that they did.

Margrit was alive and in the hospital. She needed her. Jo, her mother — they needed her.

She couldn't fall apart.

I'm going to have to tell Mama about Luiza.

The thought shattered her all over again.

Sibi wanted her mother so much in that moment that it was a physical ache inside her.

Her head dropped back against the top of the seat as she fought for composure. Staring straight up at the night sky that was now a roiling blood red as the smoke ceiling reflected the flames consuming the town, she willed away the tears.

I have to be calm. I have to think.

She sat up, squared her shoulders, crumpled the handkerchief in her fist and thrust it into the pocket of the jacket she wore.

No more tears. She was in control of

herself again. She would do what had to be done.

"There is — was — a bakery near the end of the street. My mother was working there. She might be there. My sister — my third sister — might be there. I have to look for them." Her voice, while not strong, was strong enough to make itself heard.

Griff glanced at her. The compassion in his expression terrified her anew. It said more plainly than words could have done that he thought her chances of finding her family were slim.

"Sibi —"

Before he could say anything more, a sharp cracking sound snapped her eyes toward it. Her heart leaped as what remained of a four-story building collapsed like a house of cards. The facade pitched forward to crash with an earthshaking boom maybe ten meters in front of them. Griff slammed on the brakes as stones, pillars, balconies and roof tiles smashed into the street in a cloud of dust.

Snapped forward with a cry as the vehicle jerked to a stop, Sibi caught herself with a hand on the dashboard. Pulse pounding, she straightened to see the *gudaris* and everyone else in the vicinity, having scattered to avoid being crushed, turning to stare at the still-settling ruins.

As she realized that all of them were now trapped behind those ruins while the fire closed in, her insides twisted with fear.

"Good God Almighty, that was close," Iverson said.

"Too close. Iverson, you're with me. Everybody else, stay where you are." Turning off the engine, Griff jumped out. Left alone in the open front seat, Sibi felt hideously vulnerable.

The dust the collapse had flung into the air mixed with the already present haze to create a silvery fog that threw an eerie, translucent shimmer over everything. Behind them, belching smoke, the growing behemoth of the fire continued to advance. Staring into its hellish depths served no purpose except to make her want to run screaming away, so after one frightened glance around, Sibi turned her back on it. In the spirit of doing what came next, she ran quick, questing hands down her legs. In case something happened, to Griff or the automobile or, well, in case she had to fend for herself, she needed to understand what she faced physically. Her stockings were torn to shreds. Beneath them, her legs were scratched and scraped bloody and, from the tenderness she hadn't noticed until now, badly bruised. But the worst thing was her left ankle. Swollen to maybe three times its normal size, it hurt so much to touch that she winced and drew back as soon as she did it. Badly sprained or even broken, was her verdict. Demonstrably unable to bear her weight. Terrifying to realize that she wasn't physically capable of making it far on her own. She wasn't capable of outrunning the fire on her own. She wasn't capable of finding her family on her own.

She needed Griff. A man she barely knew.

She found herself tightly clasping her hands in her lap as she watched him and Iverson jog the length of the debris field and exchange a few quick words with the *gudaris.*

Then the pair of them ran — *ran* — back. The very speed of their return spoke volumes. A fresh cold infusion of fear flooded her veins.

"What is it?" Sibi looked at Griff in alarm as he leaned into the automobile.

"We can't get through. Not in the car." Barking, "Let's go," at Lynch, he grabbed a canvas messenger bag and the canteen from the footwell.

"You don't want us to try to dig a path, Captain?" Lynch asked.

"No time," Griff replied. That curt assessment sent a shiver down Sibi's spine. Cramming more items in the messenger bag, he slung it and the canteen over his shoulder and reached for her. "Come here."

She was already scooting toward him, the action as automatic as breathing. The thought of abandoning the automobile was frightening, but if in his judgment that was what they needed to do, then she trusted him enough to do it.

"Go ahead with *Ama* — we will follow," Señor Elizondo said to Lynch. As Sibi grabbed Griff's shoulders and he scooped her out, she realized that the unconscious old woman must be Señor Elizondo's elegant, silver-haired mother. She'd served her in the restaurant, too, when she occasionally came in for a meal with her son and his wife. Lynch picked the old woman up as Señor Elizondo and his wife climbed out beside him.

Having shouldered a pair of shovels, Iverson came up behind the couple. "I'll see they get through."

With a nod at Iverson, Griff was on the move. "This way."

They were on foot now. Griff's loping strides ate up the distance to the far end of the debris field, where people were streaming through. Held securely in his arms,

123

grateful for his strength, Sibi looked back.
But looking back was a mistake.

10

Sibi's heart hammered at what she saw behind her. Loud and hot, the fire raged toward them, reaching threatening orange claws high into the pulsing red sky, sending hungry feelers racing out in front of it, releasing massive black clouds of smoke. Fiery sparks and flakes of hot ash flew everywhere. The haze around them grew thicker, thick enough to make her eyes water, to make her cough.

"The fire's catching up," she said in Griff's ear, terrified by the mammoth wall of it roaring behind them.

"We'll make it."

It was meant to reassure her, she knew, but still her stomach curled with fright. Right now the fire was behind them, but if this was a race they were barely winning.

They clambered over a line of rubble that was high enough so that, as they reached the apex, she was afforded the chance to get a good look around. Her heart stuttered as she perceived how vast was the lake of fire engulfing the town. Gushers of flame shot up in so many different places that she didn't think there was a neighborhood that had been spared. Up ahead the way was clear, but that could change at any moment. All it would take would be for another building to fall or —

"Where can we even go that's safe? The whole town's burning," she burst out.

"Not everywhere. The convent where the hospital is located, the Casa de Juntas, the munitions factory, the area around the Renteria Bridge — they weren't hit and they aren't burning. At least, they weren't when we came into town."

"How long ago was that?"

"A couple hours."

"Anything could have happened. They might be burning now."

"I'll get you out of this alive, I promise. Whatever it takes."

It was a measure of the faith she had in him that she accepted that.

"The bakery where my mother worked — it was along there," she said as they reached flat ground again and he broke into a steady jog. A gesture encompassed the area ahead of them where she thought the bakery had been. Narrowing her eyes, she strained to make sense of the jumbled ruins. There — or there? That pile of stones or the next? A bright flare-up from the fire cast a glaring scarlet spotlight over everything. It was accompanied by a blazing hot gust of wind that made her cringe and tighten her hold on him.

"Where, precisely?" Griff sounded faintly breathless.

"On the right side of the street. One of those." She'd narrowed it down to a debris field encompassing maybe four buildings — which was still an unbelievable amount of wreckage. Her stomach sank as she realized how impossible finding anyone in it might be.

"Do you *know* that your mother was in there when the bombs hit?" Griff missed a step on the broken cobblestones.

"No." It was a reluctant truth. She felt the savage twist of despair. "She was working. She should have been there. I have to —"

Something caught her eye, silencing her in midsentence.

"Have to what?"

Sibi was so focused on trying to ascertain exactly what she was seeing that she didn't answer, didn't notice the waves of heavy smoke rolling ahead of the fire to form a thick black cloud above their heads, didn't notice the increase in Griff's pace or the heightened intensity in the cries of those coming behind them.

Every bit of her attention concentrated on a shadowy flurry of movement, which resolved into a small animal digging furiously at a section of wreckage where the bakery might have been. Back curved up and tiny nose pointed down, it had floppy ears and a furry tail and —

It was a puppy.

With a jolt of emotion that was some awful, mixed-up combination of hope and dread, she recognized it.

Ruby.

"Griff, there!" Sibi pointed toward where Ruby continued to dig. "Jo — my sister — is there! She has to be. See that puppy? It's hers."

"You sure? Lot of dogs running wild out here." Casting a quick look toward where she pointed, Griff, running now, skirted a drift of fallen stone. Lynch and Iverson, with Señor Elizondo and his family, somehow managed to stay close behind.

"Yes!" Certainty lent urgency to her voice as they got close enough so that she could get a really good look at the puppy — and she spotted the rag wrapped around its back paw. *Luiza* — the stab of grief brought on by the sight of that rag she shoved aside. All she could do now was try her best to save those who were left. "Yes, I'm sure. Why else would Ruby — the puppy — be there? If Jo's there, my mother must be there, too!"

"Sibi —" His arms tightened around her as she all but bounced out of them in her agitation. The uncertain shadows veiled the finer points of his expression, but there was no missing the quick twitching together of his brows. "There could be a thousand reasons for what that dog is doing. It doesn't necessarily mean —"

"Yes, it does," she cried as he showed no sign of heading in that direction or even slowing down. The ceiling of smoke was building up like a thunderhead. The smell was awful: acrid, sweetish, nauseating. The heat felt like a thousand suns at her back. The sound was a constant, rumbling thunder. Having almost reached the barrier created by the fallen building, the towering fire lit up the sky. "You have to *stop.*"

His mouth thinned. "Look, we're running out of time. And the chances of finding anybody under there, much less anybody alive, are —"

"I don't care about 'chances.' " She was frantic as he gave every indication that he meant to rush on by. "I know they're there. My mother! My sister! *I can't leave them!*"

He shot her a look. His eyes were dark and hooded, impossible to read. His mouth was an uncompromising straight line.

"Griff, *please.*"

One corner of his mouth turned violently down.

"All it's going to take is for that fire to flash over and —"

She slammed her palm into his shoulder. "You don't want to stop, then put me down and I'll go myself. *My mother's trapped under there.*"

"Damn it." He changed course, veering toward where Ruby still dug. "We'll look. Fast." Over his shoulder he yelled, "Iverson, bring me a shovel."

"Jo!" Sibi screamed as they reached the edge of the ruins. Ruby didn't even look around as she attacked the debris with the same desperation Sibi felt. If this was the bakery, the place where she was digging would have been the front room, with its glass display cases, Sibi calculated. The staircase to the living quarters above the bakery — the sole remaining upright part of the building — stood no more than two meters away from where Ruby dug. She remembered that staircase, she realized as she looked at it. Last night, when she'd visited the bakery with Mama and her sisters, she'd noticed it at the side of the showroom.

Griff deposited her on what was left of the stone steps that had once led to the now-nonexistent front door. *"Mama! Jo!"*

"You *seen* that fire?" Iverson ran up to them. "Bad damn time for a pit stop."

"You think I don't know it? Give me one of those." Griff grabbed a shovel from Iverson. "Here." He thrust the messenger bag and canteen he'd been carrying at the other man, who pulled the straps over his head so that they hung cross-body from his shoulder, while at the same time gesturing to Lynch, who'd yelled at him from the street, to go on. To Iverson he added, "Take her —" a nod indicated Sibi "— and get out of here. I'll catch up with you and Lynch at the hospital."

"No, I'm not leaving! My family's under there." With a shake of her head at Iverson, who'd made a move toward her, Sibi scooted out of his reach and screamed, *"Jo! Mama! If you can hear me, try to make some noise."*

"Best guess is we have about five minutes before that fire catches up to us, so let's do this fast and get us all out of here," Iverson said to Griff.

If Griff answered beyond a grunt Sibi missed it, but she heard Iverson say, "You thinking that hole's where the dog dug itself out?"

"Yep," Griff said and, lifting Ruby out of the way, started to dig into the rubble. Iverson followed suit.

Clinging to the steps, Sibi watched them with bated breath.

The fire blazed up brighter than ever. Ruby sat on her haunches and howled. The men dug.

"Wait! Stop!" Holding up a hand, Griff crouched while Iverson paused with his shovel suspended in midair. Griff carefully pushed some debris aside and then looked at Sibi. She saw his expression, saw his mouth moving, but the sudden ringing in her ears prevented her from hearing anything he said.

She didn't need to hear him: she could see the pale oval of the face he'd uncovered for herself.

Pain skewered her heart.

"Mama!" Swarming over the rubble on hands and knees, Sibi never even felt the sharp edges cutting into her skin. She reached her mother, touched her face. Cold. So cold. Her heart shattered into a million

tiny pieces. *"Mama!"*

"Sibi." Griff was there, leaning over her, his arm sliding around her shoulders. He said something else to her. It didn't register.

Nothing registered except the beloved face so hideously altered by death.

"Mama —" Her voice broke. She was on her knees, curled above her mother, who was still buried in rubble to the neck. The whimpering sounds she heard made her think of some poor wounded creature until she realized that they were emerging, without volition, from her own throat. Eyes stinging with tears, barely able to breathe around the tightness in her chest, she stroked her mother's cheek, her hair. The feel of death, the look of it, was unmistakable: blue lips, ashen skin, closed eyes.

Sibi felt the world recede, and found herself all alone in a place she'd never been before.

Hail Mary, full of Grace . . .

Griff was talking to her, his hand sliding up and down her arm.

Iverson yelled, *"There's a little girl under here."*

Sibi looked in his direction. He was lifting a child. There was no mistaking the long dark braid that trailed over Iverson's arm. *Jo.*

A flash of white-hot light turned the night instantly bright as day. The *boom* that accompanied it blasted her eardrums. Something — the automobile with its gas tank? — had exploded, fueling the blaze to gargantuan proportions in the blink of an eye. Geysers of fire shot over their heads.

Screaming, Sibi ducked as the ceiling of smoke was obliterated by a crackling sea of flame.

11

"Get down." Griff threw himself over her, shielding her from the blistering shock wave that followed.

Sibi felt the searing heat, heard the almighty roar and realized that this was what he'd feared. The very sky was on fire —

A vortex of intense heat swirled around them as if the fire were creating its own whirlwind. It seemed to be sucking up all the oxygen in the atmosphere. The air was so hot it scorched her lungs.

"We've got to go." Griff rolled to his feet, gathered Sibi up.

"Jo!" Heart pounding, pulse racing, Sibi had eyes only for her sister, who looked like a discarded rag doll as she hung unmoving, head and limbs dangling, from Iverson's arms as he raced away, with Ruby barking wildly at his heels.

"Do you think she's alive?" Sibi asked, holding on for dear life as Griff pounded after Iverson.

"Iverson wouldn't be taking her out of here if she wasn't."

Behind them, beside them and shooting past on both sides of the street, rivers of flame rolled across the top of the fallen buildings, sending fiery waterfalls tumbling down the sides.

"Keep your head down." Griff's breathless warning had no sooner left his mouth than something big exploded off to their left. Sibi cringed as the fire that was now all around them erupted into an inferno.

"What was that?" she gasped.

"Incendiary, most likely." He must have picked up on her lack of comprehension, because he added, "Bombs designed to start fires on impact. I saw some unexploded ones caught up in the rubble. Fire reaches them, they go off."

"You mean another bomb could explode at any moment?"

His grimace was her answer: *yes*.

"You got a backup plan? 'Cause it don't look like we're gonna make it," Iverson yelled over his shoulder at Griff.

At the stark fear in Iverson's voice, Sibi's focus catapulted forward, and at what she saw she forgot to breathe. Roaring through the debris on either side of the street, the fire was ahead of them now, pincering in front of them, the two sides racing to come together at the end of the street where the lines of rubble nearly converged. If that happened, *when* that happened, there would be no way out.

"Yeah. *Run faster,*" Griff yelled back. Iverson didn't reply. Instead he put his head down and pounded toward the funnel-like opening.

Chest heaving, arms locked around her, Griff ran like their lives depended on it, which they did. The thud of his boots on the cobblestones echoed the pounding of her heart.

Around them, men, women and children ran for their lives. The *gudaris* fled along with everyone else.

"Quick! Quick!" A man carrying a toddler dragged an older child by the hand.

"*Mami!* Hurry!" A young boy in short pants and a filthy, torn shirt looked behind him at two women, one middle-aged and one older, laboriously running arm in arm.

"Go on, Manuel! We will catch up," the middle-aged woman called back, although it seemed impossible that they could.

"Thank you! Oh, God bless you!" a woman cried to a soldier who snatched the two children she was carrying out of her arms and ran with them while she grabbed on to the back of his jacket so as not to lose him, or them, in the chaos. He pulled her along. Her feet barely touched the ground as she somehow managed to keep upright.

Sibi's arms tightened around Griff's neck as one of the two flaming arms racing furiously along the top of the debris reached the critical juncture, blazed up and curled back over the street, eliciting screams and shouts as the ceiling of fire passed dangerously low over the heads of those cringing beneath it.

"When I tell you, close your eyes and hold your breath." The rasp of Griff's breathing made his words uneven. Shiny now with sweat, his face was set in harsh lines. Holding on to him like a limpet, she could feel the tension in his arms and shoulders, feel his straining muscles, feel the jolt of his every footfall as he pelted toward the only way out. Flames almost completely surrounded them now, forming blazing walls and a ceiling driven by a searing wind.

Not far ahead, Iverson reached the opening and, with Ruby at his heels and a motley rush of others storming after him, dashed through the curtain of thick black smoke that veiled it.

"They made it," Sibi gasped.

"We will, too." His voice was grim.

This time, she wasn't sure she believed him. It was too easy for her to see for herself what they faced.

Behind the curtain of smoke, an opening of only a few meters remained — and the wind blew the two wildly flaring sections of fire toward one another like a pair of hands trying to clasp. It was, she feared, only a matter of seconds until they succeeded and the opening disappeared.

"Hang on." Griff's arms tightened around her. She could feel the desperate surge of adrenaline through his body.

Her heart leaped into her throat as the two giant flaming hands touched almost directly in front of them and started to entwine. A thin sheet of flame flickered across the opening, blazed hot, intensified with a crackling *whoosh* —

"Now. Close your eyes. Hold your breath."

She barely had time to comply before he charged into the curtain of fire.

12

The heat blistered. The smoke suffocated. There was no air.

"You can look now." A heartbeat later, Griff's voice as they burst out the other side of the death trap was hoarse and gravelly and quite possibly the sweetest sound Sibi had ever heard. Lifting her head from where she'd tucked it into the hollow between his neck and shoulder, she opened her eyes onto a hellish red darkness that was rife with destruction and multiple blazing fires and still felt about a thousand times less threatening than the inferno they had just escaped.

A finger of flame raced up the back of Griff's shirt. Horrified, she slapped it out, fiercely but wordlessly because she was racked with coughing, because her throat was burning raw, because she was too shaken to even try to speak.

At the same time, a stride or two behind

them, the soldier with the two children in his arms and their mother hanging on like a tail on a kite barreled through. A man who followed on the heels of the soldier, a young man with curly dark hair, emerged shrieking with his hair and clothes alight. Sibi could only watch in horror as the flames consumed him in seconds and he collapsed in a fiery heap.

No one else escaped. The fire accelerated with a roar as the flaming hands clasped, firmly and unbreachably, making it impossible for anyone else to get through. An eerie, agonized howling from those left behind to burn made her stomach knot. The sound would, she knew, haunt her for the rest of her life.

Just like this night would haunt her for the rest of her life.

The black gleam of the River Mundaca was visible beyond the destroyed train station. Ordinarily it would have been blocked from view. The Hotel Julian — she had to look away from the terrible scene out front. The facade had collapsed, leaving the interior of the four-story building open to the night. Firemen and soldiers worked together to pull victims from beneath the crumpled stone. From the look of the small bodies being laid so tenderly in the street, a number of children had been killed.

She had to concentrate her thoughts on Jo, who was alive, although for the moment she and Iverson were lost among the tide of shell-shocked survivors cramming the narrow street. She needed to concentrate on Margrit, who was alive.

At least, they were alive as far as she knew.

At the thought of the alternative, Sibi felt hysteria bubble up inside her. She couldn't even begin to allow herself to entertain the possibility that one or both of them might have died, or might still die.

Mama. Luiza.

A thousand images of them, a lifetime's worth of memories, spun through her head in an instant. Her warm, impulsive, beautiful mother. Her sister: adversary, deputy, confidante.

Reality hit her like a punch to the stomach.

I'll never see them again.

Her heart broke. She could feel the physical pain of it, the knifelike stab of agony beneath her breastbone, the hollow throbbing ache as if a part of herself had been ripped away.

Griff looked at her. He was walking now. His face was black with soot. Lurid, flickering light from the fire made it impossible to read anything in the dark gleam of his eyes.

She doubted he could read anything in hers, either, but wrapped in his arms as she was it was impossible for him to miss the long shivers that she couldn't control.

"My mother died when I was six," he said. "I remember what it felt like. Worst thing that ever happened to me in my life."

At his unflinching reach into the heart of her suffering, her surroundings went slightly out of focus. She felt like she was shaking to death inside, like one wrong word, one wrong thought, would destroy her.

She inhaled, closed her eyes and fought against the dizziness that assailed her. Slowly, slowly she let the air back out and opened her eyes again.

What she saw was Griff. He was in focus for her, even if nothing else in that hellish landscape was.

He kept talking. His tone was matter-of-fact. "Spanish flu took her. She went quick, four days. Everyone was still celebrating the end of the Great War, we were all happy, she was happy — and then she got sick. She was twenty-five when she died, same age I am now. I was her only child, and my dad wasn't around, so it was just the two of us. You couldn't pry us apart. They wouldn't let me see her, after she got sick. I wasn't able to say goodbye. Bothers me to this day."

The tautness of his jaw, the thinning of his mouth, the narrowing of his eyes, all spoke of remembered pain. Her raw and eviscerated heart experienced an instant, instinctive pull toward the wound in his. Her lacerated soul cried out for solace. Knowing that he had once suffered as she was suffering was not enough, not nearly enough, to ease her pain but it did give her something: it made her feel less alone.

"Yes," she said, meaning, *I understand.* Getting out more than a single syllable seemed beyond her for the moment.

"Last thing she said to me was, 'Be good for Mrs. Morris.' Because she was sending me to stay with a neighbor when she started getting sick." He grimaced. "Not much of a note to end on. But that's the ending we got. Her name was Antonia. Her friends called her Annie."

"Marina," Sibi said.

"Pretty name."

"Yes." Sibi took a breath. The tightness in her throat was slightly less unbearable than it had been. "Last night — my mother told the little girls a story." Her voice was small and scratchy, but she was relieved to be able to string words together to form coherent sentences again. "By the time she finished, everybody was asleep except me. She walked to the door and stopped to look at us — all four of us tucked up in bed — and told us she loved us. *Love you always,* she said. She says —" Sibi faltered "— *said* that every single night. For as long as I can remember. Last night none of us said it back. I didn't say it back. I would give anything if I'd only said it back."

He said, "You didn't have to say it. She knows."

"How? She's *dead.*"

"Still."

Marina's faith, that abiding faith she had worked so hard to instill in her daughters. Their father's contemptuous lack of it. Her cruel, senseless death — and Luiza's. The horror that had been visited on all of them, on the town — all of that swirled into a mighty storm that rocked the foundations of everything Sibi had ever known or believed. Questions of God, of the rightness of the world, of order and stability and good and evil, of what it all meant, shook her to her core.

"Do you really think so?" Her eyes searched his face. She could feel the hot prick of tears in them — tears she was determined not to shed. Because, really, what good were tears? They brought no one back. They didn't change anything at all.

"I do. Nothing's ever really lost, you know? And love — love never is. Even now, everywhere I go, I carry a little piece of my mother with me. A little piece of her love. I think you'll find that the love you and your mother shared stays with you, too."

"Always." It felt like a vow, a promise to her mother that wound itself around her heart. She hadn't answered Marina last night, but with that she did. It was a pledge of love meant to last through all eternity.

Goodbye, Mama. Love you always.

"Yeah," Griff agreed. His lips twisted into a small, wry smile as their eyes met in a silent acknowledgment of mutual grief and loss. "Always."

Sibi's lips trembled. She pressed them together, swallowed hard. Her eyes stung. She blinked furiously. But hard as she fought against it, there was nothing she could do to keep the tears from overflowing.

With the best will in the world not to do so, she laid her head on the broad shelf of Griff's shoulder and cried like she would never stop.

She gasped and sobbed and shook while he murmured comforting things she was too overwhelmed to hear and held her close and patted her clumsily and kept walking,

walking, walking. When at last she was all cried out, she stayed where she was, with her head on his shoulder and her arms locked around his neck, because she was simply too exhausted to move. She felt like an empty shell of herself, as if every ounce of life and energy had drained from her body. Once she moved, once she lifted her head and took stock of their surroundings and the situation, she would be forced to acknowledge the terrible realities of the present — and confront the future.

And she just didn't think she had the strength to do any of that.

13

"Cuidado!" Watch out — the cry came as two men bearing a third on a stretcher ran past them up the hospital steps. Like the Santa María church, the Carmelite Convent had somehow managed to escape destruction. The massive, multistory stone building had been transformed into a hospital when the first casualties of the war had been brought into town. Now it stood solid, a large, dark rectangle wreathed in smoke and painted red by the towering flames. It was far enough from the fire itself to make it a refuge amid the devastation. That it was full to overflowing was made clear by the dozens of casualties lying in the open air, on the thick carpet of grass that was the hospital's front lawn. The Carmelite sisters in their white habits flitted about among them, lending what aid they could.

"Sibi! Sibi, is that you?" Coming at her from just inside the hospital's propped-open door, the greeting caused her to glance eagerly toward its source.

"Emilio." For a moment, a fleeting moment, the world spun backward to that bright, golden afternoon when the handsomest boy in school had come up to her and asked if she wanted to go to a dance. She felt a desperate need to grab on to that moment, to grab on to the girl that she had been, to grab on to the Before and never let go. But then he turned so that the light hit him and any illusion she had about a return to that earlier innocence was shattered. His face was streaked with soot, ash matted his too-long black hair and his clothes were rumpled and torn. A bloody gash on his cheek had crusted over. But what struck her most were his eyes. Even in the uncertain light, she could see that they were glassy with horror.

A horror that she — that they all — shared. The hard truth of it settled like a rock in her stomach: they could never unsee, never unfeel, never go back. They were forever changed.

"Thank the Blessed Mother you're alive," Emilio said. As Griff stopped to let them talk, his gaze swept her. "You're injured?"

"Nothing to speak of. My ankle. I can't really walk." She looked him over. "You?"

"Like you, nothing to speak of." He shook his head. "I thought, when you ran out and the airplanes came — well, I thought . . ."

"I managed to make it into a shelter with Margrit. My sister."

"The little, noisy one? I saw her inside."

"You did? Where? How is she?"

"Upstairs, at the back near the supply cabinets. I can't tell you how she is. She was just lying there with her eyes closed." He flicked a frowning look past her at Griff. "A man I never saw before was with her. I heard one of the sisters say he was an American."

"Yes. They saved us, these Americans." She, too, looked at Griff. "This is my friend Emilio."

"Captain James Griffin, USAAC," Griff introduced himself.

"What are you Americans doing here?" Hope brightened Emilio's face. "Are you part of the International Brigades? Are you joining the fight?"

"I'm the assistant military attaché, assigned to our embassy. The men with me are part of the ambassador's staff. The United States has chosen to remain neutral in the conflict. We're here to observe only."

"Observe." Anger sparked in Emilio's eyes. "If that's what you're doing — if that's *all* that you're doing — then at least tell them — tell the world — *this.*" A gesture encapsulated the devastated town. "Tell them what the Whites have done."

"It wasn't the Whites." His anger ignited Sibi's own, and her voice was sharp with it. "It was the Germans. I know, I know the airplanes. I saw them."

"The *Germans*? You are sure?"

"I'm sure."

"Filthy Nazi swine." Emilio's mouth twisted bitterly. "May they burn in the same hell they have created for us here." A group of people brushed past, causing him to move a little to one side. He took a breath. The anger drained from his face. "I came to the hospital searching for my father, but he isn't here. He was on his way home from the boatyard when the bombing started. Nobody's seen him since. I have to find him, my mother and sisters are distraught. Have you by any chance seen him?"

Emilio's father was a wealthy shipbuilder and a well-known figure around town. Emilio was his only son, and they were close. Looking at Emilio with compassion, Sibi shook her head. "No. I'm sorry."

"Then I must go." Emilio flicked a quick, assessing glance at Griff before looking more closely at Sibi. "You've found your people? You'll be all right?"

Sibi discovered she couldn't bear to speak of Mama or Luiza, so she simply nodded.

Lifting a hand in farewell, he ran down the steps and into the night.

The smell — a rank combination of what she tentatively identified as sweat, blood and all manner of bodily wastes, plus the acrid scent of smoke that was everywhere — hit her instantly as Griff carried her on inside the hospital. There she was struck by the ghastly quality of the light. There was no electricity, she realized: the lines must have been destroyed along with everything else. Lanterns, torches, candles, burning rags in bowls of grease — anything that could possibly provide illumination had been pressed into service.

Hair-raising screams from someone in a back room split the air. Looking sharply in that direction, she found a closed, battered wooden door with a hand-lettered sign on it. The length of the room was such that she had to squint to read it. It said Operating Theater.

Compressing her lips, Sibi tried not to hear the screams. The night had already held so much horror that she felt she could bear no more of it.

Upstairs, the ward they walked into was

almost identical to the one on the floor below. Here, too, each cot was full; many held more than one sufferer. In some places, bare mattresses lay directly on the floor. Broken bodies crowded close together atop them. Bloodied, charred, with gaping wounds — the people she saw as they made their way through the ward included, she was sickened to discover, a number of her friends, classmates, neighbors. Even the pompous Eduardo Montoya, one of the richest men in town, and the gossip Señora Ortega, spreader of some of the worst of the rumors about Marina — they were there, laid out on cots, in no better case than the lowliest *paysun.*

They were all equals now.

"At the back near the supply cabinets," she reminded Griff, and he nodded.

Sibi craned her neck as she looked around. "Jo — shouldn't she be here by now?"

"I'm sure she's here somewhere. Iverson probably didn't have the advantage of running into someone who could tell him where your youngest sister is." Griff navigated through the rows of closely packed cots as he spoke, carefully stepping over the injured on the floor. The dark wood of the supply cabinets stretched along the far wall. Above them, a line of high square windows, glossy black with night, looked out on that horrible livid sky.

Sibi had to glance away. If the fire should spread in this direction . . .

"If the fire comes this way, what will they do? They'll never get all these people out of here." Her stomach turned inside out at the thought.

"Pray that it doesn't," he said grimly. His tacit acknowledgment that she was right, that potentially hundreds more could be lost to something as arbitrary as a shift in the wind, made her blood run cold.

Groans and whimpers and reedy voices begging for everything from water to God's help added to the misery in the air. The holy sisters glided about, their white habits ghostly in the uncertain light as they tended to the injured.

There, in the corner by the far wall —

Sibi's heart gave a great leap as her sister's curly blond head bobbed into view above the sea of supine patients. "Margrit!"

14

Margrit was conscious and mobile, and those twin facts came as an enormous relief. Beyond that, though, she was obviously frightened. Scrambling into a crouch on the iron-framed cot on which she'd been lying, her back to the rough-plastered white wall behind her, her skirt hitched up around her knees and her shirt and stockings in tatters, she looked like a small feral creature at bay.

"No, no, *no.*" Margrit shook her head vehemently at the sister who stood beside her cot.

"You must —"

"No!" Margrit had a wide white bandage wrapped around her forehead. Brown stains on the bandage above her left eye spoke of blood. Her curls were wild, which heat and sweat tended to do to them at the best of times. She was filthy, shoeless and clearly on the verge of a patented Margrit outburst. Sibi was so glad to see her it hurt.

"Margrit," she called to her. Wide with fright as the nun leaned in closer, Margrit's eyes lit up as she saw her sister.

"Sibi!" Margrit tried to scramble off the cot toward her. The nun blocked the move, grabbing at her, but Margrit dodged, clambering the length of the creaking cot and pitching up in Sibi's arms as Griff deposited her in a sitting position on the foot of the mattress. Taking note of the fact that Margrit kept one of her arms tucked tightly against her chest, Sibi carefully hugged her close. The familiar feel of the wiry little body brought a lump to her throat.

"Where have you *been*?" Margrit demanded.

"I came as fast as I could," Sibi said into that tangle of curls. They were dirty and matted and smelled of smoke and she treasured every unruly one of them.

"I woke up and I was here and my arm hurts and I was so *scared.* Did the bombs get us? Are we safe?"

"We're safe," Sibi assured her, although she wasn't entirely certain that was true.

"You look so funny. Your face is all dirty." Margrit looked at Griff. "Who is that?"

"His name is Captain Griffin," Sibi said, taking an instinctive, self-conscious swipe at her dirty face with her arm, which was useless, she figured out after the fact, because she was still wearing Griff's leather jacket and the sleeve was gritty with soot and ash. If anything, she'd probably made the problem worse. "He brought me here."

"Like Phillips brought me."

Sibi glanced at short, wiry Phillips, clearly the fourth member of Griff's party, who had stepped back against the supply cabinets, presumably to get out of the way.

"*Private* Phillips." She made the correction automatically, because Mama was — *had been* — a stickler for manners and had done her best to drum them into her girls, and — the realization came sharp as a sword — it was up to her now to continue Marina's teachings.

"He told me his name was Phillips. I asked," Margrit said. "He didn't say anything about *Private.*"

"That's true, miss." Phillips nodded affirmation at Sibi.

"So I couldn't have known," Margrit said on a note of triumph, burrowing against her. Sibi tightened her arms around her on a wave of thankfulness that the little girl was alive and well enough to be as incorrigible as ever. Although the room was stuffy and overwarm, Margrit was shivering. This further evidence of the trauma she'd suffered made Sibi's chest tighten.

"What about Luiza?" Margrit's voice was suddenly very small.

Sibi was blindsided by the question, which hit her like a blow. She should have foreseen it, she knew. Looking around for a blanket to wrap around Margrit, she saw none, and so she unzipped Griff's jacket and folded Margrit inside it, against her own body.

Margrit's face tilted up, her eyes wide and blue and questioning as they met Sibi's.

What do I tell her? Looking into her littlest sister's face, seeing the innocence and trust there, knowing that the truth would cause Margrit untold amounts of crippling pain, she also knew she had no choice. She was going to have to tell her what had befallen Luiza, and tell her about Mama, too. But when? Surely not now. Wouldn't it be best to wait for Jo, tell them together?

Unless something terrible had happened to Jo, too. Unless —

"You are a relative?" The sister asked Sibi, stepping closer. She was an old woman, Sibi saw, with an elegant face that settled into disapproving lines as she looked the pair of them over. She regarded Sibi sternly.

Grateful for the distraction, Sibi nodded. "Yes, Sister."

Margrit cast a look over her shoulder at

the nun. "This is Sibi. She's *my* sister."

Sibi couldn't see Margrit's face, but from her tone her expression was baleful. She gave Margrit the slightest, most imperceptible of admonitory squeezes. Even at such a time, respect for the nuns was mandatory.

The sister appeared to take no umbrage. She merely sniffed dismissively at Margrit, then lifted a questioning eyebrow at Sibi. "Mama? Papa?"

"Not . . . here."

Their eyes met. Whatever the sister read in hers must have been telling, because her response was a brusque nod. "I am Sister Beatrice. I am a nurse, and I am in charge of this ward. We sewed up the cut in this one's forehead as soon as she was brought in, and she was given aspirin for the pain. It would have been something stronger, but we're running critically short on medicine. I suspect she has a broken ulna — forearm — and perhaps other injuries, as well, but we haven't been able to make a definitive determination as yet. I have been trying to persuade her to let me put this sling on her arm until she can be properly examined. Perhaps you could help."

"Has a doctor seen her?"

The nun shook her head. "There is only one doctor here, and he is wholly occupied with the most serious injuries. Of which there are many, I'm afraid. The rest of us, we do what we can. We try to see to the children first. So if I may?"

"Let Sister Beatrice put a sling on your arm, Margrit."

Margrit shook her head, huddling closer to Sibi.

Sister Beatrice clicked her tongue impatiently. "Come, child, there are others waiting."

"Margrit, do as you're told." Sibi's voice was firm. She put the little girl away from her and sat back as the nun bent over her. "It's just a sling, to hold your arm steady so you won't jar it. Once it's on, it won't hurt so much."

Margrit looked unhappy, but she allowed Sister Beatrice to do what was needed. While the sling was being adjusted, Griff squatted in front of Sibi. Occupied with watching Margrit, Sibi barely noticed until he took both her hands and turned them over so that they were palms up. His hands cupping hers were big and tanned and filthy, while hers were slim and pale and filthy. The other difference was that his hands felt warm while hers were freezing cold.

He said, "You need medical attention, too. Look at your hands."

Multiple bloody slashes crisscrossed her palms, she saw with surprise. None looked particularly deep, but some still bled a little and the creases in her palm were etched with dried blood. Remembering how she'd crawled across the glass-strewn remains of the bakery, the injuries weren't surprising. What was surprising was, until that moment, she hadn't even felt them. Her knees must be in a similar state, because as she thought about them they started to sting, too. The hot tightness that was her ankle intensified into a full-blown, throbbing ache. For the first time, she realized she felt bruised and battered all over. Bending to look at her knees and ankle, she nearly bumped heads with Griff, who'd clearly had the same intention.

Their gazes met — despite its pale uncertainty, the light enabled her to finally discern the color of his eyes, which was a bright marine blue, made even more vivid by the tan complexion beneath the grime — and then he glanced past her. She started to frown as his expression changed, and then he looked back at her again and nodded in the direction of the open ward behind her.

She glanced around . . .

A warm tide of thanksgiving surged

through her.

"Jo!" But Sibi's relief at seeing her other sister was short-lived. Jo was obviously awake, but instead of hanging on to Iverson, who carried her as carefully as if she were made of spun glass and might break at any moment, she was in constant motion in his arms, hands fluttering, torso writhing, legs jerking. As they got close, Sibi recognized the small distressed sounds she was making as cries of pain.

"Sister, please." She grabbed Sister Beatrice's sleeve. The nun, who had just finished knotting the ends of the sling behind Margrit's neck, looked at her questioningly. Sibi gestured at Jo. "My other sister —"

She broke off, lips parting in horror as Jo, now only a few strides away in Iverson's arms, turned her head toward them. Jo's eyes were wide, dark pools of anguish, but what riveted Sibi's attention, what grabbed at her heart, was the state of her face. From just below the midpoint of her left eye all the way down her cheek to her jaw, and then continuing along the left side of her neck to below her collarbone, what had once been smooth pale skin was charred black, raised and rough-looking and interspersed with red, raw, weeping patches. What she was seeing, Sibi realized with a jolt of horror, was the most terrible burn.

She just managed not to gasp aloud.

"Sibi," Jo whimpered, and held out her arms. Sibi instinctively tried to leap to her feet and go to her, but her left leg gave out as soon as she put weight on it. The resultant shaft of pain made her cry out. Griff jumped up and grabbed her, kept her from crumpling to the floor, but even with his support the best Sibi could do was collapse on the edge of the cot while Iverson brought Jo to her. Margrit scrambled out of the way as Iverson laid Jo down. Against the white sheet, Jo looked small and broken.

"It's all right," Sibi said to Jo, leaning closer. Jo's lips quivered as Sibi carefully brushed the tangle of dark hair away from her face. It took every bit of willpower Sibi possessed to keep her voice steady. "I'm here. Everything's going to be all right."

"My face . . ." Jo's hand reached for Sibi's. Her voice turned piteous. "It hurts."

Even as her insides twisted with pain for her sister, Sibi squeezed Jo's fingers. "You're in the hospital now. They'll make it better."

"Oh, poor Jo!" Kneeling beside the cot, her arm in a sling now, Margrit grabbed a fistful of Jo's skirt. "I hate it that you got hurt. I'm hurt, too, but not as bad as you."

Jo's hand closed around Margrit's. Her eyes radiated pain as she looked back at Sibi. "I want Mama. Where's Mama?"

"Not here." Margrit echoed what Sibi had told Sister Beatrice earlier while Sibi, her throat closing up, tried to formulate a better answer.

"She was in the bakery with me." Jo stopped talking to swallow hard. Her lips quivered. "There was a bomb, and the roof fell in, and — and —"

"I know." Sibi tightened her grip on Jo's hand, and Margrit said, "They bombed us, too. We had to get saved."

Sister Beatrice bent over Jo, examining her injury, then straightened to look at Sibi. "She needs to go to the operating theater right away," she said. "A burn like this — the doctor needs to see it." Breaking off, she turned to Iverson. "She's too heavy for me to carry. Would you bring her, please?"

With a glance at Griff, who nodded, Iverson said, "Yes, ma'am." He pulled the straps of the messenger bag and canteen he'd been carrying over his head, said, "I'll leave this with you," To Griff as he set the items down on the cot and reached for Jo.

Jo's fingers clamped around Sibi's. Her eyes were huge. "What are they going to do?"

"Take care of you. The doctor will know what to do," Sibi said, while her hammering heart echoed Jo's fear. "We'll be right here, waiting for you."

"I'm scared." Jo reluctantly let go of Sibi's hand as Iverson gathered her up.

"You're the bravest person I know, Jo. Remember how you saved Ruby?" Margrit said.

Jo replied, but her words were lost as Iverson, in response to Sister Beatrice's imperious, "Come, now, quickly," bore her away.

15

"Is Jo going to die?" Margrit's hand crept into hers.

"No," Sibi said, and from somewhere she found the strength to sound like she meant it. "She's going to be fine. Just like you're going to be fine. *We're* going to be fine."

"A burn like that has to be cleaned and bandaged as soon as possible. That's why she needs to see the doctor straightaway." Griff's hand closed on Sibi's shoulder, gave it a comforting squeeze. "Your cuts need to be cleaned, too. Margrit, would you hand me the canteen, please? It's right there beside you."

As Margrit nodded, Sibi gave him a look of silent gratitude for his effort to distract her sister.

In the act of handing the canteen to Griff, who'd crouched in front of Sibi again, Margrit jumped and squeaked, her attention riveted on the messenger bag. On the mattress beside Margrit, it moved. On its own. As they watched, it moved again — convulsed, actually — and then a teacup-size black furry head thrust itself out of one end, right through the space where the closed flap folded over the bag itself.

"Ruby!" Margrit exclaimed. Griff took the canteen from her as the puppy squirmed its way out of the bag and she scooped it up and hugged it. Like the rest of them, it was filthy. All kinds of debris matted its coat. The long tips of fur on its ears and back and tail looked singed. The red rag — Luiza's curler; Sibi felt a rush of dizziness at the memory — that Jo had tied around its foot was missing. The cut had scabbed over, adding to the pup's general scruffiness. But as it looked up at Margrit, its dark eyes shone. Its little tail wagged like mad. "How did you get here?"

Sibi frowned at the pair of them as she fought to regain her equilibrium, then cast a swift look around. A dog in a hospital — under normal circumstances such a thing would never be allowed. Even under these extraordinary circumstances, she had a feeling that Sister Beatrice and the other nuns would object.

Ruby gave an excited *yap* and licked Margrit's cheek. The surprised delight on her littlest sister's face won the puppy a forever place in Sibi's heart. It was the first time since Luiza had fallen that she'd seen Margrit smile.

Another swift look around gave Sibi hope that Ruby might go undetected. Amid so many patients, so much confusion, such an undercurrent of noise, who could be bothered to notice one tiny puppy?

"I know you've probably been really scared," Margrit told the puppy, who won the briefest suggestion of a giggle from her as she leaped up and eagerly licked Margrit's ear. "But you don't have to worry. You're safe now."

Griff had been looking at Ruby, too, and now he glanced at Sibi.

"Stay or go?" he asked quietly, with a significant look at Ruby.

"Stay," Sibi said.

"Oh." Iverson was back, without Jo but with a blanket that he draped around Margrit. The slightly guilty sounding "oh" was in reference to Ruby, to whom he added, "I forgot about you."

"Thank you for bringing her," Margrit said to him. "And the blanket. And Jo."

Iverson nodded. Griff shot him a condemning look. "You put a puppy in my messenger bag with all those important papers?

Puppies chew. Puppies pee."

"I couldn't help it. The pup kept following us, and the little girl kept fretting that it was going to get lost or hurt and looking around trying to keep an eye on it until I picked it up and put it in the bag," Iverson said.

"Jo?" Sibi mouthed the question at him after a glance told her that Margrit was now fully occupied in combating Ruby's spirited attempts to pull a button off her blouse.

"Someone will bring her back when they're done." Iverson's reply was equally quiet.

"I'll take care of you until Jo gets back," Margrit said to Ruby as the pup gave up on the button in favor of licking Margrit's fingers. "Then we'll take care of her."

"All right, now that that's settled I need you to hold still a minute," Griff said. He picked up her hands again, turned them over in his. With him hunkered down in front of her, Sibi could see the top of his head, which was covered with flat gray flakes of ash. Peeking through the ash was short, thick tobacco brown hair that waved. "Any other injuries besides the ankle?"

As he spoke, he pulled the hem of his shirt out of his pants, wet it with a dribble of water from the canteen and gently wiped her palms. Initially surprised at this use of a corner of his shirt, she realized that it was the only clean bit of cloth he possessed. Besides being scorched in back and bearing what she saw now were bloody streaks around the shoulders from her hands, his once-white shirt was crumpled and pocked with tiny burn holes and smeared with black streaks of dirt and soot. His gray pants were in even worse shape.

"The cuts you see," she said. "And some bruises. Nothing worse, I'm fairly certain."

He was already dabbing at her bloody knees through gaping holes in her stockings. That done, he pulled the rest of his shirt free of his trousers, wet another corner and said, "Lean closer." She did, and he caught her chin and wiped her face.

"There," he said, and released her chin. The part of his shirt he'd used was now almost black with soot and dirt, so she had a fair notion of what her face must have looked like.

She grimaced. "Thank you."

"Any time." He turned his attention to her ankle. Normally delicate and well-defined, it was now easily four times its normal size. Tightly encased in the snug wool stocking, it looked like a sausage.

"Can you wiggle your toes?" he asked, taking her foot in his hands. She did. Cautiously. And winced.

"How much does it hurt?"

"Not that much, unless I try to put weight on it." The throbbing ache was bearable, for the time being. Certainly under these conditions none of her injuries were serious enough to warrant making a fuss. It was obvious from Jo, and from looking at some of those in the cots around them, that she and Margrit were in far better shape than most.

"In that case, I think we'd better wait for someone with medical training to take care of this."

She nodded, then in a low voice said, "Griff, I need to get word to my father about —" she hesitated, glanced at Margrit to make sure she wasn't listening "— what's happened."

"Lines are down. Telephone, telegraph — nothing is operational. You won't be able to get any kind of message out of here for days. Maybe longer." Her face must have fallen, because he added, "If you'll give me his telephone number and address, I'll see that he's contacted once we leave here."

"Once you leave?" A flutter formed beneath her breastbone. Of course he couldn't stay. Of course he was going to leave. She didn't know why the thought of it should come as such a blow.

Maybe because she'd started to think of him as someone she could depend on.

Before he could reply, a man's brisk voice interrupted. "Ah, there you are! I've been hunting all through the hospital for you."

16

The speaker stopped at the foot of the cot.

"Miss?" He was addressing her, Sibi realized with surprise. A slight man of around thirty, maybe, with gingery hair and sharp features, he wore a tan raincoat over a suit and looked as out of place in that noisy, dirty, chaotic setting as a racehorse pulling an oxcart. A glance was all it took for Sibi to know that he had come into town from the outside, long after the bombs had fallen and the inferno had taken hold.

He was as clean and pink-cheeked as if he'd just bathed. And his face — it was missing the fear-stunned expression stamped across the features of every single person she'd come across who'd lived through the horror.

She didn't reply, just looked at him with some suspicion. Griff let go of her foot and stood up.

The man glanced at Griff, then switched

his attention back to her.

"I was coming into the hospital and happened to pass you on the steps outside as you were talking," he said. He spoke to her in Spanish, but his accent — she thought he might be British. "I couldn't help but overhear — you can identify the airplanes that attacked the town?"

His eyes were keen on her face.

"Yes." Sibi cast a quick glance at Margrit. Her attention seemed to be entirely taken up by Ruby, who was back to worrying the buttons on her blouse.

"Who are you?" Griff's question was abrupt. He was a tall presence behind her, looming protectively close.

"George Steer. I'm here to report on what happened for *The Times.*"

"What's a reporter for a London newspaper doing here?" Griff asked.

"There's a great deal of interest in this insurrection, in Britain and elsewhere. A failed military coup against an elected government, a bloody civil war pitting the leaders of the resulting revolt and their Nationalists against the country's lawful leaders and their Republicans, the class warfare aspect, the escalating violence, the thousands of executions and assassinations on both sides. Newspapers — and war correspondents — live for conflicts like this. And it's our job to get to the truth, and get it out." Steer's gaze shifted back to Sibi. "I'd very much like to hear what you have to say. Will you tell me what you saw?"

Sibi hesitated, glancing at Margrit again: the last thing she wanted was for the little girl to overhear. The blanket was gray, threadbare and wrapped around Margrit from her ears to her knees so that she looked like a woolly little bear with only a few golden curls sticking out. Ruby was on her lap inside the blanket. Seeing Sibi's expression, Iverson sat down on the cot beside Margrit and started talking to her as she played with the puppy. Between Iverson and Ruby, Margrit was well occupied and unlikely to pay attention to anything that was said, Sibi judged.

"It's important," Steer said. "Please?"

Looking back at Steer, Sibi gave a jerky nod. Then, speaking quietly, she described what had happened from the time the first airplane dropped its bombs on Station Plaza to the moment Luiza was shot. Her voice shook and she had to break off as she recounted that last. Mama and Luiza — her heart broke with the knowledge that they were irretrievably lost. What had been done to them was brutal and barbaric and unconscionable and undeserved. They, and the untold numbers of others who had died so horribly along with them, no longer had a voice. They were not there to speak for themselves, to rail at the injustice that had been done them, to point accusing fingers at their murderers.

But she was still here, and she could speak for them.

"My sister was thirteen. The airplane that killed her swooped down until it was no more than twenty meters above the street. The pilot — there is no doubt in my mind that he saw her clearly. He knew — he had to know — that she was just a harmless young girl. Running away. And he shot her with a machine gun," she said to Steer, who wrote busily in a notebook as she spoke. Her voice stayed quiet, but as she continued it turned steely with anger and grief. "As low as they were, all the airplanes that strafed the town had to know that they were shooting unarmed, ordinary people who were running for their lives. And no matter what people think they weren't Whites. They weren't Nationalist airplanes. They were Heinkels — He 51s — German fighter airplanes. *Germans* did this."

Steer quit scribbling in his notebook to stare at her.

"And although I did not get as close a look at them as I did the chaser that killed my sister, I am as certain as can be that the bombers were German, too. I recognized the Junkers — Ju 52s."

The look he gave her was doubtful. "I've heard a rumor of the Germans establishing an air base in the north in support of the Nationalists but there's been no confirmation."

"I don't know about that. I am telling you what I saw. The airplanes that attacked us were German. I'm not wrong."

His eyes slid over her. The look he gave her as their gazes met again told her as clearly as words could have done that in his opinion the too-thin, big-eyed, fire-ravaged and traumatized schoolgirl in front of him could not by any stretch of the imagination be considered a reliable source on such matters. Even the careful courtesy in his tone spoke of skepticism. "And how is it that you are able to identify those airplanes, if I may ask?"

"My father designs airplane engines. I know the engines, and I know the airplanes. I've been around them all my life. The Ju 52s are trimotors. A distinctive design, a distinctive sound. And I saw the He 51s up close. I saw their design, and I saw their insignia."

"Can you draw the insignia for me? Nothing elaborate, a rough sketch will do." A hint of suppressed excitement sharpened his voice as he held out his notebook and pen toward her.

"Yes." She took them and hesitated. "Would it be all right if I used a sheet of paper for something of my own first?"

He nodded, and she scribbled down her father's name, address and telephone number, tore the sheet of paper out and gave it to Griff, who, after a glance, folded it and put it in his pocket.

Then she drew the insignia. Labeling the last of the quick drawings, she handed the notebook and pen back to him.

"What is your name?" Steer asked, his pen poised over the notebook.

Before she could answer Griff gripped her shoulder, forestalling her.

"She doesn't want her name in the newspaper," he said to Steer, and as Sibi cast a quick, frowning look at him he shook his head at her. "Trust me, you don't want that kind of attention."

17

Moments later, a series of enormous explosions not far from the hospital sent Griff and his men rushing out into the night to see what was happening. Steer went, too, along with a number of others. Although the nuns continued on with their work with outward composure, the atmosphere in the ward was thick with fear.

For Sibi, the thought of finding herself completely on her own in the midst of all the devastation and danger was terrifying. Knowing that it was up to her to protect and make possibly life or death decisions for Margrit and Jo as well as herself turned her cold and clammy all over. She wasn't old enough, she wasn't ready —

Mama, I need you. Her throat burned with the tears she refused to ever again allow herself to shed. Wishing for her mother was useless. And Papa was out of reach. She might not be ready, but the hard truth was she was on her own — and she was all her sisters had.

She felt more alone than she ever had in her life.

At some point during the next few hours, Sibi's ankle, pronounced broken, was treated, along with her other injuries, and Jo was brought back to them. Sibi's first sight of her, lying limply on a stretcher borne by an unknown old man and a young teenage boy she vaguely recognized from school but didn't actually know, both of whom had been pressed into service by the nuns, hit her like a punch to the stomach.

Jo's face was swathed in bandages. Her hair had been cut ruthlessly short. Dark circles ringed her eyes, her lips were dry and parched looking and she was almost as pale as the bandages. But she was alive, and for that Sibi was immensely grateful.

Still under the influence of whatever drug she'd been given, Jo opened her eyes and looked blearily at her as they laid her on the cot. Murmuring, "Sibi," she freed her hand from the rough gray folds of the blanket and reached out. Inhaling the faint scent of iodine that clung to her, Sibi gently took her fingers. Jo latched on as if to a lifeline and fell into an uneasy sleep. Her soft moans and restless tossings left Sibi in no doubt that whatever had been done for Jo in the operating theater, she was still in terrible pain. Tense and frightened, she watched Jo's sufferings with a sinking feeling in the pit of her stomach while knowing that she was helpless to alleviate them. Other than occasionally wetting her dry lips with water from the canteen, all she could do was watch over her and try to formulate some plan about what was best for the three of them to do.

But however she looked at it, she kept coming up against the rock-hard fact that, given her inability to walk and Margrit's dependence on her and Jo's state, all she could do was stay right where she was and pray.

Rattled by the sounds of intermittent explosions and what she was almost certain was approaching gunfire, she shivered at the thought of what the morning might bring. More airplanes? More bombs? The hospital had a big white cross painted on its roof, she knew, but would that be enough to deter the bombers if they came?

Had they escaped today's death only to die tomorrow?

"I want to go home," Margrit murmured sleepily. Wrapped up in her blanket, she curled in a little ball on the foot of the cot so as not to disturb Jo. Beneath the blanket, Ruby was tucked up against her chest. Sibi perched on the edge of the cot beside them.

"I know," Sibi said, although the dozens of images that unspooled in her mind at the mere mention of *home* made her throat tighten and her chest ache.

"I want Mama."

"I know," Sibi said again, and smoothed Margrit's hair. "I'm here. Go to sleep."

Margrit sniffled, and hugged Ruby closer. Then her eyes closed and, thankfully, she slept.

Sibi ended up on the cold, hard floor in the narrow space between their cot and the one next to it, one knee drawn up to her chest, her arms folded on top of it, her head resting on her folded arms. Her other leg, the one with the splinted ankle, stretched out stiffly in front of her. Griff's jacket was dirty and so large she was swimming in it, but there were no blankets to spare for her and at least it kept her from freezing. She'd bundled her hair into a knot at her nape, but loose strands straggled around her face and she kept having to tuck them behind her ears. She was so tired she couldn't keep two thoughts in her head at the same time. Which was, she decided, a good thing, because thinking was the last thing she wanted to be doing.

Despite her exhaustion she maintained an uneasy vigil, monitoring Jo's condition as best she could, keeping an eye on the constant comings and goings in the ward. Finally she slept because she simply couldn't hold out any longer, but it was a fitful sleep from which she was abruptly awakened by the sound of running footsteps skidding to a halt nearby.

Blinking, a little groggy, not quite sure at first where she was or what was happening, Sibi heard a young woman's hushed, frightened voice.

"Mother Superior said I should tell you — Oh, Sister, Mola's coming!"

Hearing that blurted message, Sibi was instantly wide awake. Her gaze found the speaker, a panting, perspiring novitiate. The distress in her smooth round face was obvious.

"They're fighting in the hills." The words spilled from the young woman's lips. They were addressed to Sister Beatrice, who stood frowning near the foot of the cot. "Our soldiers and the Whites. Mother Superior said I should tell you. She said I should say that the Whites are advancing toward the town and we should begin making plans to evacuate the hospital."

Sibi felt every ache and pain plaguing her disappear in the face of an onslaught of alarm. Just the thought of the savagery of the Whites toward those who opposed them was enough to make her heart race. And as for Mola himself — she shuddered.

"And what was the source of that information?" Father Ignatius, who'd spent the last several hours shuffling in and out of the ward to offer consolation to the injured and dying, came puffing up. Short, portly and balding, he'd sometimes celebrated mass at the Church of San Juan, which they'd attended, so Sibi knew who he was, although she was quite sure he didn't know her.

"I couldn't say, Father." The novitiate bobbed a curtsy and shook her head. "It was Mother Superior who was given the message, and it was Mother Superior who asked me to bring it to Sister Beatrice. She was quite adamant that it should be acted upon immediately."

"Then that is what we shall do," Father Ignatius said. He looked at Sister Beatrice. "Sister —"

Sister Beatrice's sweeping gesture encompassed the ward. "Father, we cannot possibly evacuate all these people. There are too many — and too many are seriously injured. Too seriously injured to move. And we have no method of transporting even the ones that can be moved. And if we did have a means of transporting them, where would we take them? We are in the midst of a war, with an enemy army almost at our door."

"We must do the best we can."

By way of an answer, Sister Beatrice made a sound that, to Sibi, was very reminiscent of a snort.

Father Ignatius blinked at her.

Another of the nuns hurried up.

"Father, a patient is asking to give his confession."

"Is he . . ." Turning away from Sister Beatrice with what appeared to be relief, Father Ignatius raised bushy eyebrows at the newcomer.

"Yes, Father. Death appears imminent."

"I'll be right there." As the nun bowed her head in acknowledgment, he turned back to Sister Beatrice. "I will leave the details of this evacuation in your hands."

"I told you, such a thing cannot be done." Her voice was sharper than before.

"With God, all things are possible." The merest glimmer of a twinkle appeared in his eyes as he met the nun's forbidding stare. "And also with you, Sister Beatrice, as I and many others have learned over the years. And also with you."

■ ■ ■ ■

"Mola's coming! Our Reds are falling back. The Whites are advancing on Guernica!" The news flashed around the ward until the air itself seemed to shiver with fear. Patients who were aware of what was happening were restless and frightened, with some trying to get up and others calling out to each other and the nuns. Family members and friends who'd remained at the patients' sides gathered in little knots, heads together as they conferred, as the uncertain light cast jumping shadows over all. A team of nuns entered the ward and went from cot to cot, assessing each patient, tagging some cots by tying a piece of string around the top iron rail of the footboard. It didn't take much concentrated observation for Sibi to conclude that the string marker went to patients the nuns judged stable enough to be evacuated. The others — and there were many — would be staying behind.

As Jo was in the last cot at the very back of the ward, patients cleared to leave were already being taken out by the time the nun who was making such decisions for their row reached her. Looking up from the clipboard she carried to introduce herself to

Sibi as Sister Fernanda, she barely glanced at Margrit, who was asleep, before bending over Jo. Jo muttered and shifted uneasily as the nun examined her, but didn't awaken, which worried Sibi. Jo was always the lightest of sleepers.

"How is she?" Sibi looked anxiously up at Sister Fernanda as, after completing the examination, the nun jotted something on the clipboard that was already thick with notes.

"Feverish." Sister Fernanda, who was tall, spare and middle-aged, spoke in a clipped voice that matched her brisk manner. "With a burn like hers, shock is the biggest danger. Infection is next. She needs to be kept warm and still, and the wound needs to be kept clean. The night is cold, and most of our vehicles are open. The journey will be rough and dusty and it will be almost impossible to keep the dust from seeping beneath the bandages. If dirt gets in the wound, there's little that can be done to prevent infection. If that happens, well —" The nun shook her head. "I am afraid she will be one of those staying here. You and the little one, however, must go."

Sibi's stomach clenched. "I'm not leaving my sister."

"You can do no good if you stay. And what

of the other one?" Sister Fernanda cast a glance at the shabby gray ball that was Margrit. "Will you send her off alone with the other evacuees? Or will you keep her here, to greet Mola?"

Sibi's breathing quickened at the thought of Mola. Then an instant image of Margrit being torn, screaming and kicking, from her side flitted through her head. Just as she would not leave Jo, Margrit wouldn't willingly, either. Nor would Margrit willingly leave her. And even if she could be forced to go, Sibi was wary of sending her away with strangers.

But to stay meant finding themselves at the mercy of the enemy, who had none. Limpieza Social, or the cleansing of society, was the policy of the Whites. There was no mercy for women or girls. No mercy for children or nuns. What they did was wholesale slaughter. Their advent was called the White Terror for a reason.

Sibi started to sweat. The fate she and Margrit were likely to suffer at Mola's hands didn't bear thinking of. As for Jo —

"We're all going. Jo comes with us," Sibi said.

Sister Fernanda shook her head. "There are only a few vehicles left and only so much space is available in them. It has to be allocated to those most likely to survive the journey. I know leaving a sister behind will be hard, but you must think of the little one — and yourself. And you may be sure that we will take the very best possible care of this one that is left."

"No," Sibi said. "I won't leave her. She comes, too."

"That won't be possible. I'm sorry." Sister Fernanda's tone had gentled. Her eyes softened, too, as they met Sibi's. But the shake of her head was final, and she turned away without tying the piece of string that Sibi now coveted around the foot of the cot.

"Sister!" Starting up only to fall back again as stabbing pain reminded her that she couldn't, Sibi called after Sister Fernanda without result. But her voice was loud enough to rouse Jo, who turned her head in Sibi's direction.

"Is . . . something wrong?" Jo's eyes were open. Slightly unfocused, they looked as if, in the few hours since her injury, they'd sunken deep in their sockets. She wet her lips with her tongue. "Sibi?"

"No, nothing," she lied, summoning a weak smile for her sister. "How are you feeling?"

"My head feels . . . heavy. And my face —" Jo broke off. "Am I going to die?"

"*No.*" Sibi's denial was perhaps fiercer than it needed to be, but Jo didn't seem to notice. She exhaled, a small sigh of relief that wrung Sibi's heart because of the evidence it provided of the extent of her sister's trust in her. Jo's hand still lay atop the blanket where it had been left when Sister Fernanda had finished taking her pulse. It flopped toward Sibi, who took it in hers. Earlier Jo's hand had been icy. Now the skin felt hot and dry.

Sibi's fear for her ratcheted up a hundredfold.

"Where's . . . Margrit?" Jo's lashes fluttered again. She wouldn't be awake for much longer, Sibi thought, which was good: Mama had always said that sleep was the best healer. And she was very much afraid that when whatever drug Jo had been given wore off, when she really and truly woke up, she would be in agonizing pain.

"Margrit's here. Asleep, by your feet."

"Oh." Jo's eyes closed again, then opened just a little. "Mama? Where's Mama?"

Sibi's throat went dry. Her heart speeded up. Her hand tightened on her sister's. Jo was in such bad shape — and it would be such a terrible thing for her to hear.

Should I tell her? Should I wait?

Before she could decide, Jo's eyes closed

and this time they stayed closed. The tenor of her breathing changed and Sibi knew she slept.

Please, God, don't take Jo, too.

Practically jumping out of her skin with anxiety, Sibi let go of Jo's hand, tucked it beneath the blanket and looked around the ward, desperate to locate Sister Beatrice, who was nowhere in sight. If anyone could overrule Sister Fernanda, it would be her, she was sure. Sibi was prepared to beg, cry, shout, do whatever she needed to do to get Jo evacuated — including obtaining a piece of string from wherever she could find one to tie around the end of the cot herself if she had to. The ward was in such confusion now, with patients being helped or carried out while their loved ones trailed after, the sisters bustling to reassure or assist the ones left behind and more stretchers arriving with more wounded to be evaluated and kept or sent away, that getting Jo past Sister Fernanda and into a vehicle for evacuation shouldn't be that difficult, if she could only come up with a piece of string. Spotting one tied to a now-empty cot a couple of rows away, Sibi summoned every scrap of strength that remained to her, grasped the horizontal iron rail that was part of the cot's frame and prepared to use it to lever herself onto her hands and knees. Crawling would hurt, but she could do it, and — She cast a swift look around to make sure she wasn't being observed.

Griff. Instead of Sister Beatrice or Sister Fernanda, that's who Sibi saw, and her heart burst into a chorus of glad hosannas. He headed toward her, walking fast, moving with easy agility through the chaos surrounding him. He looked so vital and alive despite his soot-blackened state that she felt some of her own energy returning.

He was saying something over his shoulder to . . . Iverson, she saw, who followed in his wake.

"We get caught up in the fighting it'll cause a damned international incident." Iverson's reply was testy.

"There's time," Griff said.

"It'll be dawn in an hour."

"We'll be gone before then."

The thought of what dawn might bring — more airplanes, more bombs, *Mola* — sent a shiver down Sibi's spine.

Griff reached the foot of the cot and looked toward Sibi, who still sat on the floor. The burning intensity with which she returned his look brought a quick frown to his face.

"Take us with you," she said before he

could say anything.

"What?" There was no mistaking the surprise in his tone.

"You're leaving — you said you'd be gone within the hour. I want you to take us — all three of us — with you."

"You understood that? We were speaking English."

"Yes, I understood it. Did you understand what I just said? I want to go with you. *We* want to go with you. Wherever you're going. It doesn't matter." The urgency in her voice was matched by the fervor of her gaze. "*Mola's* coming. And they're evacuating the hospital and they said Jo has to stay and I won't — *can't* — leave her, and I can't send Margrit away without me, and . . . I want you to take us with you."

"All right."

"All right?" His easy acquiescence was a surprise. She'd expected to have to argue, maybe even beg.

"You think I'd go off and leave you and your sisters behind? With the Nationalist Army poised to invade? I was coming to get you out of here, anyway."

"Really?" Her eyes searched his.

"Yes, really."

She felt the most enormous sense of relief. "Thank you."

"You're welcome." He gave her one of those quick smiles of his. "Ah, here's Lynch," he added with a glance down the ward. Following his gaze, Sibi saw that Lynch was, indeed, hurrying toward them. "Phillips is waiting in the street with the car."

"But I thought it burned."

"We came in two vehicles. An air corps rule of thumb is, redundancy pays. You ready to go?"

"Yes. Oh, yes."

"Let's get out of here, then."

18

As they stepped through the hospital's outer door, the fire's roar formed a bloodcurdling backdrop to a thousand other sounds — voices, motors, rattling wheels, the slither and crash of collapsing buildings and, more ominously, intermittent explosions and the sharp *pop-pop-pop* of gunfire.

Sibi's heartbeat quickened. "How long do we have, do you think?" she asked.

"Before the Whites get here?" Griff shook his head. "Maybe they won't. The Reds are putting up a hell of a fight."

"If you didn't think they'd get here, you wouldn't be in such a hurry to get us out."

He didn't reply, which she took as a tacit admission that her words were true.

She concentrated on the small gray shape that was Margrit, still wrapped up in her blanket and carrying Ruby as she stomped along ahead of them, and Jo, who thanks to Iverson's long strides had already reached the street.

Every scrap of intelligent thought and focus she had remaining to her had to be devoted to them.

"Will the bombers return when the sun comes up?" she asked. They were halfway across the lawn as Griff made his way through the scattering of patients still sprawled in the grass.

"They might, in advance of Mola. But there's not much left for them to destroy."

"What about the roads out of town? They could target the evacuees." Sibi thought of Luiza, of the machine-gun fire that had killed her, and her heart lurched. "Or they could send the chasers."

"The fighter planes?" He shook his head. "With any luck, we'll be safely behind Bilboa's antiaircraft defenses before they could get here."

Sibi grimaced. "Right now I believe in luck about as much as I believe in miracles."

"Believe in this, then. I'll see you safe."

She looked at him, at this man whom she'd had no idea even existed in the universe until a few hours ago, and realized that she did absolutely trust him to do what he said: keep her and her sisters safe.

"I can believe in that," she said, and he smiled at her.

They'd nearly reached the street when it occurred to Sibi that, compared to the head-to-toe and shoulder-to-shoulder blanket of wounded that had covered the grass when they'd arrived, only about a fourth as many remained, with a single priest moving among them. She felt a niggle of surprise that any were still left outside in the cold night air, that they hadn't been evacuated or, if they were judged to be too seriously injured for that, moved inside the hospital. She'd just seen for herself that many beds were open. So why —

Glancing down at a supine patient as Griff strode past him, Sibi saw that he was a white-haired old man. His clothes were dark and shiny with what she recognized from her recent experiences was blood. He lay motionless, and . . . a bandanna covered his face.

He was dead.

Looking back over the lawn, she realized to her shock that the faces of all those who still lay in the grass were covered.

They're all dead.

A fresh wave of horror at the realization caught her unprepared. So many dead — and what would come to them? Who would care for them? Who would wash their bodies and lay them out and pray over them and bury them?

Who would do those most essential things for her own dead?

"What about my mother and Luiza?" she asked Griff, keeping her voice low to make certain her sisters couldn't overhear. "Their b-bodies. I can't just leave them — they need to be buried. I —"

Her throat closed up and she broke off, unable to go on.

"There are hundreds of dead. Maybe even thousands." His voice, like hers, was low, and husky with compassion for her. "So many that to individually bury them all would be impossible given the state of the town and with the Whites coming. When I passed the Casa de Juntas not long ago, they were already starting to bury the bodies that had been taken there in a mass grave. That would be your sister. As for your mother, I can't say."

She thought of the fire, of its fierceness and heat. "That was her funeral pyre, wasn't it? She's probably already reduced to ash."

Her voice shook on the last word.

"It's possible. At this point, there's nothing you or I or anyone else can do."

At what she recognized was the truth of that, Sibi's heart broke one more time. She wanted to scream, she wanted to cry, she wanted to curse God and the Devil and Mola, the last two of whom had in her mind become one and the same.

She wanted to —

"Are you all right?" Griff asked.

Only after he spoke did she realize that he'd stopped walking some few meters short of the automobile, which was big and black and sported an American flag on the front just like the other one. She realized at the same time that Iverson had already reached the automobile with Jo, and Margrit was just getting there, and that Phillips was waiting behind the wheel.

She realized that she was shaking, not just trembling but shaking, from head to toe.

And he'd stopped to give her time to feel what she needed to feel, away from them all, shrouded in the privacy that the darkness afforded.

"I'm angry," she whispered, and her voice shook, too. "So, so *angry*. I want my mother back. I want my sister. I can't believe that this happened. I'm so angry, and I don't know what to do."

"I know." His arms tightened around her in what felt almost like a hug. As she let the comfort he offered enfold her, she felt the weight of his cheek as he briefly rested it against her hair. Knowing that there was someone there to share it was small balm for what felt like the bottomless well of her pain, but it was *something,* and she grabbed on to it. "I know you're angry, and you have every right to be. But —"

"Sibi?" Margrit called. The little girl had come back around the front of the automobile and stopped, because beyond the headlights, which had just come on, the night with its moving, distorted shadows would be scary to her, Sibi knew. Still wrapped in the blanket, with Ruby's furry black head nestled beneath her chin, she peered in Sibi's direction, into the dark. "Are you there? I need you."

"What you do is, you go on," Griff said in her ear.

Sibi took a deep breath and nodded. Because there was simply nothing else to do *but* go on.

"I'm coming," she called to Margrit, summoning every bit of strength that remained to her to keep her voice steady.

"Hurry," Margrit said. "They said I should get in. They said we're going for a drive. But I don't want to. I want to go *home.*"

There it was: the motivation she needed. Wherever Mama was — and Sibi hoped and prayed and felt, with every fiber of her being, that somewhere her mother's essence, her soul, still existed — she was relying on her to take care of the little girls.

"Ready?" Griff asked, and Sibi nodded.

By the time they reached Margrit, Sibi was able to say, "I'm here," To her in a perfectly normal tone, followed by, "Better put Ruby down for a minute, in case there's something she needs to do. Then get in. We're *all* going for a drive."

"I don't want to go for a drive," Margrit said.

"You have to," Sibi told her firmly as Griff opened the back door and deposited her on the long bench seat.

"Do not." Margrit's reply was muffled but mulish. The child had just lived through the worst day of her life, Sibi reminded herself. And reminded herself, too, of how enormously glad she was that Margrit was alive.

Sibi crossed her arms over her chest and waited, inhaling the scent of leather and cigarette smoke that permeated the vehicle. A minute or two later she was rewarded for her patience when the little girl dropped Ruby onto the seat and climbed in after her.

By the time they pulled away from the hospital, Sibi sat pressed against Griff's side, Jo lay stretched out full length with her head in Sibi's lap and Margrit curled in the foot-well beneath Jo, with Ruby snuggled in with her. Phillips drove, and Lynch and Iverson piled in the front seat beside him.

"Where are we going?" Margrit asked. Her head was pillowed on the hump in the middle of the floorboard augmented by several folds of her blanket, and her face had turned toward Sibi.

"To another town, where it's safe."

"Safe from the bombs?" Margrit asked.

"Yes."

"We can't just go home?"

"No."

"Why not?"

"Because it's not safe."

An unknown number of vehicles loaded with evacuating patients had already left. They fell into line behind them, taking care to avoid the craters and obstacles in the streets. Joining the throng of people fleeing the town on foot and in every conceivable conveyance, they headed west, toward Bilbao.

"Where's Mama?" Thin and strained, Jo's voice coming out of the darkness was a surprise. Sibi had thought she was asleep. "And Luiza? We can't just leave them."

"Luiza got shot by an airplane," Margrit said. "She was all blood, and we left her in the street. I think she might be dead."

Sibi could feel Jo's reaction in her sudden

stiffening, in the cessation of her breathing. Her own reaction was no less physical. If they asked outright if Luiza was dead, if Mama was dead — and they *were* going to ask, the question was imminent, she knew — she was going to have to tell them.

They'd been through so much already. This would cause them such grief.

"Sibi?" Jo looked up into her face. Meeting her sister's dark eyes that were already liquid with suffering, Sibi could practically feel the portentousness in the air. The next moments were going to shatter Jo's, and Margrit's, world.

"They left ahead of us," Sibi said.

To lie might be wrong, but her every instinct told her that right at that moment, while they were in an automobile in the midst of an urgently necessary evacuation, cut off from medical attention if the shock of learning the truth should cause Jo in particular to need it, was not the time to break such devastating news.

"You two should try to go to sleep," Sibi added before they could ask her anything else. Beside her, she felt the sturdy strength of the arm she leaned against relax. That was when she realized how tense Griff had been, in anticipation, she guessed, of the little girls' reaction to learning of their mother's and sister's deaths. "It's the middle of the night, and we're going to be driving for a while."

"I'm not sleepy," Margrit said.

"Close your eyes and you will be."

"Won't."

"I'll tell you a story," Sibi offered in desperation. The memory of Mama sitting on the little girls' bed the previous night while she did just that rose vividly in her mind's eye. Her breath caught. The agony of it was so intense she could hardly bear it. Blindsided, she latched on to a fragment of that night, of the story their mother had told, of the girls' ongoing fascination with the mythical giant, and shoved the rest of the memory away. "Tartaro the giant roared loudly enough to shake the mountains as he stomped toward the village. He —"

As she spun the tale the automobile bounced and jounced over the badly cratered road, which was her first sign that the bombing had not been confined to the town. Winding through fields and then hills, the road was packed with refugees and the going was slow. Looking out at the surrounding countryside, she saw that it, too, had suffered terribly. Whole herds of sheep, their white fleece dark with blood, lay in the fields where they had been slaughtered. In other torn-up fields, lifeless, mangled people and animals were no more than dim shapes among the shadows. Burned-out trucks and automobiles lined the road. Carts lay over-turned, their contents spilled beside them. Meters-tall pyramids of fresh earth pocked the landscape, looking like giant anthills, marking, Sibi realized, more spots where the bombs had hit. The needle-shaped black pines that covered the hills had been shorn in half, most probably by machine-gun fire. *Caserios* and barns had been reduced to smoking husks. Everywhere she looked were more atrocities. The night might have hid-den the worst of them, except the night was not dark. It was alight with a pink light from the giant bonfire that was Guernica.

As the automobile topped a rise, she glanced back and saw it: the town, cradled in the valley below, ablaze from the glinting onyx thread of the River Mundaca to where the road to Bermeo disappeared into the rolling hills. Huge tongues of flame shot skyward, licking into dense clouds of black smoke streaked with flickering veins of orange. On their lowest levels, the roiling clouds pulsed scarlet like an exposed, still-beating heart. That was because, she real-ized, they reflected the raging conflagration below. What from that distance looked like glowing embers around the central fire were actually the smoldering ruins of once-teeming neighborhoods left behind as the inferno, having done its worst, passed on.

So much loss. So much pain, and grief, and sorrow.

It was only after the automobile rounded a bend and the town vanished from sight that Sibi realized she had broken off in the middle of the story.

Neither Margrit nor Jo had protested. A glance down at them revealed why: they were asleep. Their eyes were closed, their bodies relaxed. She could hear them breathing. She realized, fiercely, that she treasured the homey sounds.

19

"What . . . ?" Sibi sat bolt upright, blinking, still a little groggy but in the grip of a cold rush of fear. She was in an automobile, *the* automobile, which was overwarm and stuffy but running along smoothly now, an indication that the road it traveled over was no longer pitted and broken. In the front seat, three men, soldiers, *Americans,* talked in low voices. She remembered them, and — a sideways glance found him — Griff. She was jammed right up against his unyielding side.

His once-white shirt was gray in the dim light; the tieless collar was open and — he turned his head to frown at her — he was bleary-eyed and needed a shave and a wash, and all in all appeared thoroughly disreputable.

The wail of air-raid sirens, the boom of big guns — she'd been asleep, but she was hearing them *now.* Which meant they were *real,* not the stuff of her nightmares. What she had most dreaded — the return of the airplanes — was clearly happening. Here and now. *Again.*

Terror seized her. She couldn't get words out fast enough. Even as they struggled to force their way past her suddenly tight throat, she looked a fearful question at Griff.

"It's all right." He knew instantly what was upsetting her, even though he, like the men in the front seat, appeared unmoved by it. His grim expression softened. His voice was steady, strong. "We're in Bilbao. *Safe* in Bilbao. What you're hearing are antiaircraft guns, which means planes have been spotted in the vicinity, but they won't get too close. Bilbao's air defense system is too good, and too well known."

Unlike Guernica, which hadn't had one.

"The He 51s —" Her voice was a croak as she remembered the deadly chasers that had shot Luiza. Small and fast, they were a difficult target to hit. She'd heard talk of their prowess around the dinner table when her father's colleagues had occasionally come to the house for a meal. And her mother, beautiful and vivacious as she'd sat at the foot of the table, passing the excellent food she'd cooked with her own hands, had always steered the conversation in a different direction. *No talk of work at the table,* she'd said in her light and charming way.

And the stolid German men had laughed and agreed and changed the subject, and shot her father veiled, congratulatory looks for the acquisition of such a lovely exotic creature — those were the very words she'd heard one of the men use — for a wife.

Mama.

Harsh reality settled like a rock in Sibi's stomach. The dawning of a new day changed nothing. Her mother was still dead. Luiza was still dead.

And she was left all alone, she and the little girls. Among these strangers.

She felt like she was shaking apart inside.

"Can't get down low enough to shoot at anything," Griff said. "The pilots wouldn't even attempt it. Believe me, it's called the Cinturón de Hierro for a reason."

The girdle of iron — it sounded far more nebulous now that she was inside it and depending on it for protection than it had all those times when she'd been elsewhere and had merely heard it talked about.

The booming *ackackack* of a new round of gunfire made her heart leap, had her craning her neck — carefully, she didn't want to disturb Jo, whose head was cradled in her lap and who still slept — to look out.

All she could see were tall buildings crammed in close together, and a wide street crowded with refugees on foot and in every conceivable vehicle from trucks to oxcarts, and a sliver of brightening sky.

Her expression must have been telling, because Griff added softly, "You're safe. I promise." And smiled at her. That quick, confident smile of his that once again reassured.

Her eyes searched his face.

She'd slept for nearly an hour or more leaning against his shoulder, she realized. And realized, too, that he *wasn't* a stranger despite the brief time she'd known him. He'd saved her life, and the little girls'. He'd comforted her by talking about his own loss when she'd been imploding with grief. He'd come back for the three of them in the hospital and gotten them out of the burning ruins of their town ahead of the murderous Whites. He'd earned her gratitude, along with her friendship and her trust. A connection had been forged between them and tempered, literally, in fire. Beyond the fear and grief and misery flooding her every cell, that was what stood out.

Pushing the tangled mass of her hair away from her face, she returned his smile with a slight, almost tentative one of her own.

I will be strong. I must.

"You'll get used to it." Iverson glanced around at her. Like Griff, like them all, he was looking decidedly the worse for wear. "The sound of the guns, I mean. And the sirens. If you're here very long. They go off ten times a day in Bilbao."

"I hope we're not here very long. We *can't* be here very long." A different kind of panic seized her as she realized that she and her sisters had nowhere to go, no money, nothing except the clothes — with a quick grimace she amended that to nothing except the torn and filthy rags — on their backs.

How were they going to survive?

"I need to make a telephone call to my father," she said to Griff in a voice that was admirably composed, she thought, considering everything. He nodded.

"What the heck?" Lynch leaned forward to peer out the windshield.

Something fluttered past the windows. All the windows. A lot of somethings, pouring down, white and awkward as they twirled through the air like giant, ungainly snowflakes.

Iverson cranked down the front passenger window, thrust out a hand and caught one. The waft of fresh, sea-tinged air that blew in through the open window was welcome.

It helped clear her head.

"Leaflets," he said after a glance, and read from it aloud, "*If submission is not immediate, I will raze Bilbao to the ground* — that from the great General Mola himself!" With a sound of disgust, he dropped the leaflet back out the window.

An icy tremor slid down Sibi's spine. Once she might have discounted such a statement, but the annihilation of her small, peaceful town proved it was no idle threat.

Had death followed them? Was it hovering even now, poised to fall at any time?

"Will they come — to Bilbao?" She looked at Griff, her voice low.

"Not today," he said. "And almost certainly not for a while. They know they'll have a real fight on their hands when they do."

But they would come. Everyone knew that the Whites' true target in the north was Bilbao. And Mola's leaflets had just borne that out.

The sirens screeched anew, followed by the staccato burst of another round of gunfire. Sibi flinched and clutched Griff's arm.

"Nothing to be alarmed about." He covered her hand with his. She had a feeling that the panic she was doing her best to hide

212

blazed at him from her eyes. If her fingers that were digging into the hard muscle of his forearm hurt, he gave no sign of it. "A couple of enemy planes are apparently overhead, yes, but to succeed in avoiding the guns they would have to be too small and fast to carry bombs, and too high to strafe anybody. Any lower and slower, and the guns would bring them down. The pilots know it. All they're doing is dropping those leaflets."

But chasers are hard to hit . . .

Sibi realized that she was rigid as a board, breathing too fast — and holding on to his arm like she never meant to let go.

Margrit sat up in the footwell, rubbing her eyes. "Are the airplanes back?" Her voice quavered.

"We're safe," Sibi assured her, even though her own heart still pounded. She forced herself to release Griff's arm. "The airplanes can't get us here."

"Are you sure?" Margrit's eyes were big with fright as she took in the wailing sirens, the booming guns.

"Yes."

"I'm hungry." Margrit's lips quivered piteously. Her hair had frizzed out into a nimbus of golden ringlets that framed her woebegone little face. Sibi ran a soothing hand over the top of those springy curls. "I want Mama."

"I know." Sibi would have gathered her littlest sister up in her lap, but she didn't want to disturb Jo, who was moving restlessly but other than that gave no indication she was actually awake. She nodded at Jo. *"Shh."*

With a quick glance at Griff, Margrit tugged urgently on Sibi's skirt. Sibi ducked her head toward her in order to hear.

"I have to go peepee," Margrit whispered. Ruby was awake, too, sitting on Margrit's lap, eyes bright, tongue lolling. Probably, Sibi thought, Ruby was thinking the same thing. *She* was thinking the same thing, although given the fact that someone — *Griff? Not if she could avoid it* — was going to have to carry her to the bathroom she meant to hold out for as long as she could.

Sibi nodded her understanding at Margrit, straightened and looked at Griff.

He'd apparently overheard, because he said, "We're almost there," To her, then redirected his attention to the front seat. "Phillips, how much longer?"

"We're close," Phillips replied. "A few minutes."

"A few minutes to where?" Sibi asked. Jo's eyes were still closed, but she was moving, small jerky twitches that told Sibi she was in pain. She dreaded to think how bad it would be when her sister woke up. Burns were, she knew, among the most agonizing of injuries, and the medication she'd been given under the Carmelite sisters' care had to be wearing off. Lightly touching Jo's hand, she was alarmed to find that it was burning up. "We need to get to a hospital."

"That's where we're going," Griff said. "Hospital de Basurto. I know somebody there."

Sibi exhaled in relief. In another heartening development, the guns had stopped firing, and the sirens were dying away.

Please, God, keep the airplanes away.

"The Nationalists have Bilbao surrounded from the south." At the tinny, staticky, disembodied voice, Sibi looked sharply toward the front seat, only to discover Lynch fiddling with a radio dial. *"A blockade of Port Bilbao has the city cut off from the north. The town is being assaulted from all sides as the Nationalists try to either batter or starve it into submission. Last night, a mere thirty-five kilometers away, Guernica was attacked and des —"*

"Turn it off," Griff said sharply, his eyes on her, and Lynch instantly complied. Sibi, who'd stopped breathing as the word *Guer-*

215

nica spilled from the radio to take on form and shape and life in her mind, started breathing again, erratically, and slumped back against the seat while cold shivers chased themselves over her skin.

They'd escaped the town, yes, but not the war. Not Mola and the Whites.

"Mama?" Jo opened her eyes. She sounded, and looked, disoriented. Putting a hand to the bandage on her face, she started plucking at the strips of gauze.

"Don't do that." Sibi caught Jo's hand and held it. "Everything's all right, I'm here."

Jo's fingers twitched in hers. They felt small and frail, like twigs. Small and frail and hot. Moving her head from side to side, Jo moaned, "My face — what's wrong with it? It hurts so much."

"You got burned," Margrit said.

"Hush." Sibi shot her littlest sister a quelling look. That Jo didn't seem to remember what had happened terrified Sibi. She did her best not to let it show. Her hand tightened on Jo's. "We're going to a hospital. They'll take care of you, make you feel better."

"Where's Mama?" Jo looked up at Sibi in a way that made Sibi think she might not be actually seeing her. Her tone was fretful. "I want Mama."

"So do I," said Margrit, also looking at Sibi.

So do I. Sibi barely managed not to say it out loud.

"We're here," Phillips said.

Glancing out the window, relieved at the interruption, Sibi saw that they were pulling up to a long, four-story redbrick building with two attached wings and several entrances. The C-shaped drive curving up to the imposing front door was jam-packed with vehicles of every description. As traffic congestion forced them to stop, her eyes were drawn to the flood of people milling around on the grass lawn that stretched across the entire front of the block-long edifice.

So many — and most were as dirty and bedraggled and hopeless-looking as she felt.

"I'm going to go in and try to find my friend and see if she can get some beds ready before we go carrying your sister in there," Griff said to Sibi, and got out. As Sibi nodded, he looked at Margrit. "I'm pretty sure there's a bathroom just inside the door, if you want to come with me."

Margrit looked for permission at Sibi, who hesitated a moment — she wasn't completely sure Griff was up to dealing with

Margrit — then, recognizing the urgency of the situation from Margrit's expression, said, "Stay with Captain Griffin," in her sternest tone.

She then switched her attention to Griff as, apparently experiencing a similar qualm himself, he said, "Iverson can come with us. He can wait outside the bathroom door, then bring her straight back to you."

"I'll be good," Margrit promised. Iverson opened the door nearest her, and Ruby promptly jumped out.

"Ruby, wait!" Abandoning her blanket cocoon, Margrit scrambled after her.

It took a few minutes, but Ruby — hopefully having taken care of the same business that concerned Margrit — was restored to the automobile, the door was shut on her, and Margrit, a small, bright-haired figure between the two men, trekked toward the hospital.

Then Sibi couldn't worry about Margrit any longer, because Jo started plucking at her bandages again and making distressing little sounds of pain.

20

Soothing Jo took every bit of Sibi's energy and focus.

She talked. She stroked, hair and uninjured skin. She sang.

Jo was no sooner quiet and apparently asleep once more, and Sibi had no sooner collapsed back against the seat with exhaustion, than Margrit reappeared. A quick, apprehensive glance past her curly blond head as it popped into view confirmed that Margrit hadn't lost her escort. Iverson was a couple of steps behind her, Sibi saw, and saw, too, that Margrit was carrying something, very carefully.

"Shh." Sibi put her finger to her lips and cast a significant look at Jo as, Iverson having caught up and opened the door for her, Margrit climbed into the spot Griff had vacated. Her sling put whatever it was she held at risk, but in the end she managed to scoot in next to Sibi without dropping it.

"I brought you some breakfast." Obediently whispering, Margrit held out the thing she'd been carrying — a thick piece of black bread.

Sibi was touched. "Margrit! Thank you."

"You're welcome."

The bread was coarse and felt way too hard to be edible as she took it. Didn't matter: the mere sight of it made Sibi's stomach growl. She looked from it to Margrit, who watched her gravely. Her heart swelled with tenderness for this small sister, and simultaneously ached with the knowledge of all she — they — had lost.

Sibi held the bread out to her sister, because Margrit needed to eat more than she did. "You take it."

Margrit shook her head. "I had some," she said. "With honey."

"You got honey?" A happy note in the midst of a nightmare. Sibi smiled at her in conspiratorial delight.

Margrit nodded. "They said a boat got through with stuff yesterday, and it brought some. I asked the lady to put it on your bread, too, but she wasn't listening anymore."

"This is fine just like it is." Breaking off a piece, taking care that the crumbs didn't fall on Jo, she put it in her mouth, chewed.

The bread was coarse and hard. It was also dry as dust. She was so hungry it didn't matter.

"And there's coffee to go with it." Iverson leaned in to hand Sibi a tin mug.

"A feast." Sibi thanked Iverson with a quick smile, then glanced down at Jo with the thought of sharing the bread with her. But she didn't want to wake her, and in any case it would probably be wiser to wait and see what a doctor had to say about her condition before trying to get her to eat.

Under Margrit's unwavering gaze she ate the bread and tossed the crusts to Ruby, who'd watched her consume every bite with such a hopeful expression that it would have taken a far harder heart and emptier stomach than hers to deny the pup. Then she drank the coffee. It was weak and flavorless, nothing like the strong thick brew the Basques generally preferred, but it was hot and she swallowed it gratefully.

"It's really crowded in there," Margrit said. "Did all those people get bombed, too?"

"I don't know." Sibi finished the last of the coffee. "Some of them did, I expect."

"I hate the airplanes."

"I do, too."

Then Griff was back. There was a bed being readied for Jo, and she and Margrit could be treated in the infirmary, he told Sibi as he gathered her up. Being carried by him felt familiar now, and comfortable, and she wrapped her arms around his neck with as little thought as she breathed. Iverson took Jo, who remained asleep and hung limp and still, arms dangling, head flung back, in his arms, which Sibi found terrifying. Margrit, not in the sunniest mood because she was tired and scared and Ruby had to be left behind in the care of Phillips, who stayed with the automobile while Lynch came with them at Griff's behest, stomped along a couple of steps behind Iverson and Jo as they all headed across the lawn toward a side entrance.

"My friend's going to meet us there," Griff said. Unforgiving daylight poured over them, and his features took on a harsher cast because of it. His eyes were deep-set and unsmiling beneath thick straight dark brows, his nose was a blade, his mouth tight-lipped and grim.

"Are you here a lot?" she asked, curious as to how he'd come to have a friend — a woman friend; he'd said "she" before — in the town.

"In Bilbao? Since Mola turned his attention to the north, we've been coming up every couple of weeks to keep an eye on things."

"Observing."

"Yep."

"What does that mean exactly?"

"We talk to the locals, the mayors and politicians, the militias, a lot of different people, to get their take on what's happening. We chart troop movements, verify rumors and *observe.*" He threw her a glinting look. "It all gets written up in a report and presented to my boss."

"And then?"

"The information gets disseminated however he sees fit. A lot of governments, including my own, are interested in the outcome of this war."

"Just not interested enough to do anything about it."

"No."

That "no" was faintly rueful, but still it was enough to make Sibi bristle as it hit a vein of bitterness in her she hadn't even realized was there. She'd heard enough talk to know that none of the major powers — the United States, Britain, France — had answered the Spanish government's frantic pleas for help to quash the rebellion. They chose instead to let the fighting rage, to remain neutral and *observe* while tens of thousands died.

She was so angry suddenly she couldn't speak. Couldn't look at him, even though she knew, *knew,* that it wasn't his fault, that he wasn't responsible for his government's decisions. Compressing her lips, she glanced away and told herself to breathe.

"I'd change things if I could," Griff said quietly as he carried her up the steps and inside the door Lynch held for them. "For the record, I think nonintervention is a poor choice."

Apology and regret and sympathy were all wrapped up together in those words. Nothing that had happened was his doing, she knew. She made a face at him, in a kind of apology of her own.

He smiled.

The nurse who met them inside the hospital introduced herself as Ruth Temple. Everything from her brief greeting, in English, to her appearance made it obvious that she was another American. Sibi was briefly surprised by her presence until she remembered that dozens of foreign nurses, like the foreign soldiers who made up the International Brigades, had thumbed their noses at their governments' policies of noninterference and traveled to Spain to offer their services to the beleaguered country.

With her curly auburn hair cut in a fashionable short style and soft gray-blue eyes, Ruth was tall and sturdily built and very pretty in her nurse's uniform. Sibi judged her to be in her early twenties.

"I have something for you," she said to Sibi — her Spanish was not nearly as good as Griff's, but it was serviceable — and pointed to a wheeled chair that waited just beyond the door. It was made of wicker, upright in design, with separate footrests for her feet and big metal wheels on either side. Griff set her down in it. The seat and arms were well-worn, and she could tell that it had seen a lot of use.

"Go see if Father Ramon has any information for Fuqua," Griff said to Lynch in a low voice. Lynch nodded and took himself off.

Then, to the tune of the chair's creaking, Griff pushed her along through the hustle and bustle of the busy hospital as Ruth — she told them to call her that, and Sibi was too tired and in the grip of too many conflicting emotions to worry about the niceties of address any longer — motioned them all to follow her. They went through a door into a ward that was much like the one in the convent, except it seemed more organized and less makeshift. And it smelled better, more sharp and acidic like the medicinal scent of iodine and less like the dreadful stench of bodies that had been ripped open and burned and otherwise mutilated. Jo's bed was pointed out — it was one of the few empty ones — while Jo herself, at Ruth's direction, was carried on through a second door.

"In there, a doctor will look at her straight-away," Ruth said. "Because there are so many of them, we've created a separate unit to handle the burn victims. Saline baths, which have proved quite effective in treating burns, have been set up and a variety of other therapies are available, as well. She'll be brought back out here onto the ward when they've finished and you can visit her then. In the meantime —" she looked from Sibi to Margrit, who clumped along in uncharacteristic silence with a hand on the arm of Sibi's chair "— you both need to be examined by a doctor, too. Fortunately, I don't think you'll have to stay overnight." The panic-inducing corollary to that statement hit Sibi — *where are we to go?* — at the same time as Ruth said to Griff with a beaming smile, "I know how busy you are. You can get on about your very important work and trust me to see that these young ladies are taken care of."

Sibi glanced up at Griff, to find that he was smiling back at Ruth with a look in his eyes that she hadn't seen in them before. Despite how dirty he was, and the execrable state of his clothes, he exuded a kind of rough and ready charm. His wild hair and bloodshot eyes and unshaven jaw notwithstanding, he actually looked very handsome.

Ruth certainly seemed smitten with him.

Watching them smile at each other, Sibi felt the tiniest pang of something she couldn't quite identify.

"My arm hurts," Margrit said.

Sibi forgot about everything else. "I know," she said to Margrit. Then, to Ruth, "Will a doctor be available to see this one soon?" It was all she could do to keep the anxiety out of her voice.

Ruth nodded. "I'll take you both back to the infirmary now."

She walked around behind Sibi's chair, smiled at Griff and took over the chair handles from him.

"Hold on a minute," he said to Ruth, then crouched beside Sibi. "I'll come back in a few hours," he told her. "Make sure you girls are all right."

He pressed something small and sharp-cornered into her hand, closed her fingers around it. Glancing down, Sibi saw that they were pesetas. The multiple banknotes were folded into a compact square a little smaller than her palm. Her cheeks burned at the sight of them.

"You don't need to. Come back, I mean." Her reply, hasty and ill-considered as she instantly realized it was, because they had no place to go and no money and no one else to turn to, was prompted by . . . pride, she supposed. Even though she knew what desperate straits they were in, to be so utterly dependent stung. "If there's a telephone I can use to call my father —"

"The telephones in the hospital aren't working this morning," Ruth said. "I don't know if they're overwhelmed because so many people are trying to make calls, or if the lines are down because of what happened in —"

A quick shake of Griff's head stopped her. The silence that followed was unmistakably awkward. Griff had been aware of her earlier reaction to hearing Guernica spoken of, and was trying to protect her, Sibi realized. She also realized that hiding from the grim reality wasn't going to be possible.

All the avoidance in the world wouldn't change a thing.

Iverson returned just then and Griff stood up without another word. Sibi felt the sharp corners of the banknotes poking into her palm and knew that not even her pride was going to compel her to give them back. It was humiliating that Griff had felt sorry enough for her to give her money, and she doubted that Ruth had missed the gesture and that made it even more humiliating. But for Margrit's and Jo's sakes as well as her own, she would accept. The world was a scary and uncertain place, and the money at least insured that, for a little while at least, they could eat.

"A doctor was coming in to look at your sister as I left," Iverson said to Sibi.

"I'll get a message to your father for you." Griff dropped a hand onto Sibi's shoulder. "And I *will* be back. You can count on it."

She looked up at him. His gaze as it met hers was as steady as it was intent. The bond of trust that had grown between them over the course of the night was there for her in his eyes.

Some part of her that had been wound as tightly as a cheap watch relaxed a little.

She nodded. His hand on her shoulder tightened, then lifted.

"What about Ruby?" Margrit's mouth quivered as she looked at Sibi. "I want her."

"I don't think they let dogs in this hospital," Sibi said.

Ruth shook her head in confirmation.

Before Sibi could reply, Griff said, "We'll watch Ruby for you, Margrit, and bring her back when we come back. Would that be all right?"

Margrit looked at him, seeming to weigh him and the offer. "Promise?"

"Promise," Griff replied. "We'll take good care of her."

Margrit pursed her lips. Then she nodded.

To Sibi, he said, "A few hours."

With a smile for Ruth and a gesture at Iverson to follow, he left.

21

Curled up at the foot of Jo's cot, Margrit slept for most of the afternoon. Golden sunlight slanted through dusty windows, warming the space and making it look incongruously cheerful despite the fear and suffering that hung like a cloud in the air. Wearing a hospital-provided clean night-gown, her shorn head turned to one side and a blanket tucked up around her, Jo slept, too — or was, more aptly, uncon-scious. Her burns had been cleaned, treated and rebandaged, and the anesthesia she'd been given was not expected to wear off for several more hours. On one side of her, a young woman with heavily bandaged arms hadn't opened her eyes or made a sound since she'd been brought in. In the cot on the other side, an old woman lay moaning beneath a sheet that had been propped up tentlike so that it touched no part of her body, leading Sibi to assume that her injuries were extensive.

Sibi kept dozing off in a chair beside Jo's cot. It was an ordinary upright chair, her wheelchair having been appropriated by Ruth for a patient whose need for it was deemed greater. Every so often her head would drop forward so that her chin rested on her chest before something — the guns and air-raid sirens that went off with stomach-churning regularity, a shout or shriek from a patient, a dropped pan or slammed door — startled her awake and upright again. Her broken ankle had been set — a harrowing procedure — and reinforced by a plaster cast. She'd been given aspirin for pain because anything stronger was in short supply, and outfitted with a pair of crutches for mobility. Her other injuries had been pronounced minor. Both she and Margrit, who did indeed have a broken arm as Sister Beatrice had predicted and was now in a cast supported by a sling, were bruised and sore, but expected to fully recover.

Jo's prognosis was different.

Brusque with lack of sleep, the doctor came out to tell Sibi that Jo's recovery would be a long and painful process — if she recovered at all.

Sibi's heart seemed to stop. "She . . .

might not recover? Do you mean she might die?" Her horror was such that she blurted it out, only to cast an appalled glance at her sisters, neither of whom, fortunately, stirred.

The doctor, T. Navarro according to his name tag, shrugged. "Your sister's burns are severe. I have done my best for her. Now it is up to time, and her own body, and God," he said.

Sibi was busy beseeching God for this one gift when she fell asleep.

When she woke up, Griff stood at the foot of Jo's cot looking at her.

"I talked to Ruth," he said. Sibi was too groggy to do more than blink bemusedly at him. She could tell from the grave way he was looking at her that, despite the fact that she'd managed to wash her and Margrit's faces and hands and twist up her hair into a relatively neat knot, her appearance was concerning. Not a surprise — she felt awful. Sick, tired, heartsore, defeated. "She gave me these." He held up a brown paper bag. "And I bought you these." He held up a box.

"What are they?" She frowned at the items.

"Fresh clothes, for you and Margrit. And these are shoes. For you."

"You bought me shoes?"

233

He nodded. "If you're going to be walking around on your own, you need shoes." He looked at her feet. One was still encased in the torn and dirty black stocking. The other was partially covered by a cast that reached halfway up her calf and from which her bare toes protruded. "*A* shoe," he amended.

"I do. You're right. Thank you." She was fully awake now, which meant her head ached and pretty much every part of her body hurt and her ankle felt like a dog had mistaken it for a bone and was gnawing away at it. Worse, her fear for Jo came flooding back, coiling around inside her stomach so that she was instantly nauseous, but there was no doing anything about that, just like there was no doing anything about anything that had happened. Yesterday, in the span of a few short hours, her and her sisters' world had been shattered, and this new world order meant that terrible things could, and did, happen out of the blue, with no rhyme or reason.

Just, please, God, spare Jo.

Griff handed her the box. "Put your shoes — shoe — on. I have a hotel room, and I'm going to take you and Margrit there and leave you to it. You need rest, and food."

Sibi had been pulling the shoes — silver leather pumps, completely unsuitable to the

234

circumstances — out of the box as he spoke. She looked up at him, shook her head. She was so tired she was dizzy with it. And she *was* hungry, although she hadn't realized it until his words had made her think about food. But —

"I can't leave Jo."

"Ruth said she probably won't wake up for hours."

"It's that *probably* I'm worried about. I need to be here when she does."

"You can hardly keep your eyes open. And you've got to be starving. You won't be any good to Jo if you can't function yourself."

"Did Ruth tell you — ?" She broke off as her throat tightened. But the stricken look in her eyes must have told him what she meant.

"That Jo's condition is serious? Yes. But that doesn't mean she won't recover, and it does mean she's going to need you — and need you fully functional — when she wakes up. And what about Margrit? Come on, Sibi. You know you both need a hot meal, and a few hours' solid sleep."

Sibi hesitated. Then she nodded, because everything he said was true. "All right. Thank you."

"Put your shoe on. I'll be back. I need to talk to Ruth."

As he walked away from her, she almost tangentially absorbed the breadth of his shoulders, the athletic swing of his stride, the energy he gave off despite how exhausted he, too, had to be. It was only then, as she watched him go, that it hit her that while he was once again wearing his leather jacket, which still bore a few burn marks, although the worst of the grime was gone, the white shirt he wore underneath was not the scorched and crumpled one he'd been wearing earlier: this one was whole and clean. His pants were whole and clean, too, and dark taupe instead of gray. Minus the ash and soot, his hair, brushed back from his face, was tobacco brown, coarse and thick. His skin was tan, as if he spent a great deal of time outdoors. And except for a bruise on his cheekbone and a small cut on his chin, his face bore no marks of their ordeal. He was even clean-shaven. Obviously, he'd made use of his hotel room to shower and change. At the same time as she was registering all that, she was unbuckling the shoe and slipping it on over her remaining stocking. Fortunately, the heel on the silver pump was low and square, and the shoe was a reasonable fit. She had it on and was upright and balancing on her crutches when Griff returned.

"Ruth says she'll keep a close eye on Jo until you get back," he said.

"If you should see her before I do, please thank her for me." She turned more fully to face him — not that easy a feat — and kept her voice low. "Did you reach my father?"

"I tried telephoning several times, but none of the calls went through. I ended up sending him a telegram at the address you gave me."

"So there's no way to know if he's heard."

"I'd be willing to bet he's heard about —" he hesitated "— what happened. A number of reporters are in the area now, and the people I've talked to say the story's gone out to newspapers all over the world."

Her stomach clutched. "What are they saying?"

"Total destruction. A massacre."

Sibi closed her eyes as her surroundings seemed to shimmer. Her bandaged hands tightened on the grips of the crutches until she could feel her nails digging into the wood. It was all she could do not to sway.

"Look, right now you're experiencing what will probably be some of the worst moments of your life, but you're going to be all right." His voice was low and rough with compassion.

She opened her eyes, met his.

237

"Yes," she said. The fierceness her subconscious packed into that single syllable surprised her. But she meant it, she realized. The determination to not let what had happened break them — not just herself, but Margrit and Jo, too — rose in her like a surging tide. Total destruction, a massacre — that apocalyptic description might apply to the town. She refused to let it apply to her family. To what was left of her family. To her and her remaining sisters.

Whatever it takes, the three of us are going to make it through.

Her chin came up. "And Guernica — what of it?"

For a moment he simply looked at her.

"What? Do you think not talking about it makes any difference? The only thing to do with facts is face them head-on."

He gave a brusque nod: acceptance and agreement. "What's left of it is still burning."

At those words, a thousand thoughts and feelings and images flashed through her mind. What they boiled down to was this: Luiza, buried now in a mass grave; Mama, incinerated in the hell that German airplanes had made of her hometown.

She could feel her pulse pounding against her eardrums. Conversely, her heart seemed to slow down and steady, like it realized how very important it was to keep beating.

I will survive. We will survive.

"Sibi —" Griff frowned at her.

She took a deep breath.

"I'm all right." And she was, because she had to be. "Let me get Margrit, and we'll go."

He nodded.

Meaning to wake her, she maneuvered toward Margrit, which was tricky because it involved a narrow space and turning sideways and a plaster cast coupled with a shoe that had never been meant to be paired with a thick wool stocking or crutches. Seeing a telltale uptick in the corners of his mouth as he watched her, she gave him a narrow-eyed look in return.

"Go ahead and laugh if you want to. I've never used crutches before. And I'm not that good with high heels at the best of times."

"I'm not laughing," he said. Which was true, although his smile was wider than before. "As for the shoes, they were all I could find that looked like they'd fit. Because of the blockade, there's not much to choose from in the shops."

"Oh, believe me, I'm grateful for them. It." She made a wry face at him. "Every-

239

thing. You."

His smile disappeared. "I'm not going to just abandon you, you know. I mean to make sure you and your sisters are all right."

She thought about saying something along the lines of, *We're not your responsibility.*

Instead she simply nodded, because the connection between them was strong enough to allow her to rely on him without hesitation or guilt.

Then she bent over her sister, touched her shoulder. "Margrit. Wake up. We're going."

The Torrontegui Hotel, eight stories tall with a popular restaurant on the top floor, was a beautiful art deco building at the corner of a three-way intersection that, as they drove through it, was packed with traffic of all descriptions, from long Mercedes limousines to desperate pedestrians pushing everything they owned in handcarts. The streets had not quite descended into chaos, but as the sirens and antiaircraft guns sounded at closer and closer intervals, the sense of crisis that hung over the city was palpable.

Inside the hotel, the atmosphere was more restrained. Even while the windows rattled, even while the crystal prisms on the swaying chandeliers overhead tinkled madly from vibrations caused by the booming guns, the staff and guests carried on as though nothing out of the ordinary was occurring. Sibi tried not to look wide-eyed at the fashionably dressed guests strolling through the lobby, at the crowded dining room and busy bar, but she must have failed miserably because Griff, who carried a tail-wagging Ruby tucked under one arm, leaned down to whisper in her ear, "Don't look so worried. None of the chandeliers has fallen yet."

"It's not the chandeliers I'm worried about." It was the airplanes, the bombs, the guns, but she didn't say any of that because she didn't want to alarm Margrit, whose fist was bunched in her skirt as she trailed behind them.

He said, "I told you, this place is safe."

For now, was what she read in the shadows at the backs of his eyes.

"Captain Griffin! Ladies!" The lift operator, a small, round man with a dashing mustache, greeted them jovially as they stepped inside it. As the door closed and the lift started to rise, his eyes ran over them and his expression changed. "I have heard . . . terrible things." His voice dropped to a confidential hush as he addressed Griff. "About Guernica. Are they true?"

241

Sibi felt a now-familiar tightening in her chest. Margrit shrank against her side.

Griff nodded curtly.

"And the Whites? Where are they? Have they overrun the town yet?"

A shake of Griff's head. "Not yet."

"It is close, though?"

"A few hours. Although the resistance is fierce."

"Ah." It was a sound of lamentation. "We are next. I know it. People say Bilbao is impregnable because of our natural defenses — the mountains, the sea. They say in all of Spain's history our city has never fallen to an enemy. They speak of our brave soldiers, our guns, of the Cinturón de Hierro, tell each other that Mola cannot break through — none of it can stop what is coming. I feel it in my bones. And my bones, Captain Griffin, my bones, I assure you, are never wrong."

The elevator pinged to a stop, and the door opened.

"Let's hope that this time they are." Griff ushered Sibi and Margrit out of the lift. "Take care of yourself, Julio."

22

As they entered Griff's hotel room, Sibi made a beeline for the telephone. "May I call my father?"

"Be my guest." Griff put Ruby down and closed the door.

"Do we have to telephone Papa?" Voice tremulous, Margrit dropped to sit cross-legged on the carpet while Ruby frisked around her. "I don't want him."

Busy giving the number to the operator, Sibi didn't reply.

The call didn't go through. Anxiety had her biting her lower lip as she slowly replaced the receiver.

"You asked them to keep trying. They will, and sooner or later they'll get through. They'll ring the room, and you can talk to him." Griff's tone was bracing as he deposited the bag of clothes and his messenger bag beside the telephone and reached for the receiver she'd just replaced. "In the meantime, how about I order you and Margrit some food?"

Sibi glanced at her sister. Margrit now lay on her side on the carpet, one arm flung over Ruby, both of them to all appearances on the verge of falling asleep.

"Yes, please." Keeping her voice low, she put her crutches aside and sat on the edge of the bed.

After a brief discussion about what they both liked to eat, Griff placed the call. While he ordered — the food was to be brought to the room — her eye was caught by a book near the telephone. It lay on top of a folder full of papers, and its title, *My Ántonia,* in English, big gilt lettering on brown binding, made it seem out of place in this quintessentially Spanish room. It was, she felt, a surprising choice of reading material for someone like him, but the English title left her in no doubt that it *was* his. With a glance at him asking permission — he nodded — she picked it up and opened it.

For My Antonia, Happy birthday to the love of my life, Dan was scrawled in a bold hand inside the front cover, along with the date: November 16, 1918.

She looked a question at Griff as he hung up.

He took the book from her, ran his thumb

over the inscription, gave her a crooked half smile.

"My father gave it to my mother for her twenty-fifth birthday. It's just about the only thing of hers I have left."

Even now, everywhere I go, I carry a little piece of my mother with me. He'd told her that. She'd thought he was speaking figuratively. Looking at the book, and the tender way he handled it, she realized he'd meant it literally, too.

"Your father must have been heartbroken when she died."

He made a scoffing sound. "So heartbroken he married again a year and a half later. His new wife was the *next* love of his life. She didn't want any reminders of his first love, and that included me. Her name was Gertjan, she was German, and the one good thing about their marriage was that by the time I lit out of there I'd learned to speak the language. Comes in handy, as you saw."

"How old were you?"

"When I left our happy little family? Twelve."

"How did you survive?"

"Worked in the oil fields for a while. Took a job with a couple of crop dusters. Learned to fly a plane. That came in handy, too." He laid the book down, picked up the folder on which the book had previously rested and put it inside the messenger bag.

When his hand reemerged, something dangled from his fingers.

"What's this?" he asked, peering at it.

Sibi took one look and felt the blood congeal in her veins.

It was the red rag curler that had been tied around Ruby's foot.

Luiza's curler. A flash memory of Luiza as she'd looked with those rags tied up in her hair making butterfly wings that stood out all over her head was like a knife to the heart.

"It's mine." She held out her hand for it. Her voice was raspy, scratchy, and he frowned at her as he handed it over. Closing her fingers around the now-precious strip of cloth, she shook her head at him: she couldn't face the ordeal of talking about it.

After all, what was the point? Talking changed nothing. Just as grief changed nothing.

A knock on the door announcing the arrival of the food was a welcome interruption.

Knotting the rag around her wrist, she called to Margrit, who sat up groggily.

"I have to go. I'll be back before dark to

check on you," Griff said. "If you need anything in the meantime, more food, somebody to take the puppy out, anything, just dial zero on the telephone and ask for the front desk. I'll make arrangements with them for you to have whatever you want. Ruth knows where you are, and she'll telephone you here if there's any change with Jo."

Sibi nodded her thanks, and Griff left.

"Are we going to stay here long?" Margrit asked some ten minutes later. Face and hands washed now, her hair brushed free of tangles courtesy of the unauthorized use of what had to be Griff's hairbrush that had been left out by the sink, she sat at the table the waiter had brought tucking hungrily into a bowl of her favorite lamb stew as Sibi, all washed and brushed, too, emerged from the bathroom.

"Probably not." Sibi sat and started in on her own dish, which was a hot, savory bully beef. In an effort to turn Margrit's thoughts in a more cheerful direction, she added, "Did you see how big the bathtub is? You can try it out after we eat."

Margrit's scowl wavered: she loved taking a bath. "What if I get my arm wet?"

"We'll make sure you don't. And you need

a bath. Badly enough to risk it."

"I washed my hands. And my face."

"That still leaves a lot of you that needs to get clean."

"What about you? You need a bath, too."

"I'm not sure I can get in and out of the tub with my leg in a cast."

"I'll help you."

Sibi smiled at her. Margrit's innate sweetness could be counted on to surface often enough to keep her from being a total pest. "I know you will. Thank you."

They ate for a moment in silence. Then Margrit said, "Is Jo going to die?"

"No." Sibi's stomach cramped as she was plunged right back into a place she didn't want to go. "She isn't."

Margrit dropped her spoon back into her almost empty bowl with a clatter. "You can tell me the truth, you know. I'm *five.*"

"I know." No longer hungry, Sibi put her own utensils down. Her attention was caught by Ruby, sitting beside the table with shining brown eyes that moved beseechingly from her to Margrit, and she took the opportunity to, hopefully, redirect the conversation. Summoning a smile for Margrit, she said, "Ruby looks hungry, too, don't you think?"

As Margrit nodded, she leaned down to

put her plate on the floor.

"Is Mama coming soon?"

Margrit's question landed like a blow. Sibi's throat went tight. Straightening, she looked at Margrit, all big blue eyes and irrepressible ringlets and small but sturdy bones, and recognized that this was another of those Before and After moments. What she was getting ready to say would change Margrit forever. It would shatter her heart and alter her existence and plunge her into a world that was darker and more filled with evil than anything that existed in even the scariest Tartaro story.

"Margrit —"

Sibi broke off as the words that had to come next choked her. In that instant she realized why she had been working so hard to avoid saying them. Once she did, what had happened — their mother's death, Luiza's — became irreversible in a way that, up until then in her own mind and heart and soul at least, it hadn't really been. Telling Margrit made it official: after that, there was no pretending it hadn't happened, no hoping against hope for a miracle, no going back. She soaked up the questioning innocence of her sister's face, holding on to the last moments of the Before as greedily as if they were precious jewels.

"What?" Margrit frowned at her.

Sibi took a deep breath. Her chest ached. "Mama — and Luiza — they weren't as lucky as you and Jo and I. They weren't able to escape the airplanes like we did." Margrit started blinking, and Sibi knew she could sense what was coming next and that made getting the rest of it out even harder. "*Maitea* — they're dead. Mama and Luiza are dead."

For a moment Margrit simply continued to blink at her, and Sibi began to wonder if she'd understood. Then her lips trembled.

"Mama?" High-pitched and quavering, it was the most piteous sound Sibi had ever heard, and it wrung her heart.

She nodded. Tears welled in Margrit's eyes, spilled over to roll down her cheeks. Her shoulders shook. She gave a great, gasping sob.

"I'm so sorry." Sibi came out of her chair and, using the table and bed for support, managed to make her way around the table more quickly than she would have thought possible. Dropping to her knees beside Margrit's chair, she put her arms around her little sister.

"I want *Mama.*"

"I know."

Margrit collapsed against her, crying, and

250

the two of them sank in an untidy heap to the floor.

"Luiza — it happened because of *me.* I ran out of the shelter to go to Mama and she yelled at me to come back and I didn't and she ran after me."

"It's not your fault."

"It *is.* I didn't listen and she's dead."

"It's the fault of whoever shot her."

"The airplane." Margrit's voice shook with sobs. "I *hate* the airplane. I hate the bombs. I hate Mama and Luiza being dead."

"I know."

With the bed propping her back and Margrit sprawled across her, Sibi rocked her sister in her arms and said every comforting thing she could think of to say and felt destroyed all over again by Margrit's grief and pain. But she didn't give in to it, she didn't cry; she willed ice into her veins and steel into her spine because Margrit needed her, Jo needed her. There was no one else now, and for them she would stand tall and fast and resolute if it killed her.

Which it felt as if Margrit's heart-wrenching sobs might do.

After the worst of Margrit's tears subsided, as she lay limp and heavy against Sibi's chest, she asked in a small, watery

251

voice, "Who's going to take care of me now?"

Sibi hugged her. "I am. I'm going to take care of all of us."

Margrit's arms tightened around her. A long shudder racked her. "I love you, Sibi."

"I love you, too. We're going to be all right. You'll see."

They fell asleep like that, wrapped in each other's arms.

Ruby's urgent barking woke them. Margrit sat up in Sibi's lap, blinking and rubbing her eyes.

Sibi sat up, too. Margrit's curls were right under her nose, tickling, and she put a hand on top of her sister's head to get them out of the way as she looked toward the door.

It opened.

Planted in front of them, ears and tail up as she faced whoever was entering, Ruby barked hysterically.

A man walked into the room. Impeccably dressed, of medium height and sturdy build, he had blunt, pugnacious features, a ruddy complexion and short, graying blond hair that, if it hadn't been slicked close to his head, would have been curly.

Sibi gasped. "Papa!" She would have jumped to her feet, except jumping was beyond her at present.

"Quiet, dog." Conrad Helinger snapped impatient fingers at Ruby, who, dancing around, redoubled her efforts at noisy protection. Mouth tightening, his gaze swept Sibi and Margrit.

"Gather your things." His tone was brusque. "We leave at once."

■ ■ ■ ■

PART TWO:
BERLIN

■ ■ ■ ■

23

May 10, 1937

"He keeps his promises."

The man's booming voice was loud enough to be heard through the floorboards of their small stone house in Mitte, one of Berlin's central boroughs. It belonged, Sibi was almost sure, to Dr. Ludwig Busch, an industrial chemist who was a longtime crony of her father's. She winced at the sheer volume of it, and glanced down at Margrit, whose drooping eyelids and deepening breathing told her that the child was, thankfully, *almost* asleep. *Almost* being the operative word.

". . . and the starlight fell onto Ariadne, and in the blink of an eye she turned into the fairy princess she really was, and . . ." Sibi kept her voice low and soothing as she continued with the story she was telling.

"Give me four years — that's what he said — and by God he's done it. The economy is transformed. Employment is increasing every day. Germany's days of international humiliation are *over.* Our military is strong again, and growing stronger. It once more commands respect." The answering voice — Dr. Kurt Langsdorff, biochemist, she was almost sure — was as loud as the first, and even more exultant. "The bad days — the bad *years* — are behind us."

The scent of the bratwurst the men had had for dinner reached her along with their voices, making her nose wrinkle.

Sibi sat on Margrit's narrow bed in the room she shared with Jo, although with Jo still being treated in the hospital Margrit currently occupied it alone. Only the dim lamp beside the bed was on, and the room was full of shadows. Her back rested against the headboard. Her legs stretched out on the mattress in front of her. Her crutches were propped against the wall within reach. She was still fully dressed except for her single shoe, which she'd kicked off beside the bed, while Margrit, in her nightgown with her head on her pillow and the covers drawn up around her shoulders, huddled close against her side. Since they'd arrived home again, some twelve days ago now, Jo had rallied under the care of Berlin's best doctors, and she was not only expected to survive but to be released as soon as the end of the week.

Except for her arm, which was healing, Margrit was fine physically, but she was uncharacteristically subdued, and had trouble falling, and staying, asleep. Nightmares troubled her, and Sibi had lost track of the number of times she'd had to rush to Margrit's room in the middle of the night in response to the little girl's terrified screams. But there was school tomorrow, the first day back since their return, and along with that came a strict bedtime to be observed. Sibi had found that if she stayed with Margrit, telling her stories, she fell asleep more easily, so that had become their routine.

"They say the führer is furious about the latest disaster. He is blaming the captain, Pruss." The voice of this third man — Dr. Albert Meyer, a theoretical physicist who was also a professor at Friedrich Wilhelm University — was quieter, because public discussion of the disaster he mentioned was not welcomed by the government, but still Sibi heard. She knew what he was referring to from the few photographs that had made it into the newspapers and from fragments of the conversations that constantly bubbled up around her father. It involved the airship

Hindenburg, which on the previous Thursday had crashed in a ball of fire as it attempted to land in the United States. Thirty-six lives had been lost, which was dreadful and too many. But the public uproar over the more than sixteen hundred souls who had perished as a result of the "Tragedy of Guernica," as it was being called, overshadowed all other news of the day, including that of the *Hindenburg.*

Since they'd been back, the newspapers, the radio channels, even the loudspeakers on the lampposts on the street corners that the government used for its most important announcements, had broadcast sensational stories about the destruction of the "sleepy little Basque town" with all the accompanying gory details repeated nonstop. Most were either wrong or flat-out lies, but they were devoured by a sensation-hungry populace. Instead of dying away, the story kept growing until it was bigger even than when Germany marched into the Rhineland last March, or the coverage of the previous summer's Olympics.

At first she'd been eager for news, and when she'd learned that Mola had overrun Guernica on the day after they'd gotten out of Bilbao she'd been mad to learn the fate of everyone left behind. But there'd been no "survivor lists" in the newspapers, no news about which friends and acquaintances who through either choice or circumstance had been unable to escape before the Whites took control. The information that did get out, such as the number of deaths, was so horrifying that, unable to bear the constant reminders, Sibi had closed her mind to it. Dwelling on what was done served no purpose except to drag her back into the yawning pit of grief that she feared was now a permanent part of her soul, so she did her best not to.

"The captain of a ship is always responsible for its fate," her father said now. "But there is talk of sabotage, and from the descriptions I've heard of what happened, that seems quite possible. It's difficult to see how Pruss can be blamed."

"Pruss is fortunate in his injuries," Dr. Busch said. "It is said he will require weeks if not months of hospitalization in America, yet he is expected to survive. By the time he is able to return home, perhaps all will be forgotten."

"Herr Hitler is not a man who easily forgets," Dr. Meyer replied. His more measured manner of speaking gave his words weight.

"That is true. But given the magnitude of

the world's reaction to what happened in Spain, the government has its hands so full with that particular public relations disaster that Pruss may very well escape any consequences. Goebbels —" Dr. Langsdorff broke off, then after the briefest of pauses continued awkwardly, "Ach, Helinger, I'm a bigmouth fool. I was forgetting that you lost your wife and daughter in the tragedy. I am really most truly sorry for your loss. I apologize for my maladroitness in referring to it so thoughtlessly."

"Apology accepted. Please think no more about it." Papa's tone was brisk. Although he had organized a memorial service for Mama and Luiza in their token Lutheran church — and Sibi had herself gone in secret to the Catholic church her mother had actually attended and arranged for the appropriate rites and prayers for their souls — and had made inquiries about the recovery of their remains (the very word made her shudder), which so far had not resulted in any kind of action, he had exhibited no signs of grief that Sibi had seen.

His granite-jawed nonreaction to their deaths had widened the gulf that had sprung up between them over the months of separation. He and Sibi had never been precisely *close* — he was not a warm man — but they had shared a common interest in how and why things worked, and her aptitude, alone among her sisters, for the subjects that were his life's passion had earned his approbation. He'd enjoyed teaching her things, and she'd enjoyed following him around and learning from him. But now she regarded him with a kind of wary distance disguised beneath a cloak of outward filial deference.

The only time that cloak had slipped was when, at the hotel in Bilbao as he'd spirited them away so hastily, he'd decreed that Ruby was to be left behind and directed Margrit, who'd been carrying Ruby, to put the puppy down in the street. They'd been about to climb into the automobile he'd hired to transport them out of the city, and Margrit had burst into tears and clutched Ruby closer. Taking one look at the pair of them — Margrit's devastated face and the bright-eyed pup that had already proven herself to be a loyal friend — Sibi had cast in her lot with Margrit and turned on their father. She'd put an arm around her sister and told him with quiet determination that Ruby was part of their family now and if the puppy was to be left behind, then neither she nor Margrit was going with him, either. Papa had fixed her with a look that was intimidating enough to make her knees knock, which, with a lift of her chin, she had withstood. Faced with Margrit's tears and her intransigence, he'd glanced around at the doormen, at the driver, at everyone near them on the crowded street, some of whom were openly listening and some of whom were listening while pretending not to, hesitated, then given in with a growled, "So. You girls want the dog? Bring it." They had, and Ruby was right at that moment curled up asleep in a cushioned box beside Margrit's bed. But Sibi was quite sure that Papa had not forgotten her defiance, and the knowledge made for an uneasy dynamic between them.

"Some say static electricity sparked off hydrogen that was leaking from one of the cells, and that caused the fire," another man, one she didn't know, said. "A blue rectangle of flame was reportedly seen on the outer skin before the entire ship erupted."

There were, perhaps, nine or ten guests of her father's downstairs. She knew a few from the Before, when he would have her follow him around the labs where he designed his airplane engines, which he did as an adjunct to the classes he taught. Her job was to listen to him ruminate, and to take notes that he would dictate to her as he worked out the finer points of whatever problem currently concerned him. What she knew of tonight's gathering was that these men were her father's colleagues, all highly regarded scholars and researchers, members of the prestigious Society of German Scientists and Physicians. This was one of their regular meetings, which were held several times a year, almost always at the Helinger house because Papa was the society's current president.

This particular meeting happened to have been scheduled for this particular evening, not quite two weeks since Mama and Luiza had died, sometime previously. Although Papa couldn't have known what was coming when he agreed to the date, that he hadn't canceled bothered Sibi. It was part and parcel of his attitude toward the loss: carry on as usual. Sibi felt it showed a lack of caring, and respect.

"Please keep your sister and the dog quiet and out of the way," he'd said that morning when informing her of tonight's meeting before leaving for his post as head of the physics department at Friedrich Wilhelm University, where he'd received his doctorate in physics some years before. Sibi had had no difficulty complying. Margrit was nervous of Papa and actively avoided him,

265

and Ruby went where Margrit went.

"Whatever the cause, I fear that this will be the end of the dirigibles," Dr. Meyer replied.

"They were never practical. Too slow, and too costly," Papa said. "It was crazy to have expended so much effort and money on them."

"Not like your rockets to the moon, eh?" Dr. Busch's tone made it a good-humored gibe.

The sound Papa made in answer was derisive. "The Treaty of Versailles left rocket technology off the list of weapons Germany was forbidden to develop, so that is the path we pursued."

"Ah. So you, too, were crazy." Dr. Langsdorff sounded amused. "Crazy like a fox."

"You might say that."

The men laughed, and Sibi heard the sound of clinking glasses.

"Gentlemen, can I offer you more?" The voice belonged to Frau Skeller, the plump, gray-haired housekeeper Papa had employed to come in a few times a month while his wife was away. Since their return she'd been there nearly every day to watch Margrit during the hours Sibi spent at the hospital with Jo. Tonight she had stayed late to prepare and serve a special meal for Papa and his guests. Sibi was never to learn what she was offering them more of, because Frau Skeller was interrupted by a knock — a loud banging, really — on the front door.

A late guest? Probably. Although whoever it was seemed very insistent on being admitted. The banging came again before the first sounds had even died away.

A quick, nervous glance down at Margrit revealed that, voices or no voices, banging or no banging, she'd fallen asleep.

Sibi sighed with relief, then swung her legs off the bed, slipped her good foot into her own flat black shoe — she wore a stretched-out sock on her other foot, over her cast — picked up her crutches, turned off the lamp and maneuvered her way out of the room, closing the door behind her. Her bedroom, the room she'd shared with Luiza that now belonged to her alone, was right next door, which was a good thing because she could hear Margrit through the wall if her sister should cry out in the night. Leaving Margrit's door open wasn't an option. Ruby had developed a distressing tendency to chew on things — shoes, purses, furniture legs, basically anything she could get her little puppy teeth around — which meant that giving her the unsupervised run of the house was an invitation to disaster.

Entering her bedroom, she switched on the overhead light and closed the door. Turning, she caught a glimpse of herself in the oval mirror above the dressing table against the far wall, the dressing table that she and Luiza had shared, the one that separated the two single beds. It had a set of drawers on the left and another on the right. She'd taken the ones on the right, while Luiza had used the ones on the left. A brass hook adorned either side of the mirror. Each girl had claimed ownership of the hook on her particular side, hanging their various necklaces and bits of jewelry from it. Luiza's hook still held a gold chain with a small, dangling gold heart, and a black velvet ribbon choker to which she'd attached a flower for a long-ago party. The flower was gone now, crumbled to nothingness, but the ribbon remained.

Luiza's red rag curler was there, too. Sibi had tied it to Luiza's hook the first night she'd been home. Having it there made her feel as if Luiza was close, although it squeezed her heart whenever she looked at it.

But then, so did the room itself, with its blue striped wallpaper that the two of them had argued over — Luiza had wanted pink roses on a cream ground — and lace curtains and matching quilts. They'd shared it almost since Luiza had been born, and every time she stepped inside it, now, Sibi was reminded of her sister and crushed all over again by the magnitude of her loss.

Wallowing in pain was fruitless — she felt like she told herself that a dozen times a day lately — so she dragged her eyes away from the jaunty red bow she'd made of the curler and her mind back to the present, focusing on her own reflection as she swung toward the dressing table. The forest green dress she wore was belted at the waist and wasn't in the latest style, but then none of her clothes were and at least this one had long sleeves and a pleated skirt, both of which were useful when paired with crutches. Once one of her favorites, it had been left out when she'd packed for what she'd thought at the time would be a relatively short visit to Guernica. The dress still fit, but it made her look pale and, she thought critically, rather sickly. Certainly way too thin. She'd dropped weight she hadn't needed to lose over the past weeks: her cheekbones were too prominent, her chin too sharp. Her eyes looked huge because of the bruised-looking shadows that had settled in beneath them. Her hair had been cut in anticipation of her return to school. It was shoulder-length now and slightly mussed from her sojourn on Margrit's bed. Balancing carefully on her crutches, she was just running a brush through the mass of coffee-colored waves when a quick rap at her door had her glancing over her shoulder.

Papa pushed through the door before the words, "Come in," had gotten all the way out of her mouth.

Even as she turned to face him, she knew something was wrong. First, he never came to her in her bedroom. Second, there was an air about him, a certain set to his shoulders, a tautness to his face, a purposefulness to his movements, that set off warning bells inside her. Her pulse skittered as he closed the door, then crossed the room in three long strides to catch her by her upper arms. His grip was hard, urgent.

The hairbrush fell from her hand to land with a clatter on the floor. "Papa, what —"

"Keep your voice down," he said, low. "Did you speak to a reporter in Guernica, after . . . what happened?"

She remembered the ginger-haired Englishman and the conversation in the hospital. "Y-yes."

He bared his teeth, let his breath hiss out between them. His normally florid face was pale. "Did you tell him that the attack was carried out by Germans? And identify the airplanes involved as German?"

"Yes."

His hands tightened on her arms. "My God."

His grip might have hurt if she hadn't been too rattled by what she saw in his face to notice.

Her heart thumped. "What of it?"

"Downstairs, right now in our sitting room, is Hans Kraus from the Ministry of Public Enlightenment and Propaganda. He is a special adviser to Joe Goebbels, head of the ministry, and he has with him two gestapo agents. He's come to question *you.*"

"Me?"

"Yes. He's here about a story in a London newspaper, *The Times.* Apparently it features a supposed eyewitness account of what happened in Guernica. The reporter claims to have conducted the interview in Guernica on the night of the tragedy and describes the eyewitness as a young girl whose father designs airplane engines. This girl told him with certainty that German airplanes carried out the attacks, and claimed to know enough to be able to specifically identify some of those airplanes as He 51s and Ju 52s." His eyes flared at her. "And it's well-known that I design airplane engines, that my wife and daughters were in Guernica when it was destroyed and that my wife and one of my daughters were lost. Our government is livid about being accused by the international community of being responsible for the tragedy, livid enough to launch an investigation into the sources of some of the stories, which they deny unequivocally. That investigation has brought them here to us. To *you*."

24

Sibi wet her lips. Then squared her shoulders. "I have nothing to hide. Every word I told that reporter was true. Those airplanes — those German airplanes — bombed us unmercifully. They shot Luiza. They killed her and Mama and many, many others. They burned Guernica to the ground. Why should I not say so?"

"Because if you say so you will ruin us. Do you not understand?"

"They deserve to be exposed for what they've done! Papa, you must listen —"

He gave her a little shake. He'd never handled her so roughly before, and her eyes widened in response. "No, *you* must listen. It is *verboten* to make statements against the Reich. I have to be able to earn a living, to keep a roof over our heads and food on our plates and to provide for such things as Johanna's very expensive medical treatment. You and your sisters have school, friends, each other. We have a good life here. A *future.* If you are found to be the source of that story, if we run afoul of the government in that way, we stand to lose all that. I could lose my position. We could lose this house. Everything we have. We may stand to lose even more."

Sibi felt a flutter of fear. "What do you mean?"

"That reporter — the one who wrote the story — has been put on a secret Wanted list. A list that party leaders maintain of persons who are to be detained immediately if they should be encountered. Detained, tried and *punished.*" He took a deep breath. "Do you not remember what happened to Paul Schneider, the preacher? He is still in prison for no more than making what some felt were anti-Nazi comments. I fear that Kraus would not have brought the gestapo with him if he did not intend to make an arrest. Perhaps of you, perhaps of me for being your father since you are underage, perhaps of both of us. I am respected in the scientific community, but I'm not rich enough or powerful enough to deter them from carrying out whatever course of action they choose to take."

"How can they arrest someone for telling the truth?"

"They can do anything they like. These are strange times. Passions are high. What we must do to save ourselves is convince Kraus that you were not the source of that story."

"You want me to deny what I saw?" Mama's gray face as she lay dead in the burning rubble; Luiza falling beneath an onslaught of bullets, her blouse blossoming red: those images flashed across the screen of Sibi's mind, and a bitter anger twisted her insides. Something in her expression must have conveyed what she was feeling, because his eyebrows snapped together and his mouth thinned.

"It's the only way."

"Those airplanes killed Mama and Luiza!"

"Keep your voice down." He spoke in a harsh whisper. "Think of your other sisters. They've been through so much already. If something happens to you, to me, if we're taken away, what will become of them? Especially since, by association, they will have been labeled enemies of the Reich?"

Angry as she was, as full of the need to accuse the guilty, for them to be held to account, Sibi reluctantly recognized that there was a more urgent priority: the little girls.

"What must I say?"

His hands dropped from her arms. "You must deny that you spoke to the reporter. That you saw the airplanes. That you could identify them so precisely even if you did see them. After all, how likely is it that you could? Most girls your age have no interest in airplanes or anything of that nature, and most fathers would not share such technical aspects of their work with their daughters. They have no way of knowing that we are any different."

"I —" Sibi began, only to be interrupted by a knock on her bedroom door. Both she and Papa cast quick, fear-filled looks toward it. It was the raw fear she saw on her father's face when she had never known him to be afraid of anything that cemented for her how truly dangerous their situation was.

"Yes, what is it?" Papa called.

"Herr Kraus has sent me to fetch you, Dr. Helinger. He says, will you please bring your daughter *now,*" Frau Skeller said through the door.

Sibi's eyes met her father's. In that moment, all that had divided them was put aside. They were joined by a common goal. Survival.

Papa's jaw tightened. "We're coming."

"I will inform Herr Kraus," Frau Skeller replied, and in the silence that followed Sibi could hear her retreating footsteps.

"We must go," Papa said.

Swallowing hard, she nodded.

As they moved toward the door he added in a hurried whisper, "You should know, the official government story is that, while Franco's Nationalists might have had a German airplane or two in their arsenal, and while it might have been those airplanes that flew over initially to drop a few bombs on the bridge out of town to block the Republican Army's retreat, it was the Nationalists who did it, not Germans, and minimal harm was done to the town at that time. The true destruction of Guernica — the bombings, the burning, the deaths — was caused by the Republicans, the Reds themselves, who set off dynamite in the streets and blew up and burned their own town and in the process murdered their own citizens, as they retreated. They then falsely blamed the atrocity on German pilots attacking with their German airplanes at the behest of the Nationalists."

Sibi stopped as he reached past her to open the door. "That's a *lie.*"

"Shh." His warning was fierce. "Lie or not, that's the story our government is telling the world. For all our sakes, you must stick to it as best you can."

■ ■ ■ ■

"You say you never spoke to this reporter — this *Steer.*" Herr Kraus said the name like it left a bad taste in his mouth.

He stood with his back to the fireplace, his hands clasped behind him, his eyes keen on her face. Because it was night, the curtains over the big window fronting Sophienstrasse were closed. Warmly lit by an overhead fixture plus a pair of large *capo di monte* lamps that Sibi found overly ornate but that Mama had loved, the sitting room was comfortably furnished. Herr Kraus had not invited her to sit down, and although it was her own house she had not felt able to do so without his leave.

She stood just inside the doorway facing him, wishing the lighting was not so good, praying that her face would not betray her. Papa stood, too, close beside her, as though to support her if she should overbalance on her crutches. His real purpose in staying so close, she was almost sure, was to attempt to physically intervene on her behalf if something should go awry. His guests were nowhere to be seen. She suspected they had departed shortly after Herr Kraus had entered the house. Even eminent scientists, apparently, did not want to find themselves caught in the crosshairs of the Reich.

"No." Sibi shook her head. The surging fear that had nearly overwhelmed her as she'd stepped into the sitting room to find this beady-eyed, balding little man and his two hulking henchmen waiting for her had been replaced by a precarious calm. She had known from the moment Papa had said, "Herr Kraus, this is my daughter Sibil," and Herr Kraus had turned his hard, assessing gaze on her that Papa had not exaggerated the peril they were in. Her stomach had dropped to her toes — and then she had instinctively reached out to her newly minted army, her fledgling angels, Mama and Luiza, for help, and had felt wrapped up in a comforting warmth that she could only think of as their arms embracing her.

"No?" Herr Kraus's mouth tightened. Reaching into the right front pocket of his double-breasted suit, he pulled out a folded piece of paper and snapped it open inches from her face. He stood so close now that the scent of his cologne — 4711, she recognized it because Papa had once possessed a bottle, given to him as a gift by Mama, which, for a brief time, he had assiduously used — was so strong she found it difficult to breathe. "So how do you explain this?"

"This" was a sheet of notebook paper covered with images hand-drawn in black ink. Sibi recognized it instantly: the page out of Steer's notebook on which she'd drawn sketches depicting the attacking airplanes' insignia. Her heart lurched. Her mouth went dry. Had she written anything else on the paper? Anything that could possibly be used to identify her?

The memory returned in vivid detail. She'd scribbled down Papa's name and address for Griff, but that had been on a separate sheet that Steer had never seen. But that first sheet of paper had still been in Steer's notebook when she'd written Papa's name and address on it. She'd then torn it out, handed it to Griff and made her drawings on the sheet of paper beneath it. Could an impression of what she'd written have been left behind on the second sheet, the sheet she'd drawn on, the sheet in his hand? Panic at the possibility sent icy tendrils racing over her skin. Beside her, Papa made a sudden, restive movement as if he somehow sensed her alarm and the danger of the moment.

Help me, she begged Mama and Luiza silently, and once again felt that comforting sense of their arms enfolding her.

A rush of courage drove out panic.

"I can't explain it." She frowned slightly as she looked from the paper to Herr Kraus, cool as could be and never mind her pounding heart. "I don't know what it is."

"Drawings of airplane insignia. From the Condor Legion's He 51s and Ju 52s. Made as part of an interview the reporter conducted while in Guernica." He watched her intently as he spoke. Her insides twisted tight, but outwardly, she hoped — she *prayed* — she conveyed polite innocence. "When the Nationalists overwhelmed Guernica, which I believe occurred some two days after the tragedy, the coward Steer fled, leaving behind a notebook. The notebook contained his handwritten account of your interview, along with *this.*" He waved the paper. The slight breeze it created was like a cold wind — a cold wind scented with cologne — blowing in her face.

Her heart thumped so hard she feared he might hear it. It was all she could do not to shiver. *Betray any sign of weakness and all is lost.* With his eyes on her, she felt like a frozen-in-place rabbit with a hawk wheeling in tightening circles overhead. Thank God — *thank God* — Griff had prevented her from giving Steer her name. Taking a firm grip on her emotions, she shook her head. "With respect, Herr Kraus, it was not *my*

281

interview. And I have no knowledge of your paper, or your reporter, or of anything connected with that at all."

He frowned. Then he tapped his mouth with his forefinger, watching her all the while. Her pulse thundered in her ears but, outwardly untroubled, she said nothing and simply waited. Making an impatient sound under his breath, he folded the paper and thrust it back into his pocket.

"If you please, tell me one more time what you saw."

Sibi barely stopped herself from wetting her lips. She'd been through this with him already. Would she make a mistake, get something wrong, forget a detail that would contradict what she'd previously said, thus confirming what he obviously suspected — that she was lying?

"As I told you, I saw very little. I ran into a shelter when the church bells first sounded, and was knocked unconscious and then trapped when the building collapsed from being hit by a bomb. I did not see the airplane that dropped the bomb, or any other airplane. By the time I was rescued, it was late at night. A few fires were burning and people were rushing around trying to put them out. The hospital was already full of wounded soldiers, so those who needed treatment were taken to Bilbao and I was, too. Other than that I have no firm recollection of what happened."

"If you have no recollection of what happened, you possibly could have talked to this Steer and not remember it."

"No." Sibi's voice was firm. "That I *would* remember."

"What of your surviving sisters?"

Fear pierced her like a knife. Papa had said everyone knew that his wife and daughters had been in Guernica, and that his wife and one daughter had died. Of course Herr Kraus would know that, and know of her two remaining sisters. A split second's reflection found the danger if he questioned them: there was no knowing what Jo had seen, but she didn't know one airplane from another and thus couldn't have been the source of Steer's story. Margrit, on the other hand, was more of a risk: she couldn't identify airplanes, but she had witnessed Luiza's death. And she'd been present and awake when Sibi had talked to Steer, although Sibi didn't think she'd been paying attention. But with Margrit, one could never be sure. What she knew, or what she might say.

Herr Kraus's gaze sharpened on her face. Her eyes — what could he read in her eyes?

"They are five and nine years old, Herr Kraus," Papa said before she could answer. "Too young to have spoken to a reporter, certainly. And they are injured, the nine-year-old quite badly. And heartbroken by the loss of their mother and sister."

Herr Kraus shifted that fish-eyed gaze of his to Papa. "Nevertheless, I should like to speak —"

"There were explosions," Sibi interrupted, desperate to turn Herr Kraus's thoughts in another direction. Her blood ran cold at the thought of Margrit or Jo facing this man. As Herr Kraus's gaze returned to her — as all the men's gazes fastened on her — she frantically clawed through her memory for what her father had told her of the official government story. Blinking rapidly, she did her best to give the impression that a curtain had just lifted in her mind. "As we were leaving Guernica. Huge explosions, one after another, as if the whole town was being blown up. They shook the automobile I was in, and lit up the sky. I . . . remember now. I was so frightened. I must have blocked it out."

His lips pursed. "These explosions came as you were leaving? What time was that?"

"After midnight, I'm almost sure." She hesitated, as if dredging her mind for details. "It seemed like they were blowing up everything. Whole blocks at a time. As the automobile was driving away, I looked back and saw that the entire sky was lit up. The town was red from burning, and the sky above it was red, too."

"Now this I find extremely interesting." Herr Kraus's face remained impossible to read, but his eyes — something about the look in them as they bored into hers made her pulse pound. "This 'they' that you say were blowing up everything — did you see them? Can you tell me who they were?"

Sibi felt something inside her shrivel up and die.

"The soldiers," she said. "The Republicans. I . . . saw the red stars on their caps."

"Ah." He smiled at her, a cold and wolfish smile that sent chills chasing over her skin. "Please continue."

25

It's all right. He went away, Sibi told herself. Then of its own volition the chilling corollary followed: *for now.*

Had she convinced him? Would he be back?

There was no way to know.

Nothing inside her bedroom had changed: her hairbrush still lay on the floor where she'd dropped it. The jaunty red hair curler still adorned Luiza's hook. Had it been less than an hour since she'd gone downstairs for the confrontation with Herr Kraus? It felt as if several lifetimes had passed, at least.

Taking a deep breath, she crossed the room, intending to keep to the routine she'd established: pick out her clothes for the next day — the first day of a return to school for her, too — then bathe and go to bed.

Routine, she'd discovered, was an antidote to grief and anger. Routine required getting up and getting moving and putting one foot in front of the other, over and over again. Routine, like faith, provided a bridge across the swamp of heartbreak and grief until firmer shores were hopefully reached.

She made it all the way to the closet and got the door open before she started to shake. Reaction, she knew, but that didn't make the tremors any less unpleasant. Gritting her teeth, closing her eyes, she hung her head and waited for them to pass.

I'm a coward.

A braver person would have refused to be intimidated, would have denounced the Nazi interlocutor to his face, would have shouted the truth about what had really happened in Guernica for the whole world to hear.

Instead she'd given in to fear and corroborated the government's lies with lies of her own.

And had thereby, she was almost certain, escaped disaster by the skin of her teeth.

At the end, when Herr Kraus had said, "Thank you for your cooperation, Fräulein Helinger, Dr. Helinger," and added a brisk, "Heil Hitler," with the usual straight-armed salute, she and Papa had saluted in return and replied with their own Heil Hitlers and stayed behind in the entry hall as he'd walked out of the house with his henchmen in tow. Afraid until the last possible second that he would order them brought along for further interrogation, she'd been light-headed with relief when the door finally closed behind them. Papa had dropped his hand onto her shoulder, murmured, "Well done, daughter," so only she could hear, then gone into the adjacent dining room where Frau Skeller was clearing away the plates, to pay her for her services and dismiss her for the night, Sibi presumed.

And she had come upstairs.

Opening her eyes, she breathed in and out, fighting for equilibrium as the last of the tremors died away, letting the faint scent of lavender from the sachets Mama had tucked inside the closet soothe her. Without really seeing them, she stared at the row of clothes hanging in front of her. Luiza's were on the left, hers were on the right, separated by a pink velvet party dress that had been given to Sibi by their now-deceased paternal grandmother and subsequently passed down to Luiza. Both of them had considered it hideous. Both of them, at separate times, had worn it to please their grandmother. Both of them had wanted to purge it from their closet. It was still there only because whenever one of them would attempt it Mama would shame them by asking if, deep inside, didn't they really have too much respect for their dead grandmother to throw it away?

The truthful answer, *no,* was something that, of the four of them, only Margrit would have been blunt enough to say.

Every time she or Luiza had gone into the closet they'd shoved it toward the other's side.

Remembering, Sibi succumbed to the faintest of barely there smiles. As unlikely as it seemed, that ugly dress was a dear treasure now, the catalyst for a thousand memories.

Lu. I miss you.

At some point — not now, but when she could face it — she was going to have to pack away or give away or throw away Luiza's clothes. Mama's clothes.

An unexpected rush of anger shook her. As violent as an erupting geyser, it made her see red, made her face flush, made her lash out in a furious gesture with her crutch that smacked with a sharp crackle into the paper bag plopped on the bottom of her closet.

The bag flew onto its side and a silver shoe tumbled out.

Griff.

Picturing the man who'd given it to her,

289

she felt the hot jet of sudden rage start to cool. *What you do is, you go on* — she could almost hear him saying it. "Go on" was exactly what she intended to do. She looked up at the closet's top shelf: the silver shoe's mate was there, because that was the shoe she'd worn when Papa had whisked them out of Bilbao straight to Santander, a journey of less than two hours, then flown them himself in a tiny, single-engine Taifun loaned to him by the German Air Sports Association, of which he was a member, through the night to reach Berlin. The reason for the urgency had been twofold: to escape Bilbao before Mola could turn the full force of his army toward it, as he was expected to do, and to get Jo to Berlin's best hospital, the Charité, where she was now, as quickly as possible.

Leaning down, Sibi righted the bag that held the ruined clothes she and Margrit had been wearing when they'd left Bilbao — she hadn't yet been able to bring herself to so much as look at them, much less do anything with them — and gasped in dismay at what she saw when she glanced inside it.

Griff's mother's book: *My Ántonia.* The gilt lettering gleamed faintly as the light caught it.

Somehow it had gotten thrown into the bag.

Oh, no. What must Griff think happened to it? How do I get it back to him?

She picked it up, ran her thumb over the rough-textured binding, the gilt lettering. The knowledge of how irreplaceable the book was, how precious it was to Griff, how sick he must feel at its loss, made her stomach churn. How it could have ended up with their things she didn't know, but however it had happened it had to be returned to Griff as soon as possible.

Unfortunately, she had no idea how.

He'd been nowhere around when they'd left the hotel, nowhere around when they'd picked up a heavily sedated Jo from the hospital. She hadn't seen or spoken to him since he'd left her and Margrit in his room after the food had arrived. Papa had been in such a hurry, stressing the vital necessity of reaching Santander before nightfall when roving bands of Red soldiers and White soldiers and local brigands and myriad other dangers made the roads through the Cantabrian Mountains too dangerous to attempt, that there'd been no chance before they'd left to do anything except hurriedly ask Ruth to give Griff a message. Which was what she'd done, asking the nurse to tell

Griff that their father had come and they were leaving with him, and thank you. For everything.

Ruth had promised to pass the message on.

When they'd left Bilbao behind, Sibi hadn't expected to ever again have any contact with the man who'd saved her and Margrit's and Jo's lives.

But now, getting in touch with him was vital. Looking down at the book, Sibi pondered: she knew his name, that he was a military attaché and a captain in the USAAC and that he worked under the auspices of the American embassy in Spain.

Her best course of action would be to write to him in care of the embassy, she decided. She wouldn't send the book with the note, in case it shouldn't find him, but she could tell him she had it and ask for an address where she could send it. Then she would wait for his reply.

Carefully holding the book, she crossed to the small desk at the foot of her bed, sat down, put the book on a corner out of harm's way and opened a notebook. Grabbing a pen, she started to write.

Dear Griff . . .

She was still busily writing when Margrit screamed.

As many times as this had happened since they'd been home, Margrit's terrified screams still had the power to electrify her.

Caught in the wedge of light that poured in from the hall as Sibi burst through the door, the little girl was sitting bolt upright in bed, fists clenched at her sides, eyes wide open but glassily unseeing, shrieking as if every monster that had ever existed in the universe was poised to pounce on her.

On the bed beside her, whipping around as the door flew open to face the threat the newcomer posed, Ruby barked frantically.

"Hush, Ruby. Margrit, it's all right, I'm here." Sibi threw herself onto the bed beside her sister and wrapped her arms around her.

"Sibi?" The screams melted into shuddering sobs as Margrit turned into her embrace. Ruby stopped barking, prodded Sibi's arm with her cold little nose, then pawed at Margrit, who gathered her close.

"Yes." Sibi rocked the pair of them, sister and dog, back and forth. "You had a bad dream."

"I want Mama. *I want Mama.* I don't want her to be dead."

"I know. Shh, everything's going to be all right." Glancing up as a shadow fell across the bed, Sibi saw their father silhouetted in the doorway. She couldn't see his expression, and he didn't say anything, just stood there watching them.

Margrit reclaimed her attention by burrowing closer into her shoulder. "Everything's *not* going to be all right. How can it be, without Mama?"

"It will be. I *promise.*"

"Sibi — do you think it hurt Luiza to be shot?"

The unexpected question felt like a stab to the heart. "No, *maitea,* I don't. I think it happened so fast that Luiza was with the angels before she could feel anything."

The disappearance of the shadow on the bed coupled by a quick glance at the door told Sibi that Papa was no longer there.

"And Mama?"

"I think the angels came just that quickly for her, too."

Margrit said nothing else. Her sobs dwindled into a series of gasps and sniffles until finally the little girl's limp weight told Sibi she'd fallen asleep. Careful not to wake her, she settled Margrit back down in her bed. Ruby cuddled up next to her, and despite Papa's edict about the puppy not sleeping on the bed Sibi left the pair of them as they were, and tucked the covers up around them both.

In her view, Margrit needed all the comfort she could get.

Later, after she'd picked out the next day's clothes and washed and changed into her nightgown, Papa tapped on her door. She was just signing off on her letter to Griff: *Your friend always,* (with a line under *always* for emphasis, as a reminder to herself as well as him of the connection they shared) *Sibi.* Because she didn't feel like explaining to Papa about the book and its significance, or talking about the letter or Griff, she covered the letter up with her notebook before she went to open the door.

"Margrit's asleep?" was how Papa greeted her. He looked tired, and far older than his forty-five years.

Sibi nodded.

"I've decided to keep her home from school for the foreseeable future. I don't think she's ready to go back. I've asked Frau Skeller to come in during the day to watch her while you're at school."

Caught by surprise, Sibi hesitated. In the Before, he'd been the ultimate authority and she never would have openly questioned his decisions. But now, with Mama gone, she had to speak up about what she felt was best for her sisters. She understood Margrit and Jo far better than he did, and there was no one else to look out for them.

"I'm sorry, Papa, but I think it would be best if she does go to school. I know it's only her first year, but since the school here is going to allow her to complete the classes she began while we were gone, and there are only a few weeks left, it would be a shame not to let her finish. She'll have her friends, and it will give her something else to think about besides —"

He interrupted with a harsh sound that caused her to break off. "She needs to stay at home." His tone brooked no argument. The look he gave her was quelling. When Sibi frowned as a prelude to protesting further, he added abruptly, "There was a telephone call. After you went upstairs. Herr Kraus wishes you to present yourself to him at his office at the Ordenspalais tomorrow at half-past four."

Sibi's stomach clenched. She looked a question at him.

"I was not invited to accompany you. I will, of course, drive you there, and wait outside." From his grim tone, Sibi knew he was as alarmed as she was. "Margrit cannot go to school because she cannot be allowed to talk about how Luiza died, or about what else she saw that day in Guernica. She's young, and too impulsive and outspoken to trust that cautioning her to remain silent will be enough. In time her memory will blur, and the government's focus on the tragedy will lessen. But for now it's too dangerous. For all our sakes, it's imperative that there be no contradictions to the story you told, and will continue to tell, Herr Kraus."

26

After a night of little sleep, Sibi passed the following day in a state of cold dread. She went through the motions, rising early to dress in the white blouse, tan pullover and gray skirt she'd chosen to wear her first day back, leaving her letter for Griff on the hall table for Frau Skeller, who arrived promptly at six, to mail, then sliding into the new Volkswagen Papa had bought during the months they'd been away to be driven to school because he felt that, given her crutches, it would be too difficult for her to negotiate the tram. That meant she and Papa together stopped by the hospital to visit Jo, who was sitting up in bed eating a breakfast of *Brötchen* with marmalade, chewing slowly and carefully because of the restrictive bandaging that was scheduled to be removed later in the week.

Jo put the roll down as they appeared in the doorway. Sibi saw the apprehensive look in her sister's eyes as she spotted Papa, and sighed inwardly. In a time of so much upheaval Jo and Margrit's discomfort around their father was low on her list of problems, but because it made her little sisters feel even more bereft without their mother it was something she hoped could be improved upon. The difficulty lay in Papa's linear thinking and rigid personality, which contrasted so vividly with Mama's warm devotion that for all their lives the girls had instinctively turned to her and avoided him. Combined with the fact that he had always seemed to have little interest in his younger daughters, it made for a less than easy relationship. Sibi was the only daughter with whom he'd interacted on a more than perfunctory basis, and that was only because they shared an aptitude for science and math, she knew.

"And how are you today?" Papa asked Jo, his tone a little too hearty for the circumstances because he had no idea how to talk to this daughter he barely knew, while Sibi handed over the colored pencils and tablet she'd brought her sister, who liked to draw, to help her pass the time.

"I'm better, Papa, thank you." Quiet and shy as usual in Papa's presence, Jo cast a quick look of appeal at Sibi. Message: *please take him away.*

"Did you sleep well?" Sibi asked. Pale and bone-thin now, with her new glasses perched crookedly on the end of her nose because of the interference of the thick bandages and her dark brown hair cut as short as a boy's, Jo looked fragile as a piece of fine china.

Jo nodded. "You're on your way to school? What about Margrit?"

"Margrit needs a little more time," Papa said. "She will start back again with you, in the new fall term."

Jo's eyes widened. She cast a quick, questioning glance at Sibi but said nothing.

"It's for the best," Papa said, and the conversation moved on.

"Is something wrong with Margrit?" Jo whispered to Sibi as Papa, having announced that it was time for them to go, walked away, leaving Sibi to follow.

"She's a little emotional still. Nothing else."

"Poor Margrit." Jo's eyes clouded with the certain knowledge of why Margrit was emotional. When Sibi had broken the news about Mama and Luiza to Jo, a few days after their return to Berlin because up until that point her condition had been judged too serious for her to bear such terrible tidings, Jo had surprised her by telling her that she already knew: *Mama told me. She came to me in a dream. She said she's with Luiza, and they're all right.* Sibi had been at first unsettled and then comforted by Jo's revelation, while at the same time reserving judgment on whether it was a dream or an actual visitation as Jo clearly believed. Now she made a sympathetic face at her sister as Jo added, "Poor *us*."

"We're going to be fine." Sibi gave Jo a careful hug and stepped back. "I have to go. I'll see you later. Have a good day."

"You, too."

That was clearly not going to be possible, but there was no point in letting herself dwell on how frightened she was of what was to come later. Instead Sibi took comfort from how much Jo had improved. Her life was no longer in danger, and that was a huge relief considering the state she'd been in when they'd arrived in Berlin. Reassured that she would be allowed to come home once the bandages were off, Jo endured the painful treatments and enforced confinement with a fortitude that belied her age and delicate appearance.

Despite the inner quaking that had her feeling as if she could jump out of her skin at the slightest provocation, Sibi managed to keep up a calm facade as she returned to her old school, the rigorous Berlinisches Gymnasium zum Grauen Kloster, in which she was in her *Unterprima,* or second to last year. Her best friends, Heide Fritsch and Ilsa Raeder, welcomed her back with excitement while at the same time tearfully commiserating with her over the loss of her mother and Luiza, but the fourth member of their longtime quartet of friends, Talia Kushner, was missing. She was, Ilsa informed her, no longer a student there.

"This last year, she struggled to fit in," tall, honey-blonde Heide confided over lunch in the noisy, crowded cafeteria. "She was getting poor marks, and some people were, well, not very nice to her." She lowered her voice, glancing around nervously, as if she wanted to make sure she wouldn't be overheard. "Because her family is Jewish, you know."

"She's at the Goldschmidt School now." Ilsa's voice was equally low. The curvy ash-blonde was the daughter of a general in the Wehrmacht, and as such was a favorite of the school's administration. "I saw her last week. Her mother says they're thinking about emigrating."

"It's best if we don't talk about it," Heide warned when Sibi, flushing a little, opened her mouth to say something. She was indignant on Talia's behalf, but at Heide's reminder she thought of Herr Kraus and felt a swirl of fear: perhaps silence *was* best, for now at least.

The conversation turned to lighter topics — primarily whether or not Friedrich Gruber, the school's handsomest football player, liked Ilsa — but as the hours ticked down Sibi's nervousness ratcheted up until she found it almost impossible to concentrate on her classes. By the time school was out and she slid into the Volkswagen beside Papa, her stomach churned.

The route took them along Berlin's main boulevard, Unter den Linden, a wide and busy thoroughfare that ran east to west, bisecting the city from the Brandenburg Gate with its magnificent Quadriga to the Berliner Stadtschloss, the City Palace, once the residence of the rulers of Brandenburg and now, sadly, home to a rabbit warren of government offices. The nearby Lustgarden had seen most of its lush greenery paved over for use as a parade ground. As they passed it, a regiment of the Hitlerjugend in their brown shirts and black short trousers marched enthusiastically up and down. That was not the only chilling addition to what was for Sibi, who'd lived in Berlin most of her life, a familiar landscape. Hanging from every building, everywhere she looked, enormous scarlet banners with the central image of a black swastika centered in a white circle rippled in the breeze.

It was the same emblem that had marked the airplanes that had destroyed Guernica and killed Mama and Luiza.

Just looking at them made her dizzy.

Papa said, "We're here," and stopped at the corner of Wilhelmplatz. "I'll be waiting."

Sibi nodded and got out.

For this time of year, the day itself was nothing out of the ordinary: sunshine, blue sky with clouds like fluffy little lambs gamboling across it, a pleasant breeze. Cool, but not cold.

Why did the worst things always seem to happen on perfectly ordinary days?

The beautiful old building that was the Reich Chancellery, where the führer had his offices, had dozens more of the ten-meter-long scarlet swastika banners fluttering from it. So, too, did the adjacent Ordenspalais, which housed the Ministry of Propaganda.

Sibi did her best not to see them.

Moving carefully lest her crutches get caught in the cracks between the sections of pristine pavement, all too conscious of the need to keep her expression untroubled and refrain from doing anything that would reveal the tension that was making her palms sweat, Sibi made her way past the neat rows of military motorcycles parked along the sidewalk, past the scores of people hurrying in and out of the building, past the poker-faced soldiers in their gray-green uniforms guarding the colonnaded, classical portico, and into what she, with her fluttering stomach and quickened breathing, could only think of as the heart of darkness.

Inside, a woman waited. A severe-looking woman, blonde, unsmiling, in her thirties, perhaps, wearing a tailored black suit.

"Fräulein Helinger?"

Unable to find her voice, Sibi nodded. She caught herself tightening her grip on her crutches and deliberately relaxed her fingers.

"Please follow me."

Sibi did. The sound of the woman's high heels clicking briskly over the marble floor made her think of a clock ticking down to doomsday.

The woman stopped, knocked on an office door, then, when bidden "Enter," opened it and made a gesture for Sibi to walk through, which she did.

"Fräulein Helinger," the woman announced. Sibi thought her heart might explode as the door clicked shut behind her. She could hear the muffled *tap-tap-tap* of the woman's heels walking away.

The room smelled of a combination of cigarettes and 4711 cologne, and was brightly lit from both the overhead fixture and diffused daylight filtering in through blinds covering the single window. As she stopped a few paces inside the door, her eyes fell on a large watercolor of a bird propped on an easel near the window.

"Fräulein Helinger." Herr Kraus had been seated behind a large desk when she entered. He rose as he spoke and walked around it to greet her. As he drew closer the smell of the cologne intensified. "I see you're admiring my painting."

His painting? From the pride in his voice, there was only one possible response. "Yes, indeed, Herr Kraus."

"Do you know anything about birds?"

"No, Herr Kraus."

"Ah." A wealth of disappointment in the syllable. "I study them as well as paint them. This is a bar-headed goose, *Anser indicus,* and is of particular interest because of the extreme altitudes it can reach when migrating across the Himalayas, which it does every year." Stopping in front of the easel, he touched the goose's head, which was white with a pair of black stripes running horizontally across it. "See these black bars? The bird takes its name from them."

"I will remember that, Herr Kraus."

"Yes, well, I did not summon you here to provide you with a lesson in identifying bird species. No doubt you are wondering why I did summon you."

Her throat was tight. She did not dare swallow. *Stay calm. Be alert.*

"Whatever the reason, Herr Kraus, I am glad to make myself available at your request."

"Excellent." His eyes were stone gray, stone hard. "I wish to once again go over what you told me about your experiences in Guernica."

The metallic taste in her mouth was fear. It was, she knew, as much as her life was worth to let it show.

"Very well." Her mind raced as she tried to recollect all the details of what she'd said. The look on his face made cold sweat prickle to life around her hairline, and that terrified her still more. My God, would he see it?

"We will begin with the reporter, Steer. I only seek to uncover the truth, you understand, so I ask that you be totally honest with me now. You spoke with him, did you not?"

Give the wrong answer, and Sibi knew in some deep, visceral part of her being that she, and probably her father and sisters along with her, was lost.

"No, Herr Kraus. I did not."

He looked at her, a long, penetrating look that seemed to bore right into her soul. She returned his look calmly, steadily. Inside, she felt faint with fear.

What does he know?

"I am pleased to have that confirmed." He turned and walked away, went behind his desk while Sibi battled the buzzing in her ears and fluttering in her stomach that afflicted her despite having made what she recognized as the right choice in continuing to deny her interaction with Steer. The frightening part was, the interview was not over. She had little doubt that there would be more potentially catastrophic choices to be made, more deadly pitfalls to be avoided. "The reason I sent for you today is that Dr. Goebbels wishes to meet you. He feels, and I agree, that the account of an eyewitness like yourself would be most helpful in getting the truth about the tragedy in Guernica before the public. You *do* know who Dr. Goebbels is, I am assuming?"

Dr. Goebbels, the Minister of Public Enlightenment and Propaganda. One of the führer's top aids. A towering figure in the Reich. A terrifying figure in the Reich.

Just the thought of being quizzed by him made her knees go weak.

She did her best to keep her face impassive. "Yes, of course, Herr Kraus."

"I thought so. But you are quite young, and the young can sometimes be . . . astoundingly obtuse."

The look he gave her as he said that last told her that there was a significance in it. But what? Mentally she floundered about, trying to decipher the underlying meaning, to recognize what she feared was the trap before she stepped into it.

He went on. "Before I take you in to see him, I wish to go over the details of your experience with you one more time."

"Very well, Herr Kraus." She couldn't help it: before she could catch herself, she swallowed hard.

He saw it. She could tell by the sudden flicker of his eyes, the twitch at the corner of his mouth.

"You are overwhelmed, I can see, by the prospect of meeting Dr. Goebbels."

Sibi might almost have described his tone as affable if she hadn't been able to see his face. His expression was intent, predatory even. She got the spine-chilling feeling that he was weighing the nuances of her response down to her every blink.

He'd seen her swallow, must guess that it was the result of nerves. *Use it.*

Her voice faltered slightly as she said, "I never expected — it is only that it is such an honor, Herr Kraus."

"Just so." He came out from behind his desk again, this time with a sheet of paper with typing on it in his hand.

What is that? What does it say? Panic bubbled up inside her.

Sibi tried not to look at the paper, because she didn't want him to think she could possibly be worried about anything that might be written on it. She tried not to let any emotion other than polite interest show on her face. She tried not to grip her crutches too tightly, let her breathing accelerate, blink too often or too fast.

"I took the liberty of writing down what you told me last night. Suppose I read what I heard you say back to you, and then you may correct me if there's anything I have here that's wrong."

"All right." Was he hoping to trip her up? *Please, God, help me remember everything I told him.*

Kraus looked down at the paper, started to read.

"I, Sibil Helinger, was present in Guernica on April 26, when the tragedy occurred. At around 4:30 p.m. warning bells sounded, and I took shelter in a building that subsequently was hit by a bomb and collapsed. I did not see the airplane that dropped the bomb, or any airplane. After being trapped for hours, I was rescued and conveyed out of town for treatment because the hospital was full of soldiers wounded in an earlier skirmish. At that time, which was approximately midnight, Guernica had suffered only minor damage from the afternoon's bombing. The majority of the buildings were still standing and if there were fatalities I was unaware of them. Certainly there were no mass fatalities. As I left Guernica, explosions started going off in all quarters. I personally saw soldiers of the Republican Army dynamiting some buildings and setting others on fire. From what I witnessed, the destruction and burning of Guernica, along with the many deaths that resulted, occurred at that time, at the hands of the Republican Army." Kraus paused to look up at her. "Did I get any of that wrong?"

His eyes held hers. The gleam in them was

a warning — no, a threat.

Her heart thundered. Her pulse raced. She felt light-headed, as if she stood on the edge of a precipice afraid to look down. She saw it now — what he wanted. What he required from her, if she wished to be allowed to go on as before, to walk out of this building, to be allowed to live her life, and for Papa and her sisters to be allowed to live their lives, in safety and peace.

The price for her freedom, their freedom, was this lie. This terrible, monstrous lie. She must agree with this statement he had constructed, must hold fast to her claim that it was the Reds who had destroyed Guernica. Must hold fast to the official Nazi Party line.

She'd caught her breath as she'd listened to him read, and now, with his eyes on her, she slowly let it out.

"No, Herr Kraus," she said. "You got nothing wrong."

"Excellent." He smiled at her. It was a thin, cold smile — a smile that let her know he was as aware as she was of how truly powerless she was. "It requires only your signature, and then we'll release it to the newspapers. I suggest you read it — *carefully* — before you sign it. It's possible that you'll be asked to meet with selected reporters to talk about your experience, although that isn't up to me. You won't want to get the details wrong."

He put the paper on his desk and motioned her toward it. Sibi moved to the desk and stared down at the paper. She wasn't reading it: the words blurred before her eyes. To exonerate the murderers of her mother and sister and so many others, to falsely accuse the victims — how could she do such a thing?

What choice did she have?

In a word, none.

The bitterness of it burned like acid in her stomach.

"Fräulein Helinger?" His voice behind her acted as a prod.

Sibi picked up the pen that lay on his desk and signed.

"Excellent," he said again. Retrieving the paper, he made a gesture for her to precede him from his office. "Dr. Goebbels is expecting us." He opened the door for her. "Down the hall to the right."

A few minutes later they were inside another office, being escorted to a door at the far end of it by a smiling secretary. Sibi had seconds to absorb her surroundings — a busy anteroom with a large Nazi flag in one corner and a potted plant in another, five desks, four secretaries busily working away while the fifth led them across the room, the clatter of multiple typewriters, the ringing of a telephone — before the secretary rapped on the door and, in response to a masculine, "You may enter," opened it for them.

Sibi went past the secretary into a large, elegantly furnished office: glass-fronted bookshelves, multiple framed landscapes, a giant photograph of the führer taking pride of place in the center of one wall, a smaller photograph of a blonde woman with her arms around a cluster of beaming blond children on a corner of a long, trestle-style table that served as a desk. She had no time to take in more details because her attention almost immediately focused on the three men standing behind that desk.

They looked her over appraisingly as she approached.

The man in the middle was Joseph Goebbels. She'd seen his picture in the newspapers. In person, he was small, thin, with jet-black hair slicked close to his skull, a long cadaverous face and burning dark eyes. His blue double-breasted suit was immaculate. The men on either side of him she didn't recognize. They were larger, balder, more corpulent. They, too, wore suits, although not such nice ones. The man on the left was missing an arm. The sleeve of his suit was pinned up to compensate.

With the weight of their eyes on her, Sibi felt as if she would suffocate, as if there was no air in the room.

"This is Fräulein Helinger," Kraus announced from behind her as she came to an uncertain stop in front of the desk. From the way he said it, they all knew who she was, why she was there. The man in the middle — Dr. Goebbels — came out from behind the desk. He had a pronounced limp. She tried not to notice it.

"Ah, yes. The girl from Guernica," he said, and introduced himself. She nodded in response.

"Walther Funk, our *Staatssekretar,* and Max Amann, president of the *Reichspressekammer.*" Dr. Goebbels gestured at the other men, introducing them in turn. "We found your story most compelling, Fräulein Helinger. Would it be too much to ask if we could hear it from your own lips? If you please?"

His very politeness, when everyone in that room including herself knew he could order her arrest or worse for no other reason than he wished it, made her skin crawl. She was as certain as it was possible to be that, if he didn't like what he heard, the consequences would be dire.

The whole time she was telling them the story that they wished to hear, the lie that she, under their questioning, embellished with even more lies, she was thinking of Scheherazade, forced to spin ever more elaborate tales to survive.

At last it was over. Herr Amann said he would see that the world press received her statement right away so that the truth could finally be heard. Dr. Goebbels thanked her for her time.

As she left the office under Herr Kraus's escort, she overheard Herr Funk say, "She's just what we need. If she has her *Ahnenpass*?"

The racial passport recently required of all German citizens to certify that they were of pure Aryan descent: Sibi shivered inwardly.

"She does," Herr Amann replied. "Though it's a pity she isn't blonde."

"You did very well in there," Herr Kraus told her as they parted in the hallway. He awarded her a thin-lipped smile. "I'm pleased with you, Fräulein Helinger."

Sibi held on to her composure, her air of deference, her sense of self-preservation, with both figurative hands. She lowered her eyes modestly. "Thank you, Herr Kraus."

Then she was permitted to leave.

By the time she made it back to the automobile, she thought she might be going to be physically sick. She opened the door, shoved her crutches into the middle and collapsed bonelessly on the seat. Crossing her arms over her chest in an effort to combat the persistent chill she couldn't shake, she closed her eyes and let her head drop to rest against the seat back and told herself to breathe.

"Sibi, thank God!" Papa started the engine at once, clearly as anxious as she was to get away. He'd been worried the whole time she was inside, she knew, and he was worried still. She could hear the tension in his voice, feel it in his eyes as he kept glancing at her while pulling out into the busy street. "What happened in there?"

"They wanted me to lie about Guernica. They wanted me to say that the Republicans were responsible for murdering everyone and bombing and burning the town. So I did." She drew a deep, shuddering breath, opened her eyes and sat up. The Volkswagen was just one of dozens of vehicles on Unter den Linden as they headed for home.

She looked at the huge, rippling swastika banners hanging from the buildings and felt a flash of rage as red as they were.

Papa said, "I know how difficult that must have been for you."

"Herr Kraus was pleased with me. He told me so. So were Dr. Goebbels and Herr Funk and Herr Amann, although Herr Funk thought it was a pity I'm not blonde. They were all there, all four of them, listening to the lies I told, asking questions. They're going to get my story out to the newspapers right away so I can tell 'the truth' to the world."

"Sibi —" Papa frowned at her, clearly troubled by what he heard in her voice, saw in her face.

"It's all right. I did what I had to do. You know that, and so do I. There was no choice."

"No," Papa said. "There was no choice."

They drove the rest of the way home in silence.

27

The next few days passed in a blur of school, hospital visits to Jo, time spent with Margrit — and the appearance of her "eyewitness account" in what seemed like every major newspaper in the world. *Der Stürmer, Der Angriff, Völkischer Beobachter, Frankfurter Zeitung, The Times* of London, *Le Populaire, Ce Soir, L'Humanité,* the *New York Times,* the *Washington Post* and many more featured her tale prominently on their front page. Sibi knew, because the Office of Propaganda obligingly sent over clippings, along with a note from Herr Kraus informing (warning) her that several in-person interviews were being arranged for her in the coming days. He meant for her to study the clippings so that there would be no mistakes, she knew. She couldn't even bring herself to look at them.

Grief, anger, shame — the maelstrom of emotions she experienced from seeing the lies she'd told in print for everyone to read and believe sent her into a frenzy of activity. Long walks, alone or with Ruby and/or Margrit, homework marathons, alone or with Heide and Ilsa (her grades went through the roof), journaling, house cleaning, reading and math tutoring sessions with Margrit (only to have an ungrateful Margrit complain, "Don't you ever get tired of school, Sibi? 'Cause I do.") were how she tried to cope.

On Friday, she put all other concerns aside and left school early to be with Jo while her bandages were removed.

"I can't wait to go home." As soon as Jo said it, her face clouded over. Sibi knew without having to be told what she was thinking — that home would not be the same without Mama and Luiza in it — and reached over to clasp her sister's hand. Jo's fingers felt cold and frail. Sibi rubbed them absently even as she sought to distract her from the unhappy thought.

"Margrit's so excited to see you that she can't sit still." Sibi perched in the small, straight-backed chair beside Jo's hospital bed while Jo, fully dressed, packed and ready to go, sat on the bed. Papa was signing papers at the nurses' station at the far end of the floor. The other bed in what was designed to be a shared room was empty, so the two sisters were alone. The doctor who was to remove her bandages and release her was expected at any minute. "She's been playing with Ruby, but since she dressed Ruby up in all her best doll clothes and Ruby chewed them to pieces she's given up on that. She's been trying to teach her tricks, but Ruby so far has resisted all her efforts."

"We can teach her together." Jo smiled. It was a crooked smile, because the injured side of her face was still numb and had not yet recovered its full range of movement, but it was achingly sweet for all that. The doctor had told them that, only a few weeks after the injury, such numbness and lack of mobility was only to be expected, but still to see Jo's lopsided expressions hurt Sibi's heart. "I can't believe Papa let us keep Ruby. He doesn't like dogs."

"He doesn't like *mess*," Sibi corrected. Bridging the gap between her sisters and their father was an ongoing process. Neither party understood the other, and both were cautious in their dealings with one another. To Papa's credit, he was at least trying. "He's been very good about Ruby, really."

"He —" Jo broke off as the doctor, followed by a nurse pushing an instrument cart and Papa, entered the room. Jo's hand tightened on Sibi's: it was time. Sibi squeezed her fingers, then let go.

"You ready to get those bandages off?" Dr. Schultz was portly, jolly, with a pink, round face. Jo nodded, and the doctor got down to business. Jo held very still through every metallic *snip-snip* of the scissors. When at last the doctor began to peel away the thick layers of tape and gauze, the first thing Sibi noticed were the traces of fine yellow powder — sulfanilimade, Dr. Schultz identified it as in response to Papa's question — stippling Jo's flesh.

The next thing she noticed was the nature of the flesh itself.

Difficult as it was, she tried not to let any trace of what she was feeling show.

Jo lightly touched the new skin over her cheek. Her eyes widened and flew to Sibi's face.

"Sibi." Jo's voice was high-pitched with distress. Her fingers recoiled from the discolored flesh, then curled and dropped. She looked horror-stricken. "How bad is it?"

"It's not bad," Sibi said stoutly. "It's still healing, is all."

"It feels cold and slick — like lizard skin."

"Your sister is right. You're still healing."

Dr. Schultz gave Jo a hand mirror. Sibi caught her breath as Jo looked at her reflection.

But there was no help for it: there was no hiding the truth of what had happened to her face from Jo, and it was probably better that she discovered it now, while the doctor was at hand to explain how much better (surely) it was going to get.

The burned areas were covered in swaths of shiny purplish skin. A long rectangle of discolored flesh stretched across the left side of Jo's face from just below her cheekbone to her jawline and from a few centimeters beyond the corner of her mouth almost to her ear. A second purplish patch covered the left side of her neck to slightly above her collarbone.

The results were far, far worse than anything Sibi had been anticipating. They were disfiguring.

"I look like a monster."

The mirror wavered alarmingly. Sibi reached for it, removing it from Jo's slackened grip before it could fall.

"Don't exaggerate." The frown Papa directed at Jo was stern. Sibi thought his intention might be to buck Jo up, but the effect was intimidating. "You look like a little girl whose face was burned but who is recovering."

Jo's lips quivered.

"It'll get better." Sibi reached for her hand again. Jo's fingers fastened convulsively around hers. "You'll see."

". . . fortunate the skin grafts took as well as they did," the doctor was saying to Papa at the same time. "When she first arrived, I wasn't sure we were even going to be able to save her life. But here she is. She's made excellent progress, and I expect her to continue to improve."

"I won't always . . . look like this?" Jo's eyes were imploring.

"No, no. You'll have some scarring — no getting around that, I'm afraid — but over time it will become much less noticeable." The doctor wagged a playful finger at her. "You'll grow up to be as pretty as your sister here, never fear."

Jo's death grip on her fingers eased. Sibi summoned a small, perfunctory thank-you-for-the-compliment smile for the doctor, who beamed at her, and a more genuine one for Jo, who managed a weak near-grimace in return.

"See there?" Papa reverted to his hearty voice. "You're going to be fine."

After receiving instructions on wound care and a time to come back for a checkup, they left for home.

Margrit was in the front hall, throwing a ball for Ruby as they came in the door. The scent of dinner — Frau Skeller stayed until the meal was eaten and the dishes cleared — was in the air. Hoping for a letter from Griff, Sibi cast a quick glance at the mail tray on the table against the wall — nothing — only to be distracted by an unexpected volley of barking from Ruby. Apparently recognizing Jo, Ruby abandoned her mad scramble after the ball to race toward her.

"Jo." Margrit ran to her sister, too, enveloping her in a fierce hug. Still barking excitedly, Ruby was already there, leaping up around Jo's legs. "Ruby and I have been waiting and *waiting* for you."

Jo hugged her back just as fiercely. "I've missed you." She glanced down at Ruby, who was up on her hind legs pawing at whatever part of her she could reach, and patted the furry black head. "I've missed you, too, Ruby. Oh, I'm so glad to be home."

Margrit said, "We're glad you're home, too," and the two of them clung together while Ruby, still barking, danced around them.

Sibi looked at Jo's shorn dark head pressed close to Margrit's curly blond one, at Jo's taller, toothpick-thin frame clasped to

Margrit's shorter, sturdy one, and felt a lump rise in her throat. Here they were together, safely home at last, the three of them, and that was such a miracle she could only be thankful.

But she couldn't help thinking also of the two who would never come home again. Mama and Luiza should have been there with them, in that hall, in that house. Their absence created a void in their family that could never be filled. Her heart ached with grief for the two who were missing even as she rejoiced in having Jo back and seeing the little girls reunited.

Papa said, "Margrit, no more playing ball with the dog in the house," as he moved past them. Sibi saw that he held the small red ball, which he'd apparently caught, in one hand. "And could someone please make it stop barking?"

His voice was gruff. As he disappeared into the kitchen the little girls, abashed, stepped apart, with Jo going down on one knee to pat Ruby while Margrit, leaning over the two of them, whispered, "Hush, Ruby. Hush."

Sibi cast a frowning look toward the kitchen, where she could hear the back door being opened followed shortly by a muffled *thump,* which made her think that Papa had thrown the ball out into the garden. She was reluctant to approach Papa about the effect his abruptness had on the little girls, but to see them go from joyous to downcast in a matter of moments because of the tone he used when speaking to them bothered her.

Before she could ponder the problem at greater length, Frau Skeller appeared in the doorway and summoned them to eat.

Over the next few weeks, life took on a certain rhythm. All the residents of the small house on Sophienstrasse were busy adjusting in his or her own way to the new normal. Papa worked more than ever and was rarely home. Margrit's nightmares decreased in frequency but didn't go away, but on a positive note her arm was pronounced healed and she had no more need of the sling. Jo's skin grafts lost some of their harsh purple color but were still glaringly apparent to the most casual glance, and as a result Jo didn't like to leave the house. Jo, Margrit and Ruby spent a great deal of time playing in the back garden. Sibi tried to keep them on top of their lessons, but after a short time decided that what the little girls needed most at that juncture was time. Time to play, time to be together, time to heal. Schoolwork could wait for the fall term, and if the girls ended up having to repeat a year, then so be it. As for herself, she got her cast off and was relieved to be able to walk normally again. Other than that, she was so busy that she scarcely had time to think, which was the idea.

As he'd promised (threatened), Herr Kraus arranged for her to give interviews to reporters from the newspapers that mattered to him, with the result that on one particularly dreadful day as she walked to catch the tram to school, she passed one of the red metal newspaper boxes that stood on all major street corners only to see her own grainy, black-and-white face looking back at her through the glass window beneath a headline that screamed Guernica Survivor Blames Tragedy on Reds.

The instant upsurge of rage and heartbreak thus invoked upset her so much that the world went out of focus, and she was obliged to sit down on the nearest bench until she could once again get her more extreme emotions stuffed back into the mental box where she kept them and function normally again. As a result, she missed her tram and therefore her first class, and had to tell the headmaster she'd been late because of a headache and go in early the next day to make the class up.

June was another month that put her emotions through the wringer. On the third, Mola died in an airplane crash. To rejoice in such a thing was wrong, a sin, she knew, but she couldn't help but feel an almost savage satisfaction in the murderer's violent (and karmic) end. On the nineteenth, after a long and bloody battle, Bilbao fell to the Whites. Sibi thought of Griff, from whom she'd heard nothing, and hoped desperately that he and his men hadn't been there, and gotten caught up in the fighting. She thought, too, of Ruth, and Julio the lift operator, and the townspeople and all the refugees, and the town itself, and feared for their fate, and wanted to weep.

On June 22, she had her birthday, turning seventeen. She could hardly face it without Mama and Luiza, but put on a happy face for the little girls' sakes through a celebratory family dinner. Mama's own birthday came three days later, on June 25. It was a Friday, Sibi's last day of school for the year, and despite her friends' jubilation and the fact that she'd passed all her exams with top marks she couldn't help but feel the weight of loss throughout the day. After school was out, Heide and Ilsa went with a group (including Ilsa's now-boyfriend Friedrich Gruber) to the cinema with the intention of going later to their favorite café in the Tiergarten for a meal. They begged her to come along, but Sibi had no heart for it. Instead she went home.

She changed out of her school clothes into a cool summer dress, sleeveless with a square neck in a soft shade of lemon, and tied back her hair with a blue ribbon because it was hot enough to make the thick mass of it feel as stifling as a coat. Then she went in search of her sisters, finding them, as expected, in the garden, which was small and fenced and sadly overgrown because it had been Mama who had tended to the plants, which she'd loved and which the rest of them had no talent for. Actually, the girls were sitting on the wooden steps with Ruby between them, and even from the back looked so despondent that Sibi's first words on stepping out onto the stoop were, "What's the matter, *mein Schneckes*?"

Both girls looked around at her.

Beneath her glasses, Jo's eyes glistened with unshed tears. Her mouth trembled. Margrit's nose was red and tears slid openly down her cheeks.

"Oh, dear, what's happened?" Sibi asked in a far different tone as she hurried over to sink down on the top step behind them.

"It's Mama's birthday, and we were having a ceremony for her, and we forgot to watch Ruby and — and —" Margrit broke off on a sob. Unable to continue, she held something up for Sibi to see.

As Sibi registered with growing horror exactly what it was that Margrit was showing her, Jo added despairingly, "Ruby found one of Papa's shoes and chewed it up. And Papa came in and caught her and let out this big roar and chased Ruby outside and now he said she has to go!"

"Oh, no." Sibi took the shoe from Margrit. It was one of Papa's best brogues, of fine brown leather, highly polished — and now it had tattered shoestrings and a ragged nub of a tongue and unmistakable doggy teeth marks all over it. Perfectly able to picture how explosive Papa's reaction must have been, Sibi could only wince and shake her head. The culprit looked around at her, eyes bright, tongue lolling, not a trace of remorse to be seen. "Oh, Ruby. Bad dog."

Ruby wagged her tail.

"She didn't know any better," Jo said. "It's our fault. We should have been watching her. I tried to tell Papa that, but —"

"He yelled," Margrit said. "He said we had to give her away. But I *love* Ruby." With a sob, Margrit wrapped Ruby up in a hug. Ruby licked her cheek.

Shoe in hand, Sibi stood up. "I can fix this. I'll talk to Papa. He was just . . . upset. He won't really make us give Ruby away."

"He will, too," Margrit said. "He said so. He doesn't like Ruby."

"He doesn't like *us,*" Jo muttered.

"Yes, he does." Sibi was stung into fierceness. "He loves us. He loves both of you. He just . . . doesn't always show it. I'll go talk to him right now."

"He's not here. He left."

"Oh." Sibi looked down at her sisters, irresolute. "I'll talk to him as soon as he gets back, then."

"I picked some flowers to put on Mama's grave, but I dropped them when Papa started to yell," Margrit said. Now that Margrit pointed it out, Sibi saw a handful of orange lilies scattered on the brick walk that led away from the steps.

"Were you thinking Mama's in the cemetery with Oma?" Jo scoffed, referring to their paternal grandmother who was buried in Berlin. "She's not. She doesn't *have* a grave."

Margrit's eyes went round. "She *doesn't?*"

Fearing that Jo, whose understanding of precisely what had happened to their mother was much more detailed than Margrit's, was about to enlighten their littlest sister, Sibi said hastily, "I know what we should do. For her birthday, we should make our own memorial for her and Luiza. Margrit, why don't you gather up your flowers again, while Jo and I go find something small of theirs, and we'll take it out to the park and bury it beneath our tree. It'll be our own memorial."

"My face," Jo objected in a small voice.

"You can wear your sun hat." To combat Jo's reluctance to go out in public, Sibi had bought her a wide-brimmed straw hat at the outdoor Hackescher Market, and added a ribbon band anchoring a veil. The result was pretty, summery, and helped hide her injury from view. Once she saw how well the hat served its purpose, she went back and bought similar hats for herself and Margrit, so Jo wouldn't feel conspicuous when she wore it. "We'll all wear our sun hats. It's so hot out, we need them."

28

The park consisted of a soft green meadow with many large, leafy trees for shade, well-trimmed hedges and colorful flower gardens that perfumed the air. Birds chirped, butterflies fluttered and squirrels chased each other through the treetops. The centerpiece was a pond in which cattails grew and ducks paddled and an occasional shiny silver flash spoke of the fish that lived beneath the surface. Today, an old man sat on the bank fishing and a trio of boys piloted remote-controlled toy boats over the glassy surface. A miscellany of others, singly and in groups, sat on benches or took advantage of the neatly laid-out brick paths that meandered through it all.

"I'll dig the hole." Margrit took the trowel from the cloth bag that hung from Sibi's arm. They'd just stepped beneath the sheltering branches of *our tree,* the giant oak that, in summers past, would often shade their picnics.

Without the sun beating down on them, the air immediately felt many degrees cooler. Jo held Ruby's leash, while Sibi carried the small box in which a brooch of Mama's and Luiza's black velvet choker with its pin for that long-ago flower were tucked away.

"Close to the base of the tree. Yes, that's good," Sibi said as Margrit found a spot, dropped to her knees and set to work with the trowel. The slight earthy scent and rustle of leaves as the barely there breeze wafted through them created an illusion of peace. The sounds and activity of the park, the bustle of the city, seemed far away.

"Are you going to carve something on the tree?" Margrit asked as Jo allowed Ruby, busy sniffing the ground, to tug her around the tree. One of the reasons they'd chosen the tree for their picnics was because it was inscribed with a variety of markings, from lovers' names to hearts to dates of significant events. They'd loved pointing to one of the carvings and having Mama make up a story to explain it.

By way of an answer, Sibi fished the penknife she'd brought along from the bag and held it up for Margrit to see.

"Remember the last time we were here?"

Jo emerged from the other side of the tree at a trot as Ruby, eyes trained upward, followed the adventures of a squirrel in the branches with enthusiasm.

"A bee crawled up Luiza's skirt." Sibi smiled at the memory even as she scratched an *M* for Marina and then an *L* for Luiza into the rough gray bark, which was harder work than she'd anticipated. On that summer's day two years before, they'd all been sitting beneath the tree, four little girls picnicking with their mother, when Luiza, who'd edged off the blanket onto the grass because there was not, she complained, enough room for so many, had jumped to her feet, screaming like a steam whistle and tearing at her clothes. The resulting commotion had created a scene for the ages.

"I remember that." Margrit had been not quite four at the time, so for her to remember it said a great deal. "Luiza danced around in her underpants."

"And an old lady scolded Luiza for being indecent and Mama got so mad," Jo put in, and they all laughed.

"Ready," Margrit said.

They put the box in the hole and covered it up. Then Margrit laid her flowers on top. The beauty of the orange blooms on the raw dirt tore at Sibi's heart as the three of them joined hands and said a prayer for their lost loved ones.

"Love you always," Sibi concluded. Her voice was thick.

"Love you always." With tears trickling down their cheeks, Jo and Margrit echoed the words they hadn't said to their mother on the night before she died. Sibi felt sure that somewhere Mama and Luiza heard and sent the same love radiating back at the three who remained.

"What are you girls doing?" Papa spoke from behind them a few minutes later, catching them all by surprise. Sibi, who'd been frowning ferociously as she attempted to carve more letters into the bark, jumped and dropped the penknife.

"Making a memorial for Mama and Luiza," she said. She could only suppose he'd seen them as he arrived home: a slice of the park that included the tree was easily visible from the sidewalk in front of their house if one turned and looked.

"M and *L."* Papa picked up the dropped knife and handed it back to her, then traced the letters she'd carved with a blunt forefinger. She'd intended to go with their full names, Marina and Luiza, but realized shortly after she began that the hardness of the wood was going to make that too dif-

ficult. "And what's this?" He touched the third letter she'd almost finished. It was an *A,* slightly crooked, larger than the *M* and *L,* and located beneath them.

"Always," Sibi said. "I'm writing *always.*"

He held out his hand for the penknife. She gave it to him, and a few quick strokes later he'd carved an *L* beside the *A* and moved on to the *W:* in an unexpected gesture, he was finishing the word for her.

"Because we'll love Mama and Luiza *always,"* Margrit said. She was on her feet now, frowning up at Papa as he worked, all traces of her earlier tears gone. Her hat hung from its ribbons down her back, a smudge of dirt was on her nose and the skirt of her blue dress bore grass stains. The top of her head wasn't much higher than his waist. With her halo of curls, rosy cheeks and bright blue eyes, she could have been mistaken for a cherub by anyone who didn't recognize the significance of her jutting chin and narrowed eyes. Sibi knew that look, though, and tensed with apprehension even as Margrit planted her fists on her hips. "We love Ruby, too. You can't make us give her away. We *won't.*"

Jo's expression of alarm at Margrit's open defiance mirrored Sibi's reaction. Papa stopped what he was doing to frown ominously at his youngest, who frowned just as ominously back. Their mutual scowling expressions as their eyes clashed so exactly mirrored one another that Sibi might have smiled if the situation hadn't been so fraught with potential disaster.

"I told the girls that you didn't really mean it when you said we had to give Ruby away," Sibi said to Papa, while at the same time dropping a reproving, and hopefully silencing, hand on Margrit's shoulder. "I told them that you were just upset about your shoe."

Papa transferred his scowl to her. Despite her trepidation at the thought of how he might respond to what he could easily perceive as her insubordination, she met his gaze unflinchingly.

Papa's lips compressed.

" *'Anger is a wind which blows out the lamp of the mind':* that's Ingersoll, young ladies." His gaze swept the three of them. "I let my temper get the better of me earlier, I confess. I would not deprive you of your pet." He gave first Margrit and then Jo a severe look. "Although from now on I expect you to supervise the dog when it's in the house."

"We will," Margrit said, and Jo nodded fervently.

Papa glanced at Sibi, who smiled gratefully at him, then turned back to the tree and his carving. Glancing over his shoulder as he worked, he said, "Did you girls know that I first met your mother when she was seventeen? Just your age, Sibi. I was studying the viability of using air vehicles in combat in conjunction with the Aeronautica Militar — the air branch of the Spanish Army — when I went up in a hot-air balloon with another pilot on a test flight. To make a long story short, we hit bad weather, crashed just outside of Guernica and were immediately surrounded by marveling residents, one of whom was your mother. They pulled us from the wreckage and got us to the hospital. Your mother visited me every day, brought me special food, played cards and other games, read to me. By the time they said I was well enough to leave I didn't want to. Well, not without her. Marina Diaitz was the most beautiful girl I'd ever seen in my life." He stopped talking, stopped carving and rested his forehead against the tree.

Sibi watched his hand tighten around the hilt of the knife, watched his back rise and fall with the sudden increased force of his breathing, and felt her heart constrict. She wanted to pat his shoulder or put an arm around him, but to do anything of the sort

340

felt awkward — their relationship was never like that. Before she could settle on a response, he straightened and turned to sweep them with another encompassing glance.

"I miss her very much, you know," he said. "Her and your sister."

Handing Sibi the knife, he walked away with an almost military precision. Sibi's breath caught as she watched him go: How had she not realized that their strong, self-contained father was grieving, too? Jo also seemed to be much struck as she followed him with her eyes.

"Papa!" Margrit ran after him, caught up and tucked her hand in his. "Don't be sad. We'll take care of you."

He stopped but said nothing, just looked down into Margrit's upturned face.

Then he smiled at her. "How about we all take care of one another?"

She nodded, and he ruffled her curls. Glancing around at Sibi and Jo, he said, "I propose we all go get *Eis am Stiel.* At Gunther's, up the street."

As it worked out, Papa took Margrit and Jo for the promised treat of ice cream on a stick, while Sibi stayed behind with Ruby — dogs weren't allowed in Gunther's — to finish her carving. It was one of the few times he'd ever been alone with the little girls, and it would, she thought, be a promising step forward in their relationship.

She was digging away at the last little bit of the final *S* when Ruby leaped barking to her feet.

Glancing around, Sibi saw a man walking purposefully toward her. A frisson of alarm caused her to stiffen as she registered how deserted the park now was. It was nearing dinnertime, she realized, and there was no one else in sight. But when she saw who it was —

"Griff."

Joyous, welcoming surprise colored her voice. He was looking her over, and she could only hope that she didn't have a smudge on her nose or grass stains on her skirt, as Margrit did. She knew her face had to be flushed, and that curling tendrils of her hair had worked their way loose from the confining ribbon to cling damply to her cheeks and neck. Her fallen hat lay on the ground at her feet, near the cloth bag and the trowel and the shrilly barking dog now straining at the leash.

"Hello, Sibi." His eyes crinkled at the corners as he smiled at her. Now that he was closer, she could see how vividly blue they looked against the deep tan of his skin.

His hair, cut short and brushed back from his face, waved in the heat. Casual in trousers and a short-sleeved shirt that hugged his broad shoulders, he looked young and fit. And handsome. She'd actually forgotten how handsome.

A messenger bag — *the* messenger bag — hung from his shoulder.

Memories slammed into her like a freight train, along with the emotions that came with them: a searing jumble of pain and fear and loss that could cripple her if she let it, if she did not force the feelings away. She did, by focusing on Griff instead.

He'd saved her life, then seen her through the worst moments she ever expected to endure, and the bond they'd forged as a result felt like a soul-deep connection.

"Planning to gut me with that knife?" He flicked a look at the open blade she clutched.

"No." Her knife hand dropped. Her smile went wide. "What are you doing here?"

"Thought I better come check on you."

"I wasn't sure I'd ever see you again. How long are you here for?"

"I got here this morning, I'm leaving tonight."

"That's not much time. *Hush, Ruby,*" Sibi said in an aside to the still-barking dog.

343

"Ferocious as ever, I see." Griff also addressed Ruby as he bent to pat her. Given that Ruby was about the size of a cat, she could try for ferocious all day long and not get there. "Hello, Ruby."

"Really, what are you doing here?"

"I told you, I came to check on you. Grabbed a few hours out of a trip to Switzerland."

"What were you doing in Switzerland?"

"Business." He straightened.

"Oh, my, you've come for your mother's book, haven't you? I'm so sorry I took it! It was a mistake — it got caught up in our clothes and I didn't notice until we got home. Oh, and I'm sorry we left without seeing you, and without even saying goodbye. Everything happened in such a rush and —"

"Wait. Slow down." He stopped her in midspiel. "You don't need to say *sorry* to me. I understand exactly how it happened. I'm just glad you got home in one piece. And I didn't come for the book. Like I said, I came to check on you. And Jo. And Margrit. How are they doing?"

She told him about Jo's recovery, the grafts and the skin that would hopefully improve with time, about Margrit's arm.

"And how are you?" He sent a swift glance

down to her previously broken ankle. Her full skirt ended at midcalf. Below it, in deference to the heat, her slender legs were bare.

"All better, as you can see." She wiggled her foot in its soft brown sandal to demonstrate. Then she thought of all the things she was dying to know. Her eyes flew to his face. "How are Sergeant Iverson and Private Lynch and Private Phillips? *Where* are they? What happened to Ruth? And Sister Beatrice, and —"

He held up a hand, grinning at her. "You expect me to answer all that?"

She made a face at him. "Yes."

"Fine. I'll see what I can do." He cast a look around, as if to assure himself they were alone: they were. A woman pushing a pram along the sidewalk across the street from the park was the only person in sight. "Iverson and Lynch and Phillips are fine. I left them at the embassy in Barcelona. Ruth got out on a ship and is now in, I think, Málaga, although she may have moved on from there by this time. As for Sister Beatrice, I heard she met Mola's officers at the front door as they reached the hospital. She stood her ground like the general she was obviously meant to be and told them there was typhus in the hospital, but they were free to enter if they wished. Needless to say, they did not, and Sister Beatrice and the hospital were left in peace."

Sibi smiled. "I'm not even surprised. That sounds exactly like something Sister Beatrice would do."

"She should be running an army somewhere, that one." His eyes met hers. "I saw your cover girl turn in the newspapers. That was quite a story."

Her smile dimmed, then disappeared altogether. The memory of how Steer had questioned her and how Griff had kept her from giving him her name, along with the knowledge of what the consequences would have been if she had been identified as the source of his story, flashed between them.

She found she could no longer meet his gaze. Her voice dropped to a near-whisper. "I had no choice."

"I know."

If he'd read the story, he did know — both the truth and what she'd done. Shame burned in her stomach.

"I hate myself for doing it. Almost as much as I hate them." Her voice was low, grim.

He was serious now, too. "Hate them if you want, but don't hate yourself. There was nothing else you could have done."

"I know. But it makes me feel awful. Physically sick, actually, whenever I think about it."

"In that case, the best thing you can do is *not* think about it. You did what you had to do, and there's an end to it." He looked at her for a moment without saying anything before his gaze dropped and he smiled. "Expecting trouble?"

He was looking at her knife again and thereby, she realized, changing the subject.

"Carving." Closing the blade, she dropped the knife into one of the two patch pockets on her skirt and indicated the tree.

"Ah." His expression changed as he saw the chiseled letters, and she realized that their import wasn't lost on him.

"They didn't get to come home." She knew he knew who she was talking about. "I — *we,* Jo and Margrit and I — wanted them to have some sort of memorial." Her gesture encompassed the flowers and dirt as well as the tree. "We buried something belonging to each of them, and . . . did this. Papa helped with the carving."

Griff was still looking at the tree. She realized that, besides herself and Margrit and Jo, he was the only person left in the world who knew exactly what that *Always* meant.

"Sibi, I've got something for you. Not a

present exactly. But . . . something."

His eyes were grave and his mouth was unsmiling. Reaching into a pocket on the messenger bag, he withdrew a twist of tissue and held it out to her.

She took it. "What is this?"

"Open it."

She did. When she saw what was inside, her breath caught and her heart shook. Her eyes flew to his face. They must have asked the question she couldn't put into words, because he said, "I went back, after I left you at the hotel. To Guernica. That's where I was when your father came."

"And you found . . . this?" If her voice was the merest whisper, the wonder was that she could speak at all. She felt unmoored, as if she were in danger of being swept away on a dark and tempestuous sea. "This" was her mother's locket, the silver one with all their initials that Marina had always worn. That she'd been wearing the night she died.

He nodded.

"How?"

"The fire had mostly burned itself out, in that section where . . . she was." From his expression she could tell that he was choosing his words carefully. "I had some people with me, and we got her out. She —" He broke off. "I had her buried, sweetheart.

Where your sister is. The necklace was still on her. I thought you might want it."

"Griff." His name came out sounding strangled. After that, her voice deserted her entirely. Opening the locket, she saw that the picture — she and Luiza, standing close together, behind Jo sitting on a bench beside Mama with baby Margrit on her lap — was unharmed. She closed the locket, and closed her hand around it, holding it as if it were the most precious thing she ever had possessed or ever would possess. Her eyes clung to his. Her lips stayed parted even though no more words could pass the constriction in her throat.

"I had it cleaned," he said. "And a priest was there when your mother was put into the ground. It was the best I could do. For her, and for you."

She breathed. In, then out. Slowly and deeply and deliberately, because her surroundings had gone all blurry and the ground seemed to undulate beneath her feet and there was this annoying buzzing sound growing louder in her ears.

"Sibi."

She must have swayed, because he reached for her, pulling her into his arms. She let him take her weight, thankful for his solid strength, for the safe harbor he provided against the raging waves of emotion that threatened to swamp her, for the absolute certainty that he *understood.* She closed her eyes and let the worst of it crash over her and waited, for the tempest to subside and the buzzing in her ears to stop and the pain, the piercing sense of loss, all of it, to ebb until it was once again at a level she could live with, manage, contain.

Until she didn't feel as if she would die of grief.

When at last the storm passed, when she could hear and think and function more or less normally again, she became aware of a number of things: the firmness of his chest beneath her cheek, and its steady rise and fall as he breathed. The hard muscularity of his arms around her. The slight scent of what she thought was soap, and man.

Sibi was all at once aware of how absolutely plastered to him she seemed to be. They couldn't have been any closer if he'd been paper and she'd been ink.

She looked up, only to find that he was looking down at her. Their eyes met —

Self-conscious suddenly, she took a step back — he let her go — and promptly stumbled over Ruby, who jumped sideways with a yelp. Griff grabbed her upper arms, catching her, steadying her.

He didn't pull her close. Of course, this time there was no need. She wasn't reeling from shock or awash with emotion, nothing like that. She'd stumbled, was all.

If, before, something had passed between them — and Sibi wasn't absolutely sure that something had — the only thing she could find in the frowning look he was giving her now was . . . a frown.

"All right?" he asked.

She nodded. And stepped away from him.

He said, "I didn't mean to upset you. I . . . thought you should know she'd been decently laid to rest. And I thought you'd want her necklace."

"I'm not upset. I'm glad you told me. And I do. So much." Sibi took a deep breath, tried for a smile. "Thank you." The smile faltered, and she looked at him earnestly. "Actually, the words *thank you* aren't nearly enough. What you did — it means the world to me."

He nodded. That was all. But she understood: no *thank you* needed, no *you're welcome*s required. Long ago, he'd lost his mother, too. He'd done what he did because he *knew.*

The locket, with the tissue still cradling it, was tightly gripped in her hand. Her first impulse was to put it on. Then she thought

351

about the ramifications, about how wearing it would make her feel and the explanations that she'd have to offer up to her family if they noticed, which Jo at least almost certainly would, and about how it belonged as rightfully to Jo and Margrit as it did to her, and — and —

She tucked it into her skirt pocket, where it would be safe. Later, when she was ready, when she'd had time to think everything through, she might wear it. Or she might keep it tucked away, not forever, but until she and her sisters could decide together what to do with it.

"Today is her birthday, you know. Mama's birthday. You giving me her locket was like getting a gift from her."

"Jesus." His eyes were intent on her face. She didn't know what she looked like, but she knew how she felt: shaken by the absolute maelstrom of emotions she'd just experienced. Then something behind her attracted his attention, and his expression changed. Looking past her, he frowned.

"Let's walk," he said, even as she started to frown herself. Without waiting for her to reply, he quickly gathered up her possessions, plopped her hat on her head, caught her arm and steered her — and by default Ruby — onto one of the neat brick paths.

29

"Is something wrong?" Sibi asked as Griff towed her briskly along the path toward the pond. Ruby, who was fond of sniffing every tree and clump of greenery she passed and as a result lagged as far behind as the length of the leash would allow, kept up, but with obvious reluctance.

"You familiar with the SD?" He slowed as they rounded a clump of ornamental grass higher than his head. In front of them, the pond took on a golden glint as the late-afternoon sun caught it. Beyond the pond, across the street at the far end of the park, was the seventeenth-century Sophienkirche with its baroque spire that rose majestically against the cloudless sky. Where they were, a thick canopy of branches shaded the path, and the cool, mossy scent of the pond acted as a nice counterpoint to the heat. Behind them, the big oak and the ornamental grass and a hodgepodge of other trees and plantings blocked this main section of the park from the view of the street. A quick glance confirmed it: the only people in sight were a couple in a rowboat in the middle of the pond.

"Not very."

"The SD, the Sicherheitsdienst, is the security service. They gather intelligence for the Nazi Party. Their job is to determine who can be trusted, and who is to be considered an enemy of the state. Right now they're investigating your father."

She stopped dead, looking at him in alarm. "How do you know that?"

"Keep walking." Taking her hand, he tucked it into the crook of his arm and started off again. She had, perforce, to go with him. They were alone, there was no one anywhere near, but suddenly she felt as if a thousand eyes were watching. "I collect information, remember? It's my job to know things. Once you returned to Berlin, I wanted to make sure you were all right so I got in touch with a contact we maintain over here. He told me your father is under surveillance."

"But why?" Fear began to percolate inside her.

"I don't know. But they're watching him."

"What do you mean, they're watching him?"

"Keeping track of who he sees, who he talks to. Searching his office when he's not in it. Going through his files. Listening in on his telephone calls. Following him."

She was appalled. Then something in his tone struck her. "Are you saying they're following him *now*?"

"Two SD men drove past your house and were headed down the street in our direction when I hurried you out of sight. My guess is that that they'd been surveilling your father. I don't know that they would have noticed you here in the park, or even recognized you for that matter, but attracting their attention isn't anything you want to do."

"I have to tell Papa."

His mouth tightened. "I thought you'd probably feel that way. I'm not going to tell you not to tell him, but it's important that he doesn't know that you got the information from me, or that you and I met today. It's important than no one knows. In fact, the less you say about me to anyone, including your father, the better."

"I already told him about you."

"I figured you did. That happened in the past, though, in another country, in the face of terrible circumstances. You having an ongoing relationship with me would fall under a different category."

"Because you're an American?"

"And an officer in a foreign military, among other things. What you don't want is for the SD to start thinking you might be passing information along to me. And if they start looking at me — well, then my usefulness here will be at an end."

Sibi's heart sped up. "Your usefulness?"

"Like I said, I collect information. Such as, for example, the fact that German scientists took advantage of an oversight in the Treaty of Versailles that left rocket technology off the list of weapons Germany was forbidden to develop to do just that."

She'd written that to him. "You got my letter."

"I did. Don't write me another one."

"What?"

"You heard me. It's too dangerous. That's one of the reasons I'm here — to tell you not to do it again. Any mail coming into Spain from Germany risks being opened by censors on either side of the conflict, and vice versa. If anyone had read what you wrote to me, you could easily have been accused of passing on information injurious to the Reich. You could have been arrested, interrogated, imprisoned — or worse. You should consider yourself lucky no one looked at it — this time."

She might not have believed him, might have thought he was exaggerating or over-reacting or trying to frighten her, if she hadn't just experienced what she had with Herr Kraus.

A shiver slid down her spine.

Then she thought of something, and her hand tightened on his arm. He looked at her inquiringly.

"You have a contact. You gather information. You don't want anyone to know we talked." Even though she knew there was no one in the vicinity, she glanced around just to be absolutely certain. Her voice dropped to a shocked near-whisper. "Griff, are you a *spy*?"

His eyes narrowed. "Something you don't ever want to do again is ask someone if they're a spy. Anybody who'd say yes is probably going to kill you afterward for knowing too much."

She made an impatient sound. "That's not an answer."

"I'm a military attaché."

"And that's all."

"Yup."

While she mulled that over, they walked

on in silence. Ruby, in front of them now, trotted eagerly along, her ears pricked, her eyes on a pair of ducks that had just splashed down in the pond.

Sibi said, "Our military is being built up again. The Wehrmacht is stronger than ever. The Luftwaffe is back. Soldiers are everywhere. Even the children are being turned into soldiers. We have all these parades with big guns and tanks and airplanes, and martial music is all over the radio and the newpapers are full of stories about how Germany is rising like a phoenix from the ashes — what's the purpose? What's it all in aid of?"

"I don't know."

She made an impatient sound. "That's just it. No one knows. Everything is to be kept secret, or covered up. But there's a *purpose* behind it. There has to be. They're just not telling us what it is. Our government is lying to us. To the whole world."

The ghost of a smile barely curved his mouth. "Thus the need for people like me to gather information. That's how we figure out the purpose."

She took a breath, huffed it out. Her eyes fastened on his face. "I want to help you."

"What?"

"I want to help you. Gather information."

"No."

"What do you mean, no? You can't just say *no.* I can help. I can be a lot of help."

"I don't need your help. I don't want your help. You cannot help. And I can, too, say *no,* which is what I'm saying. Put it out of your head."

"Why? The information I gave you about the rockets was good, wasn't it? You couldn't have gotten that anywhere else."

"It was good, and I appreciate it. But —"

"There's more where that came from. Besides being head of the physics department at Friedrich Wilhelm University, which is a very prestigious university in case you don't know, Papa is chairman of the Society of German Scientists and Physicians. They meet every couple of months, at our house. They drink, and they talk. The last meeting, they talked about the *Hindenburg* crashing, and about how the 'tragedy' in Guernica was a public relations disaster — *that's* what disturbs them about it, that it was a public relations disaster — and about the rockets. And that's just what I picked up when I wasn't even trying to listen. Think what I could find out for you if I was."

He shook his head. "It's too dangerous. Even if your father wasn't under surveillance. Which he *is,* in case that's slipped your mind."

"It hasn't slipped my mind. I'm willing to take the risk."

"I'm not. Willing for you to take the risk. You're barely seventeen years old, for God's sake. Too young to get involved in something like this. Best thing you can do is sit tight and keep your head down and let the people whose job it is to do it worry about what's going on in the world."

"In case it's slipped *your* mind, I'm already involved. As involved as anybody. More involved than you actually. All you Americans are doing is *observing.* You can walk away at any time. I can't. This is *my life* we're talking about."

"Sibi —"

She rushed on before he could say anything more. "Did I mention that, starting Monday, because school's over now until fall, I'll be going into the lab with my father and taking the notes he dictates as he works full-time on the rocket technology we've been talking about? Where else are you going to find somebody with that kind of access?"

From the arrested look in his eyes, she knew she'd scored a hit.

Then his lips compressed. "You might be

able to acquire some useful information, that's true, but you have no safe way of getting it to me. You can't write to me, you can't telephone me — yes, they're probably listening in on all your telephone calls — and telegrams are definitely out."

"There's this thing called talking. Where I tell you what I've learned and you listen. See, we're doing it right now."

"That might work — except I'm not often in Berlin. I wouldn't be here today if I hadn't wanted to check up on you. Hard to talk to someone who isn't around."

She was briefly stymied. "There has to be some way."

His eyes flickered. It was the briefest of alterations to his expression, but she caught it. And she knew in that instant that he had, indeed, thought of a way.

"There is, isn't there? I can see it in your face."

"You can't see anything of the sort in my face."

"Griff. Let me try."

"No." From the stony finality of that, he wasn't changing his mind.

Frustration boiled up inside her, mixed with all the emotions she'd been tamping down for so long and combusted into a firestorm of anguished fury. Her spine stiffened, her fingers dug into his arm and her eyes blazed at him. She stopped walking, which meant he had to stop, too. He swung around to frown at her. With the wide brim of her hat in the way, she had to tilt her head back to meet his eyes.

"I hate them, don't you understand? I hate them so much that sometimes I feel like I'm going to explode with it." Her voice was no less fierce because she was speaking in an undertone. "They killed my mother and my sister. Killed our friends and neighbors and hundreds of people just innocently going about their lives. Killed them horribly, for no reason, in a few nightmarish hours. Jo will probably be scarred for life. Physically *and* mentally. Margrit wakes up screaming with nightmares. I know I said I'm all right, but I'm not. I'm *heartsick* with grief, and I'm scared all the time, and I'm angry. I'm so *angry,* Griff. I can't just bow down to them. I can't just go on with my life and pretend it didn't happen. I have to *do* something. For my mother. For Luiza. *I have to.*"

He didn't say anything. But there was a tightness around his eyes and a firmness to his mouth as he looked at her that made her think she might be getting through to him at last.

"Think how you'd feel if it was *your* mother they'd murdered. You'd do something. You know you would."

He grimaced.

"I *will* do something," she said. "If not this, then something. If you don't want my help, fine. It doesn't have to be with you."

Their eyes clashed. He was older, infinitely more experienced, a military officer who she'd already learned was accustomed to being in charge. She, on the other hand, meant every word. She wasn't backing down.

"All right," he said at last. Reluctance weighted every syllable. "There might be a way."

Sibi's eyes brightened. She looked at him expectantly.

"Walk," he ordered, and started off again, pulling her with him. With her hand still tucked in his arm and Ruby ranging in front of them, they continued along the path as it rounded the pond. Ruby tugged at the leash, exhibiting avid interest in the paddling ducks. Sibi's focus was all on Griff as he said, "If we're going to do this, I need your word that you'll do exactly as I tell you."

"I will. I promise."

"You have my mother's book." It was a

statement, not a question, and she nodded. "We can use it as a key."

"A key?"

"I'm not saying I think this is a good idea," he said. "Because I don't. In fact, I think it's a damned bad idea. But I'm willing to give it a try, on a provisional basis, to see how it goes. As long as you do exactly what I tell you."

"I already said I would."

"I know you did." The look he gave her was unsmiling. "We're going to use my mother's book as a cipher. Nobody knows about it except the two of us, so that's about as secure as you can get." He veered off the path, taking her with him across the grass, and stopped at a bench beside the pond. A nearby willow provided a decent amount of dappled shade. The couple in the rowboat were making slow but steady progress around the opposite side of the pond. No one else was in sight. The tall cattails growing at water's edge formed enough of a curtain so that they wouldn't be immediately apparent to anyone approaching, while they could see in every direction. "Sit down and I'll show you how it works."

They sat, and with the aid of a notebook and pencil he pulled from the messenger bag, Griff demonstrated how, by substituting numbers for letters, the text from *My Ántonia* could be used as a code.

"It's always possible that the SD or someone like them might search your house and get hold of anything you write down," he said. "A page of random numbers will look suspicious. What I think we should do is frame each word as an addition problem. Write it vertically, add a plus sign, draw a line under the last number, and add the digits together to get a legitimate sum. When I'm reading it, I'll know to disregard the answers, but no one else will. What you end up with is a code that looks like a notebook of math problems. Which, if you're ever questioned about it, you can claim you do whenever you're feeling anxious, to relax. I seem to recall you telling me that math is one of your favorite subjects. So, if anybody comes looking, it fits."

"If I've got your mother's book, what are you going to use to decode the message?"

"I'll get an identical copy. I know a bookstore that carries old first editions. I was already looking into it when I thought my book was gone forever."

"I'm sorry about that."

"I'm not. Seems like it worked out pretty well. What we've got ourselves here is a code that's going to be next to impossible to break." He put the notebook and pencil back in the messenger bag.

"How do I get the information to you?"

From the look on his face she realized she wasn't going to like the answer.

"You don't, for now. When I'm next in Berlin, we'll get together and I'll look at what you have and then we'll decide how to proceed."

Outrage caused her to sit up straight and glare at him. "What good is that? I may as well just wait and talk to you."

"It keeps you from forgetting anything important. It lets you be useful and at the same time stay safe while the SD is sniffing around your father. And it's practice, in case — well, it's practice. Think about it like learning to swim before you get thrown into an ocean full of sharks."

Her lips compressed.

"You promised to do as I told you, remember?"

"Fine. When will you be back?"

"I don't know exactly."

"Sibi!"

There was no mistaking that voice: Margrit. Sibi started, and glanced around. Through the reeds, she saw her sister pelting down the path. Ruby, whose leash she'd tied to the bench and who'd been lying at her feet, jumped up, tail wagging.

Griff stood. "I've got to go. When I come back, I'll put a bunch of flowers in front of your mother's tree. That'll be our signal. When you see them, come to the church there." He gestured at the Sophienkirche across the street. "Six p.m. that evening, if you can manage it. If not, eight the next morning. I'll be inside waiting for you. Got that?"

On her feet now, too, she nodded. He tugged one of the straggling tendrils that curled around her face by way of farewell.

"Be careful," he said, and walked away.

Of necessity, her attention immediately refocused on Margrit, who was flying toward her.

"Jo's hat came off — some boys pointed at her and said, *'Ugh'* — and she ran home and locked herself in our room and won't come out." Reaching her, Margrit skidded to a panting halt and grabbed her hand, pulling. "You need to come."

"Oh, no," Sibi said as Papa, looking harassed, came into view. A quick glance in the opposite direction reassured her that Griff was rapidly disappearing from sight. Untying Ruby's leash, she handed it to Margrit, who was, as intended, distracted by the charge. "Come on, then."

"Sibi." Papa stopped as they reached him, and ran a harried hand through his hair. "You're needed at home. Your sister —"

"Margrit told me."

"It was going well, and we were leaving, and then the door caught her hat and knocked it off. There were these boys — young boys, maybe nine or ten, and I'm ashamed to say it but I wanted to kill them. She ran off home, and I tried, but she's crying and she won't open her bedroom door and —" He broke off, shaking his head.

"I'll handle it," she said. "Let's go home."

Later, when she'd done what she could to comfort a disconsolate Jo and dinner was over and Mama's locket was safely hidden away, to be brought forth again at a more opportune time, and the two little girls plus Ruby were tucked up in bed, armed with a lie about having overheard two men in the park talking about the ongoing surveillance their colleagues were conducting, she went downstairs to warn Papa about the SD.

30

"Did you hear? The lady pilot — Amelia Earhart — is missing," Ilsa said when she, Heide and Sibi got together for a quick lunch at their favorite outdoor café in the Tiergarten on a Saturday in early July.

The sensational story was all over the newspapers and radio channels, and it was being much talked about everywhere. As it was one of her free days, Sibi was accompanied by Margrit and Jo, who, lured by the prospect of a visit to the zoo where the addition of a new baby elephant to the Oriental Pavilion–inspired Elephant House was the star attraction, had agreed to give going out in public one more try. This time her hat was tied down more securely and cosmetics had been applied to the purple patches of the skin grafts in an attempt to make them less noticeable in case of mishap. The two little girls, not at all unhappily, sat at their very own table so the older ones could talk without them listening in. Both wore their hats despite the shade that dappled the eating area.

In deference to the looks her friends had turned on her when she'd joined them, Sibi had taken her hat off. It lay on the seat beside her, ready to be donned again after lunch was finished.

"My father says her airplane has crashed into the ocean. He says every country with a ship or airplane in that part of the world is out there looking for her, at an enormous cost."

"Can you imagine trying to fly around the world?" Heide shook her head. "I could never do something like that."

"Most likely they ran out of fuel," Sibi said, having discussed the disappearance with her father and listened in as the scientists he worked with argued about it among themselves.

"My mother says it's probably just a publicity stunt, and she'll turn up again soon enough." Heide dismissed the subject with a shrug, and looked at Sibi. "Did Ilsa tell you? We saw Talia in Wertheim's on Tuesday."

"When would I have seen her to tell her? What with one thing —" swallowing a bite of her meal, Ilsa cast a significant look at Jo and Margrit "— and another, she's too busy to even talk on the telephone."

"I'm sorry." Because it was true, Sibi's tone was contrite.

Ilsa brushed her apology off with a gesture. "Don't worry, we understand."

"But back to Talia," Heide said. "They're moving to France. She and her whole family."

"When?" Sibi asked, intrigued.

"In a few weeks. They're packing up now. Her mother doesn't want to go, because all their family is here, but her father's making them. He says Germany is not a good place for Jews anymore."

"I'll get in trouble if my father finds out we stopped to talk to her, so don't go telling everybody you see that we did. He told me I wasn't allowed to talk to her ever again. And you shouldn't, either." Ilsa frowned reprovingly at Heide.

"But why? We've been friends with her since we were little," Sibi protested.

"My father says she and those like her are *Untermenschen.*" Subhuman.

"That's not true," Sibi said, aghast. "You know it's not. We —"

"*Shh,* you'll get us all in trouble." Shushing them with a gesture, Heide glanced nervously around.

"True or not, it's best that they leave," Ilsa said. "Anyway, I have something more important to talk to you about. Friedrich has a friend. He wants to go out with you."

Sibi blinked at the sheer unexpectedness of it. "What?"

Ilsa nodded, grinning. "His name's Wernher Oberth, and he is *cute*. He saw you walking out of the assembly with us when he came to pick us up the last day of school. He's starting at Friedrich Wilhelm University in the fall."

"It's so perfect because you'll be going there, too, in another year, and then you'll both be there together," Heide said.

"Maybe we'll all be there together," Ilsa said. "Although my father says going to university is a waste of time for women. He says we should all embrace marriage and motherhood and produce four children for the glory of the Thousand Year Reich. Fortunately for me, my mother doesn't agree. But about Wernher —" she lowered her voice, and cast a quick glance around at the occupants of the nearby tables to make sure no one was listening "— we're all going to a swing club next Saturday night and he wanted me to ask you along as his date."

"A swing club?" Due to her nearly year-long absence, Sibi had never been to one.

While she'd been gone, they'd sprung up like mushrooms all over Berlin and were now the rage. They were considered decadent, a pastime for wild youth. To go to one, especially as the date of a cute boy who'd specifically asked to meet her . . . she was tempted. Excited at the prospect, even. Or at least, she would have been Before. But now things were different. *Everything* was different. Everything had consequences. The Reich frowned on swing clubs — *verboten* was the word most often associated with them — and with all that was happening in her and her family's life, provoking the ire of anyone (such as the SD) who might be looking at them didn't seem wise. Add to that the fact that most of her free time was given over to the little girls and, well —

She shook her head. "I can't. But it was nice of him — and you — to ask."

They tried to persuade her, but she continued to refuse, and eventually they gave up.

"For now," Ilsa warned as they parted. "But don't think this is our last word on the subject. You can't live like a nun forever."

"What did she want you to do?" Jo asked as Sibi herded her sisters away from her friends and onto the tram that would take them to the zoo.

"Go on a date with some friend of her boyfriend."

"Are you going to go?" Jo asked the question as they settled into their seat, but both girls instantly made her the focus of their complete attention.

Sibi shook her head.

"Why not?" Margrit asked.

"It's because of us, isn't it?" Jo's tone turned earnest as she continued with, "You can't sacrifice your life for us, you know. We don't want you to."

"Yes, we do," Margrit said before Sibi could reply, and frowned at Jo. "We *need* her. You know we do. Otherwise we'd only have Papa to take care of us."

The little girls looked at each other. Sibi was between them, and as their gazes met across her she could feel the slight shudder with which Jo acknowledged the force of Margrit's argument.

"But it's not fair to her," Jo said to Margrit. "She —"

"I'm not going anywhere." Sibi intervened before the discussion could deteriorate, which Margrit's darkening frown warned was getting ready to happen. "And I'm not sacrificing my life, either. I didn't want to go on this particular date. When I get asked out on a date I want to go on, I'll go."

"Promise?" Jo asked.

"Yes," Sibi said.

Then the tram reached their stop, and they got off. In the excitement of seeing the baby elephant and all the other animals, then visiting the aquarium, the topic was forgotten.

The remainder of July was busy for all of them. Margrit had her birthday, and much fuss was made of her as she turned six. Jo had various doctor's appointments, which left her discouraged, because the one thing she wanted — for the skin grafts to heal to the point that they were unnoticeable — the doctors couldn't give her a time table for, or even promise her would ever happen. Sibi spent most of her free time with her sisters. Four days a week she went with her father to Heeresversuchanstalt Kummersdorf, a top-secret Wehrmacht research facility not far from Berlin, where he was part of the liquid-fuel rocket program and she acted as his assistant. Papa's workweek was six days long, but both he and she thought that Jo and Margrit needed more of her time than the typical Nazi sixty-hour workweek allowed, so hers was cut short by two days.

As she had predicted, her job consisted of following him around and taking down the notes he dictated, and listening to his ruminations as he worked through problems he encountered out loud. In the process she learned a great deal about liquid-fuel rockets — not the least of which was that potato schnapps could be distilled into rocket fuel — and the difficulties associated with getting them to fly. She also learned a great deal about Heeresversuchanstalt Kummersdorf in general. When she came across something she thought was important, she would sit down that night and write out a coded message to Griff in the notebook she kept for that purpose. Although the process was laborious at first, she found that before long converting words into math problems by way of *My Ántonia* became almost second nature to her.

A dedicated train ran from Berlin to the facility with a commute of forty-five minutes each way, so the days when she went to work with her father were long ones. Fortunately, she didn't have to worry about her sisters while she was gone. Frau Skeller agreed to come in full-time, and so was there in the house while she was absent. Also, after consulting with their schools, Papa had decreed that Jo and Margrit should have lessons at home during those same four days that Sibi worked so that they could move on with their respective classes in the fall instead of repeating the year. He hired a teacher for them to that end, so the little girls were busy, too.

One side effect of the commute was that Papa noticed her random math problems notebook — not the coded one she compiled for Griff, which she kept at home, but the one she made up to lull the suspicions of any investigators who might be watching, and took with her pretty much wherever she went — and scoffed at the simplicity of the math therein. Instead he set her to solving some of the problems he and his team faced, such as, for example, how to determine what kind of engine to use to lift various payloads into space. As a result, the notebook contained an interesting mix of the simple and the complex that was guaranteed, she thought, to lull the suspicions of the most skeptical investigator.

As she worked out various calculations while the train rattled over the tracks, the thick woods and sparkling blue lakes of the countryside to the south of Berlin passed by, largely unseen by her, outside the windows. Papa maintained a running discourse on everything — from Newton's

Third Law of Motion (*For every action there is an equal and opposite reaction*), to how rockets worked (basically, hot gases shot out the back end of a metal cylinder at enormous speed, propelling the rocket forward) — so the trips to and from work were an education in and of themselves.

"You have the mind for this, Sibi," Papa said one evening as they were nearing the end of their train ride back to Berlin. The car they were in rocked back and forth, the dim overhead light swayed in time to the rocking and the rhythmic clicking of the wheels filled the air. She had just impressed him by correctly calculating the amount of thrust needed to achieve liftoff for a particular rocket they were building, and he sat back on the hard bench seat — they always occupied a private compartment so he could work — and eyed her with satisfaction as she sat across from him. "If you weren't a girl, I would very much encourage you to follow in my footsteps."

"What does me being a girl have to do with it?" Sibi was tired. Her fingers hurt from all the notes she'd been taking at his behest, and her brain hurt, too, from all the thinking. She bristled at him.

He shrugged. He'd been inside so much over the last few weeks that his face had lost much of its usual ruddiness, and his hair was slicked down close to his head so that it appeared straight, shiny and almost dark. He looked older than when they'd arrived home and, like Sibi, tired. "Girls grow up to be women, and women want a family. It's hard to work the kind of hours this field requires and have one."

"*You* have a family."

"I do, yes, and a lovely one, too." He smiled at her, but she thought his eyes were tinged with sadness. "But we both know that until — recently — I played only a small role in it. Your mother would get upset with me because I worked such long hours and was so rarely home, but that's what this profession demands. As she would say, it's not so much a profession as an obsession." He shook his head. "To be so focused on work is not a life I would want for you."

"Was that what caused the problems, between you and Mama?" Once Sibi would not have dared to ask him such a thing, but having had to come together to face the outside threat posed by the Nazi Party, they now operated almost as a team. Their mutual grief coupled with a shared concern for the little girls plus the hours they'd spent working together had fostered a rapport between them that had been lacking before.

He looked at her without speaking for a moment. She wasn't sure he was going to answer, but finally he did.

"That was part of it, certainly." He seemed to reflect. "But it wasn't entirely that. She was so warm, Marina. So lively and sparkling and full of love for everyone. She was Basque to her core, and to be here, in Germany, didn't suit her. Over time, the different way of life leached the happiness from her. Once the Nazis took power, their —" he hesitated, shooting an instinctive glance toward the door to make sure it was firmly shut; to be overheard speaking negatively of the Reich was dangerous "— way of looking at things, and doing things, appalled her. She wanted me to leave, to start over somewhere else, but how could I do that? My work is here. I had a living to make, a wife and children to support." He broke off, made a face. "We started to quarrel, as I'm sure you know. And because home had become a place of strife, I worked more, and stayed away more. By the time your mother went to visit your *amona,* having the house to myself was almost a relief. But then I started to miss her, miss you girls, miss our family. The house felt cold and empty. I asked her to come back a number of times. She kept putting me off."

380

His eyes met hers. "I'm not sure she ever would have come home."

Sibi said nothing, because she was not sure, either. The truth, which she never meant to tell him, was that Mama had been happy in Guernica, in her old home, in her old life. And she had not wanted to return.

"The moral of the story, if you would learn from my mistake, is that love is harder to find than work." He tried for a humorous smile. It didn't quite reach his eyes. "If I had it to do over again, I would have done as Marina wished and put my family first. And that is what I want you to do, someday."

To her consternation Sibi discovered that she had a lump in her throat and could not reply, so she nodded. And then they both, with what she thought might have been mutual relief, turned their attention back to the vexed problem of getting rockets that weighed approximately as much as the train car they were riding in to soar into the air and fly, and the math that, if they did it right, if they found the one perfect solution, might allow that to happen.

The next morning, they left the house shortly after six, as they always did. The day was already warm but not yet hot, and the pale ball of the newly risen sun was just beginning to break above the horizon.

Walking down the front steps, Sibi glanced toward the park and Mama's tree for any sign of flowers left at its base, but there was nothing. Once again, Griff had not come.

"You know, maybe it's not the fuel that's causing the engine to knock." His tone thoughtful, Papa came down the steps behind her. He was talking about the latest rocket he was having trouble with, she knew. "If we tighten the bolts on the cylinder block —"

He broke off as two big black Mercedes, with a screech of brakes, slammed to a halt in front of the house. Four gestapo agents jumped out and swarmed toward them.

Sibi was still frozen in place with shock when the lead agent barked, "Dr. Helinger? Fräulein Helinger? You will come with us, please."

31

"Guernica," Herr Kraus said, his voice tight, and gestured at a large photograph propped on a table behind him. "This man perpetuates the lie with his art, and the whole world is once again up in arms because of it. The only counter for a lie is the truth."

Sibi's pulse, which had been pounding at a deafening rate since the gestapo had bundled her and her father into two separate automobiles and driven off with them, thundered in her ears.

She'd been afraid that the government had somehow discovered her intention of passing on information to Griff. Her notebook filled with random math was in her bag, and her immediate fear had been that it would be discovered and she would be questioned about it. That hadn't happened; no one had bothered with her bag, or the notebook. Instead she'd found herself being escorted alone to Herr Kraus's office in the Ordens-palais, only to be confronted about Guernica, which was only slightly less terrifying.

What lie was he talking about? Surely — *please, God* — not the one she'd told about what had happened there.

"I'm sorry, Herr Kraus, I don't understand." The office was well-lit and pleasantly cool. From the gurgle of water passing through the radiator beneath the window and the slightly musty smell, she guessed that the boiler system had been changed over to run cold water through it as a defense against the current heat wave. The painting of the goose — she couldn't remember its name — had been replaced on the easel with a watercolor of a different bird, a woodpecker of some sort, she thought. Another of his paintings, without a doubt.

"Look at this." He jabbed at the glass covering the photograph with a blunt forefinger.

His desk stood between them. Sibi didn't want to get closer, so she leaned across it, peering at the photograph.

It was of a painting, and the painting was a nightmarish jumble of images: a screaming woman with a child, apparently dead, in her arms; a fallen man crying out in agony as he clutched a broken sword; a bull and a horse; disembodied faces, angular shapes, all rendered in somber tones of black, white and gray.

"Guernica," Kraus said again, this time with loathing, and from what came next she understood that was the name of the painting. "By Pablo Picasso. Commissioned by the Republican government of Spain. Just placed on display in the Spanish Pavilion at the International Exposition in Paris. They are saying he painted it to reflect the horror of what our Condor Legion did to the 'poor defenseless town.' " Those last words mocked. He slammed his fist on the table, making the photograph — and Sibi — jump. "The damned ugly thing's eleven feet tall by twenty-five feet long — the size of a wall. What poor excuse for an artist paints something like that?"

Unable to think of anything to say, Sibi said nothing. Herr Kraus turned his beady-eyed gaze on her.

"Since that monstrosity appeared, newspapers all over the world have been besieging us for comments. One reporter for the *New York Times* actually had the temerity to approach Dr. Goebbels as he walked to his house last evening to demand that he 'tell the truth' about our involvement in the 'massacre.' His first reaction was to order that the offending journalist be expelled from the country, but upon reflection it was decided that the best response would be to come together and get the truth out in front of the international community *again. You* are our eyewitness, Fräulein Helinger. Your description of what you saw is vital to preventing our enemies from tarnishing Germany's reputation any further. You'll be meeting with a select group of journalists at ten o'clock this morning to tell them what you saw. They will undoubtedly ask questions, and you will answer them. Directly afterward, we've scheduled a live radio broadcast so that your story can be heard in your own words by any who care to listen. Later this afternoon, you'll be filmed for inclusion in a newsreel about the tragedy."

Everything from the harshness of his tone to the flintiness of his eyes told her that it wasn't a request. It was an order.

She didn't just feel cool. She felt cold. All over.

"I'm honored to help in any way I can, Herr Kraus." There was nothing else she could say. She only hoped her voice didn't sound as hollow to him as it did to her own ears.

"You look nervous, Fräulein Helinger." He studied her. The glint in his eyes made her think of a predator. The curve of his mouth was cruel. "*Are* you nervous?"

It hit her then in a stunning blow: he knew she was lying. He had to know. He might not have known it when he'd come to her house that first night, but by now a man in his position would have learned the truth. He *knew* that German airplanes had destroyed Guernica and murdered over sixteen hundred innocent people. He *knew* that the Condor Legion was guilty as charged, and that the international outrage directed at the Third Reich was justified. And if he knew all that, then he also knew that the tale she'd told him, and Dr. Goebbels, and the *Staatssekretär,* and the president of the *Reichspressekammer,* was a complete web of lies.

Her stomach dropped like a rock. Her palms began to sweat. She had to stop herself from clenching her hands into fists. She had to remind herself to continue to breathe normally.

He knew.

Her mind reeled as she tried to make sense of what was happening and at the same time figure a way out. Burgeoning fear made it difficult to think clearly.

One thought clawed its way to the surface and stayed there: to confess to what she'd done would very likely prove fatal.

He was waiting with the patience of a cat at a mouse hole for her reply. He'd asked if she was nervous, and she was sure that something of her agitation must be apparent in her face or body language. The only thing to do was to play into it, and continue to act her part in the charade until he called her on it, or until some avenue of escape occurred to her. If it did. *Why was he pretending to believe her lies?* Was it a trap or —

She said, "I . . . admit I am somewhat uncomfortable at the idea of speaking before a large audience. I have never done so."

"A common fear, I believe." Placing both hands flat on his desk, he leaned toward her. Cold and hard, his eyes held hers. "I trust you're prepared to do what you must in the interests of your country."

She felt as if a giant hand was squeezing her heart. "I — yes, of course, Herr Kraus."

"Excellent." He straightened. His expression changed, and something about it brought her to a second shocking realization: he didn't care. He knew she was lying, had been lying all along, and he *didn't care.* Not as long as she acted the part and told the lies he wanted her to tell. "You have no need to worry about what you will say. My secretary has prepared a script for you along with a set of questions you are most likely to be asked and the answers you will give. Please study them, and stick as closely to the precise wording as possible. We don't want any mistakes. Do we?"

His tone was pleasant, but it was impossible to miss the barely veiled threat. Her heart thumped. Gooseflesh raced over her skin.

She shook her head. "No, Herr Kraus."

"I'm glad we agree. You may, of course, read directly from the script for the radio program." He came out from behind his desk, and gestured for her to precede him to the door. "My secretary will take you to a room where you can study, and provide you with the script. I will come for you myself at nine thirty. That will give you —" he consulted his watch "— two hours. I trust that is sufficient time?"

"Yes, Herr Kraus." She took a quick, fortifying breath as he looked past her to reach for the knob with the intent of opening the door for her. Taking her courage in both hands, she said, "My father was picked up in front of our house at the same time I was. May I ask why, and where he is?"

To ask such questions of him was bold,

and as his eyes slewed around to her his expression reflected that. She knew it would be unwise in the extreme to assume that because he was now party to her lie that she was in any way safe from reprisal. But if they were entering into some hellish bargain, the safety of her family was an implied part of his end of the deal. And she wanted him to know that.

He said, "We felt that, given your participation in today's events, some enterprising reporter might seek out your father to question him. It is better that he be under our protection for the day. He will be instructed in what to say if he should be approached in the future, and if all goes well, you will be reunited with him when you return home tonight."

If all goes well: another threat. There was no need for it. She'd already come to the fork in the road, and chosen which path to take.

"I see," she said, and he smiled at her as, with a meeting of their eyes, each acknowledged their unspoken understanding. Then he pulled the door open and called for his secretary.

Sibi arrived home at not much past the usual time, driven by the same gestapo agents who had taken her away that morning. It continued to be blistering hot, and with the automobile windows rolled down the sounds and sights and smells of Berlin at its busiest surrounded her. During this return trip she was tired rather than terrified, and the agents treated her with more respect than they had shown before.

She was greeted by Frau Skeller with the news that her father wasn't yet there, which was concerning, although not truly alarming because she'd done everything requested of her, and Herr Kraus, who'd stayed with her throughout the day's proceedings, had dismissed her once again by professing himself pleased with her. She'd meant to go directly to her room and change her clothes and perhaps lie down for a minute because her head was throbbing, but Margrit, Jo and Ruby pounced on her before she could get upstairs. After affording her just enough time to bathe her face, which was still caked with the cosmetics the filmmaker's team had insisted on, they dragged her out into the garden with them. There she was pressed into service holding one end of a jump rope while her sisters took turns and Ruby barked in exuberant, head-splitting accompaniment. In the end she wound up taking a turn, too, and by the time darkness had fallen and dinner was over and the little girls were ensconced in front of the radio listening to their favorite program, she would have been feeling significantly better if only Papa had come home.

But he hadn't.

She was in the sitting room, curled up in a corner of the green velvet sofa riffling through the pages of the latest fashion magazine *Modenschau,* and the little girls were long in bed, when at last he walked in the door. Jumping to her feet, she hurried to greet him. A hundred questions crowded her lips, but he shook his head, pressed a finger to his lips and cast a significant look up the stairs. Remembering how easy it was to hear everything that was said in this room from the little girls' room, she followed him to his study. Standing just inside the door with her hands clasped anxiously in front of her, she waited while he sank heavily into his chair, lit the lamp on his desk and looked at her.

"I heard you on the radio," he said. "You came across very well. I was told that you also were interviewed by reporters, and made a newsreel."

She had no patience for talking about her own day right at the moment. "What happened to you?"

"I won't be going back to my post at the university. I've been offered a position with the Heereswaffenamt, which I have accepted."

The Heereswaffenamt was the Army Weapons Office. "But . . . you love being a professor at the university."

With a quick grimace he both acknowledged and dismissed the importance of that. "The pay is better. And if I miss interacting with my students, at least I will have more time for my research."

"How did this come about?"

"I was taken to meet with Generalleutnant Kurt Liese. He invited me to work full-time on the army's rocket development program. From now on I'll be based at Heeresversuchanstalt Kummersdorf. Oh, and I've joined the Nazi Party. It was a condition of my employment."

Sibi looked at him in mute distress. No matter how favorably he tried to present the change to her, she knew it was not what he would have wished for.

"We're going to be all right," he said, apparently correctly interpreting her expression. "I get to work on my rockets and you get to finish school and go on to university. Your sisters get to continue their education. There will be no big changes for any of us."

"As long as we do what they want."

"Yes."

Her voice, though still low, turned urgent. "Papa . . . he knows I'm lying. About what happened in Guernica. Herr Kraus knows I'm lying. He knows the truth, and he wants me to keep on lying, anyway, because it suits their purpose. And if he knows, Dr. Goebbels and the rest of them must know."

His brows snapped together. "What makes you think they know?"

She made an impatient sound. "Because they must. I worked it out today, while Herr Kraus was telling me what the Ministry of Propaganda requires from me. I could see it in his eyes, and then when I thought about it, it became clear. Obviously the Luftwaffe knows what it did. The Condor Legion knows what it did. They know the real truth, and if they know it the top echelon of the government must know it, as well. Don't you see?"

His frown deepened as he mulled it over. Then he nodded, slowly. "Yes. You're right. They must know."

Her last, faint hope that perhaps she'd misconstrued something, missed some salient fact that pointed to an alternate conclusion, died. She tried to keep the quiver of panic that assailed her from being reflected in her voice. "What do we do?"

His hands steepled. He looked at her over them. "Nothing. We do nothing. We live our lives, and do our jobs, and keep our heads down. When asked about Guernica, you stick to the story you have told. When required to go to Nazi Party meetings, I will go to Nazi Party meetings. We do what we have to do until the storm passes. And the thing to remember, daughter, is that the storm always passes."

Her mother's face appeared in Sibi's mind's eye, as vivid as a photograph, entirely unbidden, along with the memory of the conversation she'd had with him on the train. If Papa had only done what Mama had wanted, years ago, Mama and Luiza would be alive now and everything, their whole world, would be different. They would be together, all of them, the entire family. They would be safe.

She said, "Why don't we leave?"

"Leave?"

"Like Mama wanted. Leave Germany. Go to France. Go somewhere. Anywhere but here."

He looked at her for a long moment. She could see that he was turning the idea over in his mind. Hope for the future, fear of the unknown, dread coupled with a sense of infinite possibility, all came together to quicken her heartbeat and form a knot in her stomach as she waited.

He dashed it all with a single shake of his head. "It's not possible. You know a truth that they're desperate to keep hidden. They won't willingly let you leave for fear of their secret getting out. I know secrets, too. About their rocket program and . . . other things. We could, perhaps, say we were going on a visit, all of us, and board a train to France or Spain. But we would have to leave everything behind. We would have to start completely over once we reached our destination, and we would be continually looking over our shoulders in case they decided to come for us there and silence us permanently, and we could never come back. And if they suspected what we meant to do, if we were to try to leave and fail, and be apprehended, the consequences would be catastrophic. We would face prison, or worse." He shook his head. "The risk is too great, with no certainty we would be better off. After all, your mother took you girls to Spain, and look what happened there."

As a collage of memories from that terrible night assailed her, Sibi took a deep breath. He was right. Guernica had been, for Marina, an escape. An escape that, in the end, had gone horribly wrong. That was the problem with choosing a path: one never knew where even the safest-seeming of them would lead.

32

July turned to August, and August brought with it more war. In Spain, the most notable of the battles was at Santander, where Franco's Nationalists overran the town and the province, and captured 60,000 Republican soldiers. Japan and China were at each other's throats now, too, and bloody battles in Tianjin and Beiping ended in a Japanese victory. The Sino-Japanese War, as it was called, like the war in Spain, raged on, with no end to either in sight. The newspapers and radio channels were full of stories from both conflicts. The atrocity, as what had happened in Guernica was now being called, was still front-page news, thanks to Picasso's primal scream of a painting that continued to be a central attraction at the world's fair. Newsreels and graphic photographs of the town's destruction circulated worldwide, resulting in a continual stirring up of the pot of international outrage.

Sibi found her image and her testimony being used frequently as a counterpoint to the truth. Called in by the Ministry of Propaganda to give more lying interviews, forced to keep up the lies to her friends and acquaintances and even to do her best to convince her sisters that the Republicans were behind what had happened in Guernica lest they should be asked about it and ruin them all with a wrong answer, her shame and guilt grew to the point where she could no longer look at the newspapers displayed in their red cases on the street corners because a headline might contain some reference to Guernica, or go to the cinema for fear of seeing herself proclaiming the innocence of her mother's and sister's murderers in a newsreel. Her friends, who did go to the cinema, started calling her *our movie star,* but Sibi shuddered inwardly every time she was forced to think about what she had done.

In Berlin, as in the rest of Germany, the Nazi Party stepped up its campaign against Jews. In their own park, the park with their mother's tree, where she and the girls and Ruby frequently walked, two of the wood-and-iron benches were painted bright yellow overnight and labeled Only for Jews. The rest of the benches remained unpainted and had been stenciled with the words Jews Prohibited. New signs in the park ordered Jews to sit only on the yellow benches on pain of arrest. The area had a large number of Jewish residents, and to see such evidence of the government's worsening persecution of their neighbors horrified her. Sibi hurried her sisters home upon discovering the outrage, only to learn later from her father that his friend and colleague Dr. Meyer had been summarily fired that day along with three other professors Papa had worked with at the university. Their offense? They were Jewish.

"What will they do?" Sibi asked Papa. Bluff and good-humored, Dr. Meyer had been a frequent visitor to their house over the years, and she liked him. He had a wife and two sons, and she worried for them.

"I don't know. There are private employers . . ." His voice trailed off and he shook his head. Given the current political climate, they both knew that it was unlikely that anyone would hire a Jewish scientist for fear of bringing the government's wrath down upon themselves. "Albert is a good scientist. A good *man.* This is a loss for the university. This is a loss for us all." Still shaking his head, he went into his study. When Sibi checked on him a short time later, he was immersed in his work.

It was, she knew, his panacea in times of trouble.

The six weeks of summer break ended, and school started up again. It was Sibi's *Oberprima* year, her final one before university, and in the Before she had looked forward to it with excitement and enthusiasm. Now, without her mother, without Luiza, the year stretched out before her as a gray slog and she tackled it with the same grim resolve she seemed to need to bring to bear on every aspect of her life these days.

Margrit, small spitfire that she was, was undismayed by her new classmates and teachers and the unfamiliar regimentation of the German school system and marched through the days with aplomb. Jo, more sensitive by nature and now rendered acutely self-conscious by her injuries, wilted a little bit more every day as her fellow students' eyes lingered on, and tongues whispered about, her damaged face.

The sun hat, obviously, was not an option for school. After consulting with Jo's doctors, Sibi tried her best to mitigate the noticeability of the skin grafts with specially prescribed cosmetics and a camouflaging hairstyle. The latter was made more difficult because Jo's hair was only a little more than

401

chin-length. A deep side part that allowed a heavy sweep of her hair to fall across the left side of her face helped to a degree, but even coupled with the cosmetics it was not enough to keep Jo from becoming a meek and shrinking presence whose main goal seemed to be staying out of the way of everyone who wasn't family.

September found Berlin in a state of whirlwind excitement as the city prepared for a state visit from the Italian prime minister, former teacher and newspaper editor Benito Mussolini. The previous year, Il Duce, as he was called, had joined forces with Hitler as the two entered into the Rome-Berlin Axis agreement, cementing the "friendship" between the German and Italian peoples. In anticipation of the visit, streets were swept and washed, all public places were extensively landscaped and so many enormous German and Italian flags were hung that the sound of them flapping and snapping in the breeze became as ubiquitous as the rumble of traffic.

Early in the month, Jo had her tenth birthday, which they celebrated quietly at home. Although in years past, because her birthday fell during the school year, Jo had taken in treats to share with her classmates to mark the occasion, this year she begged off doing so. When questioned, she shrugged and said she was too old for that, but Sibi wasn't fooled. The truth was, Jo didn't want to attract any extra attention to herself.

It was a troubling situation, but other than surround Jo with love, and hope that time would help, Sibi didn't know what to do about it.

Because she was interested, Papa continued to talk through the problems he was having in his work with her. She also took charge of the notes he scribbled down on scraps of paper as ideas came to him.

Toward the end of the month, the Society of German Scientists and Physicians held another meeting. Dr. Langsdorff and Dr. Busch were in attendance, as were several more men whose voices Sibi didn't recognize. Dr. Meyer was not present — she hadn't expected him to be — and she said a little prayer for him and his family even as she listened from upstairs while the men talked. She was alarmed to learn of the existence of a top-secret program devoted solely to the development of chemical weapons. What alarmed her even more was that the program was located in the spectacular Spandau Citadel right there in Berlin.

"I hear the latest gas they've developed is called Tabun," one of the men she didn't know said. "Because it's so deadly it should be taboo."

"It's true. A small amount can kill thousands in just a few minutes," Dr. Langsdorff confirmed. "They combined the molecules of phosphorus and cyanide, and what they came up with is unbelievably toxic. If it's developed correctly, and applied in sufficient quantities, it could theoretically take out whole armies without a shot being fired."

"You've actually seen it at work?" Papa asked.

"I have this directly from its inventor, Gerard Schrader, a chemist who's an old friend. He's 25,000 marks the richer for its invention," Dr. Langsdorff replied. "It was 50,000 marks, but he had to split it with a colleague."

"Oh-ho, they're paying chemists a bounty now?" Dr. Busch let loose with his deep laugh. "How do I get into that program?"

The conversation devolved into levity, but Sibi had already heard enough to send her hurrying for her notebook. Translating words into math via *My Ántonia* slowed her up a little, but she got the conversation down on paper while the vital elements were still fresh in her mind. But for days afterward her skin crawled every time she thought about a gas with the power to kill thousands being developed right there in the city.

The question she couldn't get out of her mind was, why?

The next day, Monday the twenty-seventh, was remarkable for two things: having spent the previous three days touring Germany, Prime Minister Mussolini arrived by train in Berlin. The welcome afforded him was unprecedented. The entire city turned out. Some 60,000 soldiers lined the streets, standing three-deep in unbroken rows, giving the Nazi salute in unison as the automobiles carrying Il Duce and *der Führer* went by. Packed in behind the soldiers, crowds of citizens cheered. The sun was low in the sky as the procession passed through the Brandenburg Gate, and the magnificent fountains that had been installed for the occasion shot sparkling streams of colored water high in the air. On Unter den Linden, four rows of enormous white columns crowned with golden Roman eagles created a dazzling display. That night Il Duce was to be feted at a state banquet in his honor. The following day, September 28, had been declared a national holiday, and all Berliners were expected to participate in welcoming the Italian dictator.

Of more interest to Sibi, however, was the second remarkable thing: a large bouquet of purple and white flowers rested in the grass at the base of her mother's tree.

It lacked only fifteen minutes of six when Sibi got home from taking her place with her classmates as part of the cheering crowd, which as an *Oberprima* gymnasium student she was required to do. Most of the population of Berlin had been let off work early in honor of Il Duce's presence in their city, but that only freed them to participate in creating the spectacle with which *der Führer* hoped to dazzle Il Duce and then — in her case, anyway — battle her way onto a packed tram and through the resulting traffic gridlock, which made her later getting home than she would otherwise have been.

She'd almost given up hope that Griff would come, but still she made it a twice daily ritual to glance toward the park, and her mother's tree: when she left home in the morning and then again in the afternoon when she returned.

She was so used to seeing nothing besides tree and grass that, when the blooms registered on her consciousness, she had to do a double take to be certain that the flowers were really there.

As she ascertained that they were, indeed,

there, her lips curved into a smile and her pulse quickened. Tired no longer, she hurried into the house to make sure her sisters were fine — they were, they were in the garden with Ruby — and that Frau Skeller was able to stay with them until either she returned or Papa got home. Frau Skeller agreed to stay, and with the excuse that she had to meet some friends about the part they were to play in the next day's festivities — they had been assigned to each paint and hold up a single letter in a series spelling out Berlinisches Gymnasium Welcomes Il Duce — she ran upstairs, grabbed her coded notebook, stuffed it into her bag, took a quick moment to run a brush through her hair and apply some lipstick and practically flew out the door.

A few minutes later, she was on the other side of the park. With one more glance around to make sure she wasn't being followed — she had no idea if her father was still under surveillance, or if that surveillance might extend to her, but she was cautious nonetheless — she hurried up the steps of the Sophienkirche.

Pushing through the heavy double doors, enveloped by the subtle smell of incense, she paused just inside as her eyes adjusted to the gloom of the sanctuary. Light diffused through gorgeous stained-glass windows took on mellow shades of rose and blue. The intricately carved high ceiling, the galleries looking down on the nave, created an impression of a massive space. Several people sat in the red-upholstered pews, heads bowed in silent contemplation or prayer. A glance around confirmed that Griff was not among them.

Then she saw him, walking down the left outer aisle toward her, tall and square-jawed and almost unfamiliar in a double-breasted gray suit with a briefcase and a black fedora in one hand. He spotted her and lifted a hand in acknowledgment. A warmth instantly sprang up inside her and expanded until she feared she must be glowing like the sun. Her heart beat faster and as he reached her she broke into what felt like a ridiculously huge smile.

Hello, friend.

"You're looking very distinguished," she whispered by way of a greeting. It wasn't exactly what she'd intended to say to him after so long, but his unaccustomed dapperness surprised her. It also made her feel slightly self-conscious about the frumpiness of her own attire — the gray skirt, white blouse, short black jacket, white ankle socks and flat black oxfords — that she was still

408

wearing from school.

"I have somewhere to go later." Returning her smile with a wry one of his own, he caught her arm and turned her around, taking her with him back out through the door she'd just entered. One look at his face told her not to bother to ask about the "somewhere."

The evening was crisp, and the smell of autumn hung in the air. The setting sun gave the light a deep golden tinge. As he turned them left into one of the large cemeteries that flanked the church, long shadows reached out toward them from the tall monuments and elaborate headstones that marked the final resting places of the dead.

Griff's voice resumed its normal volume as he added, "And you're looking very nice yourself."

"Very nice?" She wrinkled her nose at him. Intensely blue against the tan of his skin, his eyes twinkled at her obvious disdain for his compliment, and she was struck anew by just how handsome he was.

"Very *pretty,*" he clarified, and flicked the tip of her nose with a teasing forefinger.

The avuncular nature of the gesture earned him a frown. He was treating her like a child, which she was not.

"I'm seventeen, you know," she reminded him tartly. Their footsteps crunched on fallen leaves as they walked past the memorial to the poet Anna Louise Karsch and around a pillared marble mausoleum that looked to be about a hundred years old. She realized that he was steering her toward the glass-walled gazebo that was the centerpiece of this section of the cemetery.

"I remember. Just so you're aware, that's not as old as you seem to think it is."

"It's old enough." Her voice was flat. She had a feeling about where this conversation was going, and she didn't like it.

"Old enough for what?"

"Anything I decide to do."

They reached the gazebo, and went up the two shallow steps that led inside. It was the size of a small room, with a stone floor and stone benches, and a domed roof. Tall bushes in the process of turning a blazing red ringed the structure, providing privacy, and she realized that this was why he had chosen it. If any eyes were indeed watching, or ears listening, they wouldn't be able to see or hear them inside this outdoor sanctuary.

"Your sisters all right?"

She nodded as they sat down together on one of the benches. She could feel the coldness of the stone through the wool of her skirt. "What about Iverson and your crew?"

"Haven't seen them for a while. They were fine last I heard."

"The papers all say that Franco's winning."

"The Nationalists are better organized. And they have better weapons, and more support."

"So, yes."

"For the moment at least."

"Where have you been, anyway?" she asked. They were angled toward one another, and he was close enough so that their knees brushed. "I was beginning to be afraid you weren't coming back. I was even starting to think that *maybe* you'd asked me to write down important things I learned in a coded notebook just to keep me out of trouble, with no intention of using it or me."

He didn't say anything.

Her brows snapped together. "That's it, isn't it? You were just jollying me along."

"I'm here, aren't I?" Griff's expression, like his tone, had turned grim.

"What does that mean?"

"It means that I have real reservations about allowing a seventeen-year-old girl to put her life on the line by playing at being a spy."

She'd known it. "Our countries aren't at war with each other. In fact, America isn't involved in a war at all. You're staying neutral, remember? Anyway, I thought you weren't a spy."

"I don't think your government is going to be impressed with those fine distinctions if they should catch you passing information on to me."

"Maybe you should hear some of the information I was able to gather before you make up your mind."

Her hands rested in her lap. He picked one up, held it between both of his. Hers was slender-fingered and cold, his were large and warm.

"Sibi, look —"

He was, she could tell, in the process of trying to let her down easy. *Not in a million years.*

"Have you ever heard of Tabun?" she asked fiercely. "It's a deadly gas created by a top-secret chemical weapons program at the Spandau Citadel. It's so toxic it can kill thousands of people in minutes." She pulled her hand from his, and reached into her bag for her notebook. "Papa's been moved from the university to work for the Heereswaffenamt. I have access to his notes, and he tells me a lot about what's happening at

Heeresversuchanstalt Kummersdorf. His team was able to get an A-3 rocket aloft with a LOX/ethanol engine. That's *important*. There's a lot more that's important, and it's all in here." She held up the notebook. "Do you want it, or not?"

He took it from her, thumbing through the pages while she watched. Math problems filled them, written out exactly as he'd instructed.

"You can't get the information I can give you anywhere else," she said.

He looked at her, his mouth tight. "You think I don't know that? That's the only reason I'm even considering this. Germany's engaged in a massive rearmament program, and we desperately need to know what they're doing. But I'm not willing to let you get yourself killed in the process."

"Don't you see, the fact that I *am* a seventeen-year-old girl is actually an advantage. No one will suspect me."

Glancing at the notebook he held, he grimaced. "If they do —"

"They won't. I'll make sure of it."

He rubbed the back of his neck, made an exasperated sound under his breath, then gave her a hard look. "If you feel the least bit endangered, you destroy whatever materials you have. Everything. Including my mother's book. If I tell you to stop, that it's over, then you stop. Right then. You have no in-person contact with anyone but me. You tell no one, and I mean *no one,* what you're doing. Do you understand?"

"Yes." He was going to let her do it. He wasn't happy about it, but he was agreeing. A rush of adrenaline made her pulse speed up. She *needed* to do this. For Mama and Luiza, and Talia and her neighbors who could only sit on the yellow benches and . . . so many. But most of all, she realized with a blinding flash of insight, for herself. To knuckle down to the monsters who had killed without conscience or mercy, to stay silent and blindly accept the injustices that were multiplying by leaps and bounds in front of her — that would destroy something inside her soul. To fight back in this, her own small way, might not be much, but it was something.

"We'll try it. Temporarily." He put the notebook in his briefcase, then stood up, pulled her to her feet and pointed through the glass. "See that reclamation bin?"

The one the man had dropped the bag in. It was meant for paper and rags, she knew. The previous year, the so-called Four-Year Plan had been implemented that called for all reclaimable materials to be collected and reused for the good of the Reich; as an example, every Wednesday evening, milk bottles and other glass containers were set out, lining the street like good little soldiers until they were picked up by volunteers under the aegis of the Commissioner for Secondary Materials. All were called to do their part to, as the slogan put it, "help us make Germany independent."

"Yes," she said. Griff stood slightly behind her with both of them facing the street, and she had to turn her head and look up at him to meet his eyes.

"I want you to start dropping things off in there. Once a week or so. A bag full of rags, paper, whatever you can come up with, bring it here and put it in the bin. Make it a habit, so that anyone who should happen to be watching gets accustomed to you doing that. As far as the world is concerned, it's part of your routine. Every two months, on the first day of the month, the bag you drop off will have one of your notebooks in it. Somebody will pick it up and get it to me. December first for the first notebook, February first for the second — you get the idea."

She turned to face him. "Don't you think every month would be better? In case anything is urgent."

"I'm going to give you another way to get anything that's urgent to me. The notebooks are for regular reports about whatever you think I should know. The two-month interval is intended to throw any surveillance off the scent. After a few weeks of rummaging through your bag of 'secondary materials,' as *der Führer* calls them, any agent assigned to the task will decide he has better things to do than look through your trash."

"You think the SD is still watching?"

"Your father is no longer under direct surveillance, as far as I know. Probably they were wanting to make sure of him before pulling him in to work for the Heereswaffenamt. But make no mistake about it — they have eyes on everybody. And given the sensitive nature of your father's position, I would expect them to take up direct surveillance again at intermittent intervals, just to be safe. So be aware."

Sibi felt a nervous flutter in her stomach at the thought. "They know I'm lying about how Guernica was destroyed. Herr Kraus, Dr. Goebbels, all of them — they know, and they *want* me to lie. They even gave me a script with what they wanted me to say written down word for word." She told him about being taken to the Ordenspalais, and what had happened there.

416

By the time she finished, he was frowning. "As long as they can make use of you, you should be safe enough."

What he didn't say, but what she took away from that, was, *What happens when you've served your purpose, and they don't need you anymore?*

Fear of the answer made the skin at the nape of her neck prickle.

She said, "I asked Papa if we could leave Germany. All of us, as a family. He said they wouldn't let us go. That we knew too many secrets. I know the truth about what they did in Guernica, and he knows . . . what's in that notebook. And more. He said that if we tried to leave, and were caught, they would probably arrest us. And even if we managed to get away, they might follow us and kill us to keep us silent."

"He's right."

He must have seen the shiver that coursed through her, because he put both hands on her shoulders and squeezed. The gesture was meant to be reassuring, bracing. The size and strength of his hands imprinted themselves on her bones.

"Hitler and the NSDAP are doing everything they can to create a totalitarian state," he said. "The party's leaders are fanatics who want to stamp out even the smallest

417

flicker of nonconformist behavior or dissent. Everything that doesn't advance their vision for the Third Reich is to be eliminated. Their goal is absolute power, along with the reemergence of Germany as a dominant player on the world stage. They'll do anything they have to do to achieve it and they are absolutely ruthless. You want to remember that."

She nodded.

"Come on, we need to get you home. It's almost dark. I'll walk you as far as the tree, then watch you the rest of the way." Releasing her shoulders, he picked up her bag and his hat and briefcase, handed her bag to her, then settled his hat on his head. Together they walked down the steps and across the graveyard toward the park.

"I don't need you to walk me home. Or watch me walk home, either."

The fedora made him look different. With dusk now swallowing them up, all she could see of his face was the outline of his features against the graying twilight. They were ruggedly masculine, and looking at them she felt an odd little tug of . . . attraction. She recognized it with dismay. More by custom than design, her hand was curled around his upper arm. She suddenly became aware of how hard the muscle was beneath the fine wool, of how companionably close their bodies were, of the charm in the quick smile he turned on her.

"Not afraid of the dark, hmm?"

"No." Her hand dropped away from his arm. She felt self-conscious now. The one thing she was sure of was that she didn't want him to somehow guess what was going through her mind.

They were in the park, on the path that circled the pond. Dusk was darkening into full night. Clouds were blowing up overhead to form towering gray peaks, and a frosty moon peeping over the horizon cast a zigzag of light across the shiny black surface of the water. Somewhere a bonfire burned; the smell of smoke was in the air.

"I'm going this way, anyway. Like I said, I have somewhere I need to be."

"You said you'd give me a way to get anything that's urgent to you."

"I will. Tomorrow. Where will you be at around, say, seven p.m.?"

"Probably still at Olympic Stadium. Our school is supposed to parade in front of the grandstand holding up letters that spell out a welcome to Il Duce. I'll be the one under the *W*."

He grinned. "I'll find you."

They reached the tree. It was darker

beneath its spreading branches and as they skirted it she could see her house. The fuzzy glow of the streetlamps illuminated the long row of small brick and stone houses with their shining windows, the neat front lawns, the sidewalks and the automobiles parked along the curb.

Hard to accept that danger was building up over that quiet, peaceful street, over the city, over Germany itself, as silently and surely as the massing storm clouds.

I won't think about it. Not now.

He stopped. She stopped, too, and looked up at him.

"Go ahead. I'll wait here until you're inside," he said.

She was conscious of not wanting to leave, of wanting to stay out there in the dark with him. The connection between them was as difficult to resist as a magnet's pull to the north. With him she felt . . . different. The only way she could describe it was, more like herself. Or rather, more like the girl she had been in the Before.

Having such feelings was uncomfortable. Awkward. Embarrassing, even.

Since she had no idea what to do about them, she nodded without saying anything and walked away.

33

A million people: that's how many, according to the radio stations broadcasting the event, gathered to witness what was bruited as the historic occasion. They filled the Olympic Stadium and the adjoining Mayfield, and spilled over into almost every centimeter of the 1.32 square kilometers of the Reichs Sportsfield. They had come to hear the speeches, to see a dazzling military tattoo, to perform their part in the massive display of pageantry designed to awe the visiting Italians with the overwhelming might and magnificence of the Third Reich. The floodlights illuminating the venue shone so brightly Sibi had no doubt at all that it could be seen from space. All of Germany's radio stations were tuned in, along with twenty countries from Europe and North and South America.

"Here's your letter." Ilsa greeted her tardy arrival — she'd had to drop her sisters off at their appointed places — by thrusting the giant *W* placard into her hands. Painted red, green and white — the colors of the Italian flag — it was to be snapped aloft as they reached the edge of the stage and held above her head until they passed the reviewing stand. Like herself and the other girls from their school, Ilsa, who'd been tapped to carry the *B,* was dressed in traditional attire: a blue dirndl skirt, white puff-sleeved blouse and red vest. Being chosen to carry a letter was an honor. Sibi didn't know if she'd been asked because of her grades, her father's new position or, as she rather suspected, because she'd become seminotorious as a result of her association with Guernica. Ilsa was quite sure why she'd been selected, and made no bones about it: her father was *generalleutnant* of the Wehrmacht. Heide had not been so honored, and would march behind with the rest of the class. The lower grades were present, too, but they'd been relegated to the crowd.

The Olympic bell began to toll from high up in the Glockenturm that overlooked the Mayfield and, by extension, the adjacent stadium.

Sibi lined up with her classmates as trumpets blared and the enormous personal standards of Il Duce and *der Führer,* respectively, were hoisted into place on either side of the review stand to join the hundreds of German and Italian flags already aloft in the arena. That signified that Hitler and Mussolini and their entourages had arrived at the stadium. It also served as the signal for the parades to start.

To the rousing strains of "Horst-Wessel-Lied," the Nazi Party anthem, she and the rest of the *Oberprima* students of the Berlinisches Gymnasium fell into place with the other classes from other schools chosen to participate. Singing along with the rest, thrusting her letter aloft on cue, she did her part and marched past the stage on which the leaders were taking their seats. Behind them came the Hitlerjugend and the Deutsches Jungvolk, for boys aged ten to fourteen. The Bund Deutscher Mädel, for girls fifteen to twenty-one, and the Jungmädel, for girls aged ten to fourteen, were next. All bore signs of welcome. All except for the sign-bearers gave the required straight-armed salute as they passed the stage. The massed bands of three army corps followed, complete with brass sections, fife players, trumpets, drum corps. Four thousand musicians in all, playing as they marched. An ocean of soldiers goose-stepping shoulder to shoulder in unison flanked by more soldiers on motorcycles with sidecars circled the stadium in the bands' wake. Spotlights sent white columns of light searching the sky, which was heavy with the storm clouds that still threatened. Blowing out the eardrums of everyone within a hundred kilometers with thunderous versions of songs from Verdi's *Aida* for the Italians, and Wagner's *Rienzi* for the Germans, the bands wheeled into the center of the huge arena while, from a specially constructed arch at the side of the stadium, a regiment of Schultzstaffel bearing flaming torches paraded onto the field. As the wind caught the flames, they appeared to blend together into a moving river of fire. At the end of the display, a battalion of soldiers formed a giant *M* with its base toward the stage on which Hitler and Mussolini stood, while divisions from the army, navy and air force, each more than 30,000 strong, goose-stepped their way in syncopation around the stadium, then wheeled to the front and came to attention with the Nazi salute and a shouted, *"Heil Hitler!"*

It was a staggering display of military power, and the combination of anger and anxiety it provoked in her made Sibi's chest feel tight.

The first speaker to mount the raised dais

in the middle of the stage and address the masses was Dr. Goebbels. Arms aching from her letter-bearing, shivering a little in the cool night air because they'd been forbidden to wear coats over their outfits, Sibi barely listened. Having turned her letter back in to the headmaster when the school's part in the spectacle was played, she was crammed in with everyone else and being jostled on all sides. Ilsa and Heide were somewhere in front of her. The rest of her class was more or less together, although students from other schools were beginning to mix in. She'd gotten shoved toward the rear, not that she minded. The farther she was from the headmaster, the less likely he was to notice her inattention to the speakers, and the speeches, and scold.

She was looking for Griff.

The skyscraping searchlights came together to form a tent of light above the stage. The bands played "Deutschland über Alles." Everyone saluted. Hitler, a commanding figure in his brown party uniform with his little whisk broom of a mustache, took the podium.

"What moves us most at the moment is our deep-rooted joy to have in our midst a guest who is one of the lonely men in history," he said in his mesmerizing voice, and

425

introduced Mussolini to the crowd, which roared as the Italian dictator, a robust, jolly-looking man in a belted uniform and peaked cap, stepped up to the podium.

He no sooner began speaking than the sky split and the clouds let loose torrents of cold rain.

Like everyone else, Sibi gasped, ducked, covered her head with her hands and looked frantically for any kind of shelter.

A coat, way oversize but blessedly warm, dropped around her shoulders from behind. A hat plopped down on her head. A man's big hand caught hers, jerked her into motion, pulled her with him toward the back of the stadium.

She knew who it was even though he had his suit coat pulled up over his head as he ran, even though all she could see of him was his back: Griff.

The rain was blinding, deafening, chilling, disorienting. It hammered the ground with a sharp *rat-a-tat,* splashing everywhere as it fell in driving curtains of silvery water that instantly soaked all who were caught out in it. Griff's hand was, for Sibi, the only stabilizing thing in the sudden chaos.

Il Duce continued with his speech, undaunted, although some combination of the

426

roaring rain and a quirk in the sound system made most of what he said unintelligible. The bands scrambled to protect their instruments, the soldiers their weapons. The sodden live audience, having nowhere to go, huddled closer together, shielding themselves from the deluge with bent heads and raised arms and whatever else they could find. But they remained largely in place, held captive by fear and fervor and protocol, water sluicing down pale faces that stayed resolutely turned toward the speaker. A glance back at the now-distant stage revealed that the tent of light shone on bravely through the rain, and that Mussolini, shielded from the worst of the onslaught by a canopy protecting the speakers and apparently unaware of his distorted voice, still stood before the microphone gesticulating dramatically as he spoke.

Then Griff pulled her through an exit, along the colonnade circling the stadium and past a massive security presence that, drowning in the sudden cloudburst, too, didn't appear to give them more than a cursory glance as they exited. Running with him through the lake the pavement had turned into, feet in her flat black shoes and legs in their white stockings soaked and freezing, thankful for the hat that shielded her head and face, and clutching his coat, which still hung from her shoulders, together in front of her with one hand, Sibi didn't notice the line of automobiles until he stopped beside one, opened the door and bundled her into the passenger seat.

It felt so good to be out of the pelting rain that all she could do was sit and let water roll off her as she tried to catch her breath.

Seconds later he slid in beside her, swiping a hand over first his face, which still had water running down it, and then his wet hair, which was shiny-dark in the gloom of the automobile's interior. His clothes, a brown suit with a shirt and tie, were soaked through, and he brought the earthy smell of the rain in with him. But he grinned at her as he took the dripping hat that she held out to him, and tossed it in the rear. Cold and wet as she was, she smiled back.

Because she was really, really, *really* glad to see him.

"That was easier than I expected. The rain helped." He started the engine, turned on the headlights, pulled out into the street. She flipped down the visor and, without much help from the tiny mirror, did her best to tidy her hair, which was a little wet on the surface but not soaked through thanks to the timely loan of his hat.

She flipped the visor back into place. "Thanks for the hat. And coat."

Which she still huddled shivering inside, although he'd turned on the heat and it was at that moment blasting warm air at her. The whooshing sound it made, coupled with the swish of the windshield wipers and the splash of the tires over the rain-soaked street, made it necessary to raise her voice.

"Any time," he said.

"Griff . . . this military buildup, us joining forces with Italy, everything —" her gesture encompassed Germany's invasion of the Rhineland "— where do you think it's going? Do you think they're getting ready to involve us in another war?" *Like the one in Spain. Like the one between Japan and China.* She didn't have to spell it out, because he knew what she meant.

"It's hard to say. All I can tell you is, we're keeping a close eye on the situation."

"We?"

A quick half smile. "Us military attachés."

The look she gave him spoke volumes, and his smile widened. There was, she knew, no point in pursuing the subject.

"Where are we going?" she asked.

"Remember me promising to show you how you can contact me if something urgent comes up?"

"Yes."

"There."

"Oh." As the air around them warmed, she settled back against the seat. Between the streetlamps and the headlights reflecting off the rain she could see him quite clearly. "Just so you know, I have to be back at the stadium by the time the program's over. I have to meet Jo and Margrit and take them home."

"They're out there in that crowd?"

"All the schools were required to come. They're with their classes." The thought of her sisters being caught in the downpour made Sibi grimace. "I hope they don't get sick."

"What about your father?"

"He's there, too, but he's up in the stands with a group of scientists, in some kind of special viewing area, I think. They're going to a reception later."

"Which once again leaves you holding the bag as your sisters' keeper." There was a note of wry humor in his voice.

She shook her head. "I don't think of it like that. After what happened, I'm theirs, they're mine. We're three parts of a whole."

"Always, hmm?"

"That's right." The little catch in her heart that the word and its accompanying promise evoked she acknowledged and dismissed. "And that being the case, I mean it about needing to be back before the rally is over."

"Don't worry, I'll have you back in plenty of time." There was a pause as he braked for a nearly empty tram, then made a turn.

"So," she said, "did you make it to your 'somewhere' last night?"

He glanced at her. "I did."

She knew better than to ask for details. "And will you be going 'somewhere' tonight?"

"Actually, I'm leaving tonight."

The words landed on her like a lead weight. "Leaving? Berlin?"

"Germany."

She was surprised at how much she didn't want him to go. "Oh." Worried about how he might interpret the flatness of that, she rallied. "I never realized how much travel was required of military attachés."

"What is it they say? Something like, no rest for the wicked?"

"Oh, ha-ha."

"Come on, that was funny."

She *was* smiling again. "Maybe a little."

"Because you were looking sad there for a minute. Made me think you might be going to miss me."

He was teasing, she knew, but still that

flustered her. She frowned repressively. "I'm just wondering how it is that you're able to move in and out of Germany so easily."

"That's the advantage of being a citizen of a neutral country. Nobody hates you. See, our leaders in the good old US of A know what they're doing."

"And here was silly little me thinking that they just didn't want to get involved."

His crooked smile conceded the point. "There's that, too." His expression changed, and he nodded up ahead. "See that building? The one on the corner?"

Peering through the rain, Sibi nodded. "Yes."

"It's a post office. It's on the tram line, so you shouldn't have any trouble getting to it."

"And I need to get to it why?"

He was pulling over, parking beside the curb, cutting the lights. "This is how you're going to get an urgent message to me."

"Write you a letter? I thought there was a problem with mail being censored."

"If you reach into the right pocket of my coat you've got wrapped around you, you'll find a key."

With a lift of her eyebrows at him, she did, and came up with one. It was small and silver.

"It's to PO Box 0912. In this building," he said.

She looked a question at him. Reaching into the back, he grabbed his hat and handed it to her.

"Put it on. Let's go."

Taking it — it hadn't dried — she looked from it to the still-pouring rain. "Seriously?"

"You bet your life." He was out of the automobile as he spoke. With his head ducked against the onslaught, he ran around to her side. She didn't wait for him to reach her door. Cramming his hat on her head, she jumped out just as he got there. He caught her hand, and they ran together through the pouring rain until they fetched up beneath the awning that protected the entrance. Shaking himself much in the manner of a wet dog — she took off the dripping hat and flicked the worst of the rivulets from the coat she wore with far more dignity — he pulled the door open and followed her inside.

It was dimly lit and deserted and so quiet it reminded her of a library. If there was anyone else inside, she saw no sign of them. Sibi remembered that the day had been declared a national holiday. The long counter where mail was dropped off stood in front of one wall. Catching her elbow, Griff pulled her in the opposite direction, down a hall that opened into a large room in which brass-fronted PO boxes lined the walls. More walls with the small, rectangular mailboxes set into them divided the space into thirds.

"They're in numerical order — 0912 is on this wall." Griff's voice was quiet, and she guessed he was responding to the library atmosphere, too. They found it — it was in the third row from the bottom, and they had to crouch to reach it — and he said, "Open it."

Using the small key, she did. He made her close it, and then do it again.

"So, what —" she began, but he shook his head at her, casting a significant glance over his shoulder. She heard it then, too, the faint squeak of wet shoes on the hardwood floor, and her heart gave a nervous thump. By the time the bespectacled man with the um-brella tucked under his arm reached the room, they were already on their way out of it, circling the middle wall of mailboxes so as to avoid coming face-to-face with the new arrival as he entered.

Griff plopped his hat back on her head and tugged the brim down low over her forehead. He then positioned himself be-tween her and the man and wrapped an arm around her, pulling her in close against his side in what she recognized as a precautionary effort to keep the stranger from getting a good look at her as they passed the aisle he was in. And as large as Griff's coat was on her — it hung almost to her ankles — the man wouldn't be able to so much as gauge her size or shape even if he looked after them as they walked out.

A moment later, they were outside, running back through the rain to the automobile.

"Do you think he was with the SD?" Sliding inside the vehicle, taking off Griff's hat and fluffing her hair, Sibi was still breathing way too hard as he jumped in behind the wheel and got them going again in record time.

"I don't think so, but there's no way to be sure." The headlights sliced through the darkness and the rain, which was slackening. There was very little traffic because of the ongoing rally at the stadium. "Even if that wasn't an agent, they have a million eyes and ears now. You've heard that they're opening tip lines and offering rewards if someone turns in a neighbor or relative or friend who, among other things, commits an anti-Nazi act, which, by the way, you passing information to me would be?"

She hadn't heard. The information was chilling. "That's terrible."

"That's the world we're living in." His voice was grim. "If you ever need to drop something off back there, you want to make certain you haven't been followed. Take a roundabout route. Use windows like mirrors to take a look at the people behind you. If you think someone is following, walk around the block, turning left at each corner. If that person is still behind you after three left turns, go into another building, buy something, catch the tram and go home. Even if you're sure no one's following, that you're in the clear, get in, do what you have to do as fast as you can and get out." He glanced at her. "Now repeat that back to me."

She did, and as he nodded his satisfaction she took a deep breath, trying to keep it quiet so he wouldn't hear.

He cast a frowning glance her way, and she knew that he *had* heard.

"You sure you still want to do this? It's a hell of a risk." The grimness was back in his voice.

"Yes." She felt no doubt at all. She noticed he was taking an indirect route with a number of left turns, and realized it was designed to foil any possible surveillance.

She glanced back automatically. A few automobiles, a tram. Anyone following? The honest answer was, she really couldn't tell.

But the possibility made her insides quiver.

"Any questions?" he asked.

"Explain to me how I'm actually supposed to use the post office box."

"You need to get something urgent to me, you write it out — in our code — seal it up in an envelope like a letter, address it to Annie — that's me — and put it in the PO box. You're Rolf, by the way."

She blinked at him. "Rolf?"

"Yup. That way, if something goes wrong and they come looking, stake out the post office, anything like that, they'll be watching for a man." A smile just touched his lips. "It's been our experience that Nazis tend to be very literal-minded."

"Our? As in military attachés?"

"That's right."

She didn't believe him, but for the moment at least it wasn't important. "So I put an envelope addressed to Annie in the PO box. What happens then?"

"Somebody will pick it up and convey its contents to me within a few hours. If it's something that you feel needs a reply, make *reply* your last word, then come back to the

PO box twenty-four hours later and you'll have one."

Her brow wrinkled. "But mail delivery even within Germany takes at least a few days and —"

"It's not going by mail, and that's all I'm going to say about that."

She looked at him in silence. Asking more questions was clearly a waste of time.

"Only use this drop-off for news that absolutely can't wait," he added. "Understand?"

"Yes."

"You remember the box number? You have the key?"

As she said *yes* to both, she realized that they were getting close to the stadium. Its white glow lit up the surrounding darkness like the sun, and the searchlights were once again roaming the angry-looking clouds. She could hear the bands — they were playing "Deutschland, du Land der Treue."

"You decide you don't want to do this, you have any doubts at all, at any time, just stop."

"I will. But I won't."

Lips compressing, he gave her an assessing look. She could tell that he was having all kinds of second thoughts.

438

She smiled at him. "It'll be fine. I'll be fine."

"I hope so," he said.

A triumphant crescendo of music from the stadium had her glancing out through the windshield. They were almost there.

"I'm supposed to meet Jo and Margrit in front of the statue of Prometheus," she said. It was one of the best known of the dozens of bronze and stone sculptures that surrounded the stadium. "We're going to catch a tram from there."

"I'd give you a ride home, but —" He didn't need to finish: her sisters couldn't be allowed to see him.

"I know." They were close enough now that she could easily walk the rest of the way to her destination. Fortunately, the rain had stopped. "You should probably let me out here."

"You're going to get cold."

"I'll walk fast."

He pulled over, got out, came around to her side. She was already standing on the sidewalk sliding out of his coat by the time he reached her. It wasn't precisely dark where they were, because of the light from the stadium, but it was shadowy and gloomy and, yes, cold. The night smelled like rain. The sidewalk, like the street, was awash.

The towering Prometheus was less than a block away. She could see it clearly. A nervous glance around revealed no sign of anyone watching but . . . he'd planted the seed in her mind and it had obviously taken firm root, because her pulse raced.

Not that there was anything now for anyone to see. Just a man and a girl, standing beside an automobile, saying goodbye.

People were on the move, spilling out of the stadium in droves, surging toward their vehicles and the closest streets and the tram stop and the subway, in a hurry to get away because the low-hanging clouds promised more rain. Friends called to each other. Automobile engines turned over. Feet sloshed through puddles. The rousing martial music continued to play, probably to speed the attendees on their way, but the rally was clearly over.

"I have to go. I don't want to miss the girls." She handed him his coat. She'd left his hat behind in the car. "When will you be back?"

"I don't know. A few months. Watch for the flowers."

"I will." She didn't know what her face looked like, but his expression changed and his hand rose to slide against her cheek.

Their eyes met. Something passed between them, that same something she'd felt before. Call it an awareness, an attraction — she couldn't even give it a name. Whatever it was, there was no mistaking it this time: it was real, and immediate, and right there. Her breath caught — and then Griff leaned forward to press a kiss to her forehead. His lips touched her skin for the briefest of moments before his hand dropped and he stepped back.

It was the kind of kiss an uncle might bestow upon a favorite niece. No meaning whatsoever beyond that of a friendly, fond gesture.

At least not, as far as Sibi could tell, for him.

As for her —

Her heart thumped. Her pulse leaped. Her lips parted — before she recovered the presence of mind to clamp them together. Her hands froze on their way to clutch at his shoulders. Her eyes shot to his face. Luckily, because she didn't like to think what they might reveal, he was looking past her.

"Unless I'm mistaken, the schools are coming out," he said. No sign of a hitch in his breathing. No sign of a reaction at all. "It's quite a group."

Her hands fell. She started breathing again. Glancing around, she saw that he was right. Impossible to mistake in their traditional outfits, the schoolchildren marched out in time to the rousing music.

"Go on. I'll see you when I see you," he said, and when she looked back at him she saw that he was smiling just a little, with a wry twist to his mouth that she didn't have the time or presence of mind to try to analyze. He tweaked a loose strand of her hair. "Take care of yourself, Rolf."

At the name, her lips curled of their own volition into a quick little smile of her own.

"You, too," she said, and turned and walked away.

34

She did not look back. And did *not* feel a pang of loss when she heard the slam of the automobile's door as Griff got back behind the wheel, or have her stomach clench at the *whoosh* of tires that told her he was driving away.

As she made her way through the throng streaming from the stadium, she'd almost forgotten about the possibility of surveillance, which now that she remembered it was disturbing enough to make her skin crawl — and *truly* forget about her overreaction to Griff.

She was within a few meters of the statue when she heard it.

"You take that back!" It was an enraged cry.

Margrit. Every cell in Sibi's body went on instant alert. Even as a volley of girlish screams pierced the noise of the crowd, Sibi's head turned sharply in the direction from which her sister's voice had come.

And saw Margrit, having apparently launched herself off the pavement a split second earlier, land atop another girl, fists flailing.

"Margrit!" Elbowing her way through a crush of people, Sibi registered several things at once. The screams came not only from the girl on the ground, but also from the group of girls surrounding the battling pair, all older and larger than Margrit. People began to stop and stare, and others created an eddy in the exiting stream as they skirted the disturbance. In the near distance, what sounded like a policeman's whistle blew.

"Let go!" A couple of girls grabbed Margrit and tried to pull her away without success.

"Get the *Giftzwerg* off me!"

"Margrit, stop!" Sibi cried. She was shoving through the crowd now, and wasn't even sure Margrit heard.

"Ow! She's pulling my hair!"

"Leave my sister alone!" Jo appeared from seemingly nowhere to throw herself into the fray in defense of Margrit and was instantly caught up in her own battle as the pair of girls now pummeling Margrit turned on her.

"Oh, look, it's her! She's come back!"

"That hurts! She's hurting me! Help!"

"*Verhurtes Drecksgör!* Dirty girl!"

"Get away! Eww, she touched me!"

"Can't somebody get her off me?"

"You stupid cows, she's only six!"

"All of you! Stop this right now!" Reaching what was now a screaming, shoving, slapping free-for-all, Sibi managed to freeze Jo and her opponents in their tracks with that blast of stark outrage. "Margrit, *let go!*" She pulled Margrit off her victim. "Jo, come here!"

Scooping her glasses off the pavement, head hanging, Jo retreated to her side. Like the other girls, she was soaked to the skin. Conscious of a spurt of anger at those who would keep children standing at a political rally in the pouring rain, Sibi put an arm around her shoulders: besides being wet, Jo felt freezing cold. With one hand now firmly locked around Margrit's wrist, Sibi could feel that even her fiery littlest sister was shivering.

"She started it!" The accusation came from a multitude of mouths at once as the group glared at Margrit en masse and the girl on the ground scrambled to her feet. Her clothes were disheveled and ripped and her wet hair was a tangled mess.

"It was her!" She pointed at Margrit. "The

445

vicious little brat attacked me!"

"Miststück!" Margrit hurled back.

"Margrit!" Shocked that Margrit even knew such a word, Sibi gave her sister's wrist an admonishing squeeze.

"She *is.*"

"What's going on here?" The deep voice belonged to one of a pair of soldiers who'd shoved their way through the crowd to, presumably, break up the fracas. One had a whistle around his neck. From their uniforms, Sibi recognized that they were officers of the gestapo, and her heart stood still.

No one answered. All of them, Sibi included, were momentarily struck dumb by the realization of how much trouble they might be in.

"Yes, what is this?" That voice was infinitely more welcome because it belonged to Dr. Richter, the head of the *volksschule* Jo and Margrit — and presumably the other girls — attended. Sibi knew him from her own schooling there before she'd moved on to the gymnasium.

"She attacked me!" The girl Margrit had, yes, attacked once again pointed accusingly at Margrit.

"That little scrap?" the officer with the whistle asked on a note of disbelief. All eyes turned now to Margrit, who Sibi continued to hold shackled by the wrist as a necessary precaution. To any who didn't know her, the blond curls, still springy and bright despite being drenched, the wide blue eyes, the round cheeks, even her traditional costume, were childish innocence personified. Sibi hoped that she was the only one who could sense the furious energy that still coursed through every cell of her sister's sturdy little body.

"Yes, yes!" The other girls chimed in. "It was her! She jumped on Gretta and knocked her down."

"You called my sister names!" Margrit's fists clenched. Her eyes shot fire. "Just like you call her names at school. All of you —"

"That's enough. We're going home now." Sibi's grip tightened on both her sisters as she started pulling them away from what was fast becoming, she feared, an unmanageable situation. The presence of the gestapo made a bad set of circumstances far worse. "We'll miss our tram. This can all be sorted out when —"

"That brat knocked me down! She hit me! She pulled my hair!" the attacked girl — Gretta — interrupted shrilly. She looked to be about ten, about Jo's age. Sibi guessed that they, and probably all the bigger girls, were classmates. Wet through, her dark blond hair had once been in braids, as was evidenced by the bedraggled, beribboned remnants of the plaits. The rest of it was now a rat's nest of tangles, and Sibi had no difficulty at all attributing that to Margrit. "She deserves to be punished, Dr. Richter!"

"You started it! You know you did!" Jo's head came up. She gave Gretta a look that sizzled with anger. The glow from the stadium hit her face — and Sibi froze inside. The cosmetics Jo had so painstakingly applied earlier had vanished, no doubt washed away by the driving rain. What was left visible for all to see were the skin grafts: purple and puckered around the edges and, probably because the cold wash of rain had left the rest of her skin so pale, horribly apparent on the left side of her face and neck.

Oh, Jo. Even as Jo's hand clapped to her cheek in an attempt to hide what was there, in an obvious reaction to the expressions of everyone looking at her, Sibi's heart wept for her.

"What is wrong with her? Is she defective?" Both gestapo agents stared at Jo with a kind of fascination mixed with repugnance, but it was the one with the whistle who spoke. Jo immediately ducked her head again so that the dark wings of her wet hair swung forward to hide her face, and shrank against Sibi's side.

"No." Sibi's response was sharp, strong and immediate. It was driven by fear, because under the Law for the Prevention of Genetically Diseased Offspring persons born with a disability or suspected of harboring a genetic defect or disease could be taken into custody. The most frequent outcome was a forced sterilization with the stated goal of preventing such defects from being passed on to future generations. Even if they escaped sterilization, anyone labeled in such a way was tracked by the government and sidelined from society. Persistent rumors whispered that even harsher remedies were being considered. "It's an injury. A burn." Her fierce gaze encompassed the huddled group of girls. "My sister was trapped in the same fire that killed our mother. She was terribly brave, and if she hadn't been most heroically rescued, she would have died, too. Her face was perfect before then, and it *will* heal. She is under the care of the doctors at the Charité."

"My sister Luiza did die. She got shot by an airplane," Margrit said, her words clear as a bell in the silence that was left behind in the aftermath of Sibi's speech. Galvanized by horror at what the gestapo might make

449

of that, or what else Margrit might reveal, Sibi tightened her grip to the point where Margrit yelped and tugged at her hand in an attempt to get free.

"If you'll excuse us, we're leaving now. We can't miss our tram." Holding on to both sisters as if she feared to let them go Sibi turned away.

"Hold," the gestapo with the whistle ordered sternly. Pulse tripping with dread, Sibi stopped, turned back and gave him what she hoped was a calmly questioning look. "Aren't you the girl from the newsreels? From Guernica? Fräulein Sibil something?"

"Helinger," Dr. Richter supplied. "This is Fräulein Sibil Helinger and her sisters."

"Yes," Sibi replied to the officer. Chin up, she met his gaze even as her heart sank at the idea that they now knew who she, and by extension Jo and Margrit, were. The weak link in the hell's bargain she'd struck with Herr Kraus had always been the little girls.

"That was a most terrible thing." The gestapo shook his head. "My wife wept at your story. Please accept my condolences." His expression changed. The condemning glance he swept around the group included Jo and Margrit. "You should go home now, the lot of you. Or else we will be forced to arrest you for creating a disturbance at this most important event. You may thank Fräulein Helinger here for our forbearance."

Looking chastened, Gretta and the group of girls drew closer together. Dr. Richter's lips pursed. A long shiver ran through Jo. Margrit, as ever, remained uncowed, although she stayed closer to Sibi than even her shackled wrist required.

"Thank you for your good wishes, Officer. *Gute Nacht,*" Sibi said. Keeping her face untroubled and her voice steady was an effort. With a polite nod for the soldiers, she turned and this time succeeded in walking away with her sisters. Plunging into the departing crowd, colder than ever from the sweat she'd broken out into at the thought of being taken into custody, searched and having the post office box key found, she was sure she could still feel the eyes of the gestapo boring into her back as she and the little girls made their way toward the tram stop.

"Those girls are mean," Margrit said under her breath.

"You should have stayed out of it," Jo hissed back.

"They called you a —"

"What they called me is none of your business."

"I was *helping* you."

"No! You were —"

"*Stop. Hush.* I don't want to hear another word out of either of you." Sibi had had enough. With a sister on either side of her, maneuvering through the crowd was difficult, but she wasn't ready to let go of either one.

"Girls, can my wife and I give you a ride home?" Dr. Richter's interruption almost made Sibi jump. With a plump, dark-haired woman who Sibi presumed was his wife at his side, he'd caught up and was looking at them with concern.

Sibi shot a glance at the tram stop, which was packed to overflowing, factored in how wet and cold the little girls were and added her own and Jo's frazzled nerves (if Margrit's nerves ever frazzled, she'd never seen it) to the mix. And promptly, gratefully, accepted.

"I'll see what I can do to make things easier for Johanna at school," Dr. Richter said some twenty minutes later as Sibi, having ridden in the back seat with her sisters, prepared to exit their automobile. It was stopped in front of the house, and Margrit and Jo were already out and on their way to the front door. "I knew she was enduring some teasing, but I had no idea it had gotten so bad."

"Thank you." Sibi's words were heartfelt: she'd had no idea, either, although she felt she should have done. Bidding Dr. Richter and his wife good night, she followed her sisters into the house. Because the three of them were the only ones home, just a few lights were on.

"I had to do it." Fists planted on her hips, Margrit was there in the entry hall waiting for her as Sibi closed the front door. Margrit was whispering, but still clearly aggrieved. Jo was nowhere in sight. "You know what that girl called her? *Sackgesicht.*"

Bag face. Sibi felt sick.

"Because she said Jo needed to wear one over her face. She said looking at Jo made her want to vomit. Jo looked so sad, but she just walked away, just like she does when they call her names at school. But I couldn't. I couldn't! I wanted to kill that girl. I would have if —"

"*No.* No, you wouldn't." She knew exactly how her littlest sister felt, but for all their sakes it was her job to try to tone down Margrit's more aggressive tendencies, not reinforce them. "I understand, but you can't go around attacking people. Not even stupid

453

girls who say bad things about Jo. In future, you need to tell an adult, and let them handle it." Even as Sibi said it, she feared she was wasting her breath. Letting things pass wasn't in Margrit's nature.

"Are you mad at me?" Margrit asked, uncharacteristically humble. Sibi met her littlest sister's eyes, saw the sudden vulnerability there and sighed inwardly.

"No, I'm not mad." She gave Margrit a hug, which was fiercely returned. The little girl was no longer dripping wet. She was more clammy and cold, and *that* was something Sibi knew how to deal with. "Now go upstairs and get ready for bed. Where's Jo?"

"She yelled, 'Just leave me alone,' when I tried to explain, and ran into the kitchen. *She's* mad at me. But I only wanted to —"

"She's not mad at you, she's just upset. I'll talk to her. Go on upstairs."

Margrit went upstairs, and Sibi went in search of Jo. The kitchen was dark and empty. So was the dining room, and Papa's study. Frowning, Sibi went to the back door, and looked out through the window in its upper half.

There, barely visible in the darkness, was Jo. She sat huddled on the stoop's top step, a too-big coat thrown around her shoulders, her arms wrapped around Ruby, who pressed close against her side.

Sinking down on the step beside Jo, breathing in the fresh smell of newly fallen rain, Sibi found herself wishing so fiercely for their mother that it was a physical ache inside her. She felt inadequate in every way for the task at hand. Jo was crying, shoulders heaving amid broken sobs. In reaction to Sibi's presence, she pulled Ruby into her lap and hid her face in the dog's shaggy fur.

Putting an arm around Jo's shoulders, Sibi said, "Your face will get better. Everything will get better."

"No, it won't." Jo lifted her head. Sibi could see the glimmer of tears in her eyes. "You know I'm always going to look like this."

"You're beautiful."

"I'm a freak!"

"You are not a freak."

"Did you see the way they looked at me? Those soldiers? Like I was the most repulsive thing they'd ever seen."

"They did not —"

"They did. You know they did! Stop lying to me."

"Jo —"

"I wish I'd died, too. I wish I'd died with Mama and Luiza. I don't want to live like this. I hate living like this!" Bursting into

fresh sobs, she buried her face in Ruby's fur
again. The little dog wriggled and licked the
only part of Jo she could reach — her wrist.
Sibi could see Ruby's worried eyes gleaming at her through the darkness.

"Johanna Marie Helinger, you listen to
me." Sibi's voice was fierce. Her arm tightened around Jo's shoulders. "You almost
did die. The fact that you didn't, that you
were saved, don't you think it *means* something? There's a reason you didn't go with
Mama and Luiza, that you're still here with
Margrit and Papa and Ruby and me. You
don't know what it is yet, but I guarantee
it's out there waiting for you. A *purpose.*"

Jo sniffled loudly. She didn't look up, but
Sibi could tell she was listening.

"You know all the bad things that have
happened to you? To us? What if, in the
future, there's that much good waiting for
you? So much happiness and so many
wonderful surprises that your life will just
be overflowing with joy? Maybe this —
Mama and Luiza dying, your face being
burned — is the road you have to take to
get to all that happiness. It's not for nothing, Jo. You have to believe that."

Jo took a deep, shaking breath. "It just . . .
hurts so much. Everything. Oh, Sibi, I wish
none of this had happened. I wish Mama

was here."

"I know. I do, too." They sat there for a moment, looking out into the dark garden, listening to the whisper of the wind moving through the plants their mother had loved. It was almost as if a little bit of her essence remained. Then a cold raindrop — two, three, a sprinkle — hit.

"Quick, it's starting to rain again, we've got to go in," she said. Jumping up, she pulled Jo to her feet. The relieving part was that, instead of resisting, Jo let her, and she, Jo and Ruby rushed inside the house just as the heavens opened up once more and buckets of rain cascaded down.

Later, after she'd changed into dry clothes and tucked Margrit into bed and come back out to find Jo emerging from the bathroom, she beckoned to her sister and said, "Come with me."

"What?" Padding barefoot over the wooden floor, Jo followed her into her lamp-lit bedroom, then across to the dressing table. Standing with her back to Jo while she retrieved something from it, Sibi caught a glimpse of her sister in the oval mirror. Jo's dark brown hair was almost dry now and tucked behind her ears. Her blue cotton nightgown had long sleeves and a hem that reached her ankles. Her face was washed clean of every last trace of cosmetics and rain and tears. The skin grafts were as glaringly apparent as ever, but so were the thickly lashed brown eyes behind the glasses and the delicate bone structure and the innate sweetness of her expression. Sibi felt a rush of protective love for this small sister, and closed her hand tightly around the object she held even as she turned back toward Jo.

"I have something for you." She opened her hand so that Jo could see the silver necklace resting on her palm.

Jo's eyes widened. "Is that . . . Mama's locket?"

Sibi nodded.

"Where did you get it? She was wearing it —" Jo broke off, but Sibi knew what she couldn't say: *when she died.*

"A friend sent it to me. After she was buried."

Jo's eyes flickered. She wet her lips.

"Would you like to have it?" Sibi asked. Jo nodded, and Sibi said, "Turn around."

Jo obeyed. Sibi fastened the cherished memento around her neck.

"Why *me*?" Jo clutched the locket as it rested against the pin-tucked blue cotton just above her breastbone. "Margrit . . . or you —"

"Mama would want you to have it." *Because you're the one who needs it — and her — the most.* "She can't be with you right now, but if you're wearing her locket, some part of her will be. Whenever you need her, she'll be right there." Tapping Jo's hand that was still curled around the locket, Sibi felt the sense of their mother's hovering presence again, and added a soft, heartfelt, "Always."

Jo looked down at her closed hand. "Always," she echoed. Then she looked at Sibi. "I won't ever take it off." Frowning, she seemed to reflect. "Except when I have a bath."

Sibi had to smile. "That would probably be for the best." Then she kissed Jo's damaged cheek in a gesture meant to show just how unrepulsed she was by the injury, ruffled her hair, turned her around and said, "Now go to bed."

Jo smiled, too, a tremulous smile but a smile nonetheless, and did.

35

Sibi held her breath, but September turned into October with no apparent repercussions from what had happened at the rally. No one asked either Margrit or Jo anything about Guernica.

Jo's situation at school improved marginally. Gretta and her friends no longer openly made fun of her. Instead they, and most of the other students, studiously ignored her. Sibi hated the thought of Jo as a pariah, but Jo assured her that she didn't mind sitting by herself at lunch or retreating to a corner of the playground at recess with a book, which Margrit reported was what she did. That, and being left alone in class and in the hallways and in the gym, was, Jo said, far preferable to what had gone on before. Afraid that anything she or anyone else, such as Papa or Dr. Richter, might do would only make the situation worse again, Sibi reluctantly left it alone.

At least once a week, she dropped off a bag of paper and cloth for reclamation in the bin at the Sophienkirche. In the process of collecting said items, she ruthlessly cleaned out cupboards and closets, and went through and included most of Mama's and Luiza's garments that the rest of them neither wanted as a keepsake or would ever wear, knowing that both her mother and sister would appreciate the use of their belongings for such a cause. The pink velvet dress she kept, although not with the thought that either of her sisters might ever wear it. She simply couldn't part with it.

She was so assiduous in her efforts that Papa, who knew nothing of Griff or the true purpose behind her attack on clutter, even complimented her on her sudden dedication to housekeeping.

In the wider world, Prime Minister Mussolini returned to Italy. Not quite two weeks after his departure, on October 11, the newly minted Duke and Duchess of Windsor arrived in Berlin. The former King Edward VIII of Great Britain, known to family and friends as David, had abdicated the previous December, and subsequently married "the woman I love," Wallis Warfield Simpson, an American double divorcée. Speculation was rife that the pair held pro-

Nazi views. Although the visit was ostensibly private, they were treated like heads of state, traveling around Germany on Hitler's personal train and meeting with Hitler himself. Ilsa confided many gossipy details of Hitler's cordiality to the couple and his conviction that the duke could be considered an ally, having gleaned them from her father, who was present at their meeting and privy to the führer's subsequent musings about how best to make use of the royal couple.

At Kummersdorf, in conjunction with the scientists at the new rocket facility that was in the process of being established at the distant outpost of Peenemünde, Papa and his team were working on problems with the pitch and yaw gyroscopes and the mushroom-shaped fuel injector of the new A-3 rocket, which was scheduled for its first test launch in December. Stability was an issue, as was the duration of flight. Papa could talk of little else, and spent most of his time at home in his office going over past flights of previous aggregate rocket incarnations to see what could be applied from their successes and failures.

October turned to November with only the most ordinary of household problems, for which Sibi was thankful. Around the city, signs reading Jews Are Prohibited popped up in store and restaurant windows everywhere, and Jewish children were officially banned from the public schools. A house down the street was left empy as the Jewish family that had lived in it for many years abruptly left. Word was they had emigrated to join relatives in Switzerland.

In other news, the Republicans in Spain suffered a terrible defeat at Gijón, Japan conquered Shanghai, the Messerschmidt ME airplane flew a new world air speed record and Britain's Lord Halifax visited Berlin and met privately with Hitler. Again from Ilsa, who got it from her father, Sibi learned that this "unofficial" visit had been sanctioned by British Prime Minister Neville Chamberlain, and what the führer and his advisers took away from it was that Britain would not allow itself to be dragged into a military conflict to defend central and eastern Europe. This left Germany free to pursue its goal of *Lebensraum,* or obtaining more living space, i.e., land, which could only be achieved by an expansion of Germany's borders, without interference from Britain.

Meanwhile, as she discovered from listening in on the next meeting of the Society of German Scientists and Physicians, at the

Spandau Citadel, scientists were conducting experiments with the pesticide Zyklon-B to gauge its potential usefulness as a weapon against humans.

Gripped by the rising sense of foreboding that seemed to hum like radio static throughout the city, Sibi tried her best not to worry too much about the future while faithfully recording everything that seemed important in the coded notebook she kept for Griff.

On December 1, heart beating like a piston engine, feeling as though a million pairs of eyes followed her every move, Sibi dropped the coded notebook off in the reclamation bin. Then she went to school.

On December 2, a Thursday, while in class, Sibi was given a message that she was to meet with Herr Kraus immediately after school the following day. An automobile would be sent to pick her up in front of the school.

Her stomach dropped clear to her toes. Her throat seized up with dread.

Was the notebook found? Was I followed? What does Herr Kraus know?

Fighting panic, she waited up for Papa that night to share the bad news. He was worried, too — any summons from Herr Kraus caused anxiety — but was not nearly as alarmed as she was. He assumed, as she would have done before she'd dropped off that notebook, that it was something to do with Guernica. His worst fear was that it was something to do with *her sisters* and Guernica. As she could not tell him that another, even more potentially ruinous, danger lurked, she took scant comfort from his speculation and subsequent reassurances. She was still in a cold sweat when she finally went to bed, and tossed and turned for what was left of the night.

At the sight of the big black Mercedes waiting for her the next afternoon as she walked out through her school's walled courtyard, Sibi's chest tightened until it felt as if it would crush her pounding heart. The sky was gray, the wind biting and the scent of what, if all the signs were accurate, would be the season's first snow was in the air. Thankful for the warmth of her long black coat, she did her best not to visibly shiver as the uniformed driver got out and opened the rear passenger door for her.

Ducking inside, she checked when she saw who was already in the rear seat waiting for her. Gooseflesh raced prickling over her skin, her stomach cramped and then she was sinking down on the luxurious padded leather seat, inhaling the aroma of cigarettes and 4711 cologne, as she said, with what she considered truly commendable composure, "Good afternoon, Herr Kraus."

"You look surprised to see me, Fräulein Helinger." Lowering the typewritten pages he'd been looking through, Herr Kraus smiled a small, tight smile at her.

If this is about the notebook, I must insist, and keep insisting, that it's nothing more than practice math problems that I threw away.

It was all she could do to breathe. "I admit that I am, Herr Kraus."

The driver closed the door with a solid-sounding *thunk* and got back behind the wheel.

Herr Kraus's lips pursed as he seemed to study her face. *Whatever you do, do not show fear.*

"Would you like to know where we're going?" he asked as the automobile got under way.

"If you would like to tell me, Herr Kraus." Her voice did not shake. Her hands did not tremble. She was, she congratulated herself, outwardly as placid as a cow.

"To the Municipal Psychiatric Clinic for Children at Wittenau. I — or perhaps I should say *we* — have business there. My good friend Dr. Bonhoeffer runs a *Sonderschule* on the grounds, which may be an excellent solution for your poor afflicted sister."

36

Every cell in Sibi's body went on red alert. The metallic tang of fear tasted sharp in her mouth. Everyone knew of the special children's ward, known as Weisengrund, although such were its horrors that it was rarely spoken of.

Lebensunwertes Lebun, or "lives unworthy of life," was how the Nazis classified those with inherited illnesses, or mental or physical handicaps or disorders. Hitler was a fervent proponent of the "Utopia of human selection" and held that purging the weakest among them would strengthen society as a whole. To this end, doctors and hospitals were charged with reporting "unhealthy" newborns to the authorities, while teachers and schools were enlisted to identify those who were slow or unable to learn. In increasing numbers, those children were removed from their families, institutionalized and subjected to forced sterilization to prevent them from reproducing. Rumors abounded that Weisengrund's ultimate solution for many of their "afflicted" residents was child euthanasia.

Learning that he had discovered the notebook would have been preferable.

"I'm sorry, Herr Kraus, but there must be a mistake. I don't have an 'afflicted' sister."

"Dear me, I am rarely the recipient of mistakes of that sort." The very mildness of his tone made her pulse thunder in her ears. He looked down at the sheaf of papers in his hand. The dark blue folder that had held them lay open on his lap. "According to this report, your sister Johanna Marie Helinger, aged ten years, has been identified as a possible defective. It has been posited that she is capable of learning nonetheless, and for that reason consideration is being given to admitting her to this *Sonderschule* rather than placing her in a more — restrictive, shall we say? — environment."

"My sister Johanna suffered burns when she was trapped in a collapsed building in Guernica. She has injuries to her skin that will heal. She is not defective in the least." Placid was forgotten. Her reaction was instant and visceral. Agitation had her sitting bolt upright with her hands fisted tightly in her lap.

"Ah, Guernica. Always it comes back to that. You have another sister, do you not? A pretty poppet, six years old, I believe?" Herr Kraus's voice had turned silken. "It has been reported that she is claiming that Luiza — that *is* the name of your sister who died in the tragedy, is it not? — was, um—" he consulted the papers "— 'shot by an airplane.' "

Sibi went cold to her bone marrow. Here, then, was the fallout she'd feared. The papers he held — were they a report from the rally? Filed by the gestapo agents who'd been on hand? Most likely, although it could have been anyone, including the girls Margrit and Jo had fought with, or their parents or friends, as an act of vengeance. As Griff had warned, tip lines facilitated people turning in friends, relatives, neighbors, chance acquaintances, someone glimpsed in the street. Anyone could, and did, turn in anyone.

"Oh, that." From somewhere Sibi summoned the presence of mind to assume a relieved tone. Her posture deliberately relaxed. She made an airy gesture even as adrenaline pumped through her veins. "Margrit has nightmares. She is little, and often thinks what she sees in them is real."

His small gray eyes were cold and hard as

they met hers. "Is that what it is?"

"Yes, of course."

The automobile stopped.

"It seems we have arrived," Herr Kraus said as the driver got out and came around to open the door. Fear had consumed her to the point where she hadn't registered anything beyond the threat unfolding in the suffocating confines of the back seat, but now Sibi darted a glance out the window. The large yellow-brick building that met her gaze looked as sinister as a prison. The cold wind that blew in through the open door was warm compared to the iciness encasing her insides.

Herr Kraus returned the papers to their folder and thrust it into the briefcase at his feet. "Come, Fräulein Helinger. I would have you see this wonderful *Sonderschule* for yourself."

To go inside with him was the last thing she wanted to do. She didn't dare refuse. Jo's future, and Margrit's, might well hinge on how she handled this. Their *lives* might hinge on it, and hers, as well. Panic gripped her. Forcing it back, she got out and allowed Herr Kraus to escort her into the building. It was old, and cold, with high ceilings and white plaster walls and lots of dark wood trim and an oppressive air of gloom.

A young child's high-pitched wail along with the strong smell of a cleansing agent mixed with — was it urine? — greeted her. It was all she could do not to shudder.

"This way." Herr Kraus led her along a fluorescent-lit corridor that ran the length of the building. Glass panes set into the doors gave her glimpses of wards of small beds filled with children of varying ages. Some were strapped down. Some lay as if dead. A few were sitting up, most with vacant looks on their faces. In one room, a nurse stood beside a machine that Sibi only identified as a centrifuge after she'd already passed by it. She'd been too fixated on the dark-haired boy of about six or seven who was locked inside the machine as it rotated at a furious pace, to register what she was seeing in the moment. The child's head, the only part of his body not encased in the machine, spun like a wheel.

His eyes were open, his mouth wide. His wailing scream made the hair stand up on the back of her neck.

"It is a treatment for a mental condition," Herr Kraus said, impatient at what must have been the expression on her face, as they stepped through a doorway into a section of the hospital that had clearly been turned into a school. "Most efficacious, I've been told."

Light-headed with horror, Sibi couldn't even manage a reply.

"Hans! Good of you to stop by." A man in a white coat, short, bald and beaming, turned from a conversation he'd been having with another white-coated man to hurry toward them. Even as he approached, Sibi's gaze riveted on the children within her view. A young girl in a wheeled chair, missing her legs from the knees down. Another girl, a little older, with milk-white eyes that made Sibi think she must be blind. A teen boy with no defect that she could see, all seated in the sliver of a second room that was visible through its open door.

"The pleasure is mine, my friend." Herr Kraus pumped the man's hand. "This is Oberartz Dr. Bonhoeffer." Gesturing at Sibi, he added, "Rudolf, this is Fräulein Helinger, who has a sister who might benefit from the specialized atmosphere of your school."

"Oh?" Dr. Bonhoeffer turned interested eyes on Sibi. "It's unusual to have a family member visit us. For most of our children, no one comes. It's understandable, of course — rare is the family that wishes to claim hazardous genes. So tell me, what disability afflicts your sister?"

"My sister has no disability. Her face is marked from a burn. It's an *injury.*"

Herr Kraus said, "She is an outcast at her school. The normal children are distressed by her. The report I was given suggested that your school might be a better fit."

"No," Sibi said forcefully. Both men looked at her.

"And then there is another sister who suffers from delusional nightmares," Herr Kraus said, his eyes on her face.

Sibi's heart seized up.

"So genetics could indeed be the problem." Dr. Bonhoeffer sounded delighted. "Most interesting, a pair of sisters —"

"My family was caught up in the tragedy at Guernica," Sibi said. Her eyes clashed with Herr Kraus's. In a blinding flash of insight, she realized that her weakness was also her power: the truth. Screaming it from the rooftops would undoubtedly prove disastrous for herself and Margrit and Jo and Papa, but it would also embarrass the Ministry of Propaganda, and the Reich. It was a very small amount of leverage, but it was something, and she meant to use it for all it was worth. "My sisters are still recovering. It has nothing to do with genetics."

"I see the idea distresses you." Dr. Bonhoeffer took her hand, patted it sympathetically. "It need not. You may be correct. If you are not, our children receive excellent care. Our medical staff can evaluate your sisters and make a recommendation."

Sibi pulled her hand from his hold.

"You're looking unwell, Fräulein Helinger," Herr Kraus said before Sibi could say anything. "Perhaps it would be best if you returned to the automobile and waited for me there. My business with Dr. Bonhoeffer will be brief. You and I can discuss your sisters' case further on the way home."

Once again their eyes met. Sibi read a warning in his, and a threat. Open opposition would, she feared, be met with a crushing response.

Yet, it was clear that he recognized that in her knowledge she did indeed possess a small sliver of power. The question was, would it be enough?

Her heart drummed. *I must be very careful.*

She bowed her head in respectful deference to his authority.

"Thank you, Herr Kraus, I do feel unwell. Dr. Bonhoeffer, it was a pleasure meeting you."

"The same, Fräulein Helinger, the same."

Sibi turned and walked away.

Her stomach was a pit. Her knees felt

wobbly. She felt the men's eyes on her as she left, and kept her posture erect and stride strong until she was beyond their range of vision.

By the time she was outside again her insides had turned to jelly and all she wanted to do was collapse.

The driver leaned against the hood smoking a cigarette. He hastily dropped his hand, hiding it from her view: the Nazi Party was, officially, anti-tobacco. Sibi made a gesture — *carry on, don't mind me* — and said as she passed him, "Herr Kraus will be out shortly. He asked me to wait for him in the automobile."

The driver nodded, bestirred himself to open the door for her and then, as she collapsed on the seat, closed it again and went back to lean against the hood and enjoy his cigarette.

Sibi shut her eyes only to open them again almost at once as she fought to regain her equilibrium. It was important that she have herself well under control before Herr Kraus rejoined her. He would not appreciate her brief flicker of defiance, and he had the power to have her and her whole family arrested — or worse — if he wished.

She could only pray that his need for her testimony outweighed the risk he might feel she and her family posed.

Her eyes fell on his briefcase, left behind in the footwell. The papers he'd been looking at were in there —

A lightning glance at the hospital entrance revealed no sign of him. The driver still leaned against the fender, staring at the lowering sky as he puffed away beneath a cloud of smoke.

Quick as the thought, she opened the briefcase and grabbed the dark blue folder. *Streng Geheim* — Top Secret — was stamped in bold black letters on its front. That *almost* gave her pause.

Darting wary looks out the windows, heart galloping like a runaway horse, she opened the folder and looked down at the sheaf of papers. The top one was indeed a report of the altercation at the rally, with her, Jo and Margrit's names heavily underlined. Included was a list of witnesses, and a precise account of what was done and said. The source of the report was not clear. Its heading was Referred for Medical Evaluation.

Her chest was so tight she could barely breathe.

The papers underneath —

They were the summary of minutes of a meeting, dated November 5, 1937. The keeper of the minutes was identified as *der*

Führer's military adjutant, Colonel Friedrich Hossbach. As she skimmed the pages, Sibi's blood congealed.

This was Hitler's blueprint for war, which he stated in a presentation to a gathering of his top advisers was his fixed intention. War was necessary to provide Germany with sufficient *Lebensraum,* he said, and he would act within one to no more than five years, beginning with the seizure of Austria and Czechoslavakia and moving on to the conquest of the entirety of Eastern Europe.

There was more, much more, but a distracted glance out the windows revealed Herr Kraus already mere steps away from the front of the car. The driver, throwing down his cigarette, straightened to greet him.

Terror shot through Sibi's veins. Snapping the folder shut, she bent and shoved it back into the briefcase.

The door opened.

Sibi's heart leaped into her throat.

In the few seconds before Herr Kraus slid in beside her, she whipped back into an upright position in her seat, folded her hands in her lap and (hopefully) composed her face.

And prayed he couldn't tell that she was sweating with anxiety.

War. Hitler meant war. The memo left no doubt about that. The prospect was terrible — and terrifying. But compared to more immediate threats — to her sisters from the asylum, to herself if Herr Kraus should discover that she'd read his papers — it was something to act on later. Something to report to Griff.

"Feeling better, Fräulein Helinger?" Herr Kraus asked as the automobile pulled away, then swept along the semicircular driveway to merge into the heavy flow of traffic heading back toward the central part of the city.

"Yes, thank you, Herr Kraus. Although I was upset rather than ill." Her glance passed — oh-so-casually! — over the briefcase. Was there any sign of what she'd done? Not that she could see, but she'd returned the folder so quickly . . . Her gaze met his. "My sisters don't belong in such a place."

She could see something in his eyes — a flicker — that told her he was surprised she would address the matter so directly. To do so courted danger, she knew, and to openly pit herself against him would undoubtedly end in her and her family's ruin, but as non-confrontationally as possible she wanted to make sure he understood that the unspoken terms of the bargain they'd struck — her family's safety in return for her cooperation

— still stood.

"Perhaps, perhaps not. It is an option we will keep open, yes?"

Feeling that further defiance at this moment might be counterproductive, she didn't reply. Without conscious volition, her gaze once again touched on the briefcase. *The folder — had she put it back in the right way? Was the Top Secret stamp supposed to be facing the front or back of the briefcase? If she'd got it wrong, would he know the difference?*

"Stop!" Herr Kraus's near shout, uttered as he reached for his briefcase, made Sibi jump like she'd been scalded. Her heart lodged in her throat. "Andres, stop at once!"

The driver pulled to the curb and slammed on the brakes.

Herr Kraus leaped out, immediately tipped his head toward the sky and clapped a pair of binoculars to his eyes.

A glance down confirmed it: he'd grabbed the binoculars from the open briefcase. She could see the blue folder standing on end inside. The papers were visible, sticking out from the top — was that from her, or from his snatching up of the binoculars?

She only hoped he wouldn't know, either.

So unnerved she felt like she could melt into a puddle right there on the seat, she could only sit and wait and try to regulate her body into a semblance of calm until he got back inside.

"It was a *Schellente*," he said with satisfaction as he restored the binoculars to the briefcase and the automobile pulled away from the curb. Sibi's last glimpse of the blue folder before he snapped the briefcase shut made her stomach twist with fright: she could see the Top Secret stamp clearly now, and it was *upside down.* She'd put the folder back upside down, and that was something that his quick grab into the briefcase couldn't have done. *My God, would he notice? Would he realize?* "I've been trying to catch one in flight for ages. They got their name from their wings, which jingle like a sleigh bell when they fly, you know."

She didn't know. She didn't care. "How very interesting, Herr Kraus."

A moment later, in a completely different tone, he said, "There is another matter I wish to discuss with you. That monstrosity — that painting, *Guernica* —" his lip curled with loathing "— is being sent on an international tour. Everything — the slander, the lies — is being stirred up again. The führer himself was asked about it by Lord Halifax, with whom he recently met. He was furious, and is now most anxious that the stain on Germany's honor be eliminated, and that the world accept the truth once and for all. At Dr. Goebbels' suggestion, you are to be the face of the campaign to place the blame where it rightfully belongs — on our enemies. You will be required to give the facts again at a press conference next week. There will be other requirements, as well."

Breathe. Just breathe. "I will be ready as needed, Herr Kraus."

The automobile stopped. Sibi glanced out the window: they were in front of her house. Never had she been so glad to see it. Light shone through the closed curtains, although it was not yet dark. The driver got out —

"It is to be hoped that your young sister — Margrit, that is correct? — will have no more nightmares. It would be most unfortunate if she did," Herr Kraus said, and smiled at her. A brutal smile. A smile that belonged to the kind of man who did not mind hurting children — or anyone. Through the gray gloom of approaching twilight, his grinning face made her think of a malevolent gargoyle.

It hit her then that when he had no more use for her, when Guernica and the painting were no longer a thorn in the international consciousness, that he wouldn't hesitate to permanently rid himself and the

Reich of the threat she and her sisters posed. It would, in fact, be the prudent thing to do. Having them killed was the only certain way to make sure they never spoke out.

Sibi barely managed not to shiver as what felt like an icy hand gripped her heart.

"There will be no more nightmares, Herr Kraus," she replied.

The driver opened the door.

"Excellent," Herr Kraus said.

As she got out, it was all she could do to keep from throwing one more lighting glance at the briefcase.

But she didn't. She didn't look back.

The automobile didn't drive away until she opened her front door.

As the long black shape of it disappeared from view, she almost fell into the welcoming warmth of the entry hall.

She'd no sooner closed the door behind her than Fräulein Skeller emerged from the kitchen with the news that the little girls had not come home from school.

37

"How many times do I have to say it? It's an emergency!" Sibi was on the telephone, trying not to scream at the operator at Kummersdorf as she was told, for what must have been the dozenth time, that Dr. Helinger was in a meeting and could not be disturbed. Having sent Frau Skeller home because she didn't want a witness to any negotiating that might become necessary in case what she most feared — that Herr Kraus had had the girls picked up — should prove true, she was alone in the house. She'd passed way beyond panic when Ruby, who'd been at her feet, erupted into a frenzy of barking and shot off into the entry hall.

Jo and Margrit burst through the front door.

Hearing her sisters' voices, Sibi dropped the receiver and ran after Ruby.

There they were, both of them, slamming the door with a bang against the snow that was now coming down hard and the night that had fallen, tripping over each other, shedding coats, hats and bags, greeting an ecstatic Ruby.

"Where. Have. You. Been?"

"Sibi!" Margrit threw herself against her. Jo was already on her knees on the floor hugging Ruby, whose tail wagged madly.

"Are you all right? What happened?" So relieved she felt unsteady on her feet, Sibi hugged Margrit tightly and at the same time cast an assessing glance over Jo.

"A doctor and nurse came to school. They examined us. We had to stay after," Margrit said. "They took us into the bathroom. We had to take off our clothes down to our underwear."

"What?" The hot surge of anger Sibi felt swamped her underlying fear. She welcomed it for the strength it gave her.

"They had papers," Jo said. "Dr. Richter said he had no choice. He wasn't allowed to telephone you, or Papa." She lifted her head. Sibi saw that her face was bare of the cosmetics she now always wore to camouflage the discolorations. The skin grafts were starkly apparent. "The nurse made me wash my face." Jo's lips trembled. "I thought they were going to take us away."

Margrit said, "Then Dr. Richter came,

and knocked on the door, and said there was a telephone call. The doctor —"

"His name was Dr. Haupt," Jo interjected. "It was on his name badge."

"The doctor went out, and came back, and said we could go. We got dressed as fast as we could and ran for the tram." Margrit clung more tightly still, the smell of snow in her curls, and Sibi clung just as tightly back. "Do we have hapless genes, Sibi?"

"*Hazardous* genes." Jo looked at Sibi. "That's what the doctor said they were checking us for." Behind her glasses, her eyes were huge dark pools of fright. "Because of my face."

Oh, Jo. Sibi felt her sister's pain like a knife to the heart.

"They asked us questions," Margrit said.

"About Guernica," Jo said.

Fear wrapped tight bands around Sibi's chest. "What did you say?"

"What Papa told us to say if we were asked." Margrit lifted her head. Her expression was triumphant. "That we couldn't remember anything. We kept saying it even when they said they could tell we were lying and we wouldn't get in trouble if we would only tell the truth."

Jo looked at Margrit. "I was afraid you were going to give in, but you didn't. You were really brave."

"*You* were brave," Margrit replied.

"You were both brave." Sibi closed her eyes in the briefest moment of gratitude, then opened them as Margrit pulled out of her arms.

"I'm hungry," Margrit said, as if that was the end of that.

Margrit the dauntless, Sibi thought with a bemused spurt of affectionate admiration. However her sister had come by her resilience, Sibi mentally saluted it.

Wanting to make as light of what had happened as possible so as not to imprint the trauma on her sisters' minds any more than could be helped, she said, "I'm sure you are. What an ordeal! You both handled it in the exact right way. I'm so proud of you, and Papa will be, too. Now, suppose we go see what Frau Skeller has left us to eat?"

"I hope it's sauerbraten. With potato dumplings." Margrit headed for the kitchen.

Jo got to her feet, muttering, "Sometimes I think food is all she thinks about," and followed with Ruby frisking along beside her.

Sibi went with them, and set out the food and even made a pretense of eating. Jo, too, picked at what was on her plate. The only hearty meals were consumed by Margrit and Ruby, who got the leftovers. Afterward, when Sibi sent the girls upstairs to get ready for bed while she cleaned up the kitchen, Jo waited until Margrit had whisked out of sight before turning back to Sibi.

"Do you think they'll come back?" Jo asked.

Sibi knew who she meant: the doctors. The Nazis.

Her hands full of dishes, Sibi paused to look at her sister. Her first instinct was to stoutly say *no* so Jo wouldn't worry. But Jo wasn't a baby, and she was at risk, and her serious question deserved a serious answer.

"Not for a while," Sibi said. "Maybe not ever."

"They looked inside my locket." Jo lifted a hand to the small silver oval nestled against her sweater. "When they opened it, it was like I could feel Mama with us. I wasn't as afraid anymore. That's when the telephone call came, and they let us go."

So maybe, Sibi thought as she wrapped her arms around Jo, she was starting to believe in miracles, after all.

Later, when Papa got home, Sibi recounted the events of the day. He was as horrified as she was, and even angrier.

"We have to leave here." Putting a hand

488

on his arm, she cut through his furious diatribe about confronting Herr Kraus and Dr. Richter and whoever the hell that Dr. Haupt was. They were in his study, he in his chair, she crouched beside him. "We're all in danger. They're threatening Jo and Margrit now. And those papers I saw — there's going to be a war."

"We can't," he said. "I'm working for the military now, and the secrets I know are military secrets. I would be considered a traitor if I left the country. If I even made it through the border, which I might not because the rumor is that those of us working on this project are being watched." He frowned at her. "And once again, you know a secret, too. I don't think they're going to let you go. I could send the little girls out of the country without either of us, perhaps, but where? And to whom? Anyway, that might backfire. They might use it as an excuse to take custody of the girls."

"There has to be a way." Desperation sharpened her voice.

"I need time to think," he said. "Go to bed, Sibi. You look exhausted. You don't have to always carry the weight of everything that happens to this family on your shoulders, you know. I'm your father, I'll figure something out."

Sibi went upstairs, but she didn't go to bed. She spent the next hour or so frantically writing a coded letter to Griff. The information in the war memo she'd read was what was urgent, but she included what had happened to the girls and herself, too. Usually unburdening herself to him in her writings made her feel better, but this time it didn't help: the sense of danger closing in was too acute.

She tossed and turned the entire night. The next day, a Saturday, with the excuse that she needed to run an errand, she went to the post office with her letter for "Annie" but was too paranoid about being followed to actually go inside and drop it off.

On Sunday, the prospect of the little girls going back to school had to be faced. Although Jo and Margrit were unaware of any discussion, she and her father debated the topic in a series of tense tête-à-têtes. Papa ultimately decided that there was no help for it, the girls had to return to school. Knowing nothing of the discussions, and taking in good part Papa's stern reminder that if asked any questions about Guernica they must continue to remember nothing, Jo and Margrit seemed to accept the inevitability of the upcoming school week as a matter of course. But as night fell, Jo grew

490

increasingly subdued.

Margrit was already in bed, and Jo was in the washroom getting ready for bed, when Sibi, hearing something out of the ordinary, went to check on her. Her own stomach knotted as she stood in the dim upstairs hall outside the washroom door listening to the umistakable sounds of her sister being sick.

A tentative knock. "Jo?"

Jo opened the door. "I don't want to go to school tomorrow." Her face was as pale as the white ruffle edging the neck of her nightgown.

"Are you sick?" Sibi laid the back of her hand against Jo's forehead: no telltale heat. Her sister nodded.

Sibi had no doubt at all that Jo's symptoms were caused by dread.

"You can't stay home forever. You have to go back. And missing tomorrow will only make Tuesday worse." Sympathy softened the practical words.

"I hate school. Nobody wants me there," Jo said miserably. "And Dr. Haupt — what if he comes back?"

That thought terrified Sibi, too, but as Papa had pointed out, if Jo and Margrit stayed at home they would be reinforcing the idea that something was wrong with them. And they could not be kept out of school indefinitely. And keeping them out of school would not even guarantee that they were safe; the gestapo could come for the girls, or any of them, at any time. That being the case, it would be best, and safest, if they all stuck to their routine while Papa worked to find a way out for them.

"Everything will be all right." The promise felt as empty when she said it as it had when Papa, earlier, had said it to her. But that was the note on which she gave Jo a hug and sent her off to bed, and went to bed herself, only for them all to be jolted awake hours later by Margrit having one more screaming nightmare.

It was Wednesday on the way home from school before Sibi finally got up the nerve to put her letter to "Annie" in the post office box. Though she badly wanted to hear from Griff, she didn't ask for a reply because she was wary about returning to the post office any time soon.

Whether it was her imagination or not, everywhere she went she had the sensation of eyes watching her. It felt as though her life — her family's lives — hung by the thinnest of threads.

On Friday, she was summoned to the Ministry of Propaganda for the threatened news conference. This time they gave her a blue dress to wear — "blue photographs better," one of the assistants who helped prepare her told her — and did her hair and applied camera-friendly cosmetics to her face. She was given a script to memorize. A script in which, in addition to repeating the story she had already told, she was to accuse the Whites of murdering her mother and sister in the course of destroying their own town.

"You've been quite a success as the face of the injustice that has been done to our country," Kraus told her as he escorted her to the assembly. "A young girl who has survived a terrible tragedy automatically garners sympathy. Today, our goal is to firmly place the blame for the atrocity on our enemies where it belongs, and in the process claim some of that worldwide sympathy for Germany. Do you understand?"

Sibi nodded.

Kraus stood at the back of the room, arms folded over his chest, watching her as she performed her part for the dozens of reporters present, and the filming camera crews and the photographers who snapped pictures as she spoke. Afterward, as assistants passed out pictures of Mama and Luiza for inclusion in the stories and newsreels, it was he who whisked her away in the teeth of the continuing hubbub of shouted questions and popping flashbulbs.

"That was quite good," he said. "At the next event, you should try to show more emotion. A few tears when you speak of your mother and sister would be particularly well received, I think."

After that, Sibi no longer felt guilty for lying about Guernica. She'd finally recognized what she was engaged in: a fight for survival, by whatever means necessary.

That night, after the little girls were in bed, Papa called her into his study to tell her that he was talking to some people he knew about possibly obtaining a transfer to a research facility in another part of the country.

"I think it would be best if we got as far away as possible from Berlin." His eyes were grave.

Standing beside his desk with the lamplight pooling around them, she saw that he looked tired and drawn.

"They're still watching us." It wasn't a question, and she didn't need his answering grimace to know the answer. For him to risk taking overt steps to get them away, the situation must be even more dire than she had suspected. At the thought of what leaving

Berlin would mean — abandoning home, school, friends — she felt a pang of distress. But it was nothing compared to the cold fear that swamped her at the thought of what might happen if they stayed.

She took a breath. "Do you think it will be possible?"

"I don't know. I'm exploring every channel I can. It's difficult. I must be very careful. We must all be very careful."

She nodded. Her hand rested on the desktop, and he covered it with his.

A week passed, then another and another. Her father went to work, she and the girls went to school. Herr Kraus summoned her to give an interview to reporters from the major European newspapers to serve as a counterpoint to the upcoming tour of Picasso's painting throughout Scandinavia, which was to commence in January amid massive publicity. Through it all, Sibi felt as if she were sitting atop a ticking time bomb.

A few days before Christmas, she stood out on the back porch looking up at the soaring half-moon, which was pale and fuzzy against the black sky and reminded her of an orange slice leached of its color. The night was cold, and smelled of the snow that covered the ground and glinted silver in the moonlight, but she needed the fresh air. Jo had been teased again at school. A teacher had intervened, but the resulting unpleasantness had drawn the attention of a visiting parent, who happened to occupy a prominent position in the Nazi Party. When Jo had told her about it before going upstairs to bed, her mind had immediately shot to possible repercussions and her already frayed nerves had stretched almost to the breaking point.

So she stood out on the back porch, and looked up at the moon, and breathed, and prayed.

That's what she was doing when Papa stepped outside to join her. He, too, took a deep breath and looked up at the moon.

Then he told her that he'd been notified that afternoon that he was being transferred to the fledgling rocket development program in the remote outpost of Peenemünde.

■ ■ ■ ■

PART THREE:
PEENEMÜNDE

■ ■ ■ ■

38

August 16, 1943

Strange to think that this moon, this fuzzy pale moon playing peekaboo among the banks of dark clouds scudding across the black velvet sky, was the same moon that she had watched that long ago night from her back porch, that her friends might be viewing now in Berlin, that Griff could see from wherever he was.

Strange, but comforting, a little. Looking up at it through the window of the *Kameradschaftsheim,* the local club where she was putting in a command appearance at a party she *really* hadn't wanted to attend, and knowing that they might be looking up at it, too, made Sibi feel less cut off from the world. Less isolated on this tiny military outpost that was Peenemünde.

Less alone.

Formerly a small fishing village on the island of Usedom, just off the coast of

Germany on the Baltic Sea, Peenemünde had been her home for more than five years now. After she and her family had fled (there was no other word for it) Berlin, this place had felt like a refuge despite its sparsity. Fortunately, in the light of her father's commitment to the Reich, the headmaster had allowed her to take her exams and graduate early from Berlinisches Gymnasium. Though Papa had urged her to return to Berlin and take up her place at university once the girls were settled, Sibi had not felt able to leave her sisters so soon. There would be, she reasoned, time for all that later. But that later time had not come. She'd found herself cocooned on their small island, raising her sisters, assisting her father while learning everything he could teach her.

The combined feelings of relief and dismay with which she'd first viewed the barely populated backwater of thick piney woods and flat sandy beaches and little else that was Peenemünde had faded as seasons had passed, and birthdays and holidays and other, less joyous occasions had come and gone, and she and her sisters and Papa — and Ruby — had settled in and made a life for themselves. Over the same period, Peenemünde, like the world itself, had changed out of all recognition. Thanks to the money and manpower the Reich had poured into the burgeoning rocket program, this all but forgotten little island had been transformed into the top-secret Military Experimental Station Peenemünde. And in the meantime, the world had gone to war.

She had watched in fear and disbelief as with spasm after spasm of violence the surrounding countries were overrun. The casual brutality of the conquerers toward the conquered, mass hunger, widespread deprivation, atrocities, death: those were the whispers that reached her ears, though no one dared speak openly of such things. Sibi grew increasingly grateful for the outpost's remoteness as the horrors of war engulfed the planet.

Now four years into the conflict, the early, overwhelming success of the Nazi military machine was sputtering. In recent months, faith in the ultimate victory had been shaken as setback after setback befell the Axis powers. The Germans had tightened the noose around the occupied territories, and terror and misery were the citizenry's constant companions. Savagery toward those perceived to be enemies of the Reich had reached new heights. Food shortages

— shortages of everything — were at crisis levels.

But here at Heeresversuchsanstalt Peenemünde, there had been a different sort of change. Morale that had been low was now high. Leadership that had been perfunctory was now focused and resolute. The military that had been in near-total disarray in the aftermath of the debacle that was the defeat of the German offensive at Stalingrad in February, followed by the Allied victory in North Africa and, just the previous month, the Allied invasion of Sicily, seemed in the last two weeks to have found a new purpose and discipline.

The question was, why?

"Eureka" was the reason, Sibi was almost certain. She didn't know what specifically it referred to, but in her capacity as her father's research assistant she had been delivering a packet of fuel efficacy test results to the office of the post's military commander, Major-General Dr. Walter Dornberger, when she had overheard him and the rocket program's technical director, Major Dr. Wernher von Braun, discussing Eureka in the kind of confidential tones that immediately caught her attention.

When she further considered what they'd

said in context with General Dornberger and Dr. von Braun's July flight to visit Hitler in his Wolfsschanze headquarters from which they had returned with, among other things, a distinctive yellow folder, and the fact that the day after they returned from the flight she had spotted on General Dornberger's desk that same yellow folder with the word *Eureka* stamped on it, and added in that he immediately got up to personally (rather than call for his secretary) stow the folder away in the locked file cabinet in his office that held the most classified of the classified documents as soon as she, once again delivering a report from her father, walked in, Sibi's interest was piqued. Combine all that with the near-impossible directive General Dornberger had subsequently given her father, now head of the engine design team, that fifty A-4 rocket engines must be completed, tested and ready to go by August 18 with no reason given, the recent heightened security in the factory that produced the rockets and the arrival of four Portuguese-flagged freighters in the harbor plus her own unshakable gut feeling, and it was enough for her to conclude that Eureka was a code name for whatever it was that had spurred General Dornberger and Dr. von Braun into ramping up a program that lately had been stuck on idle. Those two had then passed their renewed energy on to the small, tight group around them, with the result that it had flowed outward from there. The subsequent frenzy of activity had been focused on the Werke Süd rocket development complex in particular.

And all that, in turn, had prompted her to send an emergency message off to Griff.

"May I take your plate, Fräulein Helinger?"

Sibi almost jumped as the waiter spoke at her elbow. Standing not quite concealed behind one panel of the open damask curtains with the floor-to-ceiling box window itself cranked open in front of her, she was awash in the scents of a summer night in Peenemünde: the perfume of flowers, salt air from the sea and the acrid fumes of the coal-fired plants where the rockets were built — the plants that, since General Dornberger's directive, now ran twenty-four hours a day at top capacity. A welcome cool breeze lifted the ends of her shoulder-length hair, which for tonight's reception for the newly arrived VIPs she wore in a half-up style, away from her sweat-damp neck. She hadn't heard the waiter's approach, and that would be due either to her own fierce concentration on the conversation just outside the window that she was straining to overhear or the band's lively version of "Komm mit nach Madeira," which they'd just struck up and which was prompting a number of couples to take to the dance floor.

She waved the waiter away while continuing to focus on the men outside. The small plate might *look* empty, but there were crumbs left from the single miniscule, sugar-and-cinnamon-filled pastry that she'd eaten with tiny bites to make it last longer. She meant to pick the crumbs up with the pad of a forefinger so as not to waste a single scrumptious particle and eat them, too, but she'd been distracted by the need to listen closely. Her allotment had been four pastries — they were scarcely bigger than a stamp — but three were at that moment wrapped in a napkin and stowed in her handbag to be divided later between Jo and Margrit, who were at home as attendance at this most select gathering was by invitation only.

". . . the balance of power will change. The world will be very different," Dr. Goebbels was saying in a low voice to Dr. Walter Thiel, General Dornberger's deputy. The men were both in uniform: Dr. Goebbels's was the standard brown Nazi Party uniform with no insignia, his only adornment being a swastika armband; Dr. Thiel wore the gray of the Wehrmacht. They stood on the veranda just outside the window, sipping snifters of fine brandy from General Dornberger's cherished personal supply as they looked out at the silver-tipped black sea less than a hundred meters away. Germany controlled a five-hundred-kilometer, unobstructed stretch of it, making it the perfect testing range for the rockets the facility was constructed to build.

Dr. Goebbels and the Minister of Armaments and Munitions, Albert Speer, along with a whole slew of adjutants and other military types, had arrived a few hours before ostensibly to watch the next day's launch of an A-4 rocket. It wasn't the first time they'd visited Peenemünde, but it was the first time they'd visited together, and huddled with General Dornberger in a secret, private meeting from almost the moment of arriving, and given off such an intense energy upon leaving that meeting that the air practically crackled with it.

"The Wonder Weapons you are creating here will give us our victory," Dr. Goebbels continued. "More, they will give us our *vengeance.*"

"Soon our enemies will be on their knees," Dr. Thiel agreed.

Sibi's scalp prickled: more confirmation that she wasn't wrong in her assessment and that whatever they were planning, it wasn't only big, it was imminent. Had Griff gotten her message? She'd sent it twice just to be sure, but still, there was no way to know. Her present means of urgently communicating with him — via carrier pigeon, because the iron-fisted security surrounding the base made anything else nearly impossible — was strictly one way.

"Fräulein Helinger? May I take your plate?" the waiter asked again. Sibi's shoulders slumped in defeat. He wasn't giving up. She turned away from the window.

Ah, she knew him.

"One second, Herr Grau." Licking her forefinger, she picked up the crumbs just as she'd intended, popped them in her mouth and placed the now-gleaming plate on his tray with a twinkling smile for the elderly man. A lifelong local fisherman before the rocket development program had moved in and taken over, he was frail and stoop-shouldered and, along with his equally elderly wife, Ada, just doing his best to survive the war. They were friends, in the same way she was friends with most of the permanent residents thereabouts.

"You should be dancing, a pretty girl like

you, not hiding behind a curtain." He gave her a reproving look.

"I'm waiting for my boyfriend to show up," she said, which was a lie, because she didn't have one, although she had gone out, in a casual fashion, with several of the men stationed on the base. But given that they were Nazis, and she hated the Nazis with a fervor that had only strengthened over the years and was spying on them to boot, the relationships had not flourished. But the last thing she wanted was for Herr Grau to try finding her a dance partner, which she suspected was his intention.

"A loyal type. That's good, that's good. Though if my grandson were here . . ."

She had heard all about his grandson, Private Franz Grau, currently listed as missing in action after the German counterattack at Kursk in July. More than four million troops had battled the Red Army, and lost.

She hated the Nazis, but not all individual Nazis. Herr Grau was a Nazi, and his grandson fought on the side of the Nazis, but she didn't hate him or his wife. Like so many in this terrible war, the side they were on was dictated by their circumstances. They were Germans, in Germany, and their choice was, basically, go along with the

Nazis or die.

"Oh, well, I'd definitely make an exception for Franz."

"When he gets back, maybe something could be arranged. You'd like him. And he's handsome! You should meet him."

"I'd love to meet him," Sibi said. Her heart ached for Herr Grau and his wife, because she knew, and she knew they knew, too, that most likely Franz wasn't coming back. The losses at Kursk had been immense.

He smiled at her, a sad little smile, and went away.

It is only those who have neither fired a shot nor heard the shrieks and groans of the wounded who cry aloud for blood, more vengeance, more desolation. War is hell. As he worked on his engines, Papa was forever muttering that quote from the American Civil War General William Tecumseh Sherman. As a result, Sibi knew it by heart.

Batting her emotions aside, she refocused on trying to glean what information she could. The men were still there, still talking, completely oblivious to her listening in from only a few meters away.

"The führer's plan is genius," Dr. Thiel said.

"The führer *is* a genius," Dr. Goebbels

replied with such utter conviction that his words were chilling to hear. "It is his vision that will propel us onward to achieve the glory of our Thousand Year Reich."

What plan? Had they discussed it while she'd been talking to Herr Grau? Had she missed it? Sibi practically gnashed her teeth.

"To the führer." Dr. Thiel raised his glass.

"The führer," Dr. Goebbels echoed. They drank. Then, in response to a query from Dr. Thiel, Dr. Goebbels began extolling the virtues of his six children.

Sibi listened intently at first, then with half an ear, but nothing was said that was worthy of being reported to Griff, with whom she remained in regular, if clandestine, contact.

Their handler-spy relationship had solidified over the years, and her reports on the developments at Peenemünde were, he told her, the source of keen interest among his superiors. Getting information to him had been relatively easy in the beginning, when the dazzling scientific facility that was being created out of desolate marshland was touted everywhere as a future prestigious center for the exploration of space and space research and he could visit the island as a tourist. Then the war had come, and the need of the military for rockets and other deadly weapons had become paramount, and Peenemünde had grown ever more locked down and top secret. Her communication with Griff had devolved from thrice yearly meetings on the island's beautiful holiday beaches, to a rushed coffee in a mainland café to make alternate arrangements when it became clear that his visits to Usedom must end, to coded messages for him left at a dead drop when she visited the mainland, to coded phrases for her in certain BBC radio programs that they were all forbidden to listen to but they all did, anyway, until it really was forbidden, to what it was at present: coded messages sent by carrier pigeon. The sheer number of birds around Peenemünde — pigeons, egrets, gulls, plovers, ducks, coots and swans that populated the low-lying coastal area by the hundreds — made the flights of the pigeons as unnoticeable as grains of sand on the beach.

As unnoticeable as Sibi herself.

Everyone from Dr. Goebbels, who referred to her as the girl from Guernica and greeted her warmly on the few occasions when he'd visited Peenemünde, to General Dornberger, to the locals like Herr Grau, considered her one of them. As Major (he'd been given military rank as the war began, and promoted since as a mark of the value of his contributions) Dr. Helinger's oldest daughter, who was also his valued assistant, not a scintilla of suspicion had ever fallen on her, not even when the gyroscopes that guided the rockets' flight malfunctioned because of slightly bent "fly legs," or the increasingly precious fuel was found to have been contaminated with rainwater, or the wires to the Oemig — the inverter system — had been disconnected, thus delaying the ambitious timetable laid out for the development of the rockets by months.

But the danger was growing worse: two suspected saboteurs had been arrested and summarily executed on Peenemünde in the last twelve months, and just this past February three members of the White Rose resistance movement, including Sophie Scholl, who at age twenty-two was younger than herself, had been executed by guillotine in Munich for no greater crime than distributing anti-Nazi leaflets. The gruesome nature of Sophie Scholl's death in particular made Sibi's blood run cold every time she thought about it, so she simply didn't. The way she looked at it was, she had a job to do.

Because she was well known to them, because she was a woman, a girl, because she was of Aryan descent and German by birth, she was in a practical sense invisible to them. And that made her invaluable to Griff, and to the cause of defeating the Nazis. Which she embraced not only for the sake of Mama and Luiza, and the hundreds of souls who had perished that night in Guernica, but also for the suffering of the conquered, the devastation unleashed upon the world and the horrors visited on the disabled, the "afflicted," the homosexuals, the Romas, the Poles and Slavics and the members of any opposition group, and most particularly on the Jews, who'd been rounded up and taken away to be imprisoned in work camps that, if the whispers no one dared say aloud were true, were really death camps, where victims were being murdered by the tens of thousands. The truth of that was impossible to determine, but the reality of the work camps was something that she could personally attest to: Peenemünde had one of its own, Trassenheide, that housed something in the neighborhood of eight thousand *Ostarbeiter,* or foreign slave workers, delivered to the island for the labor-intensive work needed to manufacture the rockets.

She could not make their lives better, she could not stop the homicidal tide of Nazi barbarity, but she could do her small bit to strike a blow against the absolute evil that was the Third Reich by sharing what scraps of information that came her way with Griff.

Still chatting about his children, Dr. Goebbels walked away, arm in arm with Dr. Thiel. Sibi stood where she was a moment longer, listening to the distant shouts of young children at play in the sports field next to the nearby school. Margrit would have been there, not as one of the playing children but as a minder, along with a group of other *mittelschule* girls, because at twelve years old she was considered responsible enough to watch the little ones. But Margrit had elected to stay home with Jo, because Jo was staying home and Papa was busy at the factory and Sibi had been "requested" to attend the reception and Margrit did not want Jo to be alone.

The question of how best to deal with an ever-more-reclusive Jo was an ongoing one that tugged at Sibi's heart, and she was frowning and thinking of that as she stepped out of the window embrasure. Thus she was not paying strict attention to her surroundings and as a result stepped right into the path of the very man she'd been making every effort, since she'd seen his name on the guest list, to avoid.

The scent of 4711 cologne wafted around her as Herr Kraus stopped short. "Fräulein

Helinger! I was assured you'd be here, but until now I hadn't seen you. Well met."

39

"Herr Kraus." Her voice sounded hollow to her own ears. Sibi hoped he didn't pick up on it.

He'd aged since she'd seen him last, which would have been in 1939 when the painting *Guernica* was sent to New York on tour. Summoned from Peenemünde, Sibi had spent several stressful weeks giving interviews and having her picture taken. Having done everything that was asked of her to promote the lying Nazi version of what had happened in Guernica, she had then been allowed to return to her family. Kraus had made no further move against the girls, although Sibi never doubted that the threat, should one of them step out of line, still existed. He hadn't, as far as she knew, attempted to stop them from relocating to Peenemünde beyond obtaining her assurance that she would make herself available whenever she was needed to tell her (their) story. Probably he'd thought that letting her go was not much of a risk because Peenemünde was so isolated that she and her sisters could not possibly talk out of turn because there was no one to talk to, while he could still get his hands on her if the international outrage over Guernica should flare up again, as indeed it had. But in the meantime, events had steamrolled.

Hitler had put his plan, the one she'd discovered in the back of Kraus's automobile, into motion with the Anschluss, the annexation of Austria into Germany, followed by the acquisition of the Sudetenland. Then Nazi forces overran Czechoslovakia and Prague, and, on September 1, 1939, Germany invaded Poland and declared war. In a period of six weeks starting in May 1940, Germany invaded Belgium, the Netherlands, Luxembourg and France, leaving Britain alone to fight the fearsome behemoth that the Third Reich had become. In September 1940, Germany acquired reinforcements when it joined with Italy and Japan to create the Axis Alliance, which went on, in June of 1941, to send a huge force of over four million troops to attack Russia. Then, on December 7, while the fighting still raged in Russia, Japan attacked the United States at its navy base in Pearl

Harbor, Hawaii. The United States declared war the next day.

Now, less than two years later, the Third Reich was fighting for its life.

And, Sibi feared, like any vicious animal backed into a corner, it had become even more dangerous than before.

Herr Kraus said, "You're looking well. Sea air obviously agrees with you. And your sisters — the poor little ones — they live with you still, I understand? How are they?"

Sibi's hackles rose. It was a not-so-subtle reminder of what he could do to them if he chose, and he'd said it deliberately, she knew. Throughout Germany, those categorized as disabled were now being ripped from their families, institutionalized and in many cases "disappeared" — the rumors of mass euthanasia were both strong and credible. The horror of it was impossible to comprehend.

"They are very well, thank you, Herr Kraus." Whatever she did, she could not let her true feelings show.

"I am Befehlsleiter Colonel Kraus now," he said. Sibi saw that he was, indeed, clad in the brown Nazi Party uniform. "But my job is essentially the same. I serve Dr. Goebbels, and I'm here to oversee the making of a film about the rockets. That's why I'm glad to find you looking so well, and why I requested your presence at this gathering tonight."

So the request had come from him. Even if she'd known it, she would have had to attend. Such "requests" from party officials were really orders.

"It was my understanding that the rockets are top secret. That the work being undertaken here is not to be shared with anyone," she said. Despite her best intentions, her tone was too cold. She knew it as soon as the words left her mouth.

His eyes narrowed at her and she almost bit her lip with chagrin. *Be careful,* she warned herself.

"That is true," he said. "But by the time the film we're making is shown such secrecy will no longer be necessary."

Hearing that, her internal antenna pricked up.

"We wish you to be a part of our film," he continued. "It is at Dr. Goebbels's suggestion. He remains most impressed with your ability to connect with an audience, and the fact that we continue to get inquiries about you and how you are doing. That you are here — well, he feels it is an opportunity not to be missed. Your story has already garnered the world's attention and sympathy. Your face, your journey, from innocent, heartbroken young girl to a strong young woman firm in her loyalty to the Reich, will make compelling viewing. The narrator will say something like, 'The girl from Guernica has channeled her grief and loss into a thirst for vengeance, as has all of Germany.' Then the camera will pan to you, standing in front of one of the fearsome V-2 Vengeance rockets. You'll say, 'Our enemies will continue to pay a terrible price,'" and then, behind you, the rocket will blast toward the sky. You will, of course, attend tomorrow's launch. Your part will be filmed then."

More alarm bells rang in her head — what were the rockets supposed to hit? — but (she hoped) she kept her face impassive. "I'm glad to contribute in any way I can, Herr — Colonel Kraus. But I should perhaps point out that the rocket that is to launch tomorrow is called an A-4."

He made a dismissive gesture. "We've renamed it. An Aggregat 4, A-4 — what does that mean? Perhaps something to the scientific community, but nothing to the world at large. The earlier version of our Vengeance Weapon, the V-1 as we're calling it, is frightening, but this new version, this long-distance missile that travels at the speed of sound and drops in deadly silence from the sky to destroy its target, will make our enemies fall to their knees and pray to be allowed to surrender. This rocket — this V-2 — is our ultimate Vengeance Weapon. And we want the world to see it, to see for themselves what it can do, and be afraid."

His words made her heart beat faster. Coupled with the fanaticism in his voice, his eyes, they made *her* afraid. His presence, the presence of Goebbels and Speer, the rush order for fifty rocket engines to be installed, in, presumably, fifty rockets, Eureka — an attack was being planned. Soon. There might be another explanation that fit all those facts, but she couldn't think of one.

"That is brilliant," she said. "The name alone certainly terrifies *me.*"

He beamed at her. It was the first time she'd seen a genuine smile on his face.

"That idea was mine," he said. "I'll send an automobile for you tomorrow at one to convey you to Test Stand VII. That should give us plenty of time to do our filming before the launch."

Which was scheduled for four p.m. She hadn't intended to be present for that, either.

"I'll be ready, Colonel Kraus."

"Excellent," he said, and left her with a bow.

As soon as she could without making it obvious, if he should be watching, that the encounter had left her shaken, Sibi slipped away.

It was after ten on a Monday night, but Peenemünde was one of those places that never slept: soldiers and workers and even the scientists and engineers labored in shifts, and particularly so now that the rocket production schedule had been stepped up so drastically, so it was no surprise as she went down the veranda steps into the darkness to find a number of people moving around outside. She'd come by bicycle — her tight-waisted, full-skirted black taffeta party dress had been chosen partially with peddling in mind — because fuel was difficult to obtain and reserved now for military use unless it was an emergency. Their house was not too far away, just to the north of the *Siedlung* where the club, school and various shops were located and where the newer housing for the scientists and administrators and others who'd come later had been built. Their own house was an older one, two stories overlooking the sea, in a sparsely populated area of similar houses. The factory area — Werke Süd —

522

was farther to the north. Also farther to the north, at the very tip of the island, was Peenemünde West, an airfield built and maintained by the Luftwaffe, while Werke Süd was under the direction of the Wehrmacht. Peenemünde West was very useful for arrivals and departures, and also for the secret testing of experimental aircraft. But the focus of Peenemünde was always the rockets.

Sibi pulled her bicycle from the rack and was just about to remove her pumps and stockings and throw them, and her handbag, in the basket behind the seat — the night was hot despite the breeze, and she found it easier to peddle in bare feet than high heels, and anyway, the nylon stockings were precious — when she heard one of the soldiers in the tight ring of security that had been added around the club for the protection of the visitors call out, "Halt!" then, "Your papers, please!"

The challenge was issued to a man who'd come striding up from the direction of the beach. He stopped. "Certainly."

His voice . . . it was crisp and deep and —

Her head snapped in his direction so fast it hurt her neck.

With the aid of an electric torch, the soldier scrutinized the man's *Soldbuch,* a brief, summarized personnel file that all military personnel were required to carry on their persons. Sibi fixated on the man awaiting the soldier's verdict. He stood with his back to her. Even with the combination of pale moonlight and diffuse illumination thrown out by the club's windows it was difficult to tell much more about him than that he was tall, well-built and wearing the blue-gray uniform of an officer in the Luftwaffe.

She frowned.

"You are on the guest list for the reception, Major Schumann?" The sentry stopped scrutinizing the document to squint at the man's face. Comparing it with the picture, of course.

"I'm not. I was hoping to get a drink."

That voice again. Narrowing her eyes, she tried to get a better look.

"I'm sorry, sir, but the club is closed tonight." The man having apparently passed inspection, the soldier handed the document back. At what must have been the expression on his face, or perhaps as a result of a significant glance cast in the direction of the clearly not closed club, the soldier added, "Because of hosting a private function."

"I see." The man restored his papers to

his pocket and started to turn away.

His profile was briefly silhouetted against the light. Sibi blinked.

"The pub's just along that way." The soldier pointed helpfully.

"Thank you." The man set off down the walkway in the direction indicated. The soldier returned to his post.

Pulse racing, hands tight on the rubber grips as she pushed the bicycle along beside her, she hurried after the retreating officer. His attention possibly drawn by either the swish of the tires over the wooden walkway or the swish of her taffeta skirt, he glanced around sharply.

As their eyes met, her heart skipped a beat.

She hadn't been wrong: *Griff.*

Catching up, Sibi took in his square jaw, rugged features, the dark glint of his eyes, at a glance. His short, thick brown hair was hidden beneath an officer's visor cap. He looked leaner, tougher, grimmer than when she'd seen him last, at that hurried meeting in the café in Greifswald not quite two years before. *Battle-hardened* was perhaps the best term: wars did that to the people who fought them.

"Well, if it isn't just the person I was hoping to find." His eyes ran over her. "Looking beautiful, Fräulein Helinger."

She didn't know what her expression looked like in response to that, but he smiled.

He *smiled.* While panic jump-started her heart, clutched at her chest and dried her mouth.

"What are you doing here?" Her whisper was fraught with alarm. If he were to be caught — she went cold all over at the prospect. Forget POW status: for an American to be discovered behind enemy lines wearing a Luftwaffe uniform was enough in and of itself to get him shot. Add in the fact that he was an officer in the OSS — the Office of Strategic Services, America's intelligence agency. He'd been an agent as far back as their first meeting in Berlin, when he'd come to her directly from Switzerland, where the OSS was just setting up offices. They'd established the truth of that in Greifswald at the same time as they'd set up arrangements for indirect communication going forward, if it should become necessary, which it had — and if *that* was discovered he could count on being brutally interrogated and tortured and . . . well, what they did to spies was too horrible even to contemplate.

"What do you think? I came to see you."

"My God." Impossible for two tiny, whispered words to convey the degree of appalled horror she felt.

"Keep that up, and I'm going to start thinking you're not happy to see me."

"Oh, my God."

At that his smile widened into a full-blown grin. His eyes crinkled at the corners and twinkled at her. All of that would have warmed her clear down to her toes if she hadn't been so completely terrified. For a moment, the briefest of moments, though, the charm of it won through: the dark and dangerous world in which she lived was eclipsed by something that felt familiar and safe. The connection — *their* connection — was intact. She no sooner recognized it than fear once again slammed into her like a freight train.

"Major Schumann?" It was a disbelieving squeak. With good reason: her throat was so tight she could barely get the words out.

"You can call me Kurt."

"You — you —" Words failed her. That he could joke under circumstances like this was beyond belief.

"Careful, now," he said, low-voiced. Although he still smiled at her, the look in his eyes had changed to something hard and watchful.

As someone brushed by her with a muttered, *"Entschuldigung,"* she understood why. A Nazi Party official, she saw from his uniform as the man strode ahead, almost certainly also leaving the reception. In front of him, heading toward town just as they were, was a group of women, all seen from the back, probably secretaries who lived in the *Ledigenheim,* which was a dormitory for many of the unmarried women who worked on the base. The Nazi official, obviously in a hurry, strode past them as she watched. Closer to town, two men strolled up the walkway toward them. Sibi felt cold all over at this reminder that she and Griff were not alone. That they were, in fact, two spies — one completely rattled — in the middle of a seething nest of mortal enemies some twenty thousand strong. One wrong move, one wrong word, and they were *dead.*

"What happens if your papers get checked by someone who knows that there *is* no Major Schumann of the Luftwaffe stationed on Peenemünde?" More of a hiss than a whisper, it was uttered only after she glanced all around.

"Oh, but there is. Or rather, there would be, had he not been captured in time for me to, uh, borrow his identity. All our guys had to do was swap out the picture. He's a pilot, shot down over water and in American hands as we speak, and actually is due to report to the air base here on Friday. Being a conscientious sort, he's arrived on the island a few days early and will be staying in a hotel while he familiarizes himself with his newest posting."

"Have you ever thought that someone in his 'newest posting' might actually want Major Schumann, Luftwaffe pilot, to fly an airplane?"

"I'll be gone before that can happen. And in any case, I *am* a pilot. I can fly anything."

"Oh, my God."

"You're starting to sound like a broken record. Here, give me that." He took the bicycle from her, shifting it to his other side so that it was no longer between them as he continued pushing it along. "Did you ride this thing to the party? What, no date?"

"No. And how could you possibly have known about the party?" She certainly hadn't told him: the message she'd sent had been necessarily brief and to the point. She took another quick look around, then resolved to stop it: even glancing around as she was doing was telltale. Her nerves were stretched so tight they jangled. *Take a deep breath. Calm down.*

"When I checked into the hotel, I heard some people talking about the party going on at the club. Once Goebbels was mentioned, I figured that's where you'd be. If you hadn't come out when you did, my next move was go find a telephone, give the club a call and ask to speak to you."

"Did it ever occur to you that if I'd taken that call I might have fainted dead away on the spot?" She was recovering her equilibrium. Her voice was thin but tart.

"Think I don't know you better than that? Look sharp." The muttered warning, coupled with a significant flicker of his eyes, had her following his glance. She caught her breath as the two men walking through the darkness toward them stepped into range of the last faint outreach of the club's light, only to be revealed as gestapo agents.

The gestapo presence on Peenemünde had grown noticeably heavier in the last several months, which Sibi attributed to the fact that the führer, originally dismissive of the program, had done an about-face and embraced the potential of rockets as weapons capable of turning the tide of the war in Germany's favor. Along with his sudden enthusiasm had come an increased concern about the loyalty of the scientists and engineers and everyone else involved in the endeavor. That resulted in a major, and dangerous, uptick in worry over the possibility of sabotage, information leakage or even spies. Security had been tightened to the point that it was impossible to move from one end of the island to the other without encountering numerous checkpoints complete with armed guards and barriers. People just walking about were frequently stopped and asked to produce their papers, and anything or anyone leaving or coming onto the island was heavily scrutinized.

Which begged the question: How had Griff gotten there? At the thought of all the checkpoints he must have had to clear to even make it onto the island, her palms felt damp.

The agents walked past with no more than a cursory glance in their direction. Sibi waited for her insides to relax. They didn't. The situation was so perilous, the danger so acute, that her every cell quivered.

She couldn't help it. She glanced around, quickly and discreetly, to make sure no one else was within earshot: no one was.

"How did you get here?"

"Parachute."

"Onto the island?" The risks involved in that took her breath. Then the truth hit her, and her heart hiccupped. "I knew it. It's big, isn't it? Whatever's getting ready to happen, it's really, really big."

"That's what I'm here to find out." Griff's tone was carefully neutral, and as far as she was concerned that said it all.

"Is it Eureka? Did you find out what that is?"

"I know what it is."

She waited a beat. "Are you going to tell me?"

His lips compressed. He didn't say anything.

She knew him well enough to know that he didn't want to endanger her any further by telling her what he knew.

They'd reached the top of the walkway, the high point above the dunes before it sloped down into the town. A viewing platform off to the side allowed one to step off the walkway and take a moment to admire the sea. He turned off onto it and stopped, looking around, and she went with him.

"I'm in this as deep as I can be, you know," she said. "Ever hear that old saying 'might as well be hanged for a sheep as a lamb'? I think that applies here."

"If we're caught at this, you're more likely to be shot." His tone was grim.

"So telling me what you know won't make a bit of difference, will it?"

He flicked a look down at her. Despite the sensation of a cold hand curling around the back of her neck, she managed a smile for him.

The smile he gave her in return was brief and reluctant, but it was a smile.

The salt-smelling breeze ruffled her hair and her skirt. The muffled music from the club mixed with the murmur of the sea. As a romantic setting, she thought, it would have been perfect. But she was pretty sure romance hadn't entered his head at all, and she felt about as romantic as a prisoner about to be executed.

Dropping the kickstand, he left the bicycle where it was to move to the edge of the platform. Once more she followed, stopping beside him. There was no one else on the platform, no one on the walkway who was anywhere near.

He said, "Eureka is the code name for a top-secret meeting of the Big Three — Roosevelt, Churchill and Stalin. Plans are in the works as we speak for them to get together in Tehran in September. Security on this is tight as a drum. Top brass thought there was no possibility of it leaking out. And yet, obviously, it has."

"I told you, General Dornberger brought back a folder with Eureka stamped on it from his meeting with Hitler. The way he acted — I knew it had to be something important. Unless he's moved it, it's in the file cabinet in his office now."

"You told me," he agreed.

"So what does this have to do with Peenemünde?"

"It's what it has to do with those fifty rockets you mentioned that's concerning."

Their eyes met, his dark and intent, hers frowning a question.

Then the answer hit Sibi like a thunderclap. Her pulse rate exploded as all the pertinent facts coalesced into one horrifying conclusion. "That's why they're here to film tomorrow's rocket launch — to use it for propaganda afterward. That's why they're calling the rockets Vengeance Weapons, and why Dr. Goebbels said the führer's plan is genius. *This* is the führer's plan — it's an assassination plot! They're going to use the rockets to try to hit that meeting, aren't they? They're planning to kill the leaders of all three countries in one attack. *That's* how they think they're going to win the war."

40

Griff's expression told Sibi she had it right even before he answered.

"That's the working theory," he said. "My job is to determine if that is in fact the case, and if the technology is capable of carrying it out."

"If by technology, you mean the rockets — oh, yes, they're capable of it. Papa developed the engines, and I was there with him practically every step of the way, so I know. Each rocket can carry a thousand-kilogram warhead, and has a range of around 320 kilometers. Their max speed is about six thousand kilometers an hour. They're designed to be almost impossible to stop once launched, and impossible to shoot down."

"If their range is —" he paused briefly, and when he continued she realized he'd been making a quick calculation in his head "— around two hundred miles, they're not getting anywhere near Tehran or that meeting."

"They use mobile launchpads. All they require is a road and they can go anywhere. And there are freighters in the harbor, *Portuguese* freighters —" that was important, because as ships from a neutral country they would be unlikely to be attacked "— that must be intended to convey the rockets, and the launchpads, to *roads* in wherever it is they're planning to launch the attack from."

"So you think it can succeed."

She hated to have to say it. "Yes."

For a moment neither of them spoke.

"Cold?" he asked as she crossed her arms over her chest and shivered a little. As he spoke, his eyes slid over her arms and neck, left bare except for a single strand of pearls by her square-necked, sleeveless dress.

The shiver had been prompted by fear rather than the cold, but that she refused to admit. Anyway, the wind blowing off the sea was brisker now. So she nodded, and he took off his jacket and dropped it around her shoulders.

"Thank you." It was an effort, but she managed to sound as calm as he did. Slipping her arms into the sleeves — she hadn't realized how chilled she actually was until the warmth of the jacket enveloped her —

she took him in with a glance. He looked broad-shouldered and strong and reassuringly capable standing there in the white shirt and black tie he wore beneath the jacket. She saw that, attached to his belt, he wore a holstered sidearm.

Please God he doesn't need it.

"What am I looking at here?" Long fingers wrapping around the handrail, he scanned their surroundings. Determined to stay as outwardly composed as he was, she told him, pointing out the important features one by one.

From their vantage point almost the entire *Siedlung* was laid out before them. The grid of it was as neat and symmetrical as the most precision-minded engineers could make it. The necessity of maintaining a near-total blackout meant that few lights were visible. But the glimmering moonlight revealed the many houses and shops and paved streets and churches and school that made up the town. In front of the town, a wide strip of white beach led down to the sea that stretched out endlessly to the horizon. In the harbor, the waiting freighters were backed up by the heavily armed flak ships deployed to protect Peenemünde from an air assault that had never come. Although, as she told him, more and more frequently in the last few months Allied bombers had passed overhead on their way to savage such targets as Munich and Stuttgart and Hamburg and Berlin. The huge smoke machines that were another component of the base's defensive apparatus blasted their camouflaging clouds into the sky on such occasions, and the searchlights meant to blind incoming hostile pilots were available to use as necessary. But something — either the fact that, from the air, Peenemünde must still look much like the sleepy fishing village it had once been, or the remoteness of the location, or the secrecy shrouding the island's true purpose — had kept the worst of the war away.

Griff scanned the town, the harbor, looked farther north to where the Werke Süd complex was visible as a mass of dark shapes augmented by a few pinpricks of light in the darkness.

"The rockets are there?" He nodded in the direction of Werke Süd.

"Yes."

"Is there any way I can get inside the factory compound? I need to look around. Tonight, if possible, because I don't have a lot of time."

It was the most heavily guarded sector on the island.

The danger of it made her heart skip a beat.

"I can get you in." She felt a wrench at the knowledge that he would be leaving soon, but because he was in mortal danger every second he was on the ground here, and because that meant she was, too, and because this war they were engaged in was nothing less than a desperate fight to save the world, she refused to let the personal get in the way.

He turned back toward the bicycle. "Let's go."

The fact that he didn't question her, didn't try to get her to tell him how it could be done, then order her to stay out of the way while he did it, underscored just how much he trusted her — and how hugely important he considered the mission to be.

"We only have one bicycle."

"Hop on." Straddling the frame, Griff patted the handlebars.

She really, really didn't like the idea. Ordinarily she would have protested. But there was nothing ordinary about any of this, and so she dropped her handbag in the basket, hitched herself and her slippery taffeta skirt onto the handlebars, parked her feet in their high heels on the narrow front fender as best she could and held on tightly while he pushed off, and the bicycle bumped its way down the narrow wooden walkway toward the street.

"This is Fertigungshalle 1." Sibi kept her voice low. She and Griff were inside the Werke Süd complex, standing in the shadowy darkness close to the gigantic former warehouse where the mass production of the A-4 — apparently now redubbed the V-2 Vengeance Weapon — rockets was under way. The building was a two-story brick rectangle with an assembly line modeled on the Volkswagen automobile plant. Even from the outside, it was noisy, smelly and unpleasant. Thanks to General Dornberger's directive, the ground-level work area was a beehive of frenzied activity even so late at night. Beneath the work area was a prison that included basement living quarters for a contingent of forced laborers with the necessary technical skills to actually work on the rockets. They had their own special detachment of SS guards who were also constantly on the premises.

The plant belched plumes of odiferous black smoke twenty-four hours a day. Loud clangs and the rumble of machinery spilled out through the windows. The heat coming from the processes required to join together the various components and secure them within the chassis radiated through the brick walls, so that where they were felt like standing close to an oven. Inside, as Sibi knew from experience, the temperature would be sweltering. Everyone in the factory, including her father, who was inside right at that moment — she could tell because the bicycle he used to get around the complex was parked in the rack not far from the door — was constantly drenched in sweat. Sleep at best amounted to a few snatched hours a night. Food for the workers was scarce, and poor. Several dropped — from exhaustion or hunger or the heat — at their posts every day. Anyone judged to be malingering was taken out to the field beside the nearby administration building and shot. In that way, production continued at the breakneck pace required to reach the goal.

"Fifty rockets by Friday," Griff mused, peering at one of the narrow, high-up, partially open windows as though he could see through the curtain that covered it. Sibi had told him about General Dornberger's directive about the engines, and that they and the other parts were being installed in the rockets on a rolling schedule. She'd also filled him in on everything else she knew, including her conversation with Colonel

Kraus and what she'd overheard from Dr. Goebbels and Dr. Thiel. "Can they do it, do you think?"

"Yes." Sibi gestured at another, nearby brick building. "That's Fertigungshalle 2. The completed rockets are stored in there. According to Papa, when he left last night, rocket number 40 had just come off the assembly line fully complete and was being hauled away to be put in with the rest."

Griff's brow furrowed as he engaged in another calculation.

"They can do two a day," Sibi assured him, and his mouth quirked in recognition of what they had long since agreed was her superior math ability.

A pair of SS guards in their black uniforms with the distinctive red Death's Head caps that indicated they were assigned to the Werke Süd complex emerged from Fertigungshalle 2 and headed down the paved corridor between the buildings toward them. Each carried a torch, which they played over their surroundings as they walked. The illumination the torches provided was pale and dim, but coupled with the moonlight it was enough to allow the guards to see them as readily as they could see the guards. She was well-known at Werke Süd and had a pass that allowed her access to this most highly secured of areas besides, but Griff — or rather, Major Schumann — wasn't and did not. Since he was with her, that hopefully wouldn't become an issue, but neither one of them wanted to chance it.

She'd skirted the difficulty of passing through the main, and only official, entrance with its stringent scrutiny that included double sets of gates and guard stations placed some twelve meters apart — anyone trying to enter had to show a pass and/or papers and was subject to search at both gates — by bringing him in through the unofficial back door. A cliff overlooking the harbor served as a section of the fourth wall for the complex, and the two rows of three-meter-tall wire fencing ended in sturdy steel posts sunk into the ground about ten centimeters short of the cliff's edge. This allowed the few people in the know — mostly children of the early scientists and engineers who worked there — to skirt around the elaborate and time-consuming entrance rituals. The key was to be careful to hold on to the poles while swinging around them. A straight, possibly fatal drop to the water below awaited anyone who miscalculated. So far as Sibi knew, no one ever had.

The difficulty lay in the fact that anyone

entering Werke Süd after hours was required to be logged in. If they were stopped and the log was checked, they wouldn't be on it.

"Let's walk," Griff muttered as the guards drew closer. With a nod of agreement, she tucked her hand in his elbow — he was wearing his jacket again because she thought he would attract less attention in it than in his white shirt — and pulled him around the corner toward another large brick building that housed the repair and maintenance shops. It was up and running, too, with more guards about, so they walked on past and turned another corner to where the administrative building stood at the edge of the complex. The SS used the building as a headquarters, and light glimmered around the edges of the curtained windows. Black-uniformed men went in and out. Red swastika banners fluttered on either side of the front entrance. The long, narrow field beside it backed up to that same fourth-wall cliff where the fencing ended. Here the drop was some twenty meters straight down into the harbor.

While relating its purpose to Griff — prisoners were taken to the edge and shot, which meant that their bodies plummeted directly into the water and, with true Nazi efficiency, were thus automatically disposed of — Sibi had to ignore her own fast-beating heart. If she and Griff were caught, that would be the kindest part of their fate.

"That folder with 'Eureka' stamped on it you were talking about — would it be in there?"

Griff's casual-sounding question a few minutes later interrupted the guided tour she'd been giving him in which she'd pointed out such points of interest as Dr. von Braun's and General Dornberger's houses — because their families weren't with them, they lived in Werke Süd itself as did a number of other scientists who'd come to Peenemünde without their families — and the hangar — "Papa calls it his toy box," she told Griff, who responded with a grunt — where her father's most ambitious creation, a hybrid rocket-airplane fighter-bomber he'd named the Silberkugel, or Silver Bullet, was housed, along with other experimental aircraft in various degrees of completion he was working on.

"Yes," she said.

Griff was looking at the long, low building that held General Dornberger's office, along with the offices of Dr. Thiel, Dr. von Braun and the section directors, of whom her father was one. It was dark and silent, because any of the scientists still working at this hour would be in the factories, and the secretaries did their work during the day. The guards patrolled it regularly because of the sensitive material it housed, and at night the outside doors as well as all the offices within were kept securely locked.

"You wouldn't happen to have a key, would you? Or do I need to break in? I need to get a look at that folder."

41

"This is suicide," Sibi hissed.

"Only if we get caught."

"Great comfort you are."

"Shh. How do you expect me to concentrate? Ah — there we go." The door clicked open.

"The file cabinet's in the corner. Second drawer down." Sibi stood anxiously in the doorway glancing up and down the dark hall in her job as lookout. They were inside the building — as her father's trusted assistant, she did indeed have a key. To the outside door, and her father's office. *Not* to General Dornberger's office, which Griff had just broken into.

"Hurry," she added for good measure. It was hot inside the building despite the windows that were kept open to allow air circulation but were too small and high up to provide access and outfitted with metal bars besides. Despite the temperature, she

was freezing, and that was from fear, she knew. She'd thought — for about one minute — about simply entering the building openly, as if she had something she needed to do in her father's office, and then letting Griff break into General Dornberger's office while they were inside. But turning on the lights at this time of night was guaranteed to attract instant attention, and bring the guards running, which was the last thing they needed and might very well keep him from getting to the file. And she never came into the building at night when it was empty, so to be discovered doing so, and in the company of an unknown Luftwaffe pilot to boot, would raise all kinds of questions in and of itself.

Creeping in under cover of darkness had seemed like a better choice at the time, but some five minutes into it Sibi was already sweating bullets. The guards' schedule was unpredictable: for security's sake, they patrolled the buildings in a different order each night, and thus it was impossible to know when they would show up. It could be a couple of hours or, alternatively, they could appear at any minute.

The uncertainty was threatening to make her hyperventilate.

"Mmm," Griff said. Bent over the file

cabinet, he didn't look up.

Each drawer of the file cabinet was locked, too, but like General Dornberger's office door it proved little challenge for the small, thin metal file Griff had extracted from the heel of his jackboot, which she'd been amazed to discover twisted to one side to reveal that it served as a storage unit for a number of tiny implements. His other heel yielded a miniscule camera, now tucked into his pocket, and an equally miniscule torch, which at the moment was held between his teeth.

"It's *yellow,*" she whispered as, removing the torch from his mouth, he ran the beam over the contents of the open drawer. She glanced down the long, pitch-dark hallway that ran at a right angle to the corridor along which her father's office was located. The building was L-shaped, and the door to the outside — the only door to the outside — was located at the far end of *this* hallway. Which meant that if the guards appeared before they were safely outside again they were trapped. And *dead.*

"Can you come here and hold the torch?" She looked back to find that the folder lay open on General Dornberger's desk. The torch, its slender beam slicing through the darkness, lay beside it. Griff was positioning the camera.

Loath to abandon the door, she hurried to his side, picked up the torch and aimed it at the open file.

"Steady." He clicked the camera, turned a page, clicked again. It was quick, almost soundless work, and by the time he was finished she was about to jump out of her skin.

"All over." Closing the file, he pivoted to restore it to the file cabinet.

"Thank God." Her response was heartfelt. "Can we go?"

"One minute. Let me have the torch." He took it from her, swept the area around the file cabinet and desk. She understood that he was checking for any telltale signs they might have left behind, knew that such deliberativeness might make the difference between having their incursion into General Dornberger's office discovered or not, but even the brief time he took to do it and then restore his spy implements to his heels made her feel like she'd aged several decades.

"Can we go now?" She was halfway to the door and shifting nervously from foot to foot as he clicked the heel that held the camera into place and followed her.

"We were right about the assassination plot." He pulled the door closed — like all

the office doors, it locked automatically —
and then they were striding down the hall
toward the exit. He still held the torch,
which provided the only illumination.
"They're going to use the rockets to —"

He didn't finish as sounds coming from
the other side of the outside door froze both
of them in their tracks. A couple of thumps,
muffled voices, a metallic rattle —

"The guards." Grabbing Griff's arm, she
pulled him back the way they had come. By
silent, mutual agreement they broke into a
run. Faster than she was in her high heels,
he outpaced her, then grabbed her hand to
pull her along. There was no doubt about
it: the guards were on their way in to do
their regular walk-through. Unless, of
course, they'd somehow been alerted to the
presence of intruders and were coming in
to hunt them down.

Her heart pounded so hard it hurt.

"Is there another way out?" His voice was
a hoarse whisper.

"No. *Shh.*"

Running flat out now, with the tiny circle
of light from the torch their only source of
illumination in the pitch-black hallway and
doing their best to be as quiet as humanly
possible, they were, in Sibi's estimation, still
making enough noise to alert a dead man.

Rasping breath, clattering footsteps, even the rustle of their clothing — how could anyone *not* hear them?

". . . your family?" one of the guards asked the other. His words were suddenly crystal clear as the heavy metal outside door swung inward. Accompanied by a gust of fresh air and a gray wedge of light that leaped down the hall in a lightning-fast stab at where she and Griff sprinted like racehorses toward the connecting corridor, it was enough to make Sibi's life pass before her eyes.

The torch went out. Griff must have switched it off. She tried not to breathe, tried to run on her tiptoes without making a sound —

"They're alive, all of them. They made it into a shelter in time. But Hamburg — it is destroyed," the second guard replied.

"God curse the Tommies. God curse the —"

Sibi missed whatever the first guard meant to curse next as Griff dragged her after him around the corner. It was so dark without the torch that they had to feel their way along the wall. Sibi was only glad she knew the layout, and where they were going. They were out of sight of the guards now, but she could still hear them talking and had to assume, from that, that they, too, could be heard if the guards actually shut up and listened.

Griff must have had the same thought, because he dropped into a fast walk and she slowed down with him. The slap of their footsteps on the wood floor was thus reduced to a kind of barely audible shuffle. But the sound of their breathing —

The lights came on. Brilliant white fluorescent bulbs in the ceiling fixtures sprang to life with a sputter, catching them by surprise. The gray metal walls, the lineup of six darker gray metal doors, all closed and presumably locked, marching like good little soldiers down one side, the white pebbly ceiling and dark wood floor, were all brightly illuminated in an instant. Barely managing to swallow a gasp, feeling as exposed as if they'd been caught in flagrante delicto, Sibi realized that one of the guards had, of course, hit the switch that turned on the lights in the hallways. She threw a single, wild-eyed look at Griff. Then, remembering the *other* key in her possession, she mouthed, "Papa's office," and let go of him to snatch the key ring back out of her handbag where she'd dropped it after using the building key to get them in, while being careful not to let the keys jingle. With Griff right behind her, she rushed toward the door. It was four down —

". . . . working tomorrow?" one of the guards asked. Sibi realized to her horror that she could hear him clearly, which meant he was close, which meant —

"Double shift," the second guard answered gloomily.

They weren't even talking loud. They were having a normal conversation, and she *could hear every word.*

She could also hear their footsteps, hear the rattle as the guards opened doors to look inside offices. The doors thumped shut again almost at once, which meant they were taking only a cursory look, but that glimmer of hope was negated by her knowledge of the offices, which were small. Unless both she and Griff were able to get away with ducking behind the door, or the desk, even once they got inside Papa's office there was nowhere to hide.

She was at his office door, her hand curling around the metal knob, her heart in her throat —

The rattle as the guards opened yet another door was so loud Sibi caught her breath.

Unless she got Papa's door open fast, she and Griff were going to be caught right there in the hall.

"I was in line for a week's leave at the end of the month. Canceled, big surprise," the first guard said. He sounded like he was steps away from the conjunction of the corridors. Throwing a compulsive look over her shoulder and past Griff — he loomed behind her, turned to face the imminent threat as if placing his body between them and her would keep them from seeing her somehow — toward where the guards would appear, she shoved the key into the lock.

Behind her, Griff unsnapped the holster that held his sidearm. Her pulse went wild.

A guard said, "It's been seven days a week for me since . . ."

She could hear the march of their footsteps, the scrape of a key going into another lock, the creak of an opening door . . .

Her own key, the one in her hand, turned with a click that made her wince. Instantly she thrust the door open, grabbed a handful of Griff's jacket to alert him and practically leaped inside. He was right behind her.

"Be glad you're not at the front." The guard's voice was so clear, so loud, that she wasn't surprised to see, as she oh-so-gently but oh-so-quickly eased the door shut again, one of them step into view at the end of the corridor. Fortunately, he was looking back at his fellow guard, but her knees threatened to give way even as the door closed, shutting the guards out, leaving her and Griff once again alone in the dark.

What now?

She could turn on the light, pretend she'd stopped in to get something from the file cabinet . . .

But the guards might see the light suddenly flip on through the cracks around or under the door. And they would certainly wonder why she hadn't turned the hall lights on.

And if they got suspicious, and searched Griff . . .

Panic sent chills racing over her skin.

Griff was shining the torch over the walls, the tiny, impossible, heavily curtained window, the two straight chairs, the file cabinet, the desk.

"They'll be here in a second." Sibi's frantic whisper came as she, too, scanned the room for any possible place of concealment. Nothing had changed: it was exactly as she remembered it. Which meant, just as she'd known, there was no place to hide.

"Get under the desk." Despite the barely there whisper, Griff's tone made it an order.

"They'll see us."

Even if it hadn't been barred, the window was too small to allow anyone bigger than a cat to escape.

"There's no us. There's you. Get under the desk." He hooked an arm around her waist and propelled her around the desk as he spoke, then pulled the chair out and directed the torch beam into the shadowy cubby beneath it. "And keep quiet."

"While you do what?" She pulled free of his hold. "Stand there and pretend to be a piece of furniture? They'll —"

"I'm going to have to kill them." The torch went out. She realized he'd turned it off. Thanks to a glimmer of moonlight sifting in around the edge of the curtain, she saw that his gun was in his hand.

Her heart hammered. Her pulse roared in her ears.

"You can't. Somebody will hear. And only one of them will open the door. The other will be in the hall. If you shoot the one, the other will shoot you. Whatever happens, every guard within earshot will come running. And even if you do get out of the building, everyone in Werke Süd, and Peenemünde, will be hunting for you."

"You have a better idea?"

She didn't. *Dear God, there has to be a way —*

"Will you just get under the desk?" Despite the fact that he was whispering, his

557

tone was savage. He gripped her arm —

"No."

"Damn it, are you really going to argue with me *now*?"

She could hear the guards talking again.

". . . . hear that Il Duce's been imprisoned by his own government?"

"Not his own government. King of Italy's back. Sent the Carabinieri to arrest him."

Given metal walls and a closed metal door, that she could hear them so clearly must mean that they were right outside. No sooner did she have the thought than she heard a rattle, saw the doorknob move —

She surged against Griff, catching him by surprise as she wrapped her arms around his neck and went up on tiptoe and lifted her face to his. "Kiss me. Hard, like you mean it."

Even as their eyes met, she heard the *snick* of the key turning in the lock.

42

Thank God, he understood instantly.

Shoving his gun back into its holster, Griff wrapped his arms around her and pulled her tight against him and kissed her like he burned with a red-hot fire for her. Closing her eyes, Sibi kissed him back the same way.

She'd wanted him to kiss her for years. She'd dreamed of it, even.

This was not the kiss of her wishes and dreams.

This was a desperate grab at staying alive.

Even as her mouth opened beneath the hard urgency of his and he bent her back until her head was pillowed on his broad shoulder and his hand slid down until it splayed over her bottom, gripping the tender curve tightly and pressing her against him, like throwing her down on her father's desk that was right beside them was the next item on his agenda, she was acutely aware of the door opening behind them. She heard the *swoosh* of it, felt the movement of air —

Her arms went rigid as they curved around his neck. Her body quaked with fear. She thought her heart might burst from beating so hard and so fast. She was wrapped in his arms, plastered against the solid wall of his body, being kissed into next week, but every iota of her focus was on the door, and her every muscle was as taut as a violin string as she waited for what would happen next.

She could feel the rise and fall of his chest against her breasts as he breathed. In carefully regulated breaths. Not rushed and ragged as her breathing was. He'd taken her plan and was executing it with a cool calculation that she was finding almost impossible to match.

He ruched up her skirt. To the point where the tops of her stockings and maybe even her garters and a glimpse of bare thighs were, she thought from the whisper of air that touched them, in full view.

He knew what the guards were seeing. He knew what he wanted them to see. Her back was to the door. What he was giving them was a carefully calibrated distraction.

Difficult as it was to force her muscles to relax, she went soft and yielding in his arms.

His mouth devoured hers. She kissed him back with a feverish ardor that was the polar opposite of the icy terror surging through her veins.

Big and warm and totally, unmistakably masculine, his hand slid under her skirt and up her thigh, pushing the froth of filmy taffeta even higher. Blocking out any thought of what the men behind them might be able to see, she responded as if what was happening between them was real, arching up against him, threading her fingers through his hair, making a small, helpless, mewling sound that was, she hoped, all about desire —

The light snapped on.

Even with her eyes closed, she knew the second it happened. Her stomach dropped. Her heart lodged in her throat.

There's no turning back. That was the terrified thought that flashed through her mind.

Griff's hand closed on the bare skin of her upper thigh. His arm around her waist turned to steel. His head lifted —

Make it convincing.

Her head snapped around toward the source of the interruption. *"Oh,"* she said, a surprised, shocked sound. Like she'd had no idea whatsoever that anyone was there.

She sucked in air, tried to look dazed, frowned as she focused on the guard in the doorway. In his black SS uniform, with his gun in his hand.

Her stomach twisted into a knot.

She dropped her arms from around Griff's neck, pushed at his chest. In an undertone deliberately calibrated to be overheard by the guard, she said, "Kurt. Let me go."

Griff's hand came out from under her skirt and the folds of taffeta, rustling, fell back into place.

"Fräulein Helinger," the guard gasped. An older man with grizzled hair and a toothbrush mustache — she knew him.

"Sergeant Muller." Twisting out of Griff's arms — he let them drop — she faced the guard. No need to pretend to be embarrassed: seeing the way Sergeant Muller and the unknown guard in the middle of the hallway gaped at her, she could feel her face heat until she knew it had to be flaming red.

"What are you do —" Sergeant Muller broke off with a cough, as it apparently occurred to him that the answer was obvious. Sibi smoothed her hair self-consciously, aware that her lips were probably tender looking from Griff's kisses and that, behind her, Griff was running his hand over his mouth as if to wipe off any trace of lipstick.

"Did you want something?" Her voice was a little high-pitched, a shade defensive, and she did her best to look as if she was trying not to look flustered.

"Sergeant," Griff said. A superior officer talking to an underling. An underling who'd just severely offended.

"M-major." Sergeant Muller shoved his gun back into its holster. "I, uh, we, uh, were just making our rounds."

"Then carry on." There was steel in Griff's voice.

"Yes, sir. Sorry for the intrusion, sir, Fräulein." His face was pink now, too.

"Sergeant." Griff's voice hadn't lost its edge. "I'm confident we can count on your discretion — for the lady's sake."

Sergeant Muller's eyes touched hers, slid away.

"Yes, sir. Of course. Uh —" He swallowed, and then his arm shot out in the usual straight-arm salute. "Heil Hitler!"

"Heil Hitler!" Griff responded, saluting in kind, and Sergeant Muller backed out and closed the door.

Sibi's knees wobbled. She had to take a step back and lean against the desk for support.

For a moment, the briefest of moments, her eyes collided with Griff's. Something arced between them — an electric spark so charged that it practically sizzled and snapped in the air — and then his eyes went opaque and he glanced toward the door.

Leaving her to wonder if maybe she'd been mistaken. If maybe that spark was something she'd imagined — or nothing more than a meaningless collateral product of the show manufactured strictly for their audience.

Something *Griff* had manufactured strictly for their audience. Because on her part, it hadn't been — at least not entirely — manufactured.

It had been real.

This isn't the time to think about that.

Not when their lives hung in the balance. Not when the situation could turn on a dime.

She focused on what was happening beyond the door, listened, but heard nothing. The silence was so nerve-racking it was painful.

Metal door, metal walls, she reminded herself. Once inside the office, she hadn't heard the guards coming until they were right outside. Of course she couldn't hear them now.

Griff picked up her pocketbook — it was on the desk, she didn't remember putting it there — and handed it to her. Then he retrieved his hat from the floor — she didn't know how that had gotten there, either, although she did remember running her fingers through his hair — and put it on.

"So, how's your belief in miracles coming along?" He spoke under his breath. It was the first thing he'd said to her since their kiss, and it broke the tension that had her hands fisted and her nails digging into her palms sufficiently to allow her to breathe normally again.

"Ask me when we're safe." She closed her eyes. Relaxed her fingers. Got a firm grip on her shattered nerves.

"You all right?" he asked.

She opened her eyes to find that he was right beside her, peering with what looked like real worry into her face.

She nodded.

"Good girl." He gave a quick, teasing tug to an errant lock of her hair.

Her brows snapped together as she frowned at him. "Would you stop doing that? I'm not *four.*"

He smiled, and with that the balance in their relationship was restored.

"I think we should go," she said, and was proud of how calm and composed she sounded. Because she wasn't sure she was ever going to feel calm and composed again in her life.

"You're very quiet." Griff took the coat she handed back to him.

They'd stopped and gotten off the bicycle and were standing at the edge of the undeveloped woods across the street from her house. The last one on a presently deserted, J-shaped street that curved around a ridge overlooking the sea, the two-story, half-timbered Tudor had a red tile roof and a hopeless back garden (hard to grow anything except scrub grass in the sandy soil; they'd given it over to chickens, which Jo raised, meant to supplement the meager amount of protein allotted by their ration cards). Right now it was dark except for a single line of light edging a curtain in an upstairs window: the bedroom Margrit and Jo shared.

She'd been hoping the girls would be asleep. But then again, they knew she'd be bringing them treats from the party.

"I'm tired," she said with a shrug as he dropped the bicycle's kickstand and pulled on his coat.

"I thought you might be upset."

She rallied. No need to let him guess how nervy and demoralized she felt. "About what? Oh, you putting your hand up my skirt?"

A corner of his mouth quirked up. "That, too."

"Or maybe I'm worried about my reputation," she said, folding her arms over her chest because, without his jacket, she *was* cold. "If those guards talk, I won't have one. Also, there's always the chance that someone will ask me to identify the man who was kissing me, and I'll either have to say I don't know, which no one is going to believe, or give up Major Kurt Schumann of the Luftwaffe, which as you know happens to be the current false identity of an OSS agent."

He had his jacket on now, although he hadn't yet buttoned it up. They were standing close, and he was looking down at her.

"All possibilities," he said, imperturbable. "But I don't think so."

"What do you think, then?"

"I think whatever it is, you need to tell me. And don't bother saying you're tired. Think I can't tell when something's troubling you?"

She looked away from him, out at the sea. It rippled in the moonlight, beautiful and serene. Impossible to imagine that terrible things could happen in a world with a sea like that. Glancing back at Griff, she sighed and gave it up. "I was afraid tonight, all right? I'm still getting over it."

His jaw tightened. "You'd be a fool if you weren't afraid. We cut it pretty close back there." He paused, glanced away, out at the sea just as she had done, then back at her. "You know, the work you've done for us has been invaluable. Maybe after this it's time to say enough is enough."

She'd been thinking that, too. For the girls' sakes, if nothing else. But — "If I weren't here passing information on to you, would anyone have found out about Hitler's plan to use our rockets to assassinate your president and the others? In time to try to stop it?"

His grimace spoke volumes: it landed somewhere between *I don't know* and *Probably not.* "When I sent word up the chain that Hitler knew about Eureka — that my contact, who my side still only knows as Rolf, by the way, knew about Eureka — a lot of five-stars started flipping their wigs."

She translated that to *important people started going crazy,* and nodded. "So you need me," she said flatly.

"We don't need you dead." His tone was surprisingly grim. In response, what felt like an icy trickle of foreboding slid down her spine. It reminded her of what Mama used to say when she had a bad feeling about something: *a goose just walked over my grave.*

"I've been thinking about that," she confessed. "But who else has the kind of unique access I do? With the kind of cover I do? I've been in place so long —"

"None of that matters compared to the risk to you. And the risk is increasing."

"As long as you're my contact, and you're the only one who knows who I am, I should be safe." It was a reasonable assumption, and arriving at it made her feel better. "Unless you mean to give me up."

The look he sent her was scornful. Well, she'd known he wouldn't. Not under any circumstances.

"It's not your decision to make," he said.

"Whose decision is it, then? Yours?"

"As your handler? Yup."

"I'm not ready to stop yet."

"Are you arguing with me again?"

"Like that went so wrong the last time."

Their eyes clashed, and all of a sudden the memory of their kiss was there between them. She saw it in the narrowing of his eyes, the hardening of his jaw, the compression of his mouth. She felt it in the quickening of her pulse, the sudden hitch in her breathing, the warmth rolling through her.

"This is one of those conversations we need to have at greater length." He still sounded grim. "And at another time. I've got to go. I've got people waiting to hear from me."

She knew better than to ask for details, but she couldn't help speculating, and while she was doing that he reached out and tugged the same curl he'd tugged on before — "Go on, I'll watch till you're inside" — then grinned as she frowned direly at him.

"Did you miss it earlier when I asked you to stop doing that? I'm all grown up, you know."

His answering smile was wry. "You know, somewhere during the course of the evening I might have noticed."

"When you kissed me —" she hadn't meant to say it, shouldn't have put what she was thinking out there in the open, but too late "— it felt almost . . . real."

"Did it?"

"Was it?"

"If I were going to kiss you for real, that's not how I'd do it."

The thumping of her heart took her by surprise. They were facing each other, and her head was tilted back as she looked up at him, and her hands — when had that happened? — rested just inside his jacket on the smooth front of his shirt. Through the fine cloth she could feel the firm muscles of his chest, the warmth of his skin.

"So how would you do it, then?"

"If I were going to kiss you, I'd kiss you like you were somebody I cared about." He slid a hand along her cheek. She felt the warm abrasion of his touch on her skin and butterflies, dozens of unexpected butterflies, took flight in her stomach. Then he leaned forward and touched his mouth to hers. As far as kisses went, it was warm and tender and over almost before it began. And still her heart pounded and her blood raced and she lost the strength in her legs. "Like that."

She fisted both hands in his shirtfront — she had no choice if she wanted to keep standing — and looked up at him. His eyes were black in the moonlight now and impossible to read.

"James Griffin." She was melting inside, her bones liquefying, her blood turning to steam. Her voice was low, husky — and indignant. "I've been waiting for you to kiss me for years and that's the best you can do?"

He blinked, looking surprised. Then he laughed.

Then he kissed her. Like she'd always

dreamed he would kiss her.
Like he meant it. For real.

43

Not much more than ten minutes later, Sibi walked into her house. Such a brief period of time, but during those few minutes everything changed. The moonlight came alive with stardust. The murmur of the sea became a song. The earth spun on its axis, and when it stopped again she was wide-eyed and tremulous, aglow with wonder, floating on a sparkling cloud of happiness that made all the darkness and danger and fear swirling around them seem impossibly far away.

Griff had gone, after parting from her with one last quick, hard kiss and a promise that he would still be around for at least another twenty-four hours. Whatever it was he needed to do would occupy him most of the day tomorrow, he said, and she had the rocket launch to attend, but he would find her.

She was thinking of that, and of him, and

of the wonderful, magical surprise that was the two of them together that life had so unexpectedly thrown in her path, which was why she was smiling as she crossed through the dark and deserted downstairs, then headed upstairs toward Jo and Margrit's bedroom. Her own bedroom, the first one at the top of the stairs, with its neatly made bed and the dressing table that was still adorned with Luiza's rag curler and the carefully arranged bookshelf where Griff's mother's copy of *My Ántonia* was, to any casual observer, just another title among the motley selection of novels and nonfiction in several languages, was dark, too.

The door to Jo and Margrit's room was open, the light on, and Margrit, fully clothed except for her shoes, lay fast asleep atop the covers on her bed. Sibi went quietly in, left the wrapped-up party treats on the small table between Margrit's and Jo's beds, and then went in search of Jo.

A soft *woof* drew Sibi's attention farther down the hall. Ruby sat at the foot of the pull-down ladder that led to the roof, plumed tail dusting the floor as it wagged, dark eyes gleaming through the shadows as they turned hopefully in her direction. Sibi reached the little dog, bent to pat her, then climbed the ladder: if Ruby waited at its foot, Jo had gone up it.

She stepped off the ladder into gossamer moonlight. This part of the roof was at the very back of the house. It was flat and hidden from any observer on the front and both sides by the peaks in the roof's design. In the way of a widow's walk, the flat part ended in a wooden railing high above the back garden. It also afforded an unmatched view of the sea. She'd seen that view countless times before, at all hours and in all weathers, but tonight — tonight! — the sight was truly breathtaking. She marveled at the endlessness of the inky waves, at the pale perfection of the moon reflected in them, before turning her attention to the girl who stood at the rail with her back to the trapdoor entrance through which Sibi had just emerged.

Almost as tall as she was now, thin and slightly angular in the way of someone not quite grown, her long dark hair blowing behind her like a banner, Jo had both hands cupped around a pigeon with whom she appeared to be having an earnest conversation.

". . . missing your friends, but they're fine and you'll be fine and —" Jo broke off as she became aware of her sister crossing the roof toward her. Still holding the pigeon, she turned to make a face at Sibi. The moonlight caught on the purple and green jewel tones of the bird's feathers and cast an otherworldly glow over Jo's delicate features. She still wore the short-sleeved floral dress she'd been wearing all day, and Mama's locket gleamed silver against the pin-tucked fabric between her small breasts. Her glasses were halfway down her nose, and she looked at Sibi over them as she held the bird out for her inspection.

"Lida won't eat. I think she's pining for Marika and Zarah."

"Oh, dear," Sibi said, and stroked the pigeon's sleek head with a gentle forefinger. Lida cooed at her in response.

"I've put an extra latch on the gate. This one is self-fastening. All you have to do is close the gate." Jo's tone was faintly reproachful.

The gate Jo referred to allowed access to the pigeon loft. It had "accidentally" been left open, thus releasing the missing Marika and Zarah, the day before yesterday.

"Good idea. Thank you." Sibi smiled at Jo. Actually, to be accurate, since she was already smiling, she smiled more widely.

"Why are you smiling at me like that?" Jo frowned and pushed her glasses back up her nose to look at Sibi more closely. "Did something happen?"

It took a conscious effort, but Sibi banished the smile. Jo was young but no fool, and she knew her older sister well. No point in putting questions into her head that didn't need to be there.

"Why are you up here?" Sibi countered. "It's a little late to be visiting with the pigeons."

The other pigeons, snug in their boxes with their heads tucked under their wings, were clearly asleep.

"I wanted to see if Lida had eaten her dinner. She hasn't."

Jo loved the pigeons. She'd named them after movie stars, and over the course of the year or so that Sibi had been using them to send messages to Griff she'd largely taken over their care. Jo didn't know their true purpose, of course: Sibi had told her that she'd purchased them along with the chickens for eggs and meat, but as it turned out they'd never had to use them for that purpose because the chickens were such good layers and the pigeons had become de facto pets. Currently they had six in keeping: Lida and Renate were the two remaining carrier pigeons, while the other four were the kind of ordinary utility pigeons that were commonly raised for meat. Mixing the types together had been Sibi's idea, meant to keep anyone from suspecting the birds' true purpose. No one ever had, and when messages had to be sent Sibi did it herself, then took the blame for carelessness when, occasionally, one or two "escaped," as Marika and Zarah had done to carry her urgent message about Eureka to Griff. The carrier pigeons, like materials for the loft they lived in and instructions for the birds' care and use, had been dropped by parachute about the time that accessing the mainland dead drop had become unworkable. She and the girls had built the loft themselves, and so far, keeping pigeons had turned out beautifully for all concerned.

"Having trouble sleeping?" Sibi asked sympathetically. Jo had been up on the roof late at night a number of times over the past couple of weeks. Sibi knew why: the start of school was approaching. Sixteen next month, Jo was going into her *Unterprima* year, and she dreaded the resumption of classes.

"Not really." Jo carefully returned Lida to the loft. As she turned back toward Sibi, a stray moonbeam caught the left side of her face. Bathed in its ethereal glow, the skin grafts stood out starkly against the smooth cream of her complexion. No longer harshly purple, they were a deathly white with rippled edges where the stitches had been. Inevitably they drew second looks, and occasionally remarks, from strangers. Jo was self-conscious about them even with people she knew, and particularly with her classmates.

"You've been staying up half the night lately," Sibi said. "Worrying about school?"

Jo gave her a shamefaced look: she hated admitting how unhappy she was in that environment. Then she nodded. "The later I stay up, the longer the days are, and the more time that gives me before I have to go back."

Sibi looked at her without saying anything for a moment. Love and compassion and anger at what fate — no, not fate, the *Nazis* — had dealt her sister rose in a fierce tide inside her.

They would all bear lifelong scars from that night in Guernica, but Jo's were the most visible.

"If they tease you, it's because of something that's wrong with them, not you."

"They don't tease me." Jo hunched her shoulders, folded her arms over her chest. "They feel *sorry* for me. That's worse, I think. Oh, they're polite. They just . . . don't include me. Sometimes I feel like I'm invisible. Sometimes I wish I were."

"Jo." Sibi put an arm around her sister.

Jo touched her head to Sibi's in an affectionate gesture, then pulled away. "Don't worry, I'll be fine. I can always join the circus and be part of the freak show."

"*Jo.*"

Swinging onto the ladder, Jo said, "I'm *joking,* all right?" Just before her head disappeared beneath the floor she added, "How was the party? Did you bring us anything?"

"Cinnamon pastries," Sibi said. She knew a ploy to change the subject when she heard one, but forcing a conversation on Jo that she clearly didn't want to have wasn't the best way to handle her sister, as she had learned from experience. "Apple strudel."

"I love cinnamon pastries," Jo said. She was out of sight now, her voice floating up through the rectangular opening in the floor, and Sibi stepped onto the ladder to follow. "Let's go wake up Margrit. She's been waiting for you to get home with the goodies all night."

44

Sibi's chest felt tight as she passed through
the multiple layers of security surrounding
Test Stand VII the following afternoon. The
fear that one of the guards from last night
might have said something to someone
about what they'd seen, and as a result
questions might be asked of her today,
turned her stomach into a pit. But as she
was admitted onto the grassy field at last
and then claimed by the film crew, who had
been impatiently waiting, it became obvious
that the focus was all on the launch that
was getting ready to happen.

". . . imperative that we don't have a
failure," Dr. Katz was saying as they hurried past him. He was in charge of the
logistics behind unloading the rocket from
the *Meillerwagen* that had transported it to
the site and positioning it correctly in its
mobile stand, and was speaking to Ober-
feldwebel Helmut Schrader, his second-in-

command for this operation, who was tasked with maintaining constant contact with the control room and the test tower. "The Reichminister of Propaganda is here. The Reichminster of Armaments is here. If this launch goes badly —"

What he thought would happen in that case Sibi never did hear, because she was hustled inside an office where she was handed a script that she was told to memorize. Once she knew her part, she was given a Nazi uniform to wear for the filming.

Back out on the field, standing in front of the newly renamed V-2 rocket in the field blue uniform — jacket, skirt and cap, worn with stockings and sturdy black shoes — of a Luftwaffe Helferin, Sibi faced the camera and recited the lines they had written for her. Behind her, the towering, fourteen-meter-high, twelve-ton rocket with its nose cone warhead (filled with sand for this test launch), black and white paint job and trio of stabilizing fins now stood straight as an arrow in its mobile launchpad.

An object of terrible beauty, a bearer of death and destruction, it was a product of the most aspirational of human hopes and dreams — the conquest of space — that had been corrupted by evil.

Knowing what the rockets could do,

knowing the murderous purpose for which these were intended, knowing the secret role she was playing in the frantic race to stop them, she stood rigid in front of this one, desperate to keep the maelstrom of emotions it evoked from showing on her face or in her manner.

It was a warm August afternoon. She was freezing inside.

On cue, she said, "Five minutes after launch, our Vengeance Weapons strike our enemies. Silent and deadly, they drop from the sky without warning."

Those words, with the memories they conjured up of another terrible bombing, made Sibi sick to her stomach. She was required to repeat them and the rest of the spiel, over and over, until the film crew — and Colonel Kraus, who had joined them and was watching — were satisfied.

She finished with the Nazi slogan: *"Ein Volk, ein Reich, ein Führer!"*

She hated every word. The sentiments behind them ate at her soul like acid. She said them anyway.

Finally she was ushered away from the rocket into the huge, concrete-and-steel observation area and control center that had been built into the horseshoe-shaped ellipse wall surrounding the launch area. It was packed with dignitaries, including Dr. Goebbels and Minister Speer and their staff. General Dornberger, Dr. von Braun and her father were also present, among many others. The room buzzed with conversation. Attention was divided between the big countdown clock — the time remaining until liftoff boomed continuously over the loudspeakers — and the rocket itself, clearly visible through the large, bulletproof glass window.

"X minus three minutes," came the count as Sibi was positioned at the edge of the window, enough out of the way so that she wouldn't impede the view of the VIPs but still angled so that the camera crew could get a shot of her in front of the rocket as it blasted off.

"There will be no retakes on this shot," the director's assistant warned her as he tugged at the hem of her jacket to straighten it. "You have only one opportunity to get it right. I will be over there." He pointed to a spot next to where the camera had been set up. "Watch me, and when I drop my arm —" he demonstrated "— look directly into the camera and speak. Understand?"

"Yes."

The director's assistant moved away to confer with the director. Colonel Kraus stepped up beside her and said, "You are doing very well, Fräulein Helinger. Everyone agrees. So well, in fact, that we may want to bring you back to Berlin with us when we leave this evening to do more of these shorts."

That caught her by surprise. "This evening? I can't. My sisters are about to start school and —"

He held up a hand to stop her. "Your sisters will be very grateful that you are helping the Reich in any way you can, I'm sure." His tone, underlined by the look he gave her, was rife with meaning.

She was thus reminded of the threat he still held over her. Over them.

"X minus two minutes."

"Of course, Colonel Kraus. I misspoke. I'm honored to help in any way I can," she said. If her tone was slightly wooden, well, she couldn't help it.

He smiled at her. "Excellent."

The director's assistant, returning, said, "Colonel, if you could please take a step back . . ."

He did.

A powder puff was whisked over her nose.

"X minus one minute."

The room fell silent. In response to a mimed direction from the director's as-

585

sistant, Sibi stood straighter, squared her shoulders, lifted her chin.

"Liftoff!"

Behind her, on the other side of the thick glass, the monster woke with an angry rumble. Sibi didn't have to look around to know that ignition had been achieved, and fiery gases were shooting out of the rocket's tail as, almost in slow motion, it rose toward this perfect summer day's perfect cerulean sky.

The assistant director's arm fell.

Sibi looked into the camera. "Our enemies will continue to pay a terrible price as we take our just vengeance." Snapping off a straight-armed salute, she concluded with a fervent, "Heil Hitler!"

The director looked up from his camera to make a gesture that meant *good job.* If he said something, she didn't hear him. The rocket's roar was now so loud it shook the floor, the building. Sibi could feel the vibrations through the soles of her shoes. It drowned out Herr Kraus's proprietary "Excellent! Excellent!" directed at her, and the clapping and cheers from everyone else directed at the rocket's successful launch.

Sibi turned in time to see the huge rocket with its long tail of orange fire and white gases, having broken free of the launchpad, as it hung suspended in midair, straining to gain height, fighting the forces of gravity. A collective hush fell over the assembly as they waited with bated breath for it to topple over, slam into the ground, explode and burn — or rise. Sibi found herself holding her breath, too, as she thought about all the work and worry that had gone into this flight — the difficulties in getting the propellant pump turbine to function properly, the calculations involved in arriving at the special mix of liquid fuel — as well as what success might mean.

If the test launch failed, would the attack on the Eureka summit be called off?

The rocket started to climb. Slowly, almost imperceptibly. Then with a mighty roar it shot skyward, streaking straight up toward the stratosphere. Sixty seconds after leaving the ground, the V-2 was designed to achieve a speed of about 5600 kilometers per hour, and though slightly delayed, it looked like this one had done so. Just as quickly as she had the thought, the rocket pierced a drift of fluffy white cumulous clouds and disappeared from sight.

The room erupted with exultation. Men slapped each other's backs. Dr. Goebbels shook hands with General Dornberger. Big smiles and hearty congratulations were exchanged everywhere.

"We did it." Papa came up behind her, placed a hand on her shoulder, squeezed. He looked exhausted, dark circles under his eyes, wrinkles where he'd had none before, but he was smiling. "Those fire engine turbo-pumps were what made the difference, I think."

With Sibi's assistance, he'd spent weeks troubleshooting a method of feeding propellants to the engine. Finally they'd discovered that the kind of high-volume, low-weight pumps they needed had already been developed and were being used in fire engines, of all things. The pumps had been shipped in, they'd worked, and here they all were.

Sibi smiled back at him. He was wearing his military uniform, which he rarely did, preferring civilian garb topped by a white lab coat, and she knew it was because of the importance of this day, and their visitors. She might hate the uniform and all it stood for, but she loved him. His interest was always in the engines, the rockets, the science of it. He had no love for the Nazi Party, she knew, nor belief in its tenets. Survival, his own and theirs, dictated his choice to be a part of it. But still she had not told him about her own activities, or about Griff. How he would react should he learn her secret she couldn't be sure. To trust, and be wrong, would be a disaster.

"Sibi! *Kaixo!*" The Basque greeting in a vaguely familiar male voice caused her to pivot with surprise toward it. The young man who beamed at her with outstretched arms was slender, black-haired, devastatingly handsome —

"Emilio!" She returned his hug, reciprocated his double air kisses. Emilio Aguire in a civilian's tan business suit was not quite the last person she would have expected to see on this occasion, but it was close. His father, having survived Guernica's bombing only to die the following year, had left his shipbuilding business to his only son, who had gotten rich selling boats to the Nazis. He'd visited Peenemünde several times before, when his ships had delivered or picked up cargo, and she'd seen him then. Their shared history made him a friend, but . . . a Nazi friend. Which meant that while she smiled at him on the surface, underneath she was cautious and wary in their interactions. "What are you doing here?"

"Those freighters in the harbor? They're mine. I'm here to supervise their loading."

Even as her interest surged, she fought to keep her face from revealing anything besides pleasure in seeing him again. "How wonderful to have you visit us!" *Pump him for any information that might be useful — like the ships' destination.* "And will you be going with your ships when they leave, on their journey to . . . ?"

"You must join us in a toast, Dr. Helinger, Fräulein Helinger," General Dornberger interrupted, stopping beside Papa and slinging an arm around his shoulders and in the process bringing him into what was now a group that included Sibi and Emilio. An aide followed him, passing out champagne. "Good to see you again, Herr Aguire! How would we Germans get on without our loyal Spanish friends and their ships?"

"Very poorly, I expect," Emilio replied, taking the flute that was offered and tipping it toward General Dornberger in salute, and they all laughed.

Sibi accepted her flute with a smile, and kept smiling when Dr. Goebbels, at the far end of the room, lifted his and shouted, "To the führer."

"To the führer!" The toast echoed through the room.

Shortly thereafter, Sibi was conscripted by the film crew to say some additional lines at various locations in the facility.

When she was able to escape, it was after

eight o'clock.

But by then she did know where Emilio's ships were taking the rockets.

eight o'clock.

But by then she did know where Kaulbe's
ships were taking the rockets.

45

I need to tell Griff.

That was the thought that kept Sibi sitting tensely erect in her corner of the crowded automobile despite the exhaustion that was doing its best to overtake her. The intended destination of the ships carrying the rockets was important information, information he needed to know. He'd said he would find her, but she hadn't expected to have to stay so late at the launch site and was terrified that he might have had to leave the island without seeing her. Although he'd promised he wouldn't — and Griff, she'd learned over the years, was a man who kept his promises.

And maybe, just maybe, she had a personal reason for wanting so badly to see him, as well.

In an effort to avoid Colonel Kraus and his threat to take her back to Berlin with him, Sibi had found her own ride home once the film crew was finished with her. She wasn't sure if Colonel Kraus was even still on the island — Dr. Goebbels, Minister Speer and their entourages had flown out earlier — but the film crew clearly was and she didn't want to chance it.

She'd changed out of the Helferin uniform and back into the simple blue dress she'd worn to the launch site before leaving it, and felt much better, as if she were once again in her own skin.

"Did you bring us anything?" Margrit called hopefully as Sibi got out of the automobile that was still packed with the secretaries it was delivering to their dorm. Thanking them for the lift with a wave as it turned and drove off, Sibi looked toward Margrit, who was playing hopscotch with friends in the street while at the same time clearly recalling the treats Sibi had brought home last night. It was nearing sunset — August had long hours of daylight — and a beautiful pinkish light fell over everything, including the group of girls.

"Sorry, *maitea,* but no." Sibi's tone combined humor with regret. Margrit's mop of curls bounced as vigorously as the rest of her as she took her turn in the game. At twelve, she was on the cusp between child and young woman, and right now the child part was very much in evidence. Still not quite as tall as Jo, her sturdy bone structure, in Sibi's opinion, indicated that in a few years she would be the tallest of the three of them. She was pretty, friendly, quick to speak up for herself and others — perhaps too quick — and popular with her peers. "Where's Jo?"

"In the garden." Bounce, bounce. The orange plaid romper she wore had a button missing that hadn't been missing that morning. Big blue eyes slashed Sibi's way. "Oh, someone telephoned for you."

"Who?" Sibi's thoughts immediately flew to Colonel Kraus, and her stomach knotted.

"Ask Jo."

Sibi went inside, through the house, and opened the door to the garden. As promised, Jo was there, in a big sun hat, an old shirt of Papa's with the sleeves rolled up and a pair of short pants, scattering feed for the chickens that scratched and pecked at the ground around her feet. Ruby lay on the back steps watching the proceedings and panting in the heat, and turned her head to look up at Sibi as she opened the door.

"Did someone telephone for me?"

"I left a message by the telephone."

Sibi withdrew, found the message, and

smiled: *Your package will be waiting at the Strandhaus at nine.*

She had no doubt the message was from Griff. The Strandhaus was one of the more obscure of the hotels left over from when Usedom had been nothing more exciting than a mildly popular summer holiday resort.

Jo and Ruby came in through the back door, bringing the scent of summer and grass and chickens with them.

"What package?" Whipping off her hat, Jo fanned herself with it. With her hair in two long braids and her glasses askew, she looked almost as young as Margrit.

"Some Mischgerat control elements we need for the rockets," Sibi said. Jo promptly lost interest as Sibi knew she would and headed upstairs.

"Did you two eat?" Sibi called after her. She'd left food in the icebox, plus both girls were perfectly capable of fixing themselves a meal.

"Yes." The reply floated back as Jo, with Ruby following, clattered up the stairs.

"I'm going out."

"Bye."

Sibi went around to the shed, grabbed her bicycle and headed out. By the time she reached the bottom of the street — it was a slope, but not a particularly steep one — she was flying, her hair streaming back from her face, her feet resting motionless on the pedals as gravity did the work for her.

There was little traffic — it was Tuesday night — and she whizzed past the closely spaced shops and the small restaurant with its delicious *Fischbrötchen* and the offices and flats where a number of the single engineers lived and thus reached the far end of the *Siedlung* where the Strandhaus was located.

It was not quite nine when Sibi parked her bicycle and climbed the steps to the front porch of the two-story board-and-batten hotel. Not much bigger than a large house, its gray paint was weathered by the sea. Window boxes full of a variety of flowers provided a cheerful note. The place didn't appear busy, but several people strolled the wide beach that stretched along almost the entire length of the northern shore of the island. When conditions were just right, the fine, sugar-white sand was said to "sing." Sibi had personally experienced the phenomenon when it occurred, although the resulting sound was more like a chorus of tiny squeaks than any singing she'd ever heard.

Beyond the beach, two children played in

the surf while a woman, presumably their mother, watched from a nearby chair. Farther out, an intrepid swimmer plowed through gentle waves. Seagulls circled and cried overhead, while brown plovers ran in and out of the surf.

"Punctual as well as beautiful, I see." The voice came from the depths of the porch.

Griff. She almost said it aloud, but caught herself in time. Instead her heart instantly beat faster and a warm glow radiated out from her solar plexus and she smiled at the man who rose lazily from a chair in the shadowy corner like he was the one person she most wanted to see in the world.

Because he was.

He smiled back at her the same way.

"Major Schumann," she greeted him as he joined her, just in case there were any listening ears nearby.

"Fräulein." His tone was formal. His eyes were anything but.

I have news. She didn't say it, wouldn't until she got him alone, but maybe her eyes did because he took her elbow and said, "Let's walk."

She nodded, and together they strolled down the steps and out onto to the beach.

Where the heels of her pumps promptly sank into the sand. So she took them off, then — "Don't look!" — rolled down her stockings and took them off, too, stuffing them into her shoes. With her shoes in one hand and her other hand tucked in the crook of his arm she walked barefoot over the warm sand with her handsome Luftwaffe officer escort until there was no one within earshot and all the other sunset beachgoers were small, distant figures and the only sounds were the murmur of the sea, the cries of the birds and the toot of a distant boat horn.

That's when he pulled her around an automobile-size rock that blocked even those tiny potential witnesses from view.

"I know where —" she began excitedly as the rock's shadow fell over them.

"Hold that thought," he said, and cupped her face in his hands and kissed her, and she not only did *not* hold that thought but forgot it completely as, shoes and all, she wrapped her arms around his neck and kissed him back.

"How was your day?" he asked, voice prosaic if a little uneven, when he left off kissing her at last. The sun was just sinking below the waves, and the sky was wreathed in rainbow colors, and the sea was as blue as she'd ever seen it, and the light spilling over the beach where they stood was indescribably beautiful.

Wonder: that, she decided, was the best way to describe what she felt as she looked up at this man she knew so well but not in this new amazing context. Wonder, because it seemed like maybe dreams did sometimes come true and miracles did sometimes happen and that happiness was possible even in the midst of all the horrors of war. She might not quite trust in all that but she did trust him. Standing there in his arms with her arms looped around his neck and her mouth soft with his kisses, she drank him in as he looked down at her with desire blazing from his eyes and his mouth just touched with traces of her lipstick. His face was hard with wanting her, his body was hard with wanting her; she could feel the hungry tension radiating from him but he wasn't doing anything about it, not any longer. He was just standing there breathing and looking at her. As for herself? She was melting inside, all weak-kneed and shaky, pressed up against him like a stamp to a letter. All she wanted to do was go up on tiptoe and start kissing him again, but there was something — something important, something that was yammering away insistently at the back of her mind — she needed to tell him first.

"Fine," she replied, and just like that her befuddled synapses reconnected again and she blurted, "Turkey."

"What?" There wasn't a speck of comprehension in the look he gave her. His eyes did, however, linger on her mouth.

"The freighters are taking the rockets to Turkey, and they'll go overland from there."

He frowned, and she could see his synapses reconnecting just as hers had done. "Turkey," he said in an entirely different tone. Then, "How do you know that?"

She told him about Emilio. "It's good information."

"Better than good." He was looking down at her still, but she could see that the OSS agent in him had taken over. "I need to pass this along right away. How about I come by your house in, say, an hour and a half? We need to talk, but I have to do this first."

"Come by my house?" She considered it with misgiving. The girls were there — and by then Papa might even be home. Although he'd been working until the small hours of the morning lately.

"The woods across the street from your house," he clarified. "Where we were last night."

"Oh." The warm memories from that came rushing back, and she smiled at him.

"All right. In an hour and a half. That would make it —"

"About ten thirty. Maybe a little later. It depends on how long it takes me to get through. Watch for me out your front window. Don't come out until you see me there. No telling who — or what — might be running around those woods at night. Last night I swear I saw a moose. Whatever it was had horns like oak trees."

"That would be a Pomeranian deer. Unless it's rutting season, they're harmless."

"Still." His hands circled her wrists preparatory to detaching her arms from around his neck — big warm hands around slender cool wrists, and that right there was enough to make her go all shivery inside — but then he paused to kiss her. Her toes curled but before she could totally lose the thread of the conversation he broke the kiss, pulled her arms down, turned her around and marched her back down the beach.

"Get through — you have a radio?" she asked as her thought processes started working again.

"Yup."

"Where is it?" Because transmissions could be traced, and to have such a thing as a radio in any place where you could regularly be found was dangerous and — Then light dawned. "In the woods?"

"Know that clearing at the top of the ridge?"

She nodded. It was one of the highest places on the island.

"There."

They'd reached the bike rack.

"Need a ride?" she asked as he pulled her bike out for her.

He shook his head. "Not in broad daylight. Much as I enjoy the sight of you balancing on the handlebars, that might attract more attention than either of us wants. I'll make my own way."

"You could always try being the one on the handlebars."

That earned her a quick smile. "Maybe one day."

"Have it your way, then." She took the bicycle from him, dropped her shoes in the basket. He caught her chin, tilted her face up and planted a quick, hard kiss on her mouth that did ridiculous things to her insides. Then he stepped away.

He left her smiling, and she caught herself smiling the whole way home. The warm bubble of happiness was so new, and felt so fragile, like handspun glass, that she treated it cautiously, afraid to think about it too much or probe the whys and wherefores of it too closely lest it shatter in the face of harsh reality — such as the knowledge that soon, in a few hours, a day, he would be gone.

It lasted until she floated up the steps of her house and opened the door on an ear-shattering volley of frenzied barking coming from upstairs.

Ruby's shrill urgency acted on Sibi like a slap in the face, brought her down to earth in an instant, made her heart leap and her pulse pound.

Margrit. Jo.

Dropping her shoes, Sibi sprinted for the second floor.

She saw Ruby as soon as she reached the top of the stairs.

The roof ladder was down. Ruby danced on her hind legs, looking up at the opening in the ceiling, pawing at the rungs. Her frantic barks sent gooseflesh racing over Sibi's skin.

46

Sibi went up that ladder like the floor beneath her was on fire.

Even before she reached the opening she could hear an angry altercation, what sounded like violent scuffling. Every single hair on her body stood on end.

"What do you want?" *Margrit.*

"Who is behind this? You will tell me!" *A man.*

"I don't know what you're talking about." *Jo.*

"Get away from my sister!" *Margrit.*

"Ow! Let me go!" *Jo.*

Sibi burst through the opening, practically leaping from the ladder to land barefoot on the warm tin of the flat roof, and found herself the instant cynosure of three pairs of eyes.

She took in the situation at a glance: Colonel Kraus — Colonel Kraus! — had one of Jo's braids twisted around his hand;

Jo, a bucket of feed at her feet, shoved at his arm as she struggled to free herself. Margrit, wide-eyed, off to one side, clutched a broom; from the pile of dirt in front of her, it appeared she'd been sweeping. A pigeon fluttered across the floor, trying to take wing but having difficulty doing so. The small green capsule affixed to its leg that was used to hold messages hung loose, open —

Zarah: one of the pair of pigeons she'd sent off three days ago to Griff.

Sibi's blood ran cold. *No. Oh, no.*

"Sibi —" A panicked quaver sharpened Jo's voice.

"Colonel Kraus! Let her go!" Sibi's voice was sharp, too, despite the terrified constriction of her throat. She planted her feet, clenched her fists, while panic turned her blood to ice. *Play innocent, stall for time.*

"*You.*" Colonel Kraus's gaze skewered her. "I can't believe it. I *do* believe it. I was on my way to your house when I saw the *Columba livia domestica* flying in from the sea. I followed it. When it came here, I thought, no, not to this house. Not to the house of those to whom we've been so generous! But it is true! You have more birds, you have a loft! Your father, your sisters, *you — who* is the spy? *Who is the spy?*"

Sibi's heart raced. Adrenaline flooded her system. *Caught, caught, caught:* it was a drumbeat of disaster pounding through her head. All she could do was try convincing him that he was wrong.

"Of course we're not spies!" Scorn dredged from the huge reservoir of fear welling up inside her suffused her voice even as she shivered and shook internally. "We raise these birds for food —"

"You think I don't know a *carrier pigeon* when I see one? You think I don't know for what purpose they are used? It is your bad luck that I do know. And that one still has its *capsule attached.* It doesn't matter which one of you is the spy. You will hang, all of you! But first you will tell me everything. You will tell me —" Dropping Jo's braid, he fumbled at his waist, yanked his sidearm free, pointed it at Sibi *"— what did you reveal?"*

Margrit hit him with the broom. Out of nowhere, with all her strength. Gripped, swung and *bam.*

"Ah!" He staggered sideways, threw up an arm —

His gun went flying, landed with a clatter, skittered to within a few centimeters of Sibi's feet.

She snatched it up.

My God, my God.
And shot him.

Pointed, pulled the trigger and fired, just like that. The recoil almost made her drop the gun. The bang was so loud it hurt her ears. Margrit squeaked and jumped. Jo gave a choked cry and stumbled back, fetching up against the loft. The loose pigeon fluttered and squawked. Ruby, on the floor below, yelped and set up a piercing howl. Colonel Kraus clapped a hand to his shoulder, straightened to his full height and stared at her, eyes blazing, face twisting with a terrifying combination of anger and hatred and shock —

"You," he growled with loathing, and lunged at her.

She shot him again.

Blood spurted from his throat. A bright crimson stream, arcing out like someone had turned on a spigot. He clutched his throat, made a horrible wet gurgling sound, took a staggering step back and fell.

Hit the roof with a crash. Rolled onto his back.

Shuddered once and lay still.

All three sisters froze in place, gaping at the fallen man. The silence that gripped them shrieked of horror.

Sibi's knees gave out. She sank into a

boneless heap where she stood. Sitting, her legs curled beneath her, her hand holding the gun limp in her lap, she felt time slow down. She felt the heat of the roof beneath her, listened to Ruby's howls and stared at Colonel Kraus, at his motionless legs in their jackboots, at his outflung hands, at the bubbling blood. So much blood.

Is he dead? Did I kill him?

She was breathing hard — the raw meat smell of blood mixed with the sharp tang of cordite overpowered the ever-present salt air of the sea — but the extra oxygen intake didn't help. She felt sick, dizzy. Her ears rang. The bitter taste of fear was on her tongue.

Holding the broom like she was ready to bash him with it again if necessary, Margrit cautiously approached the downed man.

Sibi's lips parted. She wanted to tell Margrit, *No, get away, don't look, don't get involved,* but she couldn't get the words out and, anyway, it was too late for that.

"I think he's dead," Margrit said. Her voice was hushed, and, careful to keep her distance, she poked his chest with the broom. No reaction.

I think so, too, was Sibi's response, but her throat was still too tight to allow her to say it. Colonel Kraus lay too still, his skin was too waxen, and there was all that blood. Pouring from his throat, pooling beneath his head — an ocean of blood. Nobody could lose that much blood and live.

"Who *is* he?" Margrit's head swung toward Sibi. Her eyes were wide with shock.

That's right, she wouldn't remember, she didn't know . . .

Sibi shook her head. Words still weren't coming and, anyway, she wasn't sure Margrit, or Jo, needed to know. Maybe they'd be safer if they didn't know —

Safe. They were the opposite of safe.

What have I done?

"He just stormed out onto the roof and grabbed me." Jo's voice shook. Pushing away from the loft, she hurried toward the trapdoor. "Ruby! Hush! We're all right," she called down it, and Ruby, blessedly, stopped howling. Jo crouched beside Sibi, wrapped an arm around her shoulders. "Are you all right?"

Sibi nodded. She *was* — or at least, she would be. As soon as her heart stopped pounding so hard and her pulse stopped thundering in her ears and she could breathe again without having to force the air in past the steel bands constricting her chest.

"What happened?" Sibi's voice was a

croak, but at least she was able to speak again.

"Zarah came back. Something must have attacked her. I was up here feeding them, and she landed on the loft. I could tell she was hurt, and I picked her up and was looking at her when he —" she indicated Colonel Kraus with a jerk of her head "— came out of nowhere yelling about spies." Her gaze swung toward Margrit. "How'd he even get in the house?"

"I must have left the front door unlocked," Margrit said guiltily. "Everybody went home, and I came in, and then you yelled for me to come up here and —"

"You came up and started sweeping." Jo gave Sibi's shoulders a quick hug, then stood up and crossed to Margrit's side.

"Do you think he's dead?" Margrit asked Jo, poking Colonel Kraus with the broom again. He remained as unresponsive as before, and Jo gave a decided nod.

"He's dead," she said, then glanced at Sibi, who sat boneless and unmoving still. "You *shot* him." There was awe in her voice.

"I know." Sibi took a deep breath. "I had to."

"I thought he was going to shoot *her,*" Margrit said. "That's why I hit him with the broom."

"You did, didn't you?" For Margrit, Sibi managed a feeble smile. "Good job."

"He was definitely going to denounce us as spies." Jo glanced at Zarah. The pigeon had stopped fluttering to huddle against the loft, clearly wanting in. What remained of the dark green capsule was still attached to her leg. Jo looked back at Sibi. "*Are* we spies?"

"You're not. You and Margrit are not. This is nothing to do with you. Or Papa, either." If only she could make that so. If only what she had done did not rebound on her family.

"*You're* a spy? For the Allies?" Jo asked, incredulous. Both she and Margrit stared at Sibi wide-eyed. Then Jo's expression changed. "For Mama. And Luiza." Her voice was soft with comprehension.

Sibi nodded.

"That's *smashing,*" Margrit said, looking at Sibi with admiration, and Jo nodded agreement.

God bless Margrit, with her tough, resourceful spirit. And Jo, with her quiet strength.

They're in danger — I've put them in danger. I have to try to fix this.

The thought was enough to get her up off the floor, get her moving again. Still clutching the gun that she'd all but forgotten was in her hand, she padded over to join Jo and Margrit. Together, they all looked down at what remained of Colonel Kraus.

His partially open eyes were cloudy and fixed. His mouth was partially open, too. Blood trickled from one corner. Blood still flowed from the hole she'd blown in his neck. Sibi's stomach heaved in reaction even as she crouched beside him and steeled herself to touch him, to check his pulse.

His wrist was still warm, but flaccid. There was no detectable pulse.

I killed him. I killed a man. I just committed murder.

She had to swallow hard to keep from being sick.

"He's dead," she said, and stood up. Panic welled inside her. She had to consciously battle it back.

"So now what do we do?" Margrit asked, practical even in extremis.

Good question. Great question. Sibi took a deep breath. "You two — go downstairs. I want you to do your best to forget this ever happened. It's nothing to do with either of you. You played no part in it."

"We're not leaving you," Jo said.

Margrit shook her head. "We're all in this together."

612

"For Mama and Luiza," Jo said.

"We loved them, too," Margrit said.

Sibi looked at her sisters, Margrit still clutching her broom, Jo with her glasses barely hanging on to her nose. The little girls she'd loved and protected for so long were not really little girls anymore. They were growing up, and this, difficult as it was for her to come to grips with, was their choice to make.

"They'll come looking for him. If they find him —" She broke off. *If they find him, the girls are dead. We're all dead.* She looked at her sisters. "We have to get rid of him. We have to get rid of the body."

47

The scent of 4711 cologne was everywhere. Sibi ran through the woods, through the deepening purple twilight, heading for Griff, for the ridge where he'd said he'd be, and instead of breathing in the aroma of pine or leaf mold or any of the smells normally associated with the woods she smelled that damned cologne. It was as if it were chasing her. As if Colonel Kraus were chasing her.

The thought made her shudder.

She, Jo and Margrit had rolled him up in the heavy green canvas tarpaulin that had been spread beneath the loft to catch pigeon droppings and scattered straw from the birds' boxes to soak up the blood, while at the same time engaging in a quick, desperate discussion — *no one ever comes up on the roof, why not leave him here?; throw him down into the garden and bury him there; lug him up the road to that spot that overhangs the sea and pitch him in* — that had ended

614

with Sibi deciding that the corpse needed to be gotten as far away from the house as possible as fast as possible, and that they needed help to make that happen.

Griff was the help — *a friend,* she'd told her sisters and, in answer to Jo's cautious question, said, *Yes, we can trust him* — she had in mind, and she was planning to bring him back with her. The girls wouldn't recognize him, she was positive, and deciding whether or not to tell them who he was was something she could think about later. The urgent problem was, they had to get rid of Colonel Kraus before anyone came looking for him. They needed Griff to take him away, while they stayed behind to make sure no sign that he had ever been there remained.

How did Colonel Kraus get to the house? Did he walk? Where is his automobile? Those were the questions that Sibi had posed, rapid-fire, as much to herself as her sisters, as one after the other they'd popped into her mind. None of the questions had an answer: no automobile in sight; no keys in his pockets, which they checked.

An automobile with a driver?

The only thing that kept her from complete panic at that possibility was the fact that, when she'd come home, the street had

615

been deserted: no automobile, no driver, no one at all in sight.

Did anyone know he was on his way to their house?

They would have to say he'd never arrived.

Had anyone heard the gunshots?

Oh God, oh God, oh God.

Griff was down on one knee, packing something — a radio, it had to be a radio, he must be finished transmitting his message, dear God she hoped he was, because this couldn't wait — into a small wooden box when she burst from the trees into the clearing on top of the ridge. On her way out of the house she'd stuck her feet into the flat brogues she wore in the factory — no stockings, no socks, no time for either. Her passage through the woods had been largely silent: the thick carpet of pine needles and last year's oak leaves and other detritus had muffled her footsteps. It was almost dark. Long shadows from the tall pines swayed across the rocky protuberance where Griff knelt. Behind him the last bright orange sliver of the sun sank below a horizon of deep blue waves.

Griff glanced around as he heard her at last, then, clearly seeing that something was amiss, jumped to his feet as she ran to him.

He caught her by the arms. "What's happened?" His voice was sharp.

"Colonel Kraus — I shot him. He's dead." She was breathing so hard it was difficult to get the words out.

"What?"

"One of the pigeons I sent you came back. Colonel Kraus paints — painted — birds and knew what it was. He followed it to my house and found the loft. When I got home, he was on the roof with the girls. He said we were spies and pulled his gun and Margrit hit him with a broom and he dropped the gun and I picked it up and shot him."

"Holy hell."

"He's dead. I killed him. You have to come help us get rid of the body."

"*You* shot Kraus."

"Yes. Hurry." She tugged at him. "Somebody may know he was coming to our house. For all I know, he may have a driver waiting for him somewhere. Or an automobile. He didn't have any keys."

"All right, I'm coming. Calm down. Let me take care of this. One minute." He let go of her arms and turned back to the wooden box, folding something down inside it, closing the lid and snapping it shut, then picking it up and striding toward the trees.

Wringing her hands with agitation, she stayed beside him. He threw a frowning glance at her. "You're sure he's dead?"

"Yes."

He thrust the box into a hollow at the base of a tree and scooped fallen leaves and needles in front of the opening. Then he straightened and grabbed her hand and together they plunged through the trees. "Where's the body now?"

"On the roof. We wrapped him in a tarp," she said. "You'll have to carry him down a ladder to the second floor — we'll help you. He's heavy."

"I think I can manage."

"And then there's the blood — there's so much blood. We tried cleaning it up, the girls were still doing it when I left, and he's wrapped up, but he was bleeding still and the blood might get in the house and —"

"I'll look out for the blood."

"We thought about throwing him in the sea, but then I thought he might not sink or his body might wash back up, a dozen things could go wrong, so I think probably the best thing you can do is carry him deep into the woods and bury him there. We have a shovel in the shed and —"

"I'll figure it out." Despite the fact that they were half running, half fast-walking

618

through the trees, his tone soothed. She realized that she must be rattling on like she had no sense left to her whatsoever, and if she was it was because she *was* so rattled, so jolted out of any connection to normalcy that her mind was racing along at about a thousand kilometers a second and her body was battling the effects of shock. The only thing that kept her from succumbing entirely was the thought of the girls. She had to do what she could to save them from the consequences of what *she* had done.

"Sibi, listen. I think it's time to get you out of here. Staying just got too dangerous. Soon — in a day or two — I'll be making my way out of Germany. I want you to come with me. I'll see you safe."

She looked at him in surprise. They were dodging through the trees, half running, half sliding now because they were going down a slope, and he was hanging on to her hand to keep her from slipping on the wet leaves and both of them were short of breath. Despite that he was focused on her, and his expression told her that he was deadly serious. She wanted to agree so badly it was a physical ache inside her. Not until this moment, when he was offering her a possible way out, had she realized how afraid she was, had been for years now, and how heavy the weight of that fear was. These last few months had been the worst. The fate of Sophie Scholl — the knowledge that a beautiful twenty-two-year-old girl had had her head chopped off for something as relatively innocuous as distributing anti-Nazi pamphlets — had leached into her soul. She hadn't let herself dwell on it, because there was no point, but now — now —

"I can't." It killed her to have to say it. "The girls — I can't leave Jo and Margrit. And there's Papa, too. And after this —"

His lips compressed. "The Nazi leadership is already desperate. This — the attack they're planning on Eureka — is the equivalent of a Hail Mary pass." Seeing her quick frown of incomprehension at what she recognized as some kind of American sports term, he shook his head. "Never mind. But when it's thwarted, they're going to come looking for scapegoats. For spies. And with Kraus going missing, I suspect they'll focus on Peenemünde. It wouldn't require that much of a stretch for them to turn that focus to you."

The thought dried her mouth. She slid a little on the leaves, but before she could recover, could say anything, he came to an abrupt halt a step or so in front of her. His hand tightened on hers almost painfully, and then he was pulling her up, pulling her close to his side.

"Shh." It was a sharp warning uttered under his breath, and even as Sibi steadied herself by clutching at him she saw where he was looking and turned her attention in that direction, too.

A sizable swath of woods still separated them from the street and her house, but through the low-hanging branches and close-set, rough-barked trunks she could see the activity that riveted him.

Two vehicles were parked in front of her house. One was a military-style truck, and the other was a big black Daimler. The house was ablaze with light — it looked like every light in the place was on — and the front door stood open. Even as Sibi watched, an SS officer came down the front steps, cast a long look around the area as if looking for something or someone, then ducked into the back seat. She heard the slam of the automobile's door as he closed it, and then Ruby started to bark. Sibi couldn't see the little dog, but she would recognize that frantic barking anywhere in the world.

When the Daimler pulled away down the street, Ruby, furiously barking, ran after it.

An icy stab of fear pierced Sibi's heart. The only reason Ruby would be chasing after that vehicle was if Jo were inside it.

48

Griff wouldn't let her go back to the house to see if Margrit was there, or to try to find out what had happened. He dragged her farther into the woods, and held her against him as she all but fell apart in his arms, talking persuasively to her until her mind cleared enough to see the logic in what he was telling her: the fact that the truck was still there meant that soldiers were inside the house, if they took Jo they wouldn't have left Margrit, and putting herself in harm's way wouldn't help her sisters.

"What will they do to them? They're just little girls." Her voice shook. "That doesn't matter, does it? Any more than it matters that I'm the guilty party and until today the girls knew nothing about any of it."

Griff didn't reply for a moment. His arms stayed warm and hard around her. She gripped his jacket with both hands, tilted her head back as she looked into his face.

His eyes, black and glinting as deepening darkness wrapped the woods in charcoal shadows, were impossible to read. It was the grim set of his mouth that told her that his estimation of the severity of the situation matched her own, and that her pain hurt him.

"What do your sisters know exactly?" There was a careful note to the question that made Sibi's heart skip a beat. What he was really asking was, *What can they tell?* "Do they know anything about Eureka?"

"No." She thought hard. "They know that I've been acting as a spy for the Allies. They know that I've been using carrier pigeons to communicate. They know that I shot Colonel Kraus. They know I have a 'friend' I was going to get to help move the body." She had to take a deep breath before she could continue. "They don't know who that friend is. They don't know about you."

"Do they know anything about the information you've been passing on to me?"

"No. All they know is what I've told you."

They knew each other too well: she could sense him assessing what she'd said, and concluding that the potential damage to whatever plans his people were making wasn't catastrophic.

Meanwhile, two little girls were facing

torture, and worse.

"Margrit's *twelve*," she said. "And Jo —" Her voice broke. "It's my fault. Oh, my God."

"Sibi —" He pulled her more fully into his embrace. "You can't blame yourself. You don't even know for sure what's happened. Kraus didn't have a chance to tell anyone what he'd discovered before you shot him, did he? Maybe all they have is the body, and they think they're investigating a straight-up murder."

"You don't believe that. And is that better?"

"It wouldn't involve your sisters, probably. It wouldn't involve anyone except the actual murderer."

"How likely is that?" Her eyes narrowed, and she shook her head. "If they found the body, they'll have seen the loft. Even if they didn't know before, they'll figure out they're looking for a spy."

"The point is, we don't know what they know."

"Let me go," she said. "I have to find Papa and tell him what's happened. He must still be at the factory. Maybe there's something he can do."

"If they took your sisters, we have to assume they'll bring in your father, as well."

The very quietness with which he spoke struck terror into her soul. Her family — all of them, every single one who was left — might well die because of her.

To save the many at the expense of the few — all at once she knew, with a rock-solid certainty, that the cost was too high. That in the end war was personal, and she would sooner lose the whole world than her family.

"Maybe if I go to General Dornberger," she said. "And tell him that I'm the guilty one. Maybe he'll let Jo and Margrit go."

"It won't make a difference. You know that."

She did. Oh, God, she did. *What have I done?*

"Again, we don't know what they know. Why don't you let me nose around, see what I can find out?"

"While I do what, hide here in the woods?" She shook her head. Panic twisted through her. "There's no time. They took Jo, and as you say probably Margrit, too. They wouldn't have done that if they didn't mean to at the very least qu-question them." *Question* was a euphemism the authorities used for torture, but Sibi couldn't bring herself to say that. She knew the truth, but her mind shied away from it. The pictures it conjured up were too horrible.

Her heart wept.

"You know they're almost certainly looking for you by now, right? And that if you're taken, even just on suspicion of murder, they'll torture you until you confess to everything you've ever done, and then they'll execute you." It was a stone-cold statement of fact, designed to make her face reality. Sibi responded with a nod that was really more of an agitated jerk of her head: she knew. She'd known the risks from the beginning. *She'd* known the risks, and accepted them. But she'd never meant for her sisters to be the ones to ultimately pay the price.

"I don't care. I have to go."

"The intelligent thing to do right now would be to cut your losses and let me get you away from here," he said. "As you say, your sisters are young, and they've had no part in any of this. It's possible they'll be released."

Sibi dismissed that suggestion with a shake of her head. "You know they won't be."

"I know your sisters have a better chance of surviving this than you do, if you're taken."

Their eyes met as she silently acknowledged the truth of that and, still silently, answered: *it doesn't matter.*

"I'm going to Werke Süd, and I'm going to try to find my father." Her voice was steady now. *She* was steady. "If he's been taken, I'm going to look for him and my sisters. The man who got into the Daimler was wearing one of those red Death's Head caps that the SS there wear, so I'm guessing that's where my sisters are." She released her grip on his coat to push at his chest. "Let me go."

He let her go, but everything about him from the set of his jaw to his body language was grim.

"Fine," he said. "But all we're going to do is look. If we find them, then we step back, assess the situation and make a plan. None of this rushing in and screaming, *It's me you want, not them.* Agreed?"

She nodded: *agreed.* "If they catch you, they'll torture and kill you, too."

"I'm aware, believe me."

"I can't leave them."

"I know."

They looked at each other. She still couldn't read his eyes, but she didn't have to. That bond that linked them was there, she could feel it, and after last night, after today, there was more. Much more. What it added up to was, she trusted him with her life — and her sisters'. And they were in this together.

Putting a hand on his shoulder, she went on tiptoe to plant a quick kiss on the corner of his mouth. Whatever happened, they had this.

"Thank you," she said, sinking back on her heels.

A slight, wry smile. His hand was on her waist. "For getting you into this in the first place?"

"You didn't get me into this. The Nazis did, when they bombed Guernica. You've done your very best to keep me safe. What I was thanking you for was trying to get me out."

"In case you haven't figured it out by now, Fräulein Helinger, there's not much I wouldn't do for you."

Even as she answered with a quick smile it hit her that her bicycle was in the shed, and thus, because of the soldiers, inaccessible. She said so.

"I borrowed a motorbike from the hotel earlier," he said. "It's on the other side of the woods. Come on."

By the time they slipped through the back door at Werke Süd, it was gone midnight.

The sky was a clear pure black, almost indistinguishable from the sea below except for the big, bright nearly full moon that threw an otherworldly glow over everything. The complex was even busier than usual, with a lot of guards on patrol and a lot of vehicles on the move. Sibi had to fight the urge to jump at every unexpected sound, to look too hard at guards in unexpected places or at beefed-up patrols goose-stepping too swiftly as they made their rounds.

"Keep your head down," came Griff's low-voiced reminder as she craned her neck after a jeep with a blonde female — not Margrit, as it turned out — wedged in the back seat between two soldiers. She dropped her gaze to the ground.

The factories were working at full capacity. A brisk wind carried their acrid smell to Sibi's nostrils before she got anywhere near them, and the rumble and clang of the machines at work reached her at a considerable distance, too. A flurry of activity at Fertigungshalle 2 turned out to be completed rockets being loaded into trucks to, presumably, be conveyed to the freighters in the harbor. Upon reaching Fertigungshalle 1, Sibi breathed a little easier: her father's bicycle was in the rack out front. Which meant he was inside, which meant he hadn't been brought in by the SS for questioning.

She said as much to Griff.

"If they took him in for questioning, I doubt they'd bother bringing his bicycle," was Griff's rejoinder. He'd given her his jacket for the ride to Werke Süd — the wind was strong — but she'd given it back before they'd entered the complex and now he was once again the buttoned-up Luftwaffe officer complete with peaked cap and jackboots. His hand was locked around her wrist as if to prevent her from making any impulsive moves. As she saw the logic in his argument, her stomach twisted: he was right, the bicycle didn't mean a thing.

She couldn't go inside the factory to check. The security personnel on duty inside the building had to be presumed to be on the lookout for her. So did the sentries at the gates, and the guards patrolling the grounds. To think otherwise could prove fatal.

"There's a lot going on here tonight," Sibi said uneasily as, keeping to the shadows, they hurried on toward the building where her father's office was located.

"It's looking like they're in a hurry to wrap things up."

That's what she thought, too. The probable reason behind it was impossible to miss. She threw a quick glance at him. "That's it, isn't it? They're hurrying up because they're afraid of spies. They're afraid that word of what they're doing here might have gotten out."

"I'd say so. Of course, we don't know —"

Sibi didn't hear the rest. She stopped dead, causing him to stop, too, and look around at her, but she wasn't looking at him. Instead she looked past him, past the dark building that housed her father's office, straight ahead at the administrative building at the edge of the complex.

It was ablaze with light. The long, narrow field beside it, the killing field where prisoners were taken to be shot, was lit up, too.

Her heart seized up. That field was only ever lit up at night when —

Seven people were in the field. Four wore the distinctive black uniforms of the SS.

The other three were Papa, Jo and Margrit.

49

"The choice is yours, Dr. Helinger — you will tell me who your contact is, and what information you've passed on to them, or I will shoot one of your daughters. I'll even let you choose which one: the brunette with the scars, or the pretty little blonde. Of course, the one I don't shoot, I'll start cutting parts off of — her fingers, her toes, one by one — until you tell me what I want to know."

Sibi's heart was in her throat. She was cold with fear. Beside her, Griff gripped her arm hard and gave her a warning look: *stay silent. Stay still.* That was the promise she'd made to him as they'd crept through the shadows to get so near. They crouched side by side now, pressed close against the brick of the administrative building, ducked low, with only darkness and a few scraggly bushes for cover. A patrol goose-stepped smartly past the office building toward the administrative building. If it continued on its current path it soon would pass directly by them, and if any of the soldiers happened to glance in just the right direction at just the right moment . . .

She didn't care: her focus was all on Jo and Margrit. The girls were at the back side of the field, the killing side, with the sooty sky as a backdrop and the stygian darkness that was the cliff's edge only a meter or so behind them. Margrit, unmistakable in her orange romper with her mop of blond curls, appeared to be shivering. Jo had lost her glasses, and her braids had come undone. Pale and frightened looking, they clung together under the supervision of two guards. Papa was closer to her, close enough so that she could see how haggard he looked beneath the fitful glare of the single security light that illuminated the field. Two guards — actually a guard and an SS officer — stood on either side of him.

"My father's hands are cuffed behind him," Sibi whispered to Griff. Having just gotten close enough to see that detail, she felt the horror of it leach what blood remained from her face. Such a thing would not have been done lightly, not to a scientist of Papa's caliber and reputation, not here in Peenemünde. It meant there was no coming

634

back from this, the situation was beyond repair —

"Shh." Griff nodded acknowledgment even as he mouthed the warning at her. Heart pounding, Sibi pressed her lips together and shrank back against the brick. The patrol had reached the far edge of the field and was marching in their direction. The loud, rhythmic crunch of jackboots on pavement echoed the pounding of her heart.

"Which is it to be, Doctor? The blonde, or the brunette?" The speaker, the officer, had a taunt in his voice. Sibi didn't know him, but as he'd attended the rocket launch, she knew who he was: SS Obergruppen-führer und General Oswald Wirth, who'd arrived with Dr. Goebbels and Reichminister Speer. He was a beefy man, balding, with a meaty nose and a small, cruel mouth. A personal favorite of the führer, he out-ranked the Werke Süd security personnel by a considerable degree. They would do as he ordered, she knew.

"Your choice," he continued, and drew his gun.

She sucked in air, grabbed Griff's leg. The look he threw at her was hard and speaking: *do nothing. Watch and wait.* At the same time, he drew his own weapon. Sibi's heart slammed as she recognized how desperate he must consider the case to have done such a thing. With the three guards and the officer, the patrol marching past and countless other soldiers in the near vicinity who could be counted on to come running in case of trouble, for him to fire a shot would be suicidal.

"Neither! I choose *neither*! This is insane." Papa's voice was tight with anger, but Sibi could hear the fear in it, too. He still wore his white lab coat, which she took to mean they'd taken him directly from the factory. "I'm not a spy. My daughters are young girls — schoolgirls — not spies! How would they even go about accomplishing such a thing as you suggest? It's absurd."

"And yet we have our good Colonel Kraus shot dead, murdered, his body wrapped in a tarpaulin and discovered on your roof. Along with a pigeon loft and carrier pigeons. And a driver who dropped Colonel Kraus off at your house before being sent to bring back reinforcements to aid him in apprehending a *spy*."

"My daughters and I know nothing of any of that. They told you — they don't know how Kraus got on our roof, or who killed him. They were outside with friends all afternoon."

Thank God Jo and Margrit had had the pres-

ence of mind to lie.

"Is that really the answer you want to give?" His arm snapped up and he pointed his gun at Margrit, tracking her with it as, in response to his gesture, she was dragged a few paces away from Jo even as the other guard clamped a hand on Jo's shoulder to keep her from following. Both girls wept audibly. Sibi had to clap a hand over her mouth to keep from crying out. Griff gave her a fierce look, balanced his gun on his knee. She broke into a cold sweat. The patrol was almost directly opposite them now, their boots slapping the pavement as they marched past.

"You've made a mistake, you fool, and if you harm one of those girls it will cost you dearly when the truth comes out." Papa was red-faced and shouting now. "Where's Dornberger? He'll tell you that what you're accusing us of is not possible."

"General Dornberger has agreed to stand down in this matter, as it might be difficult for him to be objective. The unmasking of the full extent of your activities has been left to me." But General Wirth lowered his gun.

Sibi felt as if she might faint.

"My *activities* —" It was a roar.

"You have another daughter, as I recall. A

grown one. She was at the rocket launch, was she not? Where is she?"

Sibi went rigid. Griff's fingers dug into her arm, another fierce warning. The only thing keeping her from breaking free of him, running out onto that field and confessing her guilt right there and then was the fear that it might end up getting them all killed. And the fact that she now harbored the tiniest sliver of hope that Papa might be able to back General Wirth down.

"Not out spying, I will tell you that!" As the light struck Papa's forehead at a different angle she saw that it was shiny wet and knew that he was sweating copiously despite the fact that the night was cool and the wind brisk. "I demand you let those girls go! I demand to speak to General Dornberger! Or Dr. von Braun! Or —"

Papa's head turned sharply, and he broke off without finishing. A split second later she saw what had attracted his attention: a black streak raced across the field toward the girls —

"Ruby!" Jo cried, jerking free of the guard and going down on her knees to embrace the little dog, who leaped barking and wriggling into her arms.

"Get that animal out of here." General Wirth

gestured impatiently at the guard standing over Jo.

"It's a family pet," Papa said. "Harmless. Just as we are harmless."

The guard Jo had evaded kicked at Ruby — "Go, dog!" — even as he grabbed Jo's arm to haul her upright. Under duress, she let go of Ruby and clumsily rose — and, snarling, Ruby launched herself at the guard.

"Ah!" Jumping back, the guard kicked at Ruby again, viciously, and this time found his target. The sound as his foot connected had the sick *thunk* of a dropped melon. The dog yelped as his boot caught her stomach and sent her flying through the air.

"Ruby!" Jo and Margrit shrieked at the same time. Wrenching free of the guard, Jo darted toward Ruby, who landed with a thud to lie limply on her side in the grass.

"You! Girl! Halt!" General Wirth bawled. "Halt!"

Still racing toward Ruby, Jo looked at him, clearly startled, without the slightest break in her stride. The light hit her face, caught on the scars —

His hand jerked up and he fired. Sharp as a thunderclap, the sound tore through the air. Jo stopped as if she'd crashed into an invisible wall. Crying out, clapping a hand to her chest, she staggered back —

She's hit. She's shot.

"Jo!" Sibi's scream, instantly joined by Margrit's and Papa's echoing cries, was torn from her throat as she leaped to her feet, ran —

Eyes wide, mouth gaping as if she couldn't get any air, Jo reached the end of the field, teetered precariously, then toppled back over the edge.

50

Gone.

Nothing but empty air.

"No!" Even as Sibi flew toward the place where Jo had disappeared, a flurry of activity erupted around her: shots ringing out in quick succession; Margrit screaming; Papa yelling, "Bastard! *Drecksau!*"; more cursing; the sound of blows; the thud of running footsteps.

All but oblivious to everything else, Sibi reached the cliff's edge, slid to a halt on the short, thick grass, looked over with a thumping heart into the darkness, at the shiny black surface of the sea below. Nothing. No sign. Not even a ripple.

"Jo!"

The world stopped. Time stood still.

"Jo!"

Her heart shivered and shook.

Sibi thought she was the one screaming, but it might have been Margrit, Margrit

641

who ran up beside her and caught her arm and looked down, too, or it might have been them both, shrieking into the abyss as one —

"Jo! Jo!"

"Sibi!" Griff shouted. *"Sibi!"*

Startled out of the shock that was already beginning to encase her heart in ice, she glanced around.

"Get out of here! Go!" Griff pelted toward her, gun in hand, firing as he ran. All three guards were down on the field. General Wirth had fallen, too, but was struggling to his knees, a spreading scarlet stain on the front of his uniform proclaiming that he'd been shot — by Griff, Sibi surmised — just as Griff must have shot the guards. Blood trickling from his head, Papa lay sprawled in the grass beside General Wirth, who, even as she watched, raised his gun with an unsteady arm —

"Behind you!" Sibi shrieked. Griff looked and fired. General Wirth collapsed. They were all down, dead from the looks of them, the guards and General Wirth. In the street beyond the field, various members of the patrol reacted with obvious confusion to the mayhem, glancing around, shoving each other —

"Papa!" she cried to Griff as her gaze

landed on her father. He was moving, clearly not dead. Left behind, he stood no chance of surviving: "Griff, *please.*"

Griff cursed.

"I'll get him. Take your sister and run! Do you hear me? *Run!*" Griff screamed it at her even as he changed course to sprint toward her father.

Galvanized, she grabbed Margrit, who was inert with shock — "Come on, Margrit, we have to go!" — and, pulling her along with an arm around her waist — "Margrit, move!" — started to run. A glance over her shoulder told her that the patrol, now clearly aware en masse that something was wrong, had broken formation. They were turning back, drawing their weapons —

They had only this brief moment, this one nearly impossible chance, to try to escape.

"We can't let ourselves be caught! We have to *run!*" Sibi's grip shifted to Margrit's wrist. Margrit's gait was clumsy. She was running, but not fast enough. Not nearly fast enough. *"Run!"*

Closer at hand, Ruby got shakily to her feet and started trotting after them, clearly hurt but —

"Margrit, run!"

Guns banged even as Griff scooped her father up over his shoulder and bolted with him: the patrol, coming on fast, firing as they came. Griff snapped a shot off at them as he ran. The answering volley had Sibi swallowing a scream and ducking and forcing Margrit lower even as they raced out of the field and along the street and into the shadows in front of the office building. A glance back found more guards pouring out of the administrative building, joining the patrol in giving chase.

We're not getting away. It will take a miracle . . .

Her heart pounded. Margrit's pulse beat so hard she could feel its frantic throbbing against the fingers she had wrapped around her sister's wrist. Beyond the rasp of her breathing, Margrit hadn't made a sound. She was glassy-eyed and clammy with shock. Both of them were dazed and reeling from loss and grief and fear.

Jo. Oh, Jo.

What do we do? Where do we go? How do we even have a chance?

The back door. We have to get to the back door.

Then what?

Survive.

Another terrified glance over her shoulder reassured her that Griff was still safe, still running, gaining on them despite Papa's not inconsiderable weight hanging over his shoulder. Behind him, Ruby, clearly injured, loped panting in determined pursuit.

"There they are! Stop them!" A shout from in front of them had her head whipping back around. Her eyes widened with horror. Adrenaline shot through her veins. A fresh contingent of guards ran toward them from the far end of the street. A good distance, but they were coming on fast.

"Sibi, the toy box! Head for the toy box!" Griff yelled. The desperate note in his voice — telegraphing as clearly as if he'd spelled it out how slim he felt their chances were of getting away — terrified her almost more than anything else. Lifting a hand in acknowledgment, hanging on to Margrit for dear life, she pelted toward the next side street, where they needed to turn right to reach the hangar where the experimental airplanes were kept.

The crack of multiple gunshots had her ducking and swallowing a scream. Margrit flinched and jerked as bullets whistled past them to smack into nearby walls, gouge chunks of asphalt out of the street.

Almost there . . .

Over the desperate slap of her and Margrit's footsteps, over the throb of her pulse in her ears and the pounding of her heart, she heard something unusual, something she couldn't quite place. A deep drone. An angry, vibrating growl. Growing louder. From the sky —

Airplane engines. Lots of airplane engines.

Even as she identified the sound, even as she glanced around to be sure, the air-raid sirens went off. The hair rose on the back of her neck as the angry drone turned into a roar.

"Heavy bombers," Griff shouted. "Praise the Lord."

Bombers: a cold prickle raced over her skin. *Not again. No* —

Then it registered on her: he hadn't sounded surprised.

Another glance back: Griff was grim-faced, breathing hard but pounding along only a few strides behind them, with his gun in his hand and Papa, limp and unmoving, slung over his shoulder. Ruby, tail down, scuttled along not far behind him, limping but keeping up. The patrol, racing in pursuit, had lost their focus on them. They'd slowed down, and were bumping into each other, looking up and back just as she was, while at the same time soldiers, scientists, workers, people, poured out into the streets from everywhere.

The entire sky suddenly lit up with brilliant white lights.

"Target indicators," Griff yelled. "Run like hell."

Sibi did, and now she wasn't having to pull Margrit along: gasping, trembling, her sister ran flat out, too. The patrol chasing them scattered, running in all directions. The guards running toward them ran in all directions. Everyone ran in all directions.

The roar of the incoming bombers drowned out every other sound.

Fear gave wings to Sibi's feet.

Glancing back again because she couldn't help it, she saw a squadron of bombers pass in dark silhouette in front of the moon.

Her heart leaped into her throat. Hand tightening like a vise around Margrit's wrist, she said, "They're here," and Margrit made a squeaky little mewling sound and their eyes met and —

The bombers came in from the sea, their blunt noses soaring above the factories, their sheer numbers blotting out the moon. The night grew black; the roar was louder than a dozen freight trains.

The first bomb hit with a great crash. The ground shook. The shock of the blast slammed into them like a tidal wave of hot air, knocking them off their feet, throwing them to the ground. Windows blew out around them. Bits of glass hurtled outward, rattling like hail as they hit the pavement.

"Sibi!" Margrit screamed, the first word she'd spoken since Jo had gone, and covered her head. The memories — Guernica — the hissing sound of the incendiary bombs . . . Sibi knew how terrified Margrit was. Terror grabbed her in its cold fist, too, but she gritted her teeth and got her feet beneath her and dragged her sister up.

She yelled, "Come on, come on," at the same time as Griff was getting up, too, and jockeying Papa into position again while shouting: "The toy box. Go, go, *go.*"

Somehow they were running again, she and Margrit, arm in arm, with Griff behind them as more bombs hit and shock wave after shock wave had the ground beneath their feet rippling like the sea. Ears ringing, gasping for breath in the superheated air, they ran for their lives. Behind them, a wall of fire gave chase. Heat like a blast furnace enveloped them.

Everywhere people screamed, ran, burned.

And there it was: the smell. The sickly sweet smell of burning human flesh.

Oh, God, she remembered: it had haunted her dreams for years. Only now, once again, it was real.

Suddenly she was shaking to pieces inside.

The memories — Mama and Luiza — *Jo* . . .

Margrit. Papa. Griff. Herself. Thoughts of the living steadied her, gave her the strength to go on.

"Here," Sibi screamed as she reached the toy box, found the person-size door beside the big hangar-size one. She grabbed the knob — *hot* — but it was locked, and she didn't have her key.

Over the *boom-boom-boom* of the bombs, she screamed the bad news to Griff.

"Move," Griff yelled, and when she did he kicked the door as hard as he could. It sprang open, bounced back on its hinges.

They rushed inside. It was cooler, dark, not so terrifying with its familiar kerosene smell — until she thought that, if a bomb hit the hangar, the airplanes, fueled and ready, would explode, too, incinerating them probably instantly.

"How do you open the big door?" Griff yelled as he slid Papa off his shoulder onto the left wing of the Silver Bullet, where he sprawled on his side. It was closest to the big door; the other airplanes were lined up behind it, wing to wing down the length of the hangar.

"There's a button —"

"Hit it. We're flying out." He was on the wing, standing beside Papa's motionless body, yanking up the cockpit cover. "Margrit, come here."

"Go." Sibi shoved her sister in his direction and ran for the button, which was big and red and set into the wall. A dozen objections occurred to her, but it was clear they were fresh out of options as well as time. "How's my father?"

"Unconscious. Alive. Bullet grazed his head, knocked him out. That's it, as far as I can tell."

Thank God. Another loss — she didn't think she could bear another loss.

Jo.

The wave of pain that accompanied the thought of her sister was so intense that it was all Sibi could do not to crumple beneath it. But she couldn't, not now.

Gritting her teeth against it instead, she hit the button — the grinding sound as the door began to open was lost beneath the tumult outside — and ran back toward the airplane.

The inside of the hangar was instantly red with reflected flames. The sounds, the smell —

"Get the block." Griff had dumped Papa into the rear seat, and was helping Margrit into the airplane. Sibi knew what he meant — the wooden block that kept the wheels

from moving — and she dragged it aside. Then she was at the wing, too, and Griff held his hand down to her.

"Sibi. Get Ruby." Scrunched into the rear seat with Papa slumped beside her, Margrit looked down at her with big, piteous eyes. "We can't leave her. Please."

Sibi looked around, saw the little dog crouched behind her and scooped her up. Margrit had lost so much — they had lost so much . . .

The feel of the warm, furry body, the trust in Ruby's round dark eyes — Sibi instantly thought of Jo and another wave of pain assaulted her.

"Give her to Margrit," she said to Griff, lifting Ruby up to him. His mouth tightened, but he flicked a look at Margrit and didn't argue. Instead he took Ruby and handed her to Margrit without a word, then reached down to help Sibi onto the wing.

A violent banging sounded on the hangar's rear door. Sibi's breath caught. The single glance she and Griff exchanged said what they were both thinking: the guards had found them.

"Get in."

51

They scrambled into the cockpit.

Pound, pound, pound from the rear door. The guards would break through at any moment — or run around to the front, where the big door was now open wide.

"Strap in," Griff ordered, and yelled back at Margrit, "Strap your dad in with you," as he closed the cockpit cover. Once it was latched, they were effectively cut off from the three crammed into the single seat in back.

"Can you even fly this thing?" Sibi asked in an urgent undertone, and he flashed a quick look at her.

"We'll find out," he said, and started the engine. The sound was somewhere between a locomotive and a chain saw. Behind them, an enormous *bang* plus a change in the quality of light told her that the guards had broken through. Her heart leaped. Her stomach went into freefall.

"They're in," she yelled over the roar.

The warning proved unnecessary: a muffled, *"Halt!"* was followed by the hair-raising bark of gunfire. She had no doubt at all that the guards had spotted them in the airplane and were racing the length of the hangar, firing their weapons at the Silver Bullet as they came.

"Got that."

They were moving, rolling out the doors, rattling down the street that served as a runway with gushers of fire shooting up everywhere she looked, a ceiling of bombers above them, and gunshots targeting them on all sides, all amid the *tat-tat-tat* of distant flak. She held on white-knuckled to the edge of her seat as they picked up speed.

"It's basically an ME 163 with modifications. If you can fly one of those —"

"I can fly anything," he yelled back.

They raced directly toward the inferno, certain, Sibi thought as she sat there rigid with fear, to be hit at any second by one of the bombs that fell from the air like rain. The airplane accelerated until everything around them was a blur, eating up runway until they were almost out of room and the wall of fire was directly in front of them and . . . . kept bumping and bouncing as it went faster and faster but didn't rise.

Lift up. Lift up. Lift up. She screamed it inside, although she was too afraid of disturbing Griff's concentration to make a sound. Her heart was in her throat.

Just when she thought they would plunge straight into the heart of the fire he pulled back on the stick. She felt the afterburners kick in. The Silver Bullet leaped toward the flames, then nosed up and soared into the air.

They shot under the bombers, away from the onslaught, perpendicular to the attackers' flight. The smoke screen that was one of the island's primary defenses was up, creating clouds of silvery haze. The Silver Bullet bounced and hawed as it flew out through the rough air created by the shock waves and the wake. Flashes from ground defenses lit up the cockpit. Searchlights crisscrossed the sky, catching the bombers and the German defenders, the night fighters, indiscriminately in their beams. Dogfights with their staccato gunfire and screaming explosions tore up the night. Flak bursts spiraled past, many colors, bright as fireworks.

Still holding tight to the edge of the seat, Sibi looked down on a sea of flame. The *Siedlung* was burning. The forest was on fire. Pine trees blazed like torches. In the harbor, at least two of the freighters were ablaze.

She thought of Jo, lost beneath the waves. The heartache was almost unbearable. To be flying away without her, leaving her behind —

Mama. Luiza. Come for Jo. Take care of her.

Sparks shot past the plane.

"Tracers," Griff yelled — she knew that meant they were in some fighter plane's sights — and dived. Every organ Sibi possessed slammed into her spine as the G-forces hit and she stared, terrified, straight down into the livid red surface of the sea. By the time he pulled up and leveled out, they were so close to the water that she could have jumped, and survived.

Without warning, the radio crackled, making Sibi flinch.

"Who the hell is flying this thing?" Papa's voice, broken by static.

He's conscious, and making sense. Thank God.

Griff picked up the microphone, clicked it on. "For the safety of this aircraft, and your daughters, I'm enforcing radio silence, sir. We'll talk when we're on the ground."

"Who are you?"

"Papa, it's all right. He's a friend," Sibi yelled before Griff could click off again.

He turned the radio off, and looked at her. The two seats were side by side with the stick between them, close enough that their arms brushed. The Silver Bullet skimmed over the water, flying low, out from under the raging battle.

"You realize your father might not think I'm a friend." He had to yell to be heard over the roar of the engines.

Sibi hadn't thought of that. Her father, officially, was a Nazi officer — and Griff was on the other side.

"He's a good man. All he's ever tried to do is keep us safe. He's interested in science, not politics. He's *not* one of them."

"We'll sort it out when we get to England."

"England?" Her voice was next door to a squeak.

"Yes."

She said nothing.

"You and your sister will be fine. We'll have to see what can be worked out for your father. In any case, he's better off in England and alive than back there and dead."

As she digested the truth of that, one of the gauges in the instrument panel caught her eye.

"We're low on supplemental oxygen." She tapped the gauge, wanting to make sure he knew before he started climbing again.

"Not necessary. We'll be staying at rooftop level." Which Sibi knew was around five hundred meters. "Keep us out of the way of the fighters, and below radar. I don't know about you, but I'd just as soon not get shot out of the sky."

On that demoralizing thought they flew on over the sea through broken clouds and a strong westerly wind, their way lit by a moon so bright you could read by it.

52

By the time they were flying over land again, hours had passed. Because of mandatory blackouts, and because the water wasn't beneath them to reflect the moon, it was far darker once they were no longer above the sea. England bristled with antiaircraft defenses, Sibi knew, and knew, too, that if anyone spotted them they would be perceived as an enemy plane and treated accordingly. But she was too tired and emotionally wrung out to worry about it. She was physically numb from the aircraft's vibrations and riven by anguish over Jo.

It's all my fault, was the refrain that kept beating like a pulse in her head, followed by, *I'm so sorry* and *Forgive me.* The image of her sister clutching her chest and then falling backward to disappear into darkness was a crushing pain she knew would never leave her.

Hearing Griff click on the radio again and

start talking into the microphone — "BAD 1, BAD 1, this is Colonel James Griffin, OSS, coming in in an experimental enemy aircraft, requesting permission to land" — and the subsequent alarmingly negative answer had her sitting up straight in her seat. The following sharp exchange ended with Griff saying, "Suggest you contact Wild Bill Donovan immediately. Tell him it's Griffin and I've got Rolf. In the meantime, I need a runway. I'm low on fuel, and there are civilians on board. I'm setting this bird down."

The Silver Bullet swooped lower without waiting for a reply.

She looked at Griff. "What are the chances we get shot out of the air?"

"Toss-up."

"They know about Rolf?"

A corner of his mouth quirked up. "Yeah, they do. You're famous in certain circles, Fräulein Helinger. Wild Bill's a fan. He's the head of OSS, by the way. A great man." His face tightened, and he picked up the microphone again, roaring into it, "Damn it, where are those lights?" Then to her, "Hang on, lights or no lights, we're landing."

Sibi's heart thumped as the dark silhouettes of trees and buildings rushed past just meters beneath them. They were at approximately treetop level and she was white-knuckling it again before the runway lights, pale and sullen, flashed on at last.

Minutes later they were on the ground, bumping over the pavement, taxiing toward the end of the runway. Griff released the cockpit cover even before they came to a stop. Fresh air, cool rather than cold and bearing the scent of fuel and rain, poured into the cockpit. Wrapping her arms around herself as he killed the engine, Sibi breathed deeply, welcoming it after the stuffiness of the flight. Ahead of them, a multitude of vehicles rushed toward the aircraft.

Griff was already unstrapping and levering himself out of his seat. "Can you get yourself and your sister out? I need to talk to your father before they reach us."

"Yes."

As quick as that he was out, and helping her father out. By the time she got herself, Margrit and Ruby on the ground, the two of them were standing near the wing having what looked like an intense and not entirely friendly conversation. She had her arm around Margrit, whose eyes were puffy and swollen from crying and who was carrying Ruby, as they headed toward the men.

The vehicles — jeeps and trucks loaded

with soldiers, she saw now that they were closer — screeched to a halt not far beyond the nose of the aircraft. Margrit shrank closer against her side.

"Don't worry, we're safe now," Sibi told her, although she wasn't one hundred percent certain it was true.

"I don't want to be safe when Jo isn't."

Sibi's arm tightened around her. Her own grief felt like a vise squeezing her heart. "Jo is safe, *maitea*. She's with Mama and Luiza now."

Margrit looked up at her. "You really think so?"

"Yes, I do."

Margrit laid her head on her shoulder. Sibi thought she was drawing comfort from the thought.

". . . . you're a damned Nazi, sir," Griff was saying as she and Margrit got within earshot of the ongoing conversation between him and their father.

"I'm a *German*. I love my country. I have no love whatsoever for her government." Papa leaned a shoulder against the fuselage. His hands were still cuffed behind him. There was dried blood on his forehead, more on his white coat. He was looking at Griff, apparently oblivious to the armed soldiers pouring out onto the tarmac as he spoke. "Those murderous bastards just killed another one of my daughters. I'll see them in hell with pleasure."

"Hands in the air! Don't move!" That shouted warning came as the soldiers closed in, weapons at the ready. An officer separated himself from the pack to stride toward them, wariness evident in everything from his expression to the way he moved. It was only as she saw how suspiciously he was looking at Griff that Sibi realized he was still wearing his Luftwaffe uniform. "You the guy claiming to be Colonel Griffin? I need to see some proof."

As "guests" of the air base — Burtonwood, which Sibi was informed was the largest air base in Britain and also in Europe and had been turned over to the USAAF early in the war — she and Margrit were treated with every courtesy. Papa, on the other hand, was immediately taken away by the soldiers: a prisoner.

Her stomach roiled as she watched him being escorted away. To lose another family member — she didn't think she could bear it.

"He won't be harmed, I give you my word," Griff promised her in a quiet aside before disappearing with the soldiers.

"They'll want to question him. I'll stick close, do what I can."

She hadn't seen him, or Papa, since. She and Margrit had slept, eaten, been debriefed. To her embarrassment, she'd been given a standing ovation by the officers around the long table as she'd finished answering the questions that had been put to her.

"You're a hero, my dear," the American general who was in charge of her debriefing told her in response to what must have been her surprised expression. "Rolf has been a legend among those of us who deal in intelligence for some time. We know what you've done, and what you've sacrificed. It's an honor and a privilege to meet you and to have you here."

53

Sibi and Margrit had gone to the chapel on the base to pray and light a candle for Jo. The priest had promised that a mass would be said for her soul. Later, a tearful Margrit had been given something to help her rest. By 10:45 — which would be 11:45 Peenemünde time — Margrit was fast asleep in her room in a special section at the base infirmary, with Ruby curled at the foot of her bed and nurses available to check on her through the night. Sibi had been given the room next to hers, but she was too restless for sleep.

She showered — each room had its own en suite bath — and pulled on the pajamas that were part of the cobbled-together wardrobe the nurses had found for her. She stood at the window for a while, watching rain falling on the blacked-out buildings surrounding the one she was in, breathing in the earthy scent of it, listening to the growl of airplanes coming in overhead. Thoughts of Jo — grief and guilt and a thousand heart-wrenching memories and emotions — haunted her, and the rain pouring down like tears from heaven only made it worse. Putting on one of the two dresses she'd been given — this one was a black shirtwaist, with polka dots — she left her room. Her mission: find Griff.

She had questions. He, she hoped, would have answers.

And she just really wanted to see him.

No one was around. No surprise: it had to be close to midnight. Already more than a day had passed since Jo — no, she wouldn't think of that. The grief was too heavy to bear, and served no purpose besides. The hallway was dimly lit — like the rest of the base, the infirmary was in mandatory blackout, with heavy curtains covering all the windows and only the most essential lights turned to their lowest wattages permitted — and it took her a moment to realize that the tall, well-built man in the brown OSS officer's uniform who stepped out of the lift at the far end of it and then came striding toward her was, in fact, Griff.

She stopped, waiting for him to reach her. He saw her just about then, and smiled.

"Where were you going at this time of

night?" he asked when he was close enough.

"To find you."

"That's quite a coincidence. See, I was coming to find *you.*"

A nurse stepped out of one of the rooms along the hall, said, "Shh!" and gave them a disapproving look before hurrying away.

"I want to talk to you." Whispering, Sibi took his arm, tugged him toward her room.

Griff came inside her room with her, and stood just inside the door glancing around as Sibi turned on the lamp, which was on the bedside table and generated a weak pool of light around the bed while the rest of the room was wreathed in shadows. The room itself was small, with whitewashed walls and heavy blackout curtains over the single window. It was furnished simply, with a chest, a chair and a bed.

"How are you?" Griff asked as she turned back to face him. From his tone, she knew he was asking how she was coping with Jo's death.

"Heartbroken." It was the simple truth.

"Margrit?"

"The same. One of the nurses gave her something to help her sleep. She's in the next room." Keeping her voice low, she indicated the chair. "Sit down."

He sat, while she perched on the edge of

the bed facing him.

"How's Papa?"

"That's what I was coming to see you about."

"Is it?" A lift of her eyebrows made the question pointed.

"Among other things." His smile was wry. "Your father has managed to convince the army's top brass that he's willing to tell everything he knows about the Nazi rocket and aircraft programs, and to henceforth turn his considerable expertise to assisting the Allied war effort. They've examined his experimental aircraft, which they are very appreciative that we brought with us, by the way, and are impressed. There were some slight concerns that he might, if given the chance, turn double agent — sabotaging the projects he was given to work on, doing what he could to pass on information to the enemy — but he calmed most of their suspicions by asking me, in front of them, if I knew what he had named the aircraft we flew in on. I repeated what you'd told me — the Silver Bullet — and he then asked the assembled brass if they knew what Hitler's top-secret hideaway was called. They all did, and one of them said it — the Wolf's Lair. Your father gave this satisfied nod, then glanced around the table and said something on the order of, 'You know what it takes to kill an evil werewolf like Adolf Hitler? A Silver Bullet.' If the Nazis looked like winning the war, he said his plan was to take his Silver Bullet and crash it into the Wolf's Lair when Hitler was there, killing him. Your father's got a convincing way about him, I must say, and his assassination plot cinched the deal."

"He was planning to crash the Silver Bullet into Hitler's hideaway?" Sibi blinked in surprise, reflected a moment and nodded. "For Mama and Luiza. And now Jo. It makes sense."

Griff was looking at her, and there was something in his expression . . . She frowned at him. He hadn't kissed her, hadn't touched her, in fact, and there was something in that, too. He grimaced in the face of her frown and stood up, taking a restless turn about the room as she slewed around to watch him, then stopping to face her.

"What?" she said.

"You're going to America. All three of you. Leaving tomorrow. The thinking is that your father will be an enormous asset to us. No one outside our group is to know what's become of him, that he's working for the Allies. It will be made to appear as if he and his family were killed in the bombing of

Peenemünde. Which was, by the way, the biggest raid of the war so far — 596 bombers, 1800 tons of bombs. Those rockets, the information you gave us about their intention to use them on Eureka, all of it was that important. You may have stopped Hitler from delivering a blow that would have allowed the Nazis to win the war."

Sibi stood up. Knowing that she had made a difference would matter at some point, she knew, but right at the moment she was so shattered by Jo's death, so tired and yet so full of nervous energy, and now so rattled at the thought of the future, that she could only focus on the personal.

"We're going to America? Tomorrow?" If her voice was strained, it was because that news was the last thing she'd expected to hear, and not at all welcome.

He nodded. "They want to get you out of here as quickly as possible. Before anyone knows you're here."

"What about you? Are you coming?"

"I'm leaving tomorrow, but I'm going somewhere else." His voice was grim. "We have a war to win, and until we do my time belongs to the OSS. I go where they send me."

It took her a minute to absorb that. "So I won't see you again?"

Ridiculous after all the pain she'd endured to discover how much that hurt.

His mouth compressed. "You'll see me again. Count on it."

They were looking at each other across the bed. "When? In a year? Two? After the war, which could go on forever?"

"I don't know exactly when. As soon as I can make it happen, I promise."

"Or you could get killed."

"Sibi . . ."

There really wasn't anything else he could say. They both knew it was a possibility. Spies tended to have short life spans.

"What about us? You and me." There it was. She was too emotionally spent for subtleties.

"You'll be safe in America. And after the war —"

"I don't want to wait until after the war." She walked around the bed. Stopping in front of him, she folded her arms over her chest and looked him dead in the eye. "I want to know right now. *Is* there an us?"

His mouth curved in a way that was both rueful and tender. His hands settled on either side of her waist. "As far as I'm concerned, there is definitely an *us.*"

"All right, then." She let out a breath. Then she slid her arms around his neck, went up on tiptoe and kissed him. He kissed her back, pulling her against him, his lips slanting across hers, warm and firm and fiercely hungry. And there it was, the connection, the magic that was them, and she knew that, whatever happened, whatever war and the future might bring, that this was real, maybe the realest thing she had ever experienced or ever would experience in her life. Even if she could only have it for a little while, she would take it. Take him.

When he lifted his head at last, she whispered, "Griff, stay the night."

He looked down at her, his expression grave. Then he nodded, and kissed her again.

The hours were too short. He had to leave before the sun came up, before the base began to stir and the infirmary began to fill with people. As the minutes ticked down toward dawn, their lovemaking grew more and more desperate, more and more intense, until finally Sibi, exhausted, fell asleep in his arms.

He woke her with a kiss. "Sibi."

Her eyes fluttered open. When she saw that, despite the fact that he was leaning over her and his hard, handsome face was mere centimeters away, he was on his feet and fully dressed, she was instantly wide awake.

"Griff —"

He straightened to his full height, stood looking down at her. "It's time. I have to go."

She sat up, instinctively clutching the sheet to her chest to preserve her modesty as she caught at his sleeve. But she couldn't keep him, she knew.

"I love you," she said. "I've been in love with you for what feels like forever. Don't get killed."

"I love you, too." He leaned over, kissed her again. It was a quick, hard, possessive kiss, and brief as it was it claimed her soul. "I'll come find you when I can. Wait for me."

"I will," she promised, and then he smiled at her and was gone.

■ ■ ■ ■

Part Four: Fort Bliss

■ ■ ■ ■

54

June 22, 1945

"What are you doing here? You're supposed to be at home getting ready for my surprise party," Sibi whispered to Margrit, who only moments earlier had unexpectedly shown up in the glass-walled observation room at Biggs Field next to the east-west runway where the latest successor to Papa's Silver Bullet had just touched down after completing its first test flight.

"I knew you knew about that," Margrit whispered back. At nearly fourteen, Margrit was as tall as she was. In white short pants and a blue sleeveless top, she looked almost grown-up, and Sibi smiled at her with affection. Flushed and glowing (two things Sibi had learned since arriving: Texas in June was *hot,* even at almost five p.m., which was what time it was, and despite the heat female Texans did not sweat, they glowed), her mop of golden curls pulled back from

675

her face on either side by twin barrettes, Margrit had Ruby with her, on a leash. That told Sibi that she'd walked over from, presumably, their house, which was nearby. "Trying to keep secrets around this place is *useless.* Everybody talks."

"Did Mrs. Carter finish making my cake?" Sibi asked. "She's the only person I know who can make war cake taste delicious."

"You aren't supposed to know about that, either." Margrit shook her head in exasperation, and Sibi grinned at her. Margrit made a face, then — reluctantly — smiled back.

Margrit had lost none of her strength of character, but she was quieter and more subdued than before they'd come here, and instead of settling in with a group of giggly friends she seemed to prefer to be alone. Ruby had become her boon companion. Part of the reason might simply have been because she was well into the moody phase that was part of growing up, but Sibi attributed most of the change to Jo's death. Grief was a heavy burden that you always carried with you, as Sibi knew from her own experience, and losing Jo weighed on Margrit even more, she sometimes thought, than it did on herself. But there was no changing any of it, and she could only hope that with time more of the old Margrit would resurface.

But for now, it was Sibi's twenty-fifth birthday. It was a Friday night, and the plan (which she wasn't supposed to know about) was for a core group of friends and neighbors to gather in their backyard for barbecue and Mrs. Carter's butterless, milkless, eggless but nevertheless scrumptious cake. She and Papa, whose assistant she was, had just watched the sleek silver aircraft touch down and race past the enormous balloon (Texan for "airship") hangar on the other side of the runway. The test flight was a success, and Papa beamed from ear to ear. The mood in the room was jubilant. The base's commanding general, who was present, had only a short time earlier informed Papa that, in no little part due to the success of his contributions to the Allied war effort, a number of top German scientists were being gathered up and brought to the United States as they spoke, and would in the next few months be coming to Fort Bliss to join the new rocket program, as part of an initiative they were calling Operation Paperclip.

The twenty months since she, Margrit and Papa (and Ruby) had arrived in Fort Bliss had seen some of the bloodiest days of the war. Battles were hard fought, and an Allied victory was constantly in doubt. The raid on Peenemünde — Operation Hydra — had forced what was left of the Nazi rocket program to relocate to an underground bunker in the middle of Germany and delayed it by months, which meant that it was rendered largely ineffective. The Tehran conference between Roosevelt, Churchill and Stalin, otherwise known as Eureka, took place, although it was pushed to November 1943. With the original assassination plot foiled by the destruction of the rockets at Peenemünde, a second assassination attempt on the Big Three in Tehran had been attempted. It, too, failed. June 6, 1944, D-Day, had seen American and British troops landing on the beaches of Normandy to begin the liberation of Europe. Hitler and Mussolini were dead, Mussolini hanged and Hitler a suicide.

On April 12, 1945, President Roosevelt died of natural causes in Warm Springs, Georgia.

The world reeled. America mourned. But the war went on.

Then, little more than three weeks later, on May 7, 1945, Germany surrendered. The war in Europe was over.

And now, Sibi was smiling at her whispering little sister, and celebrating her birthday.

"Anyway, heads-up. Sally Birkett —" the

commanding general's secretary "— telephoned and asked me to come. You're supposed to be getting some sort of special birthday gift and she said I should be here for it," Margrit said in Sibi's ear as they were joined by another of the officers who'd come to observe the test launch, General Stanley Mickelson — "Who's this?" he said, looking down at Ruby; and then, as the dog was introduced with a wag of her tail, leaned down to pat her — as well as Papa and a contingent of six or so other senior officers whom Sibi didn't know.

They were presumably there to witness the test flight. But this was Papa's third prototype, and they'd all had multiple test flights, and such a large number of senior officers had never shown up to witness any of them before.

Sibi was just starting to frown thoughtfully when General Mickelson said, "Ah, yes, it looks like the birthday present we've all been waiting to see delivered to you has just arrived. You might want to step outside, Miss Helinger."

He looked out through the glass as he spoke. Sibi turned around to see that a Twin Beech had just landed and was taxiing down the runway.

Her heart started beating faster as a

thought — a hope — occurred to her. With a quick smile for the group now gathered around her, she went outside. Margrit and Ruby, Papa and the entire gathering followed. The fact that they did reinforced the hope that was now fluttering like a fledgling bird inside her. It was sunny and baking hot, hot enough to curl her hair as it fell around her shoulders and turn her cheeks the same rose-pink as the sleeveless dress she wore. Didn't matter: her steps quickened as the Twin Beech, having reached the end of the runway, turned and came back, then rolled to a stop some twenty meters away.

The passenger door opened. The steps came down. A man appeared in the doorway. A tall, well-built man in a brown OSS uniform. He hadn't even started down the steps when she began to run.

"Griff." Did she shout it? It felt like she shouted it. Whether she did or not, he looked up, saw her running toward him, rattled down the steps and came to meet her.

She threw herself into his arms. And, onlookers or no on-lookers, he kissed her dizzy.

When he lifted his head a few minutes later, her pulse was racing and her toes were curling in her strappy shoes and her heart was in her eyes.

"You waited," he said. He was holding her like he never meant to let her go and smiling down into her eyes.

"Yes, I waited. Of course I waited. I would wait forever, if you asked me to."

"You remember that. We'll be talking about it more later. For now, you want your birthday present?"

"I *have* my birthday present." She was pretty sure the way she was looking at him left him in no doubt that she meant him. "The best birthday present ever, just so you know."

He shook his head. "Nope. I've brought you something else. Something I think you're going to like even better."

She shook her head, meaning that was impossible, then was distracted by the sight of Ruby running, fast as a streak of lightning, past her.

"See for yourself." Griff let go of her, turned her around . . .

A slim young woman in a full-skirted black dress, in the process of disembarking from the aircraft, reached the bottom of the Twin Beech's steps and stepped onto the tarmac. Sibi was only peripherally aware of her until Ruby reached her and started jumping on her, yapping frantically, tail beating the air like the little dog hoped to take flight. The young woman looked down at the dog . . .

Because she was looking down, Sibi couldn't really see her face. She stared, transfixed, at a fall of long coffee-brown hair; a slim body that looked to be near her own height; a pair of black glasses in danger of falling off a delicate nose; an averted cheek with a pale rectangular scar —

Her heart clutched. The world fell away.

"Jo?" She barely managed to choke the word out. The young woman was crouching now, hugging the dog, but she looked up at that and —

"Sibi!" She jumped up.

It *was* Jo. Sibi's heart did what felt like a full stop, then surged until she thought it would pound its way out of her chest.

"Jo!"

They ran into each other's arms.

"My God, my God." Sibi hugged Jo like she never meant to let her go, and Jo hugged her back the same way. Then Margrit was there, screaming Jo's name, and Papa was there, too, and they were all hugging and crying and exclaiming, and hugging some more, while Ruby jumped up on everybody, barking and wagging her tail, until at last

Margrit, practical Margrit, still holding on to Jo's arm — they'd quit hugging, but they were all still holding on to some part of her as if they were afraid she'd vanish if they let go — said, "You were shot. How —"

Jo looked at Margrit, then at Sibi. "It was Mama's necklace." Reaching up, she pulled at the delicate silver chain that disappeared beneath her neckline. The locket came into view — the silver locket with all their initials on it and the picture of the four of them and Mama inside. Only now, in the oval's center, there was a round indentation, with, at its deepest point, a small hole. "The bullet hit it. I was wounded, but the locket kept the bullet from going all the way through so it wasn't horribly bad. I fell into the water, and the next thing I knew bombs were going off all around and these little boats were in the water as sailors tried to get off the big burning freighters and one of the boats picked me up. The sailors took me onto a freighter that wasn't burning, that was putting out to sea trying to escape. The boats belonged to Emilio Aguire — you remember him, Sibi, from Guernica; he said he knew you, that you were friends — and he was on board. When I told him what had happened he took me with them. A few days later we heard that you — all three of you — had been killed in the raid, so Emilio took me to his family in Spain and left me there and I stayed with them. After the war ended, Emilio came back and said he'd heard that a rocket scientist and his family had escaped from Peenemünde during the raid and, when he checked, it was you! He got in touch with someone he knew, and they said yes, you were alive. I was flown to Switzerland and Griff was there to meet me and he brought me here."

"Oh, my God." It seemed like it was all any of them could say.

"I owe you, sir." Papa looked away from Jo at last, offered a hand to Griff. "More than I can ever repay."

Griff returned the handshake, but shook his head. "I brought one of your daughters back to you, but I intend to take another of them in payment, so we're square."

Standing beside him, Sibi caught her breath. "You do?"

He met her gaze. "Unless you have some objection."

"I don't." The smile she gave him felt tremulous. "No objection at all."

With the fascinated attention of her entire family now riveted on them, Griff looked a little rueful, gave her a squeeze, kissed her cheek and murmured in her ear, "Another of those things we'll be talking more about later."

Sibi laughed and nodded.

Then Margrit said, "What a complete smasher of a day! And it's still Sibi's birthday! We've got *cake*!"

At the exultant note of that, they all laughed. Then they went home, and had barbecue and cake in the backyard surrounded by friends and neighbors, and talked so much that first Jo's, then Margrit's and finally Sibi's voice gave out. Tears mixed in with the laughter, and Jo held Ruby close throughout the party, and Margrit glowed with happiness, and Sibi felt her heart swell with joy.

At the height of the party, Papa called for quiet, raised his beer in a salute. "To my girls. The ones who are absent as well as the ones who are here. The treasures of my life."

"Papa." The three who were there swarmed him. He wrapped his arms around them, and they all clung together until at last Papa, with an embarrassed, *"Hmmph,"* let go.

Jo's glance encompassed them all. "I never thought I'd see any of you again. I've never been so happy in my life."

Sibi knew how she felt. Jo restored to them, returned from the dead — and Griff.

Her cup runneth over.

His arm was around her. He leaned down, said in her ear, "Believe in miracles yet?"

She looked at him, smiled mistily.

After this, after today, there was only one answer she could give.

"Always," she said.

AUTHOR NOTE

I love history. I love delving into the past, into the lives of people and the events that shaped them and that they helped shape. For *The Girl from Guernica,* I started with the actual events and people and inserted my fictional characters — Sibi and her family, Herr Kraus, a few others — into the thick of them. The attack on Guernica is, of course, real, as is Picasso's painting *Guernica,* which many regard as the most powerful anti-war painting of all time. The top-secret military facility at Peenemünde, the V-2 rockets, Operation Hydra (the raid on Peenemünde), Operation Paperclip, which brought Nazi scientists including Wernher von Braun to America, the Tehran conference between the Big Three — Roosevelt, Churchill and Stalin — otherwise known as Eureka and the November assassination attempt on them, all those are real. Coupling Peenemünde's rockets with Eureka called

687

for a little bit of poetic license, but it could have happened. And there really was a top-secret Allied mole at Peenemünde who has never been definitively identified. Another thing to remember is that this story is told through Sibi's eyes, so we only know what she knows. For example, other planes besides the Junkers and He 51s participated in the attack on Guernica, but those are the ones she saw. For the rest, I'd just like to say that I've done exhaustive research, but I've undoubtedly made a few mistakes. Any inconsistencies with the facts are strictly my own.

I hope you love Sibi and her family as much as I do. Happy reading!

ACKNOWLEDGMENTS

Writing is a solitary pursuit. Bringing forth a book in all its tweaked and polished glory is not. That requires, I won't say an army, but a team. My husband, first and foremost, makes sure I get fed and the house doesn't fall down and everything besides writing that needs to get done gets done. My wonderful editor, Emily Ohanjanians, is responsible for much of the tweaking and polishing and is the soul of patience besides. My agent of many years, Robert Gottlieb, is a mentor, friend and constant support. Margaret Marbury believed in me and my books, and gave me the space to write them. This is my huge, heartfelt thank-you to all of them, and to the entire staff of MIRA as well. *The Girl from Guernica* wouldn't exist without you.

ABOUT THE AUTHOR

Karen Robards is the *New York Times, USA TODAY* and *Publishers Weekly* bestselling author of fifty novels and one novella. She is the winner of six Silver Pen awards and numerous other awards.

The employees of Thorndike Press hope you have enjoyed this Large Print book. All our Thorndike, Wheeler, and Kennebec Large Print titles are designed for easy reading, and all our books are made to last. Other Thorndike Press Large Print books are available at your library, through selected bookstores, or directly from us.

For information about titles, please call:
(800) 223-1244

or visit our website at:
gale.com/thorndike

To share your comments, please write:
Publisher
Thorndike Press
10 Water St., Suite 310
Waterville, ME 04901